Line in

Chris Hernandez

TACT16AL

Line in the Valley
Copyright © 2014 Chris Hernandez

First Edition

Because of the dynamic nature of the internet, any web address or links contained in this book may have changed since publication and may no longer be valid.

Line in the Valley is a work of fiction. Names, characters, places, and incidents are the products of the author's imagination, experiences, or are fictitious. Any resemblance to actual events, locales, or persons, living or dead, is entirely coincidental.

The views expressed in this work are solely those of the author and do not necessarily reflect the views of the publisher, and the publisher hereby disclaims any responsibility for them.

Published by Tactical 16, LLC
Colorado Springs, CO

eISBN: 978-0-9855582-8-4
ISBN: 978-0-9898175-2-3 (hc)
ISBN: 978-0-9898175-1-6 (sc)

Printed in the United States of America

For my family.

PROLOGUE

Carlos Ramirez's phone rang in his pocket, rousing him from a half sleep, half pleasant buzz. He put his beer down, shifted in his recliner, reached past belly fat and dug his phone out. The caller ID showed it was his coworker and across the street neighbor, Andy Carter. Carlos slurred a greeting.

"Hey Andy, what's up? Why you bothering me now, when you know by this time every night I'm into my tenth beer?"

Carlos' wife gave him a dirty look from the kitchen as she washed dishes. She had complained about his drinking for years and threatened to divorce him more than once, to no avail. But she was Mexican, devoutly Catholic and wouldn't want to be stuck taking care of their kids alone. She would never leave him.

"Sober up, *pendejo*," Andy said. "You remember that little shithead Antonio Guevara you arrested last week? He's walking around by the corner, next to the Melendez's. I think he's looking toward your house."

"Shit," Carlos responded. "That little punk needs his ass kicked. Again. You see any of his little gangster friends with him?"

"*Nadie mas, hermano*," Andy answered. He was white, but like most of the white people in Arriago and all the white cops, he spoke fluent Tex-Mex Spanish. "Nobody but him. He's been walking from the corner toward your house and back, talking on a cell phone."

"A cell phone? Who did he steal that from? That little shit can't afford a cell phone."

"Who gives a fuck why he has a phone?" Andy asked. "I didn't call to talk about his phone, I called to tell you he was outside in case you want Jesse to run him off."

Carlos took another swallow from his beer. "Nah, I won't bother Jesse for this. He's the only one on duty tonight, he's probably busy. I'll go outside and run Antonio off myself. And if he wants to argue about it, I'll kick the shit out of him again."

"*Andale* Carlos, that's what he needs. Call me if you want me to come outside and videotape it."

"Go to sleep, *hermano*. Thanks for the call."

"*Hasta luego.*"

Carlos hung up and struggled out of his chair. He went to his room, pulled on a t-shirt and grabbed the flashlight and pepper spray from the duty belt hanging on his bedpost. He thought about it a moment, then went to his closet and threw a .38 sub nose into a pocket. He doubted he'd need the gun for Antonio, but you never knew how stupid a wannabe gangster could be.

Antonio Guevara was the seventh grade, fourteen-year-old head of *Los Nortenos*, a middle school "gang" made up mostly of eleven to thirteen year old mini-thugs who aspired to be real thugs someday. Since anointing themselves gangsters, they had been trying like hell to make a name for themselves in the tiny Texas border town of Arriago. Being the oldest, Antonio naturally fancied himself the leader. He and his flock, all eight of them, had been making themselves royal pains in the asses to the town's 2400 residents. They had spent the last month marking turf with their made-up gang symbol, bringing beer to school in backpacks, beating up terrified ten-year-olds and even talking trash to police whenever they saw a passing patrol car. Arriago had real gangsters, but they tried to keep a low profile. The *Nortenos* wanted everyone to know who they were.

Carlos had caught Antonio breaking into an old woman's car the previous week, and Antonio bowed up to fight. Carlos convinced Antonio that he didn't want to fight a cop after all. Antonio hadn't needed any medical attention afterward, but Carlos knew he would feel the asskicking for a few days.

Carlos walked toward the front door, past his sons playing Xbox in their bedroom, and told his wife, "I'm going outside to handle something, I'll be back in a minute." She asked what he was talking about and he ignored the question, walked out the front door and turned toward the corner, two houses away.

He didn't see anything at first. His neighborhood was poor and overgrown with brush. Then, in the pale light of a barely working street lamp, half-hidden behind a bush, he made out Antonio's baggy, rumpled outline.

"Antonio!" Carlos yelled. "You don't live here! What you want, boy? Didn't you get enough last time I arrested you?"

Antonio stepped out from behind the bush. He had a cell phone to his ear. Carlos walked toward him, fast, yelling "Hey, I'm talking to you! What you doing here, *pendejo?*"

Antonio yelled back, "Fuck you, *lambiache!*" and spoke into the phone. He didn't back away.

Antonio was a punk and a coward. He shouldn't have stood his ground. Surprised, Carlos yelled back, "Ass kisser? Boy, you better run, because I'm about to beat you to death!" He quickened his pace, ready to whip Antonio's ass again.

Before he stepped out of his yard the sound of racing engines came from around the corner. Carlos stopped, unsure what to make of it. He didn't see light from headlights, he just heard engines. Antonio looked toward the sound and didn't move. Carlos heard him say, *"Aqui, aqui!"* Right here, right here.

Two black Ford Explorers raced into view, screeched past Antonio and made the turn toward Carlos. Their lights were off. The lead Explorer covered the distance to Carlos' house in two seconds and slid to a stop. The second Explorer skidded to a stop in front of Andy's house.

Carlos felt no fear, just confusion. He stepped back, turned on his flashlight and pointed it toward the Explorer in front of his house. The SUV doors flew open. Two men in ski masks jumped out, dressed in all black with AK-47 rifles, body armor and tactical vests. Carlos shined his light on the man who had come out of the back seat. The man shifted his body so his chest faced Carlos, and raised his AK. He moved like a soldier, his actions quick and efficient.

Carlos took another step back. *What the fuck is going on?* Behind him he heard his front door swing open. He turned to see his wife standing at the front step. He looked back as two more men with rifles and gear ran toward his house.

The impulse to react finally worked its way through the alcohol. Carlos jammed his hand into his pocket and grabbed his pistol. Before he could yank his weapon free the man pointing the AK at him pulled the trigger.

A white-orange flash exploded from the rifle's muzzle. The bullet hit Carlos to the right of his sternum, punched straight through and exited his back. His vision went gray. He dropped flat onto his back, struggling to breathe. He heard his wife scream *"Dios mio!"*, then more shots. The scream stopped, but was replaced

3

by shrieks from his sons' room. He turned his head and could just make out another man in black rushing through the door. Down the street he heard more shots, more screams. Andy's screams.

He looked up. Antonio stood over him, flashed a gang sign and said, "See that, bitch? See what happens when you mess with *Los Nortenos*? Never fuck with me, bitch."

Carlos couldn't process this. His sons' screams drowned in automatic gunfire. Slow, painful recognition worked through the haze of pain and alcohol. His family had just been murdered. *He* had just been murdered. This couldn't be the work of Antonio and his band of preteen shitheads. They couldn't do this. It didn't make sense.

Antonio kicked him in the groin. Carlos' body rocked from the blow, his blurred vision bounced, but he couldn't feel the impact. He heard girlish screaming and could just make out Andy's teenage daughter running down the street. Gunfire sounded, the scream disappeared as if it had never been there. Carlos watched the young woman's blurry, ghostlike image slam facedown onto the street. He heard laughter and shouted comments in Spanish.

Carlos closed his eyes and tried to breathe. When he opened his eyes he barely saw a man standing over him holding an AK to his face. He heard Antonio's voice, but couldn't make out the words. He croaked, "Why, Antonio? Why?"

Antonio laughed. The man next to him said in Spanish, *"Muevete atras."* Move back. Carlos didn't understand him. He managed to wheeze, *"No entiendo, no entiendo."*

The man in black fired another round, from ten feet away. This wasn't the first time he had shot a man in the head with an AK. He knew to stay at a distance so the blood, bone, brain, skin and hair wouldn't spatter back on him. Carlos never heard or felt the round. It hit beside the bridge of his nose and exited the back of his skull, scattering shards of bone and tissue across the lawn.

Carlos died without knowing that all seven Arriago police officers, and all seventeen Harper County deputies, and their families, had died with him. Or that the Arriago mayor, municipal judge and twelve firefighters had been killed. Or that the same thing had happened in every Texas town along a hundred mile

4

stretch of border between Roma and Brownsville, within fifteen minutes of Carlos' murder.

CHAPTER 1

Sergeant First Class Jerry Nunez kicked open the Humvee door and stepped out. As he stretched his cramped muscles, all the old, familiar aches and pains hit. Riding for hours in full gear had always been hard on his knees, shoulders and lower back. Nunez had spent countless hours stuffed into Humvees on convoys and patrols in Iraq and Afghanistan, and didn't miss those missions or places. He took his helmet and body armor off and laid them on the seat, then grabbed his M4 carbine and headed toward his platoon leader's vehicle.

Lieutenant Rodger Quincy stood stretching by his own vehicle. His shook his head and said, "I don't believe we're doing this shit, Jerry."

"Me neither, Lieutenant."

"Jerry, quit calling me 'Lieutenant'. When the kids aren't around, just call me Rodger," Quincy said to Nunez, his platoon sergeant.

"Sure thing, LT."

Nunez and Quincy slung their carbines and walked toward the mall's main doors. The parking lot was jammed with Humvees and utility vehicles, many with sleeping soldiers draped over hoods. Police cars from several departments, some as far away as Victoria and Corpus Christi, were parked around the military vehicles.

Except for the police cars, the scene looked almost like every forward operating base Nunez had ever been to overseas. But this wasn't Iraq or Afghanistan. It was Edinburgh, Texas, within the borders of what was supposed to be the safest, best protected country in the world. And the soldiers weren't there for a training exercise. They were there because the United States of America had been attacked.

Nunez agreed with Quincy; he couldn't believe this was happening, not here. When he reenlisted in the National Guard after the terrorist attack in Houston, he had expected to be back in Afghanistan within a year. He hadn't expected to be mobilized for whatever the hell was happening on the border.

Nunez had been patrolling his beat two nights earlier when news of the border attacks broke. He and his partner watched the first reports on CNN. Local reporters repeated what little they had been told by the few refugees brave enough to stop and talk at highway rest stops and gas stations. Traumatized survivors sputtered wild stories of masked men in black mowing down women and children in quiet neighborhoods, police cars shot to pieces, bombs exploding in fire stations.

The first calls from the National Guard had come in that night. An unofficial mobilization order trickled to thousands of soldiers, including Nunez. He went home from work early, loaded his jeep while arguing with his wife Laura, and headed out.

Laura was furious, sick of Nunez leaving her and the kids alone every time the Guard needed him to do a dangerous job somewhere in the world. Iraq, Afghanistan, the attack in Houston, and now this, were too much. She didn't want him doing one more dangerous job or responding to one more call up of troops. When he left the house she warned him she wouldn't be there when he came back.

He believed her, but he didn't have a choice. He couldn't ignore attacks in America, in *Texas*, just hours from home. It didn't even matter if official orders were never cut and he wasn't paid; he couldn't sit this one out. If his troops were going, and were going to be in danger, he was going with them. He told her he'd call when he had the chance, kissed the kids, and drove away.

Nunez and Quincy checked in with guards at the mall's main doors and headed toward the Apple store, where an intelligence briefing was about to be held. Nunez was amazed at how a regular shopping mall had become a military base. Edinburgh was fewer than thirty miles from the border, and had pretty much shut down when word of the attacks spread. Any family that was able headed north to Corpus Christi, Houston or San Antonio. Refugees displaced from besieged border towns clogged every school in Edinburgh. The owners of the one mall in town offered to let the National Guard use it as a base of operations. That would prevent looting, but the shop owners must have thought the soldiers themselves would steal what was left. Merchandise was gone from almost every business, hidden in storage somewhere.

Every store they passed had been taken over by a Guard unit. Sears, the largest, was occupied by the 56th Brigade Combat Team headquarters. The smaller shops had been taken by battalion commanders and their company commanders. All the makeshift command posts were beehives of activity. Junior sergeants and lower enlisted set up maps and butcher block paper on walls and checked connections on radio antennas, preparing for the hurricane of action that was sure to come.

"Fuck, I wish the food court was still working," Quincy said as they walked past closed junk food restaurants. "I want a smoothie."

Nunez pulled out his notebook and pretended to make a note. "I'll tell your driver to get right on that, sir. 'Lieutenant Quincy wants a smoothie.' Any specific flavor?"

Quincy looked like he wanted to say something smart-alecky, but all he could come back with was "Asshole." Then he asked, "You get ahold of Laura yet?"

"No Rod, I haven't," Nunez mumbled. "She wouldn't answer my calls or texts, and the phones don't work down here so I can't even try anymore. And I forgot my phone charger and ran the battery out. But, whatever. She'll be there when I get back. Or she'll divorce me. I'll live either way."

"It won't bother you if Laura divorces you?" Quincy asked.

Nunez drew a long, slow breath. He thought of his beautiful red headed wife, and their son and daughter who looked just like her. He had almost lost them before. He and Laura had teetered on the edge of divorce more than once over the years. Sometimes his determination had saved the marriage, more often hers had. Once they were so close to ending it he packed his things and moved in with a friend. That had given him one whole day of a false sense of relief. But the thought of his wife married to someone else and his children being raised by someone else, like the ex-wives and kids of a million cops he knew, made him want to cry. So he went back, cried in front of his wife, and she cried with him. He moved back in and they stayed more or less stable, until he walked out the door with his gear and headed toward the Texas border.

The last few years had been a hard road for Nunez. He had been sent to Iraq early in the war and spent a year riding a Humvee down scarred, bomb-ravaged highways, cringing every time they passed an abandoned car or pile of trash. He had dreaded every convoy, but made it through his year whole and safe. He went home, shook off the anxiety of the war, and spent two years back on the streets of Houston. But then new orders came, this time for Afghanistan.

In Iraq, Nunez was never in a big firefight. In Afghanistan, he was in huge battles. In Iraq he never lost a soldier. In Afghanistan, his orders had cost a close friend his life. In Iraq, every mission he went on was a success. In Afghanistan, he felt like he had lost the most important fight he had ever been in. He came home physically fine, but Afghanistan left a mark he knew time wouldn't erase. He got out of the Army, pledged himself to his family and job, and moved on.

What happened a year later changed Nunez's life. It had been a November afternoon he'd never forget. Houston SWAT officers screamed on the radio as they were engaged in a brutal, close range firefight with a terrorist cell at a mosque. Nunez had charged straight into the fight. That decision almost cost him his life.

He was nearly killed several times, but was on his feet when it was all over. He had beaten the grim reaper. But there was no celebration because, as it turned out, the wars he fought overseas and at home weren't as big a threat to his life as they were to his marriage.

Nunez made it through Iraq and Afghanistan without a divorce, but his decision the day after the terrorist attack almost killed the marriage. He had rejoined the military, against Laura's express wishes. He half expected her to leave him that day. She stayed, but it had been close.

Nunez considered Quincy's question, *it won't bother you if Laura divorces you?*, and knew two things: first, he honestly didn't know if he would still be married when he got home. Second, losing his wife would tear him apart.

"Bother me?" Nunez asked. "Nope."

"You're a liar," Quincy responded.

Nunez nodded and gave a hopeless shrug. "Yup."

"Well, good luck. And if you wind up single, I'll take you to pick up some nasty, disease-ridden strippers in Beaumont. They'll make you feel better."

Nunez smiled. "That'll work, Rod. Hook me up with some woman who's so disgusting even her herpes have AIDS. It's like you looked into my soul and saw all my hopes and dreams."

Nunez's group was almost there. Other company commanders and platoon leaders, and their platoon sergeants and a few squad leaders, converged on the Apple store. Nunez saw a few dozen soldiers already inside, and when the others entered it would be almost packed. But it still didn't seem there were enough leaders to represent a full strength brigade combat team.

Nunez and his company's leaders bumped their way into the Apple store. The Sergeant First Class about to give the intelligence brief had a map of south Texas spread on a wall and was reading from a green notebook. Eight large satellite images of towns were plastered above the map. The soldier had no computer, there would be no PowerPoint presentation. This looked like it was going to be a bare-bones affair, not like the complicated intelligence briefings overseas.

The intelligence sergeant, Lacey, looked about thirty-five years old, wore a Combat Action Badge and had a 36th Infantry Division combat patch on his right shoulder. He was stocky and medium height, his light brown hair a little long, face overgrown with stubble. Nunez guessed he had been called up so quickly, like the rest of the soldiers in the room, that he hadn't had time to get a proper haircut. He looked like he hadn't slept for days. Lacey waited for the last few soldiers to trickle into the Apple store, then began his briefing.

"Good morning, gentlemen." He looked at his watch. "I mean, good afternoon. Sorry, I've been awake a long time. I'm Sergeant First Class Laccy from brigade intelligence, and guys, I have a shitload of information to give you. I'm winging this whole briefing, so you'll have to bear with me. If I fuck something up, call bullshit on me so I can get it straight."

He yawned, turned away and rubbed his eyes. When he turned back he said quietly, "Whoops. Sorry." Then he picked up his notebook and put his finger on a page.

"Alright, quick roll call. The only soldiers in here should be company commanders and below. Battalion staff and higher are getting a separate briefing from my lieutenant. If there are a few people missing I won't hold everything up for them. You guys can fill in anyone who couldn't make it." He looked at his notebook again. "Okay, from 118 Cavalry, do we have reps from Headquarters Troop?"

Hands went up and a few "Hooahs" sounded.

"Alpha troop?…Bravo?… Charlie?" Responses sounded from each unit's soldiers. Lacey went down the list for each battalion, all five in the brigade. Nunez and his group answered for Alpha Company, 4th battalion of the 112th Infantry Regiment.

"Alright, let's get started. If you guys want to get comfortable, have a seat on the floor or tables, go right ahead. Just don't fall asleep. This briefing isn't going to be some blow-off waste of time. Everything I'm about to tell you is no shit, life and death important. Your soldiers' lives, and the lives of a whole lot of Americans on the border, depend on you taking in what I'm telling you and acting on it the right way."

A few soldiers sat on the floor or jumped up backwards onto tables. Lacey looked around the room, his gaze right around shoulder level. He was looking at combat patches, taking note of how many combat vets were in the room.

"I see that most of us have been somewhere and done something before to-day. That's good, because we're going to need veterans for what we're about to do. And guys… I hate to say this, but this is going to be way different from Iraq and Afghanistan. And worse."

Lacey paused to take a drink from a plastic water bottle, then screwed the cap back on and set the bottle aside. "Okay gentlemen," he said, looking over the room again. "Here's what's up. I know you've been watching the news, and the rumors have been flying like crazy, but most of what you've heard and almost all of what's been reported has been complete bullshit. Here's the real situation."

Lacey ran his fingers through his hair. "Friday night, two nights ago, right around 2200 hours local, all the police in eight border towns were wiped out. And I mean, wiped out. All the city cops, all the deputies, all the state troopers, and we think all the constables. And their families."

Heads turned and mumbled gasps of "holy shit" and "Jesus fucking Christ" floated around the room. Nunez bit his lip. He had gone to Iraq with several soldiers from units near the border. Some of them had been small-town cops. The names came up from his memory: Arellano, Zavala, the Haynes brothers, maybe a dozen more. Good soldiers, all of them. He wondered if they were dead.

Nunez and Quincy looked at one another, and at their company command-er, Captain Harcrow. To their sides the two other platoon leaders, Lieutenants

Campbell and Belding, and their platoon sergeants, Beall and Quiran, stayed silent. Lieutenant Belding was new, having received his commission within the last two years. He had never deployed. Campbell and the platoon sergeants were Iraq veterans. Nunez didn't know any of them well.

When they were called up, the company was so understrength that almost all its soldiers were consolidated into Nunez and Quincy's platoon. The one other lieutenant, Campbell, had been thrown together with the one other platoon sergeant, a former infantry Marine named Beall. They had been given command of soldiers from other, even more understrength units who had been sent to fill out Nunez's unit in Round Rock, near Austin. Belding and Quiran were from two different infantry companies outside San Antonio. They didn't know each other or anyone else in the company.

Nunez was lucky to have Quincy as his platoon leader. They had first served together years earlier in Afghanistan. Nunez was the platoon sergeant over then-Corporal Rodger Quincy. Quincy was black, tall, and built of solid muscle. He had played college football and could have pursued a career in professional sports after graduation, but never considered it. His father, who settled down with his third and last wife late in life, had been a Marine in Vietnam. Quincy was going to be either Marine Corps or Army infantry, and that was the end of it. The National Guard offered him a good deal, so he signed up.

Three months into their Afghanistan tour, a bomb attack and ambush on their convoy killed three soldiers. Nunez led a charge to a compound the Taliban had fired at them from. When they reached the door Nunez ordered Quincy to go in first. Quincy didn't complain or hesitate, he just did it. Or at least tried to do it.

When he kicked the door in a Taliban machine gunner shot him through the thigh and helmet, barely missing his skull. Quincy was knocked out cold. Nunez picked up Quincy's machine gun and led the charge into the compound himself. Until the compound was clear and he walked back outside, Nunez thought Quincy was dead. He would never forget the relief he felt when he found Quincy alive. And never stop questioning his decision to order Quincy through the door first.

Quincy recovered, applied for officer candidate's school and found his way back to Nunez as a platoon leader. Quincy was only twenty-six now, much younger than Nunez's thirty-nine years. Quincy was single and under assault by so many awestruck women he had to choose the best two or three to sleep with every month. Nunez, on the other hand, had been married almost ten years and had two kids. Quincy worked with at-risk teenagers in his hometown of Beaumont, Texas, Nunez was a cynical cop in Houston who put those teenagers in jail. Quincy was an Adonis. Nunez was small, thin, not bad looking but basically unremarkable. But their shared wartime experience bonded them, and they were close friends as well as superior and subordinate.

The intelligence sergeant went on with the briefing, saying, "And guys, that's not all of it. Early reports say most of the mayors of those towns are dead, along with a shitload of firefighters, although their families apparently aren't. The same happened with the municipal court judges, except for the judge from Curran's Pass, 'cause he was on vacation in Galveston when everything went down. All this happened between here," he said, pointing on the map at Roma, "and here," pointing at Brownsville. "Those two cities, Roma and Brownsville, have not been attacked. That might be because there's such a strong federal government presence in those cities, but we don't know for certain. Brownsville is a lot bigger than any of the cities that got hit, and that might have something to do with it."

Lacey unscrewed the water bottle cap while he was speaking and took another drink. The liquid was dark, and Nunez figured he was overdosing on caffeine in an effort to stay awake. Lacey flipped a page in his notebook and said, "The night the killings happened, just about every surviving person from those eight towns decided to pop smoke and haul ass. Although that decision came after a little prodding. Some refugees said bad guys went house to house banging on doors, telling people to get out or they'd be killed. Locals were encouraged to tell their family members and neighbors to leave as well. Then when they got moving out of town, bad guys stopped random cars, pulled people out and set the vehicles on fire. There are a few reports of bad guys shooting the people they yanked out, but most reports say they just burned the cars. We think that was done to make it harder for help to get in, but we don't know for certain.

"And remember all the reporting we've gotten has come from refugees getting the fuck out of Dodge. There have been no cell phone or landline calls from any of those towns since that night. Some residents of those towns called family in other cities to say the shit was hitting the fan. Those calls either were cut off or ended abruptly and there was no further contact. We do know that no calls are getting through now. We think the cell towers and landline have been destroyed, but you know what that means. Think in one hand and shit in the other, and see which one fills up first."

Lacey walked to the map and pointed to highways leading away from the border. "As of early Saturday afternoon, police have had checkpoints set up on these roads, two to five miles north of each city's limits. Before anyone asks why the checkpoints are so far from the targeted cities, I'm going to ask a question. Where are the cops in here? If you work in law enforcement, please raise your hand."

Nunez raised his hand, along with several other soldiers in the room. He looked around, checking for familiar faces. He didn't know any of them.

Lacey pointed and said, "You. Sergeant, uh, Nunez. If you're a cop on duty in one town, and you hear a cop from another town screaming for help, what do you do?"

Nunez answered, "I go help him. No matter what."

Lacey responded, "Right. That's what we expect you guys to do. And that's what officers and state troopers did. But the bad guys expected it too, and prepared for it. So what happened, and this is confirmed, is that twenty-six officers were ambushed and killed hauling ass into these eight cities. In two cases, other officers were killed responding to calls for help from the first officers who were ambushed. Some civilians tried to help the officers, and some of them were killed as well, but we don't know the number. We do know that anyone who tried to get close to those officers was at least shot at, so nobody's even tried it since then."

Nunez spoke up abruptly. "So you mean those officers are still out there on the road? Nobody's recovered them?"

"That's correct," Lacey answered. "Nobody has been able to recover them so far. Some of them are near the checkpoints, but anyone who approaches gets shot at. Nobody right now has the ass to fight their way to those bodies. I can almost guarantee that will be our first mission when we head into those cities. And it won't be only those bodies we're recovering. Most of the refugees said dead civilians are all over the towns and roads."

Damn, Nunez thought. *Things must be super fucked up if the cops can't even get to the bodies of their friends.*

Nunez looked around, seeing anger on the faces of almost everyone, not just the police. Lacey held up one hand and said, "But guys, don't get so wrapped around the axle about the bodies that you miss some real important background details. Did anyone ask how the bad guys were able to carry out these ambushes? If so many officers were successfully ambushed within such a short time, that means spotters were on the highways, identifying targets for the ambushers. So this couldn't have been an afterthought, not if they were already in place when the first cops tried to respond. They showed up with that plan ready to execute. In other words, these guys don't seem stupid."

Lacey turned away from the map and looked at his notebook again. "Now, our enemy," he said. "Guys, I wish I could give you some information that's worth a damn, but we don't have shit right now. There's been a stream of refugees pouring from the border for the last two days, and the police are trying to get information from them. We're getting bits and pieces of what they're hearing, but it's a bunch of confused shit so far. A lot has been contradictory, like some of the descriptions. Most of the refugees said the bad guys are Hispanic, but some said they're white, some that they're black. One witness swore they were Vietnamese. The common threads are that these guys roll in SUVs, carry military rifles and wear military gear."

Lacey made eye contact with several soldiers before he spoke again. "This is a hell of a big deal, gentlemen. All the first responders in eight towns are gone. All the people who could pick up a phone, call the cavalry and say, 'Hey, we're under attack by such and such guys, this is what they look like, this is how many there are, this is where they are', are dead. But Roma and Brownsville haven't been touched. So what does all this mean? We don't know yet. We're trying to figure it out."

Lacey turned and tapped one of the satellite photos. "One big question mark we have is about Curran's Pass, right here. Someone in that town fought back. Refugees reported a huge gunfight inside the town, around midnight Friday night. Of course the witness stories don't add up, but we think the firefight went

16

on for about half an hour. We have no idea who fought back, or if it had any effect."

Someone toward the back of the room spoke up. "Sergeant, are these cartel guys doing all this crap? Who the fuck are these people?"

Lacey's answer was less than definite. "Well, it sure as hell sounds like cartels. Who else would have the ass to pull something like this off? And if it isn't cartels, how would anyone be able to do it without the cartels at least giving tacit approval? But on the other hand, it sure seems to me that this would hurt their business. They couldn't do all this shit and expect easier flow of drugs across the border."

Lacey ran his finger along the border on the map. "The affected area is known for drug and human trafficking. Cartels run the area, and we know they have their hands into all kinds of criminal enterprises, on both sides of the border. You don't have to be a master of intel to know that, it's common knowledge. And we know that federal law enforcement has most of that area under surveillance. So one of the first things we asked was, 'What did the feds' surveillance see before all this shit kicked off?' And the answer surprised us. As it turns out, the cameras are only covering heavy drug trafficking routes. And there was no increase in activity along those routes in the week before the attacks.

"After all this started the federal government sent up high altitude aircraft to get imagery. I haven't seen it yet, but as far as we know the aircraft aren't seeing anything other than bodies laying around the towns. My guess is that these guys are staying indoors during the day. We're hoping we get access to drones for real-time surveillance, but it hasn't happened yet."

Harcrow responded, "So what do we have in our favor, I.S.R.-wise?" I.S.R. was a term usually used only overseas, and meant intelligence, surveillance and reconnaissance.

"Captain, right now our only sources of intel are human intelligence reports and the media. And when I say human intelligence, I'm using the broadest possible interpretation of the term. The reporting we're getting isn't formal, isn't vetted, and so far isn't being collected and analyzed in any organized way. The police are overwhelmed with evacuees and can't take the time to write real reports. All they're doing is taking brief statements from people at checkpoints, writing notes and passing them up their chain. We've set up a shared command post with the state police at Edinburgh PD and we're reading their reports, but there's no way to know if this reporting is worth a fuck. Right now we could be getting a bunch of bullshit from people intentionally trying to mess up our response."

"Is that likely?" Harcrow asked. "Do you think we're getting lied to?"

Lacey rubbed his face. "No, Captain, I don't think so. My gut reaction is that we're getting honest reporting. But that doesn't mean it's true. Some people are misinterpreting what they see, or repeating secondhand information. But I think they're reporting what they honestly believe."

"And what's the media getting?" Nunez asked.

"The media's getting about the same thing the police are. We ordered some soldiers to watch the news on TV twenty-four hours a day and notify us if something major comes up. Anything important will be sent out ASAP."

Lacey took another drink, then his face lit up and he slammed the water bottle down. "Holy shit, I almost forgot," he said. "Speaking of the media, don't expect intrepid reporters to force their way into these towns at the risk of their own lives, or any of that crap. Last night a media van from Corpus Christi drove into Morenitos. That news crew hasn't been heard from since they passed the police checkpoint outside the town. Cops at the checkpoint heard gunfire in the town after they lost sight of the van, and nobody's heard shit since then. There are rumors the TV crew was feeding live video back to their station. Supposedly the newspeople watching it saw them get ambushed and killed. The station refuses to make any comment, they don't want to shake up anyone's family until they have confirmation."

"What about news helicopters?" Nunez asked. "Haven't they made flights over the area?"

"One helicopter from Corpus tried it the first night," Lacey said. "They went over Morenitos, looking for the media van. The helicopter got hit by ground fire and got the hell out of there. No injuries. The crew said they took tracer fire from several directions. It sounds like the bad guys were triangulating their fire, you know, making a coordinated effort to bring down the helicopter. It wasn't random harassing fire like we saw overseas. The airspace was shut down after that. There have been a few flights by Navy Search And Rescue helicopters from Kingsville, but they haven't seen anything that helps us. The Navy is being real careful about where they let their helicopters go, they don't want one to go down where the crew can't be recovered."

Another captain asked, "Is that the only air support we have? Just Navy SAR birds? No Apaches or Kiowas?"

"Sir, Apaches are on the way. A National Guard Apache battalion at Ellington in Houston has gotten orders. They have twenty-four birds, but six were down for regular maintenance and four others failed preflight inspections. They'll be here tonight-ish, but they're not going to be worth much. They don't have any armament at their station, the only thing available is thirty millimeter ammo from Fort Hood. That's supposed to meet them at the Brownsville airport sometime tomorrow. Maybe we'll get Hellfires and rockets for them at some point, but even if we do there's a 'no air strikes' rule in effect. Once they're in the air over the affected areas, they're much just going to be armored observation platforms."

"And fixed wing support? Air National Guard F-16s from Houston?"

Lacey shook his head. "We're working that issue. But no promises."

"Well, shit," Hacrcrow said. "Okay, so we know for the moment we have no air support. Next question. Sergeant, what's the plan for us? How are we going to be committed?"

Lacey gave a *Don't look at me* gesture, hands up and eyebrows raised. "Sir, that's the question of the year. Since yesterday the goal has been containment, which is why the first Guard troops were fed to police checkpoints in ones and twos. All they wanted was bodies, no attention was paid to keeping units together. Just after midnight this morning someone figured out that we were degrading the effectiveness of the entire force, and convinced the state disaster response people to at least keep company sized units together."

Lacey looked around and asked, "Does this sound familiar, guys? It should. This is the same shit they do to us when we deploy overseas. Our battalions get piecemealed out and can't work like they're supposed to, so all we can do are force protection missions instead of full spectrum operations. This time, there isn't anyone else available to do the full spectrum missions. But they're still parting out units as they arrive, and I guess they're just hoping that little problem will work itself out later. Expect your battalions to be split up and tasked as individual companies. I can't give you any better news right now."

A voice in the room groaned, "Geez that sucks."

Lacey said, "No shit."

A captain from one of the Cavalry troops spoke up. "Alright, this is a huge shitstorm and it's going to be a fucking mess, but what do we do? What's the first step?"

Lacey held his hand up again. "Hey sir, I can't tell you what to do. Those orders have to come from your commander. All I can tell you is what we know, and what we don't. And I suppose I can also tell you this. Forget rumors about the big Army coming to the rescue. They've been ordered to keep their hands off. *Posse Commitatus* is in effect. The federal government says this is a criminal matter that should be handled by law enforcement and Guard troops. We're just here to assist law enforcement. I hope the regular Army is at least spinning up in case things get worse, but the federal representatives have been clear about this. This is a crime, not a war. Emergency teams from the FBI and DEA are responding, plus FEMA, but they won't enter the towns until we establish a presence.

"As far as directly confronting whoever these people are, that's all on us. And because we're just here to assist law enforcement, we can't carry more than one magazine per rifle, no weapons larger than a 5.56 millimeter, no explosives, and no armored vehicles. That comes from General Landers, commander of the Texas National Guard."

The room erupted with loud exclamations of "That's bullshit!" and "Fuck that!" Lacey held up his hands and yelled, "Hey guys, don't shoot the messenger! I'm not saying those rules are my idea, I'm just telling you what to expect. I know it sucks, and I guarantee you that if I roll into one of those towns, I'm going to have more than one damn magazine. Your commanders will lay the rules out to you, then it's up to you to decide how much you can get away with. But they give the orders, not me."

The room quieted. The Cavalry captain gave a smirk and said, "Yeah sergeant, I know a little bit about where I'm supposed to get my orders from. I think I saw on TV once how the chain of command works. What I'm asking, since you know the situation better than we do, is what are we doing? What's our response?"

Lacey smirked back, "Well Captain, maybe you should ask the people you're supposed to. They'd probably tell you the first step is for the nearest available unit to go on a recon mission into one of the cities. When they get in and report what they see, we formulate a response. Until then, we're just operating on guesses."

"So which of us is the nearest available unit?" the captain asked, without the smartass tone this time.

"None of you are," Lacey answered. "This shit started Friday night. A maintenance company had already reported for drill Friday morning in Cuidad Irigoyen, about forty miles north of the border. Those guys are at about two thirds strength, and have vehicles and weapons ready to go. They're the first unit tasked for a recon, into Arriago. They were supposed to start their mission yesterday, but nobody was able to get ammo for them until today."

Jesus Christ, Nunez thought. He jerked his hand into the air and blurted, "They're sending an understrength National Guard maintenance company with no heavy weapons, unarmored vehicles and one magazine per soldier into this shit first? When do they start their recon?"

Lacey looked at his watch. "If they kept to the timeline, they hit their start point about thirty minutes ago, Sergeant Nunez."

CHAPTER 2

"Well, 9? You see anything yet?" Lieutenant DeLeon asked over the radio.

First Sergeant Olivares answered, "Nothing yet, 6. A few more bodies, no activity at all."

"Roger. Keep me updated."

Olivares tried to relax. Supposedly every time the police went south of the checkpoint they were shot at. But nobody shot at Olivares' convoy. That had to mean the enemy was gone, which was what Olivares expected anyway. Shooting cops in some Podunk town was one thing, taking on the U.S. Army was something else. Olivares didn't believe a bunch of criminals, even cartel criminals, were stupid enough to try it.

Olivares looked around from his Humvee at the front of the convoy as the outskirts of Arriago slid by. Run-down wooden shacks and overgrown junk-filled yards lined the highway. Here and there an "antique shop", which was more like a shed full of old worthless crap, stood out from other structures. If not for the handful of bodies and random burned cars, nothing would have been out of place.

The corpses, looking like piles of stained rags instead of men, women and children, were almost all face-down in the road. One fat old woman had her knees bent under her distended stomach. Olivares saw her hands still clasped behind what remained of her head. He didn't have to be CSI South Texas to know she had been executed at close range. Or that there would be more just like her less than a mile ahead, inside the city limits where smoke from several fires rose. The bodies had been stewing in the Rio Grande Valley summer heat for two days. The stench here, outside town, wasn't too bad. He expected it to be much worse by the time they reached the Arriago high school.

When his company first received the order for this mission, he had been pissed to discover that none of his soldiers were from Arriago. It would have been good to have at least one soldier who knew the town to act as a guide. Now, after spending half an hour recovering the punctured bodies of six Harper county deputies outside town, then driving past corpses of murdered residents, he was glad nobody from Arriago was on the mission. Handling the dead deputies had given his soldiers a bad case of the willies already. The last thing he needed was one of his troops going crazy after seeing his family and friends decomposing on the highway.

The convoy of ten vehicles, a mix of soft-skinned Humvees and an old five-ton truck, crept past the fat, dead woman. It was the last one Olivares knew for sure was a body. The other clumps lying in the road ahead were too far away to identify.

Olivares looked in the side mirror as the last truck weaved around the body. The convoy's spacing looked right, his soldiers had rifles pointing left and right from their windows. The last truck commander had just confirmed one of his troops had a rifle over the tailgate, covering their six. The company was keeping 360 degree security, just like Olivares told them to.

He turned forward again, looking for the city limit sign. The structures along the highway were packed a little closer now, they couldn't be far. Olivares scanned the road ahead through binoculars. Heavy brush lined the highway. He still couldn't make out the city limit sign, but he could see what looked like downtown Arriago, such as it was. Olivares had grown up in Cuidad Irigoyen, just over forty miles away, but hadn't been to Arriago since elementary school. The town was a dump then, and hadn't improved in over thirty years. Even without the burned cars, burning buildings and rotting corpses on the street, the place was a shithole.

Olivares scanned left, came back the other way and spotted the city limit sign in his binoculars. It was a few hundred meters away, nearly hidden behind a faded sign advertising a restaurant that had probably been closed for years. He pulled the Humvee's's radio handset off the sun visor and keyed up.

"Wrench 6 this is Wrench 9, the city limits are just ahead. I still don't see any activity. We're continuing on."

Lieutenant DeLeon answered, "Roger. Hey 9, um, before we get into town, you sure you don't want to dismount some guys to walk alongside the trucks? Over."

Olivares answered, "Negative, 6. We keep everyone in the trucks, just like we said before. Out."

Without waiting for a response, he stuck the handset back on the visor. Even though DeLeon was officially in charge, Olivares wasn't interested in what that weak, inexperienced shithead had to say. Olivares had the experience, so he was running the company.

When they had received the mission order, he told DeLeon the company should stay mounted in their vehicles the whole way into Arriago. Olivares had been on at least six convoys in Iraq, between Tallil and Kuwait, and that was how they had done it. He didn't see any reason to jack with success. But when they briefed the company, one of their soldiers, a former infantryman named D'Angelo, almost blew a gasket.

D'Angelo had been discharged from the regular Army, come back home to Irigoyen and checked into the Guard unit eight months earlier. He hadn't seemed like a bad soldier at first, and breezed through the National Guard mechanic's course. But after a few drills he started running his mouth nonstop. His scorn for Olivares' and DeLeon's decisions, and his loud disgust at the company's tactical training, bordered on insubordination.

Olivares and DeLeon conducted training the right way; nothing that might be dangerous, no extra risks taken, no reason to do more than the bare minimum. Olivares ignored the medical training requirements because they were a waste of time. If someone was wounded, a medic would be there to treat them. At the range they got everyone qualified, whether they could shoot or not. Soldiers who were blind and helpless with a rifle got a little extra help with a pencil on their qualification records. Rifle qualification was just a "check the block" exercise anyway. There was no reason to waste time with all that advanced tactical training bullshit the Army wanted Guard units to do now. They only needed to qualify once a year. Anything more was extra, unnecessary effort. And a maintenance company didn't need it anyway.

When D'Angelo had gone to the range with them the first time, he showed up with personalized gear, different from everyone else. Olivares had almost lost it. The company's standing order was for every soldier to set their gear up the same way. Everyone knew the military had to have uniformity. That D'Angelo was good with his gear didn't make any difference. All that mattered to Olivares was unquestioning obedience.

During the mission brief, when Olivares said every soldier in the company would be mounted in the vehicles, D'Angelo had to open his big mouth. He insisted, in front of the whole company, that keeping everyone in the vehicles was the wrong thing to do. Soldiers needed to walk alongside the convoy to give the company more flexibility and better observation. The vehicles were the biggest targets and as many troops as possible needed to be out of them if they got hit.

Lieutenant DeLeon, weak-willed as always, stumbled over a few words of halting agreement. Olivares told D'Angelo to shut the fuck up and follow orders. Then he told D'Angelo to ride in the back of the last vehicle, since he was so scared. D'Angelo had answered, "Cool, thanks Top. That'll be the best place to be when we get ambushed."

Olivares had wanted to hit him. Fucking D'Angelo. A twenty-four year old Italian who grew up in a Mexican town, spoke Spanish and looked Mexican enough to never get picked on about his background. The one guy in the company who was in shape and always carried himself like a soldier, who should have been the shining example of how to follow orders without question. He could have been an asset to the company. But he wasn't, because of his fucking attitude. He thought he knew everything about combat, just because he had been an infantryman during one tour of Iraq and one of Afghanistan. Olivares didn't care what D'Angelo knew, he wasn't going to listen to anything he said.

A few hundred yards ahead, Olivares could make out two of the burning structures. One looked like a gas station, the other a falling apart dump, maybe an old store, on the right side of the road. Dark plumes rose into the sky above Arriago, mixed with smoke from other fires Olivares couldn't see. The narrow three-lane road through downtown was obscured with it, but Olivares thought it was far short of a smokescreen, if that had been the intent. Most of the fires were on the right side, so if the convoy stayed left it should get through fine.

He looked at his map again. Preston street was just past city hall. They had to turn left there and then make the second right to get to the high school. If they reached the school, they would circle their vehicles in the parking lot, sit tight and wait for more orders. If they took fire, even one round, they were to turn around and drive back out of the town. Of course D'Angelo made some remark about the order being chickenshit, but Olivares ignored him. As far as Olivares was concerned, if D'Angelo wanted to get shot that badly he could walk into Arriago by himself.

Olivares had stuck D'Angelo in back of the last truck, under the command of Sergeant Lerma, a man he trusted. Lerma was an old-school Guardsman, from the days when soldiers did nothing at drill except get drunk. He was forty-seven, fat, lazy, slow, and wouldn't even take a dump without Olivares' direct order. So when Olivares told Lerma to keep D'Angelo in the back of the truck no matter what, he knew Lerma would keep him in the back of the truck. Problem solved.

"Wrench 9, this is 6. Do you see anything else going on up there?" Deleon asked over the radio. "The trooper here is getting a little nervous."

Olivares rolled his eyes. Deleon had a state highway trooper riding with him in his Humvee, but Olivares knew if anyone was getting nervous, it was Deleon, not the trooper. Olivares understood it to a point. Some seriously bad stuff had happened in Arriago. But still, he couldn't imagine that whoever had done all this killing would hang around and wait for the Army to show up.

Olivares grabbed the radio handset. "Negative 6, there's nothing going on. Just a few bodies around and stuff on fire. Like I told you already."

"Uh, okay, roger," Deleon said. "Make sure you tell me right away if you see something. Tell me if we need to turn around."

Olivares turned to his driver, Private Salazar, and gave a sarcastic smirk. "Roger, 6. I say again, I'll tell you if there's anything for you to be scared of. Right now I can't see much through all the smoke."

"9, can you tell how far we are from city hall? I don't want to miss the turn."

"Jesus Christ," Olivares muttered. He clipped the radio handset onto the visor and told Salazar, "Fuck that, I'm not going to answer him. He needs to quit being such a pussy and just wait for me to give him updates."

The city limits sign, advertising *City of Arriago, population 2357,* coasted past Olivares' window. The gas station map in Olivares' hand showed city hall six or seven blocks from Arapahoe street, the town's northern border. He didn't know which side of the street city hall was on. Like most small Texas towns, the old downtown area consisted of long one story buildings separated into shops.

City hall should be somewhere among those buildings. If it was on the right, they'd have a hell of a time spotting it in all the smoke. The tiny downtown area wasn't quite blanketed in it, but it looked thicker now than it had from outside the town. The left side of Nogales, the main north and south street, was still clear enough to drive through.

Salazar pointed to the right side of the road, about a block ahead. "Top, see those things on the sidewalk? What are those?"

Olivares followed Salazar's pointed finger and raised his binoculars. Through the gray haze he saw what looked like six or seven charred trash bags scattered around the pavement in front of what had been a small grocery store. Smoke rolled upward from the tops of the store's shattered front windows. He focused on one of the bags, and saw what looked like an off-white stick protruding from the side.

"Uh…that's nothing, Salazar. Just garbage bags, or something."

"Bullshit, Top. I think those are bodies."

Olivares swallowed. "Just drive, Salazar."

Deleon's voice came across the radio, shaky as usual. "9 this is 6, the command post just asked for our front line trace. What does that mean?"

Olivares turned to Salazar. "What's a front line trace?"

"Fuck, Top, I don't know. Why don't you ask D'Angelo? He'll probably know."

"Fuck D'Angelo. I'm not asking him shit." Olivares keyed his radio. "6, they probably just want to know where we are. Tell them we're at Nogales and, uh, 5th. If they mean something else they'll tell you."

"Roger."

Olivares' Humvee reached a burned car in the right lane, not blocking their path but pushing them left. The right lane was blocked and filling with smoke. Olivares was getting the urge to cough. He reached down and pulled the Humvee's's plastic window up, then struggled to zip it closed. His gunner, Rivera, coughed and ducked into the passenger compartment. Olivares shot him a quick glare.

"Rivera, get the fuck back up there."

"Shit, Top, it's smoky as hell up here. I'm gonna get sick."

"We'll take you to the doctor later. Just get your ass up there."

Rivera mumbled curses in Spanish and stood back up. The Humvee didn't have a turret like they'd had in Iraq. They had just rolled back the vinyl top so the gunner could stick his upper body out, he had no protection at all. And Rivera didn't have a machine gun, just his M16A2. The one magazine Rivera had was in the rifle, but Olivares hadn't let any of the gunners lock and load. That was a sure way to have a negligent discharge, and he wasn't about to risk that. The soldiers inside the vehicles hadn't even been allowed to insert magazines into their weapons. Olivares could just imagine what one moron could do if he accidentally fired a three-round burst inside a Humvee.

"9 this is 6, we just passed the city limits."

"Yeah? So fucking what?" Olivares said to the windshield. Then he keyed the microphone and said, "Roger."

"Hey, Top!" Rivera yelled down into the Humvee. "There's a bunch of empty shells and crap laying around! Like there was a firefight here, or something."

Olivares looked at the line of shattered windows fronting the old buildings, and at the burned cars. Bullet holes were everywhere. Olivares felt a little chill at the sight. No kidding, there had been some kind of fight there. He covered his nervousness by saying, "Gee Rivera, you think so? Damn boy, I'm gonna have to promote you to Lieutenant. You're a genius."

Rivera mumbled something in reply. Olivares couldn't understand it, but the very tone of the mumbling was disrespectful. He was about to get him back in line when Rivera yelled into the Humvee again.

"Top! Something just started burning, around the corner to the left! It's about a block up!"

Olivares looked and didn't see anything. "There's nothing burning over there, you dumbass. It's just smoke drifting over from the right."

"No Top, there's a real thick column of black smoke coming up on the left, and I know it wasn't there before! I can't tell what it's coming from!"

"Calm down, Rivera," Olivares said. "I don't see shit and you're probably wrong anyway, but so fucking what if something else is burning? Shit's burning all over the place out here."

"Top, someone just set something on fire," Rivera said. "Someone's doing something out here. Take another look, you should be able to see it now."

Olivares muttered a curse, crouched and tilted his head to get his eyes under the upper edge of the windshield. And he saw it, a solid black tower of smoke. His brow furrowed in confusion.

"9 this is 6, my gunner says he sees smoke rising on the left," Deleon said over the radio. "Do you see anything?"

"6 this is 9," Olivares answered. "Yeah, we see it too. I can't tell what it is."

"Uh…you think we should turn around?" DeLeon asked.

Goddam it. What a friggin' faggot. "No, 6, we shouldn't turn around. We'll see what it is when we pass the next intersection, and report if we need to. Got it?"

"Roger, 9. I got it."

Rivera tapped Olivares with his foot. "Top, we should stop and dismount some guys. I don't know what the fuck is going on, but we need guys on foot looking around corners and shit."

"Shut up, Rivera. I was on plenty of convoys in Iraq, and we kept everyone mounted. I know what I'm doing."

"Top, you did like five milk runs on routes where nothing ever happened. I was on a couple of those convoys, remember? This ain't Iraq, Top. This shit is different."

Olivares bit back anger. "Rivera, shut the fuck up! If we get hit I don't want to wait for guys to mount back up before we haul ass. Everyone stays mounted." Olivares turned to his driver and said, "Salazar, don't slow down. Rivera, keep an eye that direction when we get to that corner."

Rivera gave a reluctant "Roger" and hunched down, rifle ready. Salazar moved his head closer to the steering wheel, looking left. Olivares checked the side mirror and saw the convoy keeping pace and interval. That was a relief. Of the ten vehicles, only four had radios. The rest of the drivers were just following the trucks in front. He hoped none of the drivers would see the smoke and slow down on their own.

Salazar jammed on the brakes. Olivares' head rocked forward. Rivera yelled "Shit!" and Salazar yelled, "Top, look!"

Olivares looked forward. An old red Suburban, engulfed in flames, rolled onto Nogales street. The doors were open and what looked like flaming human bodies hung out. One dragged on the street. The Suburban crept on burning tires, obviously not under its own power. Its front bumper just reached the center lane before its momentum died. The vehicle coasted to a stop, less than fifty yards ahead of Olivares' Humvee. As the soldiers inside stared at it in silence, a burning corpse flopped onto the pavement. Rivera yanked his rifle's charging handle to the rear, loading a round into the chamber. Salazar put the Humvee in reverse.

"Salazar, stay put. Don't back up."

Behind them, the convoy tightened and rolled to a stop. Olivares looked around and didn't see anything. He keyed the radio and said, "6, this is 9. There's a burning vehicle blocking our path. I mean, uh… it's blocking our path now. It wasn't before."

DeLeon responded, "9, what do you mean it wasn't blocking the path before? How did it get in our path?"

"6, uh… it just came out from a side street."

There were several seconds of silence over the radio. Then DeLeon said, "9, well, what do you think we should do? Should we turn around?"

Olivares looked around again. There was still nothing going on. They could just drive around the Suburban or push it out of the way. But he couldn't understand where it had come from. And now DeLeon, that chickenshit, was asking him what to do. Fuck that, he wasn't about to make that call and be at fault for whatever happened.

"6 this is 9, that's your job. You tell me."

Several more seconds of silence followed. DeLeon finally got on the radio and managed to say, "9 this is 6, the trooper thinks -" before the first volley of automatic gunfire ripped through Olivares' Humvee from the left side of the street.

A roar punched Olivares' ears. Glass and shards of metal slapped him in the face. He jerked back and slapped his hands over his eyes in defense. Gunfire exploded above him as Rivera shouted "Motherfucker!" and opened fire. Salazar screamed "Oh shit! Oh fuck!" and stomped on the accelerator. He hadn't taken it out of reverse. The vehicle lurched backward and slammed into the Humvee behind it.

Olivares' head bounced off his seat. Blobs of steel zinged past his head.

Panic flooded his brain, all he could think to do was hide. He tried to slide onto the floorboard. Something smashed into his left forearm. It went numb and he fell back onto the seat, shielding his face with his right arm.

"Salazar! Do something! Hurry!" He tried to slap Salazar but his left arm didn't work. He looked to his driver. Salazar's upper body was slumped onto the empty space between the front seats. His head hung down and a stream of blood poured from his helmet. Rivera yelled "Ow! Ow!" above him. When Olivares looked up something heavy fell onto his helmet, knocking the rim onto the bridge of his nose.

He saw stars. Dead weight pressed Olivares' head against the flimsy door handle. The door popped open. Olivares spilled backwards and slammed the back of his skull onto the street. He lay with his head and upper back on the street, legs and rifle still in the Humvee. Hundreds of pounds pressed down on his calves, trapping them on the seat. The speaker squawked, "9 this is 6! They're shooting us! What do we do?"

The weight on his calves jerked violently several times. Something stabbed him in the right foot. He shuddered from the agony. Further back in the convoy someone yelled over the gunfire, "Top! Move your fucking Humvee!"

Olivares looked down the convoy. Soldiers were piled in clumps next to the passenger sides of vehicles. Bits of metal and plastic exploded from the Humvees, limp bodies poured from the doors. He shouted "Someone help me! Please!"

Nobody responded. Two soldiers sprinted across the street. One of them didn't have a rifle. Gunfire exploded from a roof. Puffs of concrete dust erupted around them.

The soldier with the rifle didn't make it even halfway across the road. It looked like someone switched him off midstride. He slammed down onto his face with arms limp beside him. The other soldier dropped to his knees, got back up dragging one leg. More concrete erupted around him and he fell onto his ass, then keeled over sideways.

Olivares closed his eyes and tried to shut out the terror. He didn't know what to do. Someone had to help him. His soldiers weren't supposed to leave him like this.

A burst of automatic fire rang out in front of his Humvee. Gunshot concussions slapped Olivares' skin. He opened his eyes and snapped them right. A man in black fatigues with a black mask, chest rig and M4 carbine stood at the front bumper, firing through the windshield. He looked down at Olivares. Their eyes met. The man stopped firing.

Olivares closed his eyes again. *I'm dead,* he thought. *It's over. I'm dead.*

CHAPTER 3

Corporal Marc D'Angelo crouched below the edge of the low steel wall encircling the five-ton truck's bed, keeping as still as possible. His breath was ragged and his heart pounded so hard it hurt. Of the seven soldiers in the truck bed with him, two were still making noise. One was gurgling, the other doing something that sounded like a hiccup every few seconds. One more had fallen out of the truck when he was hit. The others were silent and ripped to shreds.

The enemy had stopped shooting into the truck bed, but D'Angelo knew any movement could draw more fire. He stayed still, hoping whoever had ambushed them wouldn't advance on the convoy and shoot into the vehicles. If the ambushers' plan was to hit them and leave, D'Angelo could stay where he was, get on the radio and wait for help. If the ambushers went into the vehicles, he was fucked.

D'Angelo knew what was going to happen as soon as that fucking moron Olivares reported the burning vehicle blocking their path. A blind and deaf tribesman from the Amazon rain forest could have seen it. DeLeon should have ordered Olivares to punch it and get past the spot they should have recognized as an ambush kill zone. But Olivares had the tactical awareness of an Alzheimer's patient and DeLeon the leadership ability of a preteen girl. Those flaming dipshits just sat still and let the company get butchered.

The entire mission had been fucked from the start. The company had fewer than seventy soldiers to begin with, and when DeLeon told them they were going into Arriago a dozen suddenly developed severe medical issues. The remaining soldiers in the company had gone nuts trying to get the company's piece of shit vehicles and rusty old M16 rifles ready.

D'Angelo had been in the unit eight months, and still couldn't believe how shitty their vehicles were. He and the other mechanics kept them running well, but they had no turrets, no gun shields, no bulletproof glass, no armored doors, nothing. A blind insurgent with a .22 rifle could put a round right through them.

In Iraq those vehicles hadn't been allowed off base. And their weapons were almost worse. Old, poorly maintained M16A2 rifles with no optics that rattled like tin cans full of rocks when you shook them. They were practically muskets. The Army might as well issue ramrods and powder horns with them.

The order to carry only one magazine was bullshit. So was the order to leave the Squad Automatic Weapons. D'Angelo knew he couldn't sneak a SAW out of the armory, but he could sure as hell steal enough ammo to fill a few more magazines. A combat load was seven mags and D'Angelo had rolled into Arriago with only four, but he had four times as much ammo as everyone else.

When they mounted up in the trucks to move out, Top Olivares' brown-nosing little buddy Lerma reminded everyone they couldn't insert magazines into their rifles without permission. D'Angelo hadn't said a word. He looked Lerma in the eye, slapped a magazine into his rifle and loaded a round into the chamber. Lerma hadn't even tried to assert any of his supposed authority. He just folded, got into the front passenger seat and didn't look at D'Angelo anymore.

D'Angelo knew the company leadership was going to fuck this up. Their plan for the mission would work great, as long as nothing went wrong. Olivares assumed they'd make it to the school with no problems, Lieutenant DeLeon didn't argue. Nobody made contingency plans. Nobody went over actions on contact. Nobody rehearsed what to do in case of an ambush, or if a vehicle was disabled. There was no casualty evacuation plan. D'Angelo got yelled at by Olivares every time he brought up the possibility of a firefight.

When they climbed into the vehicles D'Angelo asked the soldiers in his truck for a mission brief-back. Some of them didn't even know where in Arriago they were supposed to go, or what the communication plan was. When D'Angelo asked Lerma for the company and command post call signs, Lerma gave him a blank look and stammered in Spanish that he hadn't asked. Lerma probably hadn't expected him to understand, but D'Angelo had grown up in Cuidad Irigoyen, married a Mexican girl he met in high school and spoke fluent Spanish.

D'Angelo wrote down the radio frequency and stayed near the cab so he could listen to the radio. He figured out their company was Wrench and the command post was Thunderbolt. He knew he better remember their call signs, because when the shit hit the fan Lerma sure as hell wouldn't know what to say on the radio.

All the way into town D'Angelo talked the guys in the back of the truck through possible scenarios. He set up a casualty evacuation team, made sure everyone knew where everyone else's first aid gear was, did everything he could to prepare his vehicle for combat. He positioned himself at the front of the truck bed, at the space between the bed and cab, where he could look through the windshield and listen to the radio. He made the soldiers lock and load their rifles. His planning wasn't perfect, but he figured he had done all he could to prepare for an ambush. It almost worked.

When the ambush started, their truck and the one in front of it hadn't been hit. All the fire came from shop windows up ahead, on the left side of the road. D'Angelo saw windows explode and rounds tear through vehicles. The convoy didn't move at all when the gunfire started, there was no attempt to clear the kill zone.

His truck's driver, an eighteen year old just-out-of-basic-training private named Kallinen, shouted to Lerma in terror, "*What do we do?*" Lerma didn't say shit to Kallinen, didn't say anything on the radio, nothing.

"Goddamn it Lerma, tell them to push through!" D'Angelo screamed. "Do something!"

Lerma froze. D'Angelo shouted at his men to stay low and cover 360 degrees, and made sure the rear guard was in place. In front of them, gunners made short but valiant last stands before being shot to pieces. M16 rifles jutting from windows recoiled from three round bursts as soldiers fought back. They and their one magazine of ammunition didn't last long. The volume of fire from the convoy died, Humvee doors opened and soldiers struggled out. D'Angelo watched most of them pour dead onto the street.

D'Angelo's friend Specialist Vicente Marroquin was the gunner on the humvee in front of D'Angelo's truck. Marroquin wasn't fired on at first. He milled around in confusion, yelled down into his humvee and then looked back to D'Angelo for guidance. They locked eyes through the windshield, and D'Angelo screamed, "Shoot, Vicente! Shoot!"

Marroquin's face tensed, he nodded to D'Angelo. Then he turned and opened fired into the shop windows ahead. Disciplined, aimed shots, one every two seconds.

D'Angelo watched a stream of bullets smash through the Humvee's windshield. A round punched through Marroquin's abdomen, just under his armor plate. Marroquin screamed, clutched his stomach and wavered like he was about to fall. Then he put both hands on his weapon and emptied the rest of the magazine. More rounds hit the humvee, Marroquin's head snapped back and he dropped into his vehicle.

D'Angelo screamed at Kallinen, "Back up, dammit! Back the fuck up!" When Kallinen threw the truck into reverse D'Angelo turned and yelled, "Get ready to dismount!"

That pulled Lerma out of his trance. He looked back and yelled, "Top said you're not allowed to get out!"

D'Angelo was about to tell Lerma to shut the fuck up when the rounds hit, from a roof on the right side of the street. The canvas sides on the truck bed were rolled up, the gunner on the roof had a perfect view into the truck and a perfect downward shot. D'Angelo recognized the sound of the RPK machine gun as the soldiers behind him shrieked and returned fire. He turned to see one man trying to hold the blood inside his throat and others rising to their feet, climbing over one another to get away.

"Get the fuck down!" he screamed. "Get below the walls!"

Bullets knocked the soldiers around the bed of the truck like bowling pins. The rear guard tried to go over the tailgate and got hung up on the nylon "troop strap" stretched sideways above it. D'Angelo saw his head jerk from a round's impact before he dropped out of sight. D'Angelo rolled to the metal wall around the bed, threw his muzzle over it and laid down a magazine on burst. The truck started to back up. Lerma's window exploded. D'Angelo jerked his head up to see Lerma flop forward until his helmet hit the dash.

Kallinen screamed, "Oh God! Oh fuck!" and spun the wheel. D'Angelo changed magazines as bullets punched through the front right door and windshield. Kallinen shrieked like his nuts were on fire.

D'Angelo dumped a second mag, pulled his rifle back into the truck bed to reload and slid up to the cab. Another burst of RPK fire smashed into the truck bed. D'Angelo heard rounds impact bodies around him. The radio squawked a frenzied message, DeLeon begging Olivares for orders.

The command post cut in. "Wrench this is Thunderbolt, give me a Goddamn situation report! What's going on?"

The truck jerked to a stop. D'Angelo flattened his body on the floor of the truck bed, found a dead torso with his foot and used it to push himself until his head stuck into the truck's cab. He was about to slide all the way into the cab when the RPK across the street ceased fire, and the gunfire from the left side of the street dropped to almost nothing. The ambush had lasted all of a minute.

He looked up. Lerma was still hunched over with the top of his helmet resting against the dash. He didn't look like he was breathing, and D'Angelo didn't have time to check. He turned left to talk to Kallinen.

Kallinen slumped in the seat with his back resting against the driver's door. His eyes were open, and he cradled what looked like a small pile of grey sausage in his lap. The area around his midsection was soaked with dark red blood. D'Angelo wasn't sure if he was alive at first, until he saw Kallinen blink and his hands shake.

D'Angelo almost said, "Oh shit," but stopped himself. He looked at the radio in the center console and saw that the handset was hooked on the dash on Kallinen's side. It should have been on Lerma's, but that fat loser had probably thought he couldn't talk on it the right way.

"Kallinen," D'Angelo said. Kallinen blinked again, and looked at D'Angelo. "Hey bro, you're good, alright? You hear me?"

Kallinen swallowed and gave a weak nod. He had a look of pure, out of control fear on his face. D'Angelo couldn't reach the handset and couldn't climb into the cab without drawing fire. He'd need Kallinen's help.

He said, "Hey Kallinen, I need you to do something for me. I need you to grab that handset and give it to me. But keep low and quiet, don't move a lot, okay?"

Kallinen barely moved his head. His jaw shivered. He rasped, "I'm gonna die."

D'Angelo looked down the length of the convoy. All the gunners were down, dead soldiers lay scattered along smoking vehicles. One torn and bloody driver had dropped out of his open driver's door. The firing had slowed to a random shot now and then. Loud voices conversed in Spanish somewhere ahead. They didn't sound panicked, so they weren't from his company. The voices weren't leaving.

D'Angelo's heart rate skyrocketed. He wasn't going to be able to sit tight and wait for help. If the enemy had planned a hit-and-run ambush, it didn't make sense for them to hang around and have a calm conversation.

He took a deep breath to steady himself. He still had to get on the radio and tell the command post about the ambush.

"Kallinen, you're not going to die. Chill out, I'll take care of you. Now give me the damn handset."

Kallinen didn't move. He looked at D'Angelo with tears running down his cheeks.

"Lean forward a little bit, reach out with your right hand and grab the handset," D'Angelo urged. "Hurry up, man."

Kallinen let go of the pile of intestines but barely reached his knee before his arm fell. Toward the front of the convoy a shrill scream rang out, followed by a short, sharp burst of fire. Someone laughed, and a gruff voice called out, *"These idiots are American soldiers? Why the fuck were we so scared of them?"*

"Kal, grab the fucking handset and give it to me. Now."

Kallinen mumbled, "I can't."

"Kal, If you don't give me the handset, I can't call you a fucking medevac. Gimme the handset."

Kallinen's eyes widened. He struggled to force himself a little higher in the seat, then grimaced in pain as he reached to the dash. His arm shook like he had Parkinson's. He made an *"uuhhhnn"* noise as he forced his hand the last couple of inches. D'Angelo flattened himself against the floor, hoping the movement inside the cab wouldn't draw more fire. It didn't.

Kallinen got his bloody fingers around the handset and just managed to lift it off the green nylon cord it was hooked onto. He collapsed back into the driver's seat, then held his shaking right arm toward D'Angelo.

D'Angelo grabbed the handset. "Thanks, Kal. Lay back and rest, alright? We're gonna be okay. Just stay quiet and don't move, okay?"

Kallinen nodded, laid his hand gently back onto his intestines and closed his eyes. D'Angelo put the handset to his ear and felt the earpiece slip around from the blood on it. He keyed the mike and said, "Thunderbolt, this is Wrench."

Thunderbolt shot back a reply. "Wrench this is Thunderbolt, what the fuck is going on? Give me a SITREP!"

"Thunderbolt this is Wrench, we got ambushed and wiped out. We need reinforcements, like now. How fast can you get someone to us? Over."

The response was delayed this time. "Wrench, we're working that issue. What do you mean, you got wiped out? What happened? Over."

"Fuck," D'Angelo muttered. "We were hit in a near ambush. The enemy blocked the road in front of us with a burning vehicle and opened up from hidden positions in the stores on our left. They also had at least one automatic weapon in an elevated position on the right. All our vehicles are stopped and I think almost everyone's dead. How copy, over."

Seven vehicles ahead, two men in black fatigues with black masks and gear sauntered into view on the right side of the convoy. They didn't seem the least bit concerned about any danger. They kicked a few of the corpses in the head, then opened the door of a Humvee. One of them stuck the muzzle of his AK into the doorway and jabbed something with it. Then they both reached in, braced themselves against the vehicle and yanked the body of the state trooper onto the street. The man's brown uniform was ripped and stained red.

One of the men reached to the trooper's belt and took his duty radio. The men moved on to the next vehicle. Three other men in black appeared behind them, grabbing rifles from dead soldiers.

D'Angelo's breath caught in his throat. Adrenaline spiked his veins. There was no question now, they were coming for him.

"Wrench, did you see any of the enemy? Can you give a description? Over."

"Thunderbolt, I see five of them now. Wearing all black BDU uniforms, black masks, black chest rigs and carrying AKs and M4 type weapons. Over."

There was another delay from Thunderbolt. Up ahead, someone yelled in Spanish, *"Hey! One of these assholes is talking on the radio!"*

The five enemy D'Angelo could see rushed to yank Humvee doors open and look inside. He blurted "Oh fuck!" and jerked his head down. He waited a moment, then eased his head up until he could barely see over the dash. More than a dozen men in black were visible now, on both sides of the convoy. They were pulling all the bodies out onto the street.

"Wrench, I need more information. Are you Wrench 6? Who are you? Over."

"Thunderbolt, I'm not 6. I'm not one of the company leaders, I'm just a mechanic. Over."

"What's your name, Wrench?"

D'Angelo didn't want to say his name over the radio. Instead, he gave the generic response, "Echo 4 Delta." Echo 4 for his rank, E-4, and Delta for the first letter of his last name.

"Wrench, give me your name in the clear. Over."

"Goddamn it," D'Angelo mumbled. He heard a wheeze and turned to see Kallinen staring at him, blue eyes full of fear. He keyed the radio and said, "Corporal D'Angelo."

"The guy talking on the radio is named D'Angelo!" a voice announced. D'Angelo thought, *Shit.*

"D'Angelo, are you secure right now? Are you safe?"

D'Angelo spat back, "No I'm not fucking safe right now, Thunderbolt! I just told you I'm looking at the enemy. And they're listening to this radio traffic."

"What's your location?"

Fuck you, D'Angelo thought. *There's no way in hell I'm going to put my location over the radio with the enemy listening.* "I'm in the area of the ambush, Thunderbolt. That's all I can say."

Shop doors flew open on the left side of the street. Men in black fatigues walked out, joined by others stepping through broken windows. Over twenty men milled around the convoy, peered into vehicles and yanked dead soldiers onto the street.

D'Angelo watched one soldier's head bounce off the concrete. The soldier cried out in pain. The man who pulled him out jerked back in surprise, then grabbed the soldier's rifle away. Others dug through the soldier's gear and pockets, pulled his helmet off and forced him to his feet. One yelled in Spanish, *"Jefe! We found a live one!"*

Jefe. Boss. D'Angelo wondered, who the fuck was in charge of these assholes? "Thunderbolt this is Wrench, they just took one of our guys prisoner. Do you copy?"

"Thunderbolt copies! Do you know who it is? What are they doing with him?"

The prisoner's back was to D'Angelo, he couldn't see the man's face. A masked man jabbed his AK into the soldier's stomach and yelled something D'Angelo didn't understand. The soldier raised his hands. Then another man with a short, paratrooper-style AK hanging on his chest walked around the front of the Humvee. This man had an entourage of four other men in black. He said something to the soldier, who shook his head furiously. Then the soldier tore open his body armor and let it slip off his shoulders. The man with the short AK looked at the man's chest, then turned to his men and shook his head. He turned back to the soldier and rubbed his hair, like he was a cherished son. The soldier recoiled in terror. The man took him by the arm and led him between the vehicles, out of D'Angelo's sight. His entourage followed. D'Angelo knew he had just seen their *jefe*.

Aw, fuck, D'Angelo thought. *The boss checked his fucking nametape. They're looking for me.*

Thunderbolt this is Wrench, I don't know who it was. They took his weapon and walked him away somewhere. Over."

"Roger. Wrench, can you stay where you are and keep reporting?"

"He's still talking on the radio," a voice yelled out. *"He's fucking watching us!"* The masked men swarmed around the vehicles, moving faster down the line toward D'Angelo's truck. As he watched, three men popped all the doors of the Humvee two vehicles ahead and pulled bodies out. He saw them tear open body armor to read name tapes.

"Thunderbolt, I don't think so. I don't have much time. I see over twenty of them now, all armed with AK's and M4 type weapons. Black fatigues with no markings. One of them fired an RPK during the ambush, I recognized the sound. They're checking all the vehicles in the convoy."

As soon as he let go of the transmit key, he saw something he hadn't expected. A man stepped into view with a Rocket Propelled Grenade launcher slung over his shoulder. His partner walked behind him, carrying a vinyl pack designed to carry three RPG rounds.

"Thunderbolt, one of these guys is carrying an RPG. They didn't use it during the ambush. You copy?"

"Thunderbolt copies. Listen to me, Wrench. Don't hang around too long if it's not safe. You do whatever you have to to stay alive. You copy? Do anything you think you have to. We're behind you and we'll get you as soon as we can."

D'Angelo's exhaled and closed his eyes. They were saying goodbye. He was on his own. He keyed up and said, "Roger, Thunderbolt, see you later. Out," and dropped the handset.

He considered his options: there were only three, and two were suicide. He could get out and run, knowing he'd be chased down and shot in the back. He could fight back and kill a few of them before being killed. Or play dead and hope they didn't check him too closely, or read his name tape. He opened his eyes to see Kallinen still staring at him with wide eyes. He said, "Kallinen, when they come to you, don't say anything about me. Just surrender, okay?"

Kallinen started mumbling something. As D'Angelo rolled onto his back and slid into the truck bed he recognized a few of Kallinen's words. "… thou among women and blessed is the fruit of thy womb, Jesus. Holy Mary, mother of God… " D'Angelo felt with his feet for a gap, then forced them under an anonymous corpse's legs. The truck bed was slick with what felt like warm oil, but D'Angelo knew what it was.

He laid his rifle on a jumble of limbs, pointed at the tailgate. Then he rolled halfway left, listening for the men to reach his truck. Their voices were still a little ways off. He reached to the sleeve of the dead soldier beside him, pulled as hard as he could. He hoped to God the RPK gunner wasn't still watching, there was no way in hell that he wouldn't spot the movement.

Nobody fired into the truck. The voices outside came closer. Kallinen still rasped a prayer, the same prayer, from the cab. D'Angelo got the body of the soldier closer and lifted one shoulder. Jesus, the guy was heavy. He got the soldier's shoulder just high enough that he could jiggle his way underneath, one tiny bounce at a time.

The truck's passenger door opened. D'Angelo froze. Someone outside laughed and said, *"Shit, I thought you had to be in shape to be in the American*

Army. Look how fat this bastard is."

He heard a scraping noise, then a wet thud as something heavy hit the ground. A voice giggled, *"Hey asshole, watch out. You hit my foot."*

D'Angelo let go of the dead soldier's shoulder and as slow as he could, laid his own left arm across his face. He turned his head a little, enough so that he didn't look like he was watching the tailgate but not so far that he couldn't see it. He quietly flipped the safety off his rifle. Outside, someone exclaimed, *"Hey look, the driver's alive, and there's a fucking radio in here! I bet that's the cock-sucker who was talking about us."*

Kallinen's voice kept repeating a Hail Mary. Orders were yelled outside, and the driver's door opened. Kallinen shrieked. D'Angelo grimaced despite his efforts to keep every muscle still. Kallinen's back had been resting on the driver's door, and D'Angelo knew he had fallen backward when the door opened. The pain in his torn abdomen must have been excruciating.

D'Angelo forced the thought of Kallinen's agony out of his mind. He let his lips part, left his eyes halfway open and tried to slow his breathing so the movement of his chest would be invisible under his body armor. He hoped he had a corpse's expression on his face.

Spanish shouts mixed with Kallinen's screams. Someone yelled in accented English, "Whas jour fucking name, boy?"

Kallinen didn't answer. D'Angelo's heart tried to smash a hole in his chest. His midsection heated, and he realized he had just pissed himself. It didn't matter, the bodies in the back had pissed themselves too. Nobody would notice.

A stern voice outside said in Spanish, *"Check his name tag."*

Oh, fuck, D'Angelo thought. *Kal, let them think you're me. If you don't, I'm done.* He cursed himself for his selfishness, but it was true. He hoped they would think Kallinen was him.

Kallinen had the new body armor, the kind that had a complicated fastening system and went on over your head instead of closing in front like the old vest D'Angelo was wearing. He tried to remember if Kallinen had a name tape on his body armor. He didn't think anyone in the company had one. As far as he could remember, name tapes were only on their uniform tops.

Kallinen screamed, "No, stop! That hurts!"

Someone yelled back, "Chut thee fuck up, *pendejo*! How you open thees fucking thing?"

Another voice growled, "Who was talking on the radio, boy?"

D'Angelo closed his eyes. *Kallinen, please, don't tell them about me.*

"It was... it... I was! I'm sorry!"

D'Angelo opened his eyes again. *I owe you, Kallinen. I owe you. For as long as I live.*

In his peripheral vision, D'Angelo saw the muzzle of an AK poke over the wall of the truck bed. He nearly shit himself, but caught it in time. Another AK joined it. Two men had climbed onto the side of the truck and were looking into the bed. One of the men said, *"One of them is still moaning. That one, over there."*

D'Angelo's heart rate shot up again. He checked himself. *Oh God,* he thought. *Am I moaning?* Then he heard it, the pathetic noise one of the soldiers in the back had been making since the truck bed was raked by machine gun fire. With all the other crap going on, he'd stopped hearing it. The other soldier, who'd been making the hiccup noise, was silent.

"I can't figure out how to open his armor, Jefe. And he's a fucking mess, his guts are hanging out. I don't want to get that shit all over my hands. He's the only white guy here, and he said he was talking on the radio."

"Does he have a wallet?"

Seconds of silence, then another scream from Kallinen. *"No wallet, Jefe."*

"Fuck it. It's him. Get rid of him, he's too fucked up to keep. We have two others anyway."

"You don't want any others?"

"No. No need for more. How were our losses?"

"Not bad, Jefe. A couple of these Americans got lucky. Two dead, one other might die. They were just throwaways, nobody important."

Outside, Kallinen screamed, "No! Please, no!"

A voice replied in Spanish, *"Calm yourself, son. It's alright."*

Two shots rang out. They sounded to D'Angelo like pistol shots. Kallinen didn't scream again.

D'Angelo felt a wave of guilt wash over him, with an even guiltier touch of relief. They had killed Kallinen, D'Angelo might be safe now.

One of the AK's pointing into the truck fired once, two feet from D'Angelo's head. His eyes slammed shut for a moment. He could have sworn his body jerked from the sudden shock of fear. The moaning from the wounded soldier stopped. D'Angelo swallowed and waited for another round to explode from the AK. Another round, for him.

Go away, Goddamn it, D'Angelo prayed. *You think you just killed the guy you were looking for, get the fuck out of here.*

The *jefe's* voice ordered, *"Take their rifles and let's go."*

The AK's pointing into the truck bed withdrew. D'Angelo swallowed again and prayed, *Please, don't come in here.*

Metal scraped metal, chains rattled, and the truck tailgate fell with a clang. A masked man hoisted himself with a groan and stepped into the bed. Heads appeared behind him, looking into the truck. D'Angelo had a sudden thought, that maybe he should have followed Top Olivares' orders to wear the same gear as everyone else. D'Angelo's gear was unique and better than everyone else's. If one of these guys decided he wanted it, D'Angelo was a dead man.

The man inside the truck picked up an M16 and handed it back. One of the heads at the tailgate pulled its mask off. Through slitted eyes, D'Angelo saw the face in the sunlight. A dark, bearded man, maybe forty years old. He took the M16 and looked it over, then said, *"What a piece of shit. I don't know why they want us to send these back, they won't sell for that much in Mexico."*

"I don't know either, Jefe."

The man in the truck grabbed another two rifles and passed them to waiting hands. The unmasked man smiled and said, *"Boys, this is a good day's work. I think God will smile on us for today."*

"Jefe, do you think this was a good idea?" one of the entourage asked. *"I understand why we killed the police, but killing American soldiers? Don't you think that will bring more attention to the border, instead of making it easier for us to move our stuff across?"*

"Miguel, I hear what you're saying," a paternal voice answered. *"Maybe it will make it harder for our business, I don't know. But you have to trust those who planned this operation, they thought about everything. It will work out for*

us. If God wills it."

Voices murmured agreement. The man in the back passed another rifle back. He stepped over another body onto D'Angelo's ankle. D'Angelo stifled a groan. The man grabbed D'Angelo's rifle by the front sight.

This was it. D'Angelo had to decide, right now, what to do. He could blast the man in the face with a burst, then take out that asshole in charge and maybe a couple of others before he was shot down. Or he could keep playing dead, let the man take his rifle, and hope nobody noticed he was alive. Every soldier he knew would want him to shoot it out, kill as many enemy as possible and die a hero's death. On the other hand, his wife, daughter and parents would want him to play dead, to reach for that one faint hope of survival.

D'Angelo didn't know what to do. The faces of his wife and daughter floated across his mind. He remembered his Vietnam veteran grandfather's advice, before his first deployment. *Never let yourself be captured, no matter what. Take death over capture if it comes to that.* And his wife's words, on that same day. *Don't be a hero. Do whatever you have to so you come home to me.*

He wished God would give him a sign, some direction. He swallowed again. His hand tensed on the pistol grip of the rifle.

The man in the truck bed lifted the rifle. D'Angelo moved his eyes, looked into the man's face. The man was looking down at the weapon, not at him.

D'Angelo took his decision, said a silent prayer, and made his move.

CHAPTER 4

First platoon huddled around the hood of Lieutenant Quincy's Humvee, staring at a map. Captain Harcrow and First Sergeant Grant stood with them. Nobody spoke as they waited for Colonel Lidell, the 56th Brigade Combat Team commander, to read a note a runner had passed to him. He frowned as he read it, making Nunez wonder what bad news he had just received.

Lidell folded the note, put it in a map case hung over his shoulder. "Go back and tell Colonel Burress he's just going to have to make do until more troops get here. We'll talk about it later."

The runner gave a "Roger that, sir," and headed through the darkness toward the mall. Nunez figured Colonel Burress, whoever he was, was bitching about having his units split up just like Nunez's battalion had been. Nunez's company received the warning order about the Arriago mission over an hour after Bravo and Charlie companies moved out from the Edinburgh mall. Bravo was sent to reinforce checkpoints around the eight affected towns, Charlie given to a scout squadron that was sending dozens of small teams to ring the towns with observation posts. At least they weren't getting some bullshit mission like guarding a police station or evacuee center, like other units were. Some mayors and police chiefs in unaffected towns near the border were making ridiculous demands of the Guard, even going so far as to insist soldiers be assigned as their personal bodyguards. The Guard's commander and the Governor weren't having any of that, but mobilized units were still being spread thin.

Arriago should have been a full battalion's mission. Instead, each of Alpha's three platoons would do the work of a company. Quincy's and Nunez's first platoon would secure the convoy, second platoon would push past and secure the area immediately around the convoy, third platoon would stand by outside town as the Quick Reaction Force. If something went wrong, Captain Harcrow could find himself running out of troops real fast.

Colonel Lidell put both hands on the Humvee's's hood. Nunez thought he looked tired and frustrated. Lidell gave a loud "Good evening, warriors," and received a chorus of "Good evening sir," in response. He looked around and gave nods to several men. The younger ones nervously nodded back.

Lidell's voice didn't reflect the fatigue Nunez knew he was feeling. They were all feeling it. Since first being mobilized two days earlier, the soldiers had only slept in brief naps of less than an hour, whenever they had a chance. Nunez knew they weren't at the stage where fatigue would cripple their ability to do their jobs, but another day without sleep would do it.

"Men, you have received the most important mission I've ever given any soldiers under my command," Lidell said. "And you didn't receive it at random. I chose this battalion for the mission, your battalion commander Lieutenant Colonel Ybarra chose this company, and Captain Harcrow chose this platoon." He smiled, then added, "Well, this was the only company left in the battalion, so it wasn't a hard choice."

The gathered soldiers laughed, a subdued wave of chuckles. Nunez thought it was an expression of their appreciation for Lidell's honesty.

"Now that I know a little about this platoon, I know we've made the right choice," Lidell said, then pointed toward Quincy. "I know it's the right choice because this platoon is led by a man who took two rounds charging through a door in Afghanistan after an IED attack and ambush, and was awarded a Bronze Star with a V and a Purple Heart for it. The platoon sergeant," he pointed at Nunez, "picked up Quincy's SAW, dumped a drum through the doorway and then led two soldiers inside to clear it. And you know what Sergeant Nunez did during the terrorist attack in Houston two years ago."

A few soldiers new to the platoon looked at Nunez. They knew the basic story, no details. Nunez kept his eyes on Lidell. He hated any mention of the attack, and refused to discuss that day with anyone but his wife and a few trusted friends. He still had nightmares about it, still went to regular appointments at the department's psychological services division to talk about the guilt he still felt. A lot of people had been killed while he was trying to figure out what to do. His soldiers had heard the story about what he had done, but not from him. He never talked about it.

Colonel Lidell pointed at another soldier. "And Sergeant Allenby ignored a serious arm wound during a firefight in Iraq so he could try to stop his squad leader from bleeding out. All your squad leaders have seen combat, almost all your NCO's have been tested in Iraq or Afghanistan, or both. So have quite a few of the specialists and corporals, and even one of the privates. And those who haven't been tested under fire aren't slackers, they're ready for what you're about to do. Other units are staging tonight to push into other towns tomorrow morning, but your mission into Arriago has priority. Remember that."

Lidell looked around again. "Men, it's up to you to recover an entire company of American soldiers who we think have been lost, and to rescue any survivors. I stress that we just think they've been lost, we don't know for sure. I know a million rumors blew through here last night after the ambush. Forget all that bullshit and listen to what I'm going to tell you, because I got this straight from the command post. Here's what happened…"

As Lidell ran down the details of the ambush, Sergeant Carillo lit a cigarette. Nunez took in the sight of geared-up soldiers crowded around a map, smelled the butane scent of a lighter mixed with tobacco smoke. He was reminded of other briefings, on other nights before other missions in other, less important places. Gatherings of tense soldiers communing with their leaders before battle had become normal in Nunez's life. The mission and place, however, were anything but.

Lidell continued, "After the gunfire tapered off, a soldier who claimed to be from the company got on the radio and started putting out information. He said the convoy had been hit by a near ambush that killed almost everyone. He saw over twenty enemy fighters dressed in black with black military gear, armed with M4 type weapons, AK's and one RPG that they did not use during the ambush. He said he heard RPK fire, but as far as the command post could tell he didn't see one. He saw one soldier captured. According to this soldier, the fire first came from shops on the east side of the street. They also took fire from a high position on the west side. He didn't give any more information after that. He had to get off the radio and we don't know what happened to him."

Lidell made eye contact with several of the soldiers again. "If this person's reporting is true, this was a well-prepared, well-executed ambush, better than anything I ever saw the Iraqis or Taliban do. The enemy prepared a kill zone, blocked the road and took out the entire company in seconds. Soldiers at the checkpoint said heavy gunfire lasted less than a minute, then was followed by short bursts of fire or single shots for a few minutes. We don't know what the gunfire after the initial ambush was for. Men, I hope to God they weren't executing our wounded, but I don't know. It's up to you to find out.

"Now, the soldier who was reporting. He said his name was Corporal D'Angelo. We got someone to the maintenance company's armory in Cuidad Irigoyen and found out there was in fact a Corporal D'Angelo on the convoy. He's a former regular Army infantryman who did one tour of Iraq and one of Afghanistan with the 1st Infantry Division. According to the soldiers still at that armory, this guy D'Angelo was sharp. We collected all the information about him that we could, and one of the Joes in my Command Post wrote up detail sheets on 3x5 cards. I'm told those cards have been issued out, Captain Harcrow?"

"Yes sir," Harcrow answered. "The key leaders have them."

"Good. Keep in mind that we don't know if the person who was on the radio was really D'Angelo. Worst case scenario, one of these fucking guys just looked at a dead soldier's nametape, got on the radio, claimed to be him and gave false information. If you find someone claiming to be D'Angelo, be real damn careful about trusting what he tells you. We don't have a picture of him, just the information you have on your cards."

Lidell leaned in toward the platoon a bit. "Men, I'm going to tell you something that doesn't go any further than this parking lot. The truth is, that maintenance company was fucked up. Their commander was a disorganized dipshit, and there are still a bunch of soldiers at their armory who weaseled their way out of that mission. One of them even said he faked an illness to get out of it, because the company commander and First Sergeant were so fucked up. That doesn't mean we won't make every effort to get to them, men. But it does mean we go in there ready for a fight, not blind and stupid like they did."

Nunez raised his hand. "Sir, how does this affect the big picture? General Landers' bullshit about only one mag per soldier and nothing larger than a 5.56 went away, but what else has changed? What about the rumor the President finally committed regular Army units?"

Lidell grimaced and rubbed his face. "Sergeant Nunez, the short answer is that a lot has changed. First, as you probably heard, General Landers has accepted responsibility for the ambush and stepped down from his position. I know some of you think that's good, but I don't. General Landers has been a friend of mine for over twenty years. I was one of his platoon leaders back when he had an infantry company, a long time ago. He's a good leader and he cares about his troops. When he gave the orders restricting ammo load and heavier weapons, he was trying to prevent unnecessary collateral damage. The order to not use armored vehicles was because we don't have many, and because he was under pressure from the Pentagon to avoid the perception that we're militarizing the border. He knew how serious those orders were, and he agonized over them. And he's agonizing over the consequences. I know you men don't care much about that, you have more important things to worry about than how General Landers is feeling. The important thing is that the acting commander of the Guard, General Koba, and Governor Mathieu have both authorized stronger measures to destroy the hostile forces. And the word they used was 'destroy'. Not 'neutralize', not 'arrest', no weak bullshit like that. The mission is to destroy them.

"And to answer your question about the regular Army, it's not a rumor. They're coming. Once the President was informed of the ambush he authorized the use of federal troops. As of four hours ago you're all under federal orders. This is no longer a criminal action, gentlemen. It's a war, or something damn close to it. Elements of the 1st Cavalry and 4th Infantry Divisions have received warning orders to head south from Fort Hood, but it's going to take some time. And remember, most of those divisions are deployed, so they only have about a brigade total strength between the two of them. All of their organic Apache battalions are overseas. Some of their troops will be airlifted in, but then they're dependent on us for support. The regular Army units can't just jump in their armored vehicles and drive down here, they have to load them up on heavy equipment transporters and organize a convoy over a five hundred mile route. I'd like to think they had plans in place before they got the order, but the bottom line is that they're not going to be here for at least a day. Then they have to figure out what units are being committed where, what the orders and rules of engagement are, how to integrate with the Guard units already operating in the affected area, everything. It's going to be a couple of days before regular Army ground units move into any of the towns. Marine Reserve infantry units from San Antonio, Houston and Austin have also been mobilized, but they'll take a little time to get here. Our National Guard 19th Special Forces Group soldiers have been tasked to recover any troops captured during the convoy ambush. Kiowas from Fort Hood will fly into the area tomorrow, Apaches from Hood and the Guard unit north of Houston will be here about a day later. Tonight we'll have observation from two Navy Sea Hawk rescue helicopters from Naval Air Station Kingsville. They don't have guns or thermal sights, but the pilots have night vision and can watch the area for you.

"For now, there will be no fixed wing support. Neither the President, the Governor nor General Koba are willing to authorize air strikes inside American towns. Same thing with the use of explosives. No hand or M203 grenades, no Mark 19 grenade launchers. That could change, depending on what happens when you and other units push into the towns. For this mission, the largest weapon you'll have is an M240 machine gun."

Nunez looked at his watch. Forty minutes after midnight. They were supposed to hit their start point at one. The Sea Hawks Colonel Lidell was talking about wouldn't be on station until 0130. A unit could have been pushed into Arriago sooner, but the senior leadership wasn't rushing anything this time. Sending another company pell-mell into Arriago could compound the problem instead of fixing it.

Nunez glanced up from his watch and saw Lidell looking at him. Lidell checked his own watch and said, "Alright men, I know you don't have much time for your last minute checks, so I'll cut this off now. I'll be with your company leadership on the highway behind you, but I want you guys to know I'm not going into Arriago with you. That's not because I'm not willing to take the risks I'm asking you to take, it's because I don't want to be a distraction to you. I don't want anyone worrying about protecting me when you should be worrying about your platoon, the maintenance company, and any Americans that need help inside Arriago. If things go bad, I'll go in with the Quick Reaction Force, either as the commander or just an extra rifle. But don't think about me while you're in there. Just do your job, accomplish your mission and make our country proud. I know you can do it, warriors. Do you have any questions for me?"

Nobody spoke. Lidell put his hand on Captain Harcrow's shoulder and said, "Alright men, that's it. Get ready to move out, and I'll be right behind you. Good luck to you."

Lidell and his entourage walked away. Harcrow gestured to Quincy and Nunez, and they gathered near him as the rest of the platoon went to their vehicles. Harcrow said, "Rodger, Jerry, I know you've been over the plan more than enough times, but I'll ask anyway. Is there anything you don't understand about what we're supposed to do?"

"No sir," Quincy said. "Second platoon secures the area, we recover the casualties, third stays on the highway as the quick reaction force. Too easy, sir."

"Alright, you've got it then. Guys, I don't have to tell you that we're not about to let ourselves get taken out the way the 336th did. I trust you both to do this right. Good luck."

Harcrow walked away. Quincy turned to Nunez and said, "I told him we're ready, but are all the squad leaders clear on the plan?"

"The squad leaders are as ready as we are. We've briefed and back-briefed them. We're all set to go."

"Okay, good." Quincy looked at his watch. "Jerry, I already know the answer to this, but any luck getting more night vision?"

Nunez gave a dejected shrug. "I begged everyone I could and looked for any that weren't tied down and under guard. There aren't any extras. We've got our two for the whole company, and we're lucky Captain Harcrow gave both of them to us for this mission. I don't think we're going to get more."

"Yeah, I know. Overseas everyone down to the lowest private gets a set, but here at home we got nothing." Quincy rubbed his chin. "Well, fuck it. The driver of the lead vehicle gets one set and the dismounted element's point man gets the other." He looked up at the lights and said, "Uh… any word on whether lights are still on in Arriago?"

Nunez's eyebrows rose. That question hadn't come up. "Well, shit," he said. "Nobody thought about that. If the lights are on, I guess our stealthy approach might be a little harder to pull off than we planned."

"Yeah," Quincy said, shaking his head. "Whatever, who cares. We'll deal with it when we get there." He rubbed his temples and said, "Jerry, if anyone, and I mean anyone, isn't clear on what they're supposed to do, tell me. We'll do a radio rehearsal on the way in."

"Got it, Rod. I'll pass the word." Nunez started to walk toward the rest of the platoon.

"Jerry, hold up."

Nunez turned back to see Quincy staring at him, eyes intense.

"Don't let me fuck this up," he said quietly, so nobody else would hear. "If I'm doing something wrong, tell me. I trusted you in Afghanistan and I trust you now. Watch my back."

Nunez grabbed Quincy's hand in a handshake. "Rodger, we all have each other's backs. Relax a little. You're doing everything a good infantry platoon leader should do. I trust you with my life. I mean that."

Quincy swallowed. "Right back at you, brother. Let's do this shit."

Nunez hesitated a moment. He was taken back to another early morning, with another platoon in another place, where another lieutenant had shaken his hand and said *Let's do this shit.* Nunez had rolled into a Taliban-held valley in Afghanistan with that platoon leader. The disaster they expected that morning failed to materialize. But odds were that a different disaster was out there, hiding on a dark street in Arriago, waiting to pounce.

Nunez gave Quincy's hand a squeeze. "Let's do this shit, Rodger."

Quincy smiled, let go of Nunez's hand and moved toward his vehicle. Nunez walked to his Humvee and climbed in. His soldiers were already there, passing a can of Copenhagen back and forth. Nunez liked the smell of chewing tobacco but couldn't imagine sticking any of that crap into his mouth.

Engines started up and down the convoy. Nunez told his driver, Private First Class Conway, to crank their Humvee. Conway flipped the start switch to stand-by, waited for the "wait" light to go out, then flipped the switch further right and let it go. The diesel engine rumbled to life.

Within two minutes the platoon was mounted in their vehicles with engines running. Radio and weapons checks had already been completed, drivers had inspected and reinspected fluid levels, personal gear was tested to ensure it wouldn't make noise, radio frequencies set and communications checks completed. The platoon was ready.

Quincy got back on the radio. "Red 4 this is Red 1, check with 6 and see if everyone's ready to move."

Nunez answered, "1 this is 4, roger." He hung the platoon radio handset back on its mount and grabbed the handset for the company net. "Rapido 6 this is Red 4."

"Red 4 this is Rapido 6."

"6, Red platoon is ready to go, request Start Point."

"Red 4, standby one."

A few seconds passed. Nunez turned back to see Sergeant Corley, the platoon's medic, check his aid bag for what had to be the tenth time that night. Corley, twenty-eight years old, was tall, thin, pasty white and professional enough to hide the fear Nunez knew he felt. Three deployments to Iraq as a combat medic had taught him a lot. He had tourniquets on the outside of the bag ready to go, needles and tubing duct-taped to IV bags inside. His red helmet light was on so he could look into his bag. He closed the bag, turned his light off and gave Nunez two thumbs up. He was ready.

"Red 4 this is Rapido 6, all Rapido elements are ready to roll. Start your move."

Nunez acknowledged and switched back to the platoon net. "Red 1 this is Red 4, Rapido is ready."

"Roger," Quincy said. "Red platoon this is Red 1, follow me."

From his position in the convoy, three vehicles from the rear, Nunez saw Quincy's Humvee at the front move out. The platoon's eight vehicles crept from their spots and followed in line as their platoon leader weaved through the parking lot and onto the highway. Nunez keyed the company radio.

"Rapido 6 this is Red 4, SP time 0058. How copy, over."

"Red 4 this is Rapido 6, I copy your SP and I'm behind you. Godspeed."

Dozens of soldiers from other units stood at the parking lot's exit, watching Nunez's platoon roll past. Nunez looked one of them in the eye as his Humvee neared the exit. A tall and heavily muscled buck sergeant, with the bearing and gear of an infantryman. The sergeant stared hard at Nunez and lifted his M4 over his head, a sign of one soldier's respect for another.

Other soldiers joined him. The last thing Nunez saw as they left the parking lot was a cluster of soldiers raising M4 carbines and Squad Automatic Weapons in the air as a silent salute.

CHAPTER 5

"Reds this is Red 1, lock and load."

Vehicles commanders acknowledged. Nunez called "Barney! Lock and load!" to his gunner, then grabbed his driver's M4, yanked the charging handle and slammed a round into the chamber. He and Doc Corley loaded their carbines and stowed them, muzzles down. They had just weaved through the police checkpoint north of Arriago, the line of departure for their mission. The town was two miles ahead, out of sight on the other side of heavy brush.

The vehicles moved slowly. They had driven blacked out since leaving Edinburgh and slowed even more to get through the mass of police and military vehicles at the checkpoint, but from this point they could speed up. The rest of the convoy would take a while getting through, but Nunez's platoon wasn't waiting for them. The other vehicles would stay behind on the road anyway, and would have plenty of time to set their positions while Nunez's platoon dismounted and walked into Arriago.

The drivers increased speed to thirty miles per hour, driving in the dark with a tiny amount of moonlight. The highway lights had been out for almost twenty miles. The lead driver had a good view through his night vision, but everyone else was doing nothing more than following the hazy outline of the Humvee to their front.

Nunez checked his GPS. Quincy's vehicle should hit the dismount point, half a mile north of Arriago, within a few minutes. He checked his handheld radio, which was jammed into a pouch on his left side. One last time, Nunez made sure his magazines were rounds-down and pointing right in the mag pouches. He slapped the forward assist on his carbine and made sure the red dot sight above his scope was on, checked his weapon and helmet lights to make sure they were in "safe" settings and wouldn't be turned on by accident. Everything was in place, he was ready.

The vehicles slowed, then the Humvee ahead of Nunez's swerved hard right.

Nunez's driver, Private Conway, said "Shit!" and spun the steering wheel to follow the other Humvee's's move. The shadow of a car floated by on the left. Nunez was looking at it when he felt the right side of the Humvee bounce over something lumpy and soft.

The scent of rotting flesh exploded in the Humvee. Barnes, in the gun turret, said "Aw, fuck! That stinks like fucking crazy!" The men inside reacted in disgust, covering their faces and gagging at the rotten stench. Conway said, "God damn Sarge, what is that?"

Nunez blew outward, tried to get the imagined taste of maggot-infested corpse out of his mouth. All he managed to do was get a nose full of his own stale breath. He said, "You just hit a dead person," as he grabbed the platoon radio handset.

"Red 1 this is Red 4, we need a heads up from your driver if you pass something in the road. We almost hit a car, and we ran over a dead body."

"4 this is 1, roger that. Correcting that problem now."

Nunez stuck the handset back on its mount. "Get a little more distance between you and the Humvee in front of us." Conway backed off. Quincy called out two more burned vehicles and four bodies during the next two minutes before he announced, "This is 1, we're stopping at the dismount point."

Nunez acknowledged. The convoy slowed and crept to the grid Nunez had marked on his GPS. No lights shone in the distance.

"Reds this is Red 1, we don't see any lights on in Arriago."

"This is Red 4, roger. I'll call it up."

The Humvees eased to a stop. Nunez turned his dismount radio on and popped his door as Doc Corley got out on the other side. Nunez told his driver and gunner, "You guys stay cool, listen to Sergeant Allenby and stay the fuck awake. We might be screaming for help real soon."

His men gave quiet assurances that they'd stay sharp. On both sides of the Humvee soldiers jogged past Nunez, headed up front. Nunez dropped in behind them and keyed the mike on his radio to report, "Rapido 6 this is Red 4, we just hit our dismount point. How copy, over."

"Red 4 this is Rapido 6, good copy."

As he jogged forward the platoon formed two columns, just as they had been told during the mission brief. They would advance into town with one column on each side of the road, Quincy leading the column on the right, Staff Sergeant Burrows leading the column on the left. Nunez would stay about two thirds of the way back in the left column and was responsible for all reporting to Captain Harcrow.

Nunez jogged to the front of the left column and spoke to each soldier, making a quick roll call, then did the same thing for the right column. Everyone was in place. He jogged to Quincy and whispered, "We're accounted for."

"Cool. Let's roll."

Quincy waved his arm forward. The signal was repeated down both columns as the soldiers began their move. Nunez fell in to the left column as the men broke into a speed walk. He held his weapon in close, muzzle down, looking everywhere into the darkness and seeing nothing. If the enemy had another well-planned ambush set for them outside town, they might lose a lot of guys.

The troops up front broke into a slow run, just faster than a shuffle. Nunez had already been hot and sweaty from the summer night humidity, but within fifty meters he felt a layer of sweat cover everything. He and the others had been without a shower for days, and he could smell his underarm stink as he bounced down the road.

Ahead of him a few soldiers mumbled something unintelligible. Nunez was pissed at the breach of noise discipline until the smell hit him, causing him to mutter "Fuck!" like everyone else. His column weaved to the right around another body. Nunez caught a quick sight of it in the moonlight. A fat old woman on her face with her knees bent under her, hands clasped behind a hollowed out eggshell of a skull. Something inside her head bounced a dull reflection into Nunez's eyes. He held his breath a second until his boots cleared the halo of stained pavement around the body, then forced himself to breathe normally again.

A man ahead stumbled, but kept his footing. Darkened shacks lined both sides of the highway. Muzzles came up to cover the structures as they passed. Each one was an ambush waiting to happen. The town stayed silent at the platoon's arrival, until a few dogs barked from a safe distance. Nunez wondered if the dogs were looking for bodies to eat.

The right column jogged around a burned-out truck. The faint odor of charred flesh hit Nunez, nowhere near as bad as the choking stench of the dead woman had been. He recognized the smell, this wasn't the first time he had been around it. The others didn't react.

Quincy's breathless voice huffed over the radio. "Red trucks, halt your move. Red trucks, halt and establish security."

"Red 3 roger." Nunez heard brakes squeak as 2nd platoon's humvees stopped less than fifty meters behind them. If the rest of the company was sticking to the plan, third platoon should be stopped about a mile to their rear. Second platoon would halt just behind first platoon's vehicles to dismount their soldiers and run into town behind Nunez's platoon.

The column slowed to a fast walk, then stopped. After five seconds everyone took a knee, faced outward and peered out into the night. A voice on the radio whispered, "Red 4 this is Red 1, come to me."

Nunez rose to a crouch and shuffled to the front of the platoon. Quincy was on one knee, looking through binoculars. He handed them to Nunez and whispered, "The maintenance convoy is about four hundred meters ahead. I don't see any activity around it."

Nunez took the binoculars. Straight down the road he was able to make out the silhouette of a five- ton truck and two Humvees ahead of it. The five-ton was at an angle, nose pointing to the right side of the road, tailgate down. Nondescript clumps dotted the street. Even though Nunez couldn't make out the shapes from this distance, he knew what they were. He handed the binoculars back to Quincy and keyed his radio.

"Rapido 6 this is Red 4, we have the convoy in sight. We're holding our position until White catches up."

"Rapido 6 roger."

A harried voice jumped on the radio. "Red 4 this is White 4, we're almost to you."

Nunez rogered. In the distance, above the dull whisper of wind noise, Nunez heard the thumping of helicopter blades. Far south, on the other side of town. He looked into the sky, knowing he wouldn't see them. The helicopters flew blacked out, lights visible only with night vision. Nunez keyed up again.

"Rapido 6 this is Red 4, we hear rotors. Can you confirm our air support is on station?"

"Red 4 Rapido 6, roger that. We just established commo with them on the air frequency."

Boots slapped concrete to the rear. Nunez looked back down the lines of soldiers and heard the noise slow and stop, but couldn't see second platoon.

"Red 4 this is White 4, we're caught up to you."

"Roger. The convoy is less than half a kilometer ahead."

Quincy stood up and motioned upward. The platoon rose as one. Quincy gave the signal to move out. Nunez stayed on his knee, waiting to fall in to his spot in the left column. He keyed up as his soldiers walked past.

"White 4 and Rapido 6 this is Red 4, we're moving to the convoy."

Nunez looked back until he saw second platoon. They were in two columns, just behind first platoon. Nunez sidestepped into his column and moved out. The highway widened in town to three lanes. The men spread out, one column on each side of the street. The platoon passed short blocks of run down restaurants and convenience stores. The scent of dead fires followed them. The black out-line of a five-ton truck rose from the darkness, a hundred meters ahead. Nunez looked up as they passed a street sign: *Nogales and 5ᵗʰ*.

Arriago was silent. Nunez's platoon slowed as they approached the five ton. Quincy keyed the radio and said, "White 1 this is Red 1, we're stopping at the convoy, flow around us."

"St-stop, motherfucker! HALT!"

Two platoons of soldiers dropped flat onto the street. The noise sounded like thunder in the dark. Nunez popped his head up, wanting to yell at the point man to shut the fuck up.

"Don't shoot! I'm a fucking American!"

"Stop! Stay where you are and put your hands up!"

"Fuck you!"

Nunez heard rapid footfalls, getting louder by the second. A figure charged them from the sidewalk. Quincy called out, "Stop, Goddamn it!"

"I'm American! Don't shoot, I need your fucking help!"

"Stop... son of a bitch--!"

The running figure fell at Quincy's feet. Quincy half whispered, half yelled,

"Shit! Zip tie this motherfucker! Sergeant Nunez, get up here!"

Nunez jumped to his feet and ran forward, hearing a voice whimper, "Don't zip tie me, man! Fuck!"

Nunez dropped to his knees at the front of the column. Quincy and two other soldiers had their carbines on a prone, dark haired man in an Army combat uniform with no body armor or helmet. Nunez looked at the two platoons stopped in the open.

"Lieutenant!" Nunez rasped. "We're in the open, we need to fucking move!"

"Shit," Quincy muttered. He keyed his radio and said, "Rapido 6 this is Red 1, we just had someone run from the convoy to us, he's being detained now! White platoon, move around us! Continue with the plan!"

"Red 1 this is Rapido 6, who ran out to you?"

Second platoon scrambled to its feet and ran past first platoon. Quincy said, "There goes the element of surprise," then keyed the radio and said, "Rapido 6 Red 1, what looks like an American soldier ran out to us. We're identifying him now." He turned to Nunez and said, "Jerry, handle this guy. I'm pushing up to the convoy."

"Roger." Nunez tapped the nearest soldier and squinted to see who it was. Corporal Mireles. He would do. "Mireles, stay with me. Search this guy, I'll cover."

Quincy led the platoon toward the convoy. Mireles jumped forward and knelt over the prone man, slung his carbine behind his back and grabbed the man's waist and pockets. Nunez crept closer and got hit hard by the combined smells of blood, piss and shit. He ignored them and asked the man, "Who are you? What's your name?"

The man wheezed, "Sergeant Briones."

"What's your first name?"

"Robert."

Nunez keyed the mike. "Rapido 6 this is Red 4, this guy is identifying himself as Sergeant Robert Briones. Do we know if anyone by that name was on the convoy? Over"

Silence followed the question. Captain Harcrow got on the radio after the pause and said, "Red 4, that's going to be a negative. I mean, we don't know.

Nobody has a roster for the maintenance company."

Nunez mumbled "Fuck" under his breath. He asked the man, "What unit are you with?"

"I'm the supply sergeant for the 336th Maintenance Company," the man said, still out of breath. In the pale light Nunez saw the man's left leg and sleeve were dark with what looked like blood.

"Do you have your military ID?"

"No, it was in my patrol pack and I think they took it."

Mireles whispered to Nunez, "Sarge, he's wounded. Back and left leg."

Nunez got on the radio and called for Doc Corley. Then he asked the man, "What happened? How did you survive the ambush?"

Mireles rolled the man onto his side so he could check the front of his waist and his front pockets. The man stuck his arms up and didn't resist. He said, "Goddamn man, I fucking played dead, waited a while and then hid in a store. What the fuck do you think I did? They tore us up, we didn't have a fucking prayer. Fuck, man, I'm relieved to see you guys. You're going to get me out of here, aren't you?"

"Yeah, brother, you're safe," Nunez said. He pulled two linked heavy-duty zip ties from a pouch and said, "Listen Briones, I have to cuff you. It's just until we confirm who you are, then we'll get them off, all right?"

"Shit, man… okay, whatever. Just, please, man, if they hit us again cut them off, okay? Don't leave me tied up. Please, man, don't let them get me like that."

Nunez handed the makeshift handcuffs to Mireles and said, "Relax, Briones. I promise you I'll cut them off if we get into a contact."

Mireles put the zip ties on, not as tight as he should have. He and Nunez pulled the man to his feet and hustled him to the sidewalk. Nunez heard running footsteps approaching on the sidewalk and looked up just in time to see Corley trip over a corpse laying half on the sidewalk, half on the street next to the five ton truck. Corley went down hard with a loud clatter, grunted a quiet curse and struggled back to his feet. He ran to Nunez and dropped his bag to the sidewalk.

"You okay, Doc?" Nunez asked.

Corley's chin oozed blood. He said, "I'm fine. Can we get this guy into a building instead of treating him out here?"

"Yeah. Watch him, Doc. Mireles, come with me."

Nunez and Mireles piled in the open door of the nearest shop. It had been a tiny craft store, and they took a minute to do a sloppy clearing job in the dark before calling Corley in. Doc got to work and Nunez heard a yelp outside.

He ran to the door. Muffled, tense words sounded from the bed of the five ton. He sprinted over.

"What y'all got?"

A staff sergeant answered, "My guys just found a live one. They're searching him now."

Surprised, Nunez asked, "Shit, two survivors? What's this one's name?"

"Don't know yet, Sarge."

A voice inside the truck gave a hoarse whisper, "Coming out, coming out!"

Two soldiers in the bed of the truck stepped to the rear, each of them holding one arm of a third man. This one was wearing body armor and a chest rig, and still wore his helmet. Nunez saw that one of his escorts held a bayonet in one hand. The man had an empty bayonet sheath on his chest.

The man was lowered to the waiting soldiers on the street. He was almost covered in blood. One of his escorts jumped down and told the staff sergeant, "He had this bayonet and one magazine, that's all."

Nunez asked the man, "What's your name?"

The man calmly answered, "Corporal D'Angelo."

"What's your first name?"

"Marc. Marcello, but everyone calls me Marc."

Nunez dug his 3x5 card with D'Angelo's information out of his sleeve pocket. "D'Angelo, what's your date of birth?"

The soldier gave a birthday that would have made him twenty-four years old. Nunez rotated the card back and forth, trying to catch some moonlight so he could read it. There wasn't enough, and he wasn't about to turn a light on. He didn't remember D'Angelo's birthday, but that sounded right. He tried to remember the other information on the card.

"What division were you with when you deployed?"

"Same division both deployments," the man said. "First Infantry."

"What's your daughter's name?"

The man looked at Nunez. Nunez could barely read his puzzled expression in the dark.

"What fucking difference does that make?"

"I need to confirm who you are. What's your daughter's name?"

"Oh," the man said. "It's Lissette."

"You got your military ID?"

"Yeah. Can I get it?"

"Go ahead."

The man dug into a back pocket and pulled out a wallet, then flipped it open and dug something out. Even in the dark, Nunez could see his hands shake. He held out a military ID card. Nunez took it and read *D'Angelo, Marcello, CPL E-4, U.S. Army.* Nunez looked from the picture on the card to the blood-smeared face on the street in front of him. He couldn't tell if it matched. Nunez considered the situation for a moment.

"Give him back the bayonet."

Just for a second, D'Angelo seemed to melt. He took the bayonet and stuck it back in its sheath, muttering, "Oh my fucking God, am I glad to see you guys." Nunez led him to the craft shop, where Corley bandaged Briones' leg. Nunez pointed at Briones and asked, "D'Angelo, you know this guy?"

D'Angelo took a step closer and asked, "Briones? That you?"

The man brightened. "Yeah, it's me, D. I lived."

D'Angelo's face scrunched in anger. "Was that you doing all that screaming, you fucking idiot? What are you trying to do, get them to come back and finish us off?"

Briones shrank and stammered, "I'm sorry man, I… I saw Americans and I just decided to run for it. I thought… I was afraid they were going to shoot me."

"They should have shot you, dumbass. Don't ever do that shit again."

Nunez keyed his radio. "Rapido 6 this is Red 4, SITREP follows."

"Send it."

"Rapido 6 this is Red 4, Red platoon is checking the convoy and White has set security. We have code name D'Angelo and the one we found earlier. No ID on the first one, but D'Angelo recognizes him. How copy, over."

"Good copy. What are their conditions? Over."

Nunez looked at D'Angelo and whispered, "D'Angelo, are you wounded?"

D'Angelo turned away. "I'm fine."

"D'Angelo's okay, no injuries. The other one's walking wounded. Over."

"Roger Red 4, outstanding. We'll pass both of them back to higher after the mission."

D'Angelo mumbled, "Fuck that."

Nunez looked at him and said, "What?"

"Fuck that," D'Angelo said. "They're not passing me back to anybody. I owe these motherfuckers. I'm not going anywhere until this shit's over."

Nunez keyed the radio and said, "Uh, roger. We'll have to talk more about that later." Then he asked D'Angelo, "Is the enemy still in the area?"

"I haven't seen or heard shit for hours, since before dark. After the ambush they took everyone's rifles and shot the radios and left. I played dead in the back of the five ton and they left me alone."

"They shot all the radios? Are you sure?"

"I'm sure," D'Angelo said. "I checked every vehicle after it got dark."

Briones spoke up in a rush. "That was you that came into the humvee? God-damn, I didn't know who it was. I was so scared I shit all over myself as soon as you left."

D'Angelo looked away and mumbled an insult. Briones asked in a weak voice, "Hey, uh, since he knows me can you guys cut these things off? Please?"

Nunez said, "Oh, yeah, forgot about those. Doc, cut them off." Then he asked D'Angelo, "Which way did the enemy go after the ambush?"

"Fuck, I don't know. I think they went south into town. Hey, who are you guys anyway?"

"Sergeant First Class Nunez, Alpha Fourth of the One-Twelfth Infantry. Out of Round Rock."

"Good to meet you, Sergeant Nunez. Sort of." He held his hand out and Nunez shook it, realizing at the last second that D'Angelo's hands were covered in blood. Nunez ignored it and keyed his radio.

"All elements, Echo 4 Delta says he hasn't heard or seen anyone since before dark. He thinks the enemy withdrew to the south after the ambush but he doesn't know for sure." Then he asked D'Angelo, "How did you make it through that

68

ambush?"

D'Angelo let his head fall back and exhaled. When he picked his head back up, he took a few seconds to run his hand over his face before he answered.

"Sergeant Nunez, I fucked up. I tried to get the guys in my truck ready for a contact, and we were okay at first, but that motherfucker on a roof with an RPK across the street had a good angle on us. When the rounds hit us, guys jumped up and started moving around instead of getting behind cover. I laid down suppressive fire, but I couldn't see the guy, you know?"

Nunez nodded. D'Angelo swallowed and said, "Everyone but me got hit. Everyone. I was about to crawl into the cab when the RPK let up, and I was able to get on the radio and put some information out."

He paused, then sank to one knee. Nunez followed him. "They were going down the line checking every vehicle, and they heard me on the radio. Thunderbolt made me say my name, so they knew who it was that was talking. That's when they started checking the bodies, and captured one guy."

"You know who they captured?" Nunez asked.

D'Angelo shook his head. "I didn't recognize him. They checked his nametape and walked him away. I thought they were going to kill him. They said something about capturing two guys, but I don't know anything about the other guy."

"So, how'd you escape?"

D'Angelo grimaced. "Sarge... I fucking chickened out and played dead. I thought I was fucked. I mean, I thought I was a dead man. Then they, they made a mistake, and... well... they killed someone else they thought was me."

"Who was that?" Nunez asked.

"After that, one of them got into the bed of the truck and started grabbing rifles," D'Angelo said, ignoring Nunez's question. Nunez knew he had hit a nerve, and didn't ask again. "The fucking guy stepped on me while he was getting the rifles. When he grabbed mine, I had a come-to-Jesus moment. I had to decide whether to shoot the motherfucker and go down fighting or wuss out, play dead and hope they wouldn't look too close at me."

D'Angelo dropped to both knees and put his hands on his face. Nunez stayed silent, letting D'Angelo get it out.

"I wussed out, Sarge. I let them take my rifle. I should have blown that one asshole away, and their fucking boss. I've never been so scared in my fucking life, laying there waiting to see if they would kill me. I felt like I had surrendered, like I put my whole life in their hands. It was pure fucking luck they didn't check me. I should have fought back, Sarge. They would have got me, but so fucking what? I should have fought back."

Nunez knelt and put his hand on D'Angelo's shoulder. "You didn't have a choice, D'Angelo. Playing dead was the only way to stay alive. Being a kamikaze or a suicide bomber doesn't help. And your wife and daughter want you to come home when this is over. That's so fucking what."

D'Angelo nodded. He asked, "Sergeant Nunez, keep me here with you guys, okay? I need to see this through. Tell higher you need more bodies, or I should be a guide because I saw the guy in charge, whatever. Just keep me here."

"You saw the head guy?" Nunez asked in surprise.

"Yeah. He was standing at the back of the truck when they took my rifle."

"Okay. You stay with us then."

Above them the sound of helicopters grew and ebbed. He wondered if they could see anything with their night vision from up there. Maybe they were just there to be a deterrent. He asked D'Angelo, "Who were the guys who attacked you, anyway?"

"You tell me, Sergeant. I have no idea."

Nunez went through a quick debrief while first platoon checked each vehicle. Everything was done in near-silence. After several minutes, Quincy's voice came across the radio.

"Reds this is Red 1, as far as I can tell everyone else is dead. Red 3, push the trucks up so we can load these men for evac. You copy?"

"Red 3 is on the move."

Minutes passed with no incidents, nothing suspicious reported by the soldiers pulling security. Invisible helicopters circled above, never dropping lower than about a thousand feet. Nunez stood at the door of the craft shop watching his men pull dead soldiers from vehicles and lay them in rows. The Humvees pulled up. Nunez got on the radio.

"Red 1 this is Red 4, our vehicles are up. We're ready to get the casualties loaded."

"Red 1 roger. We've recovered three rifles, they're going into my vehicle."

D'Angelo's head jerked up. He looked at Nunez. Nunez said into the radio, "We're going to need one of those rifles at the back of the convoy."

"Roger that. Just one, you don't need two?"

D'Angelo whispered to Nunez, "Hey Sergeant, Briones was worthless before he got wounded, he'll be worse now. Don't give him a rifle, he'll hurt himself with it."

Nunez nodded and said into his radio, "Just one rifle, Red 1. The other recovered soldier is wounded and won't need it."

Nunez watched as his men shoved the first body into a Humvee's's cargo compartment. D'Angelo said, "Sergeant Nunez, I need to take care of one of those bodies."

"No problem. Was he your soldier?"

D'Angelo said, "No, Sergeant, he wasn't," and Nunez knew right away who D'Angelo was talking about.

Nunez and D'Angelo jogged to the five ton. D'Angelo led him to a small body by the driver's door, the same body Doc Corley had tripped over. Nunez looked at the young man's face, dull and distorted in death. He looked like a child, with blond hair matted by clumps of blood. Two holes were in his face, one just above his right eyebrow, the other beside his nose. D'Angelo opened the soldier's body armor and gently lifted the front panel until it cleared his head. The back of the soldier's skull was gone, scattered across the sidewalk. Something grey was just visible under his uniform top, and a name tape was legible despite a huge bloodstain on the man's chest. Nunez leaned in close to read the name.

Kallinen.

D'Angelo cradled the remains of Kallinen's head on his forearms and reached under his shoulders. Nunez grabbed the corpse's legs, set his feet and asked D'Angelo, "Ready?"

D'Angelo nodded. They lifted the body and walked sideways to the nearest humvee. Two other men stood at the back and helped guide Kallinen into the trunk of the humvee. D'Angelo held Kallinen's head, making sure it didn't bump the metal walls. He whispered, "Be careful with this one, okay?"

One of the soldiers nodded and asked, "Was he your friend?"

"No," D'Angelo said. "He wasn't my friend."

The soldier gave D'Angelo a puzzled expression, but didn't say anything. Nunez stepped back and looked south. All the way down the convoy, first platoon loaded corpses into Humvees while second platoon held security. The helicopters passed overhead, heading southwest. Nunez keyed his radio.

"Red 1 this is Red 4, Echo 4 Delta says all the radios in the vehicles were shot. Can you confirm that?"

"That's affirmative 4, they've been checked and they're all damaged."

"Roger. Are we going to take the time to recover them?"

"Negative, 4. We're close to finishing with the bodies, the radios can wait."

Before Nunez could acknowledge, a *crack!* washed over him, followed by a *whoosh* from maybe a mile away. Nunez ducked behind a Humvee as everyone took cover. Someone nearby whispered, "What the fuck was that?"

In the two seconds between that question and the moment Nunez saw it, nobody spoke. It had already been in the air when they heard the noise. Multiple, hushed exclamations of "oh shit!" broke the silence. Nunez jumped up and keyed his radio in a rush, almost fumbling the warning, "Tell the helicopters we just saw a missile launch!"

A small orange streak tore through the darkened sky, rising from a spot a mile southeast. It gathered speed as it moved from left to right over the town. Nunez thought he heard the helicopter rotor noise change to a higher pitch, just before another orange streak jumped into the sky after it. A second *crack/whoosh* washed over the town as Captain Harcrow yelled back over the radio, "Did you say a missile launch? Where?"

Nunez stood up and said, "Shit! Shit!" as the first missile disappeared. Then a circle of orange sparks blasted outward in the sky. A swirling blob of flame tumbled from the ring of sparks, trailing fire. The sound reached them, a metallic *bang*. Choppy noise, like the sound of a rock caught in a treadmill, followed it. Nunez followed the blob of flame as it corkscrewed all the way down, until it dropped out of sight miles away. A white-orange flash lit the sky, then died.

"Red 4 this is Rapido 6, what the hell did you see? Did you say it was a missile launch?"

The sound of the second helicopter was still in the air but fading fast. Nunez couldn't see the second missile anymore. No more explosions lit the sky.

"Rapido 6 this is Red 4, we just saw a missile take out one of our helicopters! It went down about five miles west, I think."

"Motherfucker. Stand by."

Nunez was almost in shock. The men around him were talking too loud now, amazed at what had just happened. Nunez shushed them, dropped to a knee and shook his head. He looked at D'Angelo and said, "Goddamn, man, who are these motherfuckers? How are they doing this?"

Quincy ran to the back of the convoy with an old M16A2 in his hand. He dropped to a knee, handed the rifle to D'Angelo and said, "I think you're going to need this, real soon."

"Lieutenant, am I fucking nuts or did I just see one of the Navy helicopters get hit by a missile?" Nunez asked.

"You're not nuts. Unless I am too, 'cause I saw the same thing."

"Holy shit," Nunez said, shaking his head. "This is going to be a bitch. We've got our hands full already, it's going to take us forever to get all this shit done and get to that helicopter. And it's not like we can just drop what we're doing, we're not about to leave these bodies here and haul ass. One company can't do all this."

Quincy gave a helpless shrug. "One company is all we got. I guess… maybe we can leave second platoon here to finish with the bodies, we can go to the helicopter, and third can be split so half their guys go with us and half stay here."

"Jesus." Nunez took his helmet off and rubbed his head. "We're in the United States, fighting a large enemy force that's wiped out an entire company and shot down one of our helicopters. We cannot be the only fucking company available for this mission. There has to be someone they can pull off a checkpoint or something to reinforce us."

"Red 1 and Red 4 this is Rapido 6."

Quincy's hand shot to his radio. "This is Red 1."

"We got confirmation about the downed helicopter on the air frequency. Your mission just changed. Leave your dismounted element in place, have your vehicles evacuate the dead to the checkpoint then turn around and head back.

We're not pulling out of Arriago. We're going to clear this whole town, starting at first light."

CHAPTER 6

Holy shit, I'm tired.

Nunez stretched in the seat of his Humvee. The sun was almost up. First light had hit about twenty minutes earlier, but start time for the push had been delayed to 0800. At least one more infantry company was supposed to be in position on the highway into Arriago by then, but the way things kept changing who knew if they would show up. The hoped-for second added company was just a pipe dream now, Nunez didn't believe for a moment it would arrive on time.

The recovery of the dead maintenance company soldiers hadn't been as difficult as Nunez expected. He didn't let his emotions get involved. The experience of handling butchered American soldiers, some of whom had been shot in the head at close range, had been fucking horrible. He dealt with it, and didn't see anyone go to pieces. But after first platoon drove the bodies back to the checkpoint, Quincy insisted they go back and recover dead civilians. The trip back with dead soldiers had been bad enough, but was nothing compared to riding with blackened, rotting civilian corpses.

Nunez made two trips to the checkpoint on the hood of his Humvee, holding onto the side view mirror with one hand and keeping a corpse from rolling off the hood with the other. He kept himself under control well enough to ensure he only vomited to the side, not on his body. His driver, Conway, puked all over his own legs twice.

When they finished, Nunez's soldiers poured bottles of water over their hands, bodies and gear to wash the smell off. Nunez threw away his expensive tactical gloves and dug an old spare pair from his pack. He still smelled death on his hands. He smelled it on everything.

Nunez closed his eyes and tried to sleep again. His door flew open. He opened one eye, annoyed. Quincy tapped his shoulder and said, "That additional company just showed up. Let's go spin them up on the mission."

"Fuuuuck," Nunez said. "I didn't sleep at all." He rubbed his face, grabbed his M4 and helmet and stepped out of the Humvee. "We still planning on giving them two hours to get ready before we push?"

As he spoke, a Navy training jet roared through the sky over the helicopter crash site. The jets had been covering the site since about an hour after the Sea Hawk was shot down. As far as Nunez knew no ground troops had arrived to secure the site yet, and he didn't know who was supposed to. The jet pilots had reported the crew was almost certainly dead.

"I doubt we'll wait that long," Quincy said. "Someone's been leaning on Colonel Lidell to speed this up, he's been leaning on Colonel Ybarra, Ybarra's leaning on Harcrow, Harcrow's about to lean on us. I think we'll move out within half an hour."

The two men walked toward Harcrow's Humvee at the north end of town. Nunez took a look at soldiers standing outside their vehicles stretching, pissing, taking pictures, eating MRE food packets or just hanging out. He should have been amazed to see soldiers so nonchalant about the danger still around them, but he knew from experience how quickly danger became normal in combat. Enemy fighters not far from where they stood had wiped out a company and shot down a helicopter. But hell, that was hours ago. No reason to worry about it now.

Nunez and Quincy stopped at the back of Harcrow's Humvee. Harcrow, his other two platoon leaders and the other company's officers were looking over a gas station map. Their battalion commander, Lieutenant Colonel Ybarra, stood by Harcrow's shoulder. The soldiers made their introductions, and Ybarra started the briefing.

"Alright guys, our mission is a movement to contact. Harcrow's company is pushing on three parallel routes south through Arriago. To keep it simple, they're going in 1, 2, 3 order, left to right. That puts first platoon on Fannin street, the route two blocks east of Nogales, which is the road we're on now. Second will advance on Nogales, third two blocks west on Crockett. Harcrow's men will move with their key leaders and dismounts kicked out alongside their vehicles. Captain Harcrow, you're moving with your second platoon, correct?"

"Yes sir."

"Okay. Your company," he said, pointing at Captain Crow, the new company's commander, "will stay here on Nogales and on order reinforce any of platoons that make contact. I suggest you keep all your men mounted, to make your response faster."

"Roger that sir, we'll do that," Crow said.

"You'll have to be flexible about who you send as a quick reaction force. You might have to react as platoons to three separate contacts, or I might commit you as a full company. You might take over as the main effort if Harcrow's company gets bogged down and can't move. Like the Marines say, Semper Gumby. 'Always flexible.' We have to stay that way for this mission.

"The order from Colonel Lidell before he went back to Edinburgh was to clear the entire town of Arriago. Well, we're not able to at the moment, and Colonel Lidell understands that now. With the limited resources we have, it's smarter to push through the town and look for obvious signs of enemy, then maneuver and pin them down until we have enough force to destroy them. We don't have the manpower to clear and hold every structure in this town."

"Sir, what if we don't find anything?" Captain Harcrow asked.

Ybarra answered, "If we reach the south end of town with no contact, we establish a perimeter and maintain it until other forces arrive and start clearing from the north. Then we move north and meet them halfway."

Harcrow smiled and said, "Gee sir, sounds simple."

Ybarra smiled back. "Of course it's simple. Two companies without additional support, no air strikes or indirect fire, against an unknown enemy force that's already wiped out a company and shot down a helicopter? What could go wrong?"

The men gave a subdued laugh. Ybarra asked, "How much time do you men need to prepare?"

"We're set, sir," Harcrow said. "All we need to do is make sure we're synced up on radio frequencies."

Captain Crow said, "We got a brief when we left Edinburgh and we've been radio rehearsing all the way out here, sir. Everyone's mounted up except for us. We can roll in fifteen minutes."

"Okay," Ybarra said. "Any questions?"

Nobody spoke. Nunez thought, *There is no way in hell that everyone understands all the details of this mission.*

Ybarra said, "Good. Mount up and stand by to move in twenty minutes. I'll fall in behind your company, Captain Crow."

The soldiers murmured wishes of good luck to one another and headed back to their vehicles. As they walked back Nunez asked Quincy, "Didn't that seem like a real short brief for a real complicated mission?"

"Yeah," Quincy said. "The old man must be tired. So am I. I guess Ybarra knows we're going to fall back on the basics if the shit hits the fan. We'll do okay, Jerry."

"I know, Rod. Or at least, I hope."

They reached Nunez's Humvee. Nunez opened his door and Quincy said, "Hey Jerry, same deal as last night. Don't let me fuck this up, brother."

"Right back at ya, Rodger."

Nunez got into his vehicle. Corley was already awake, D'Angelo still snored. Nunez decided to let D'Angelo sleep. He had spent almost two hours being debriefed by radio about the ambush. After what he experienced yesterday and the interrogation that followed, he needed every second of sleep he could get.

Nunez turned the Humvee radio up. No traffic yet. His company would be all over the net as soon as the mission kicked off, but now he had a few minutes to rest. As tired as he was, he knew the sensation of fatigue would disappear once he was on his feet moving into town. It was just the sensation that wouldn't be there, though. The real fatigue would remain, softening muscles, paralyzing his tongue when he needed it most, throwing foolish impulses to the front of his brain. He would have to be on guard, to watch his men for the bad decisions that come from lack of sleep and hope they were watching him as well.

Minutes passed before Quincy called, "Red 4 this is Red 1."

Nunez grabbed the platoon mike. "Go ahead, 1."

"We're getting ready to move. Stand by."

Nunez woke everyone up. He felt familiar prebattle sensations, the tiny bursts of nerves in his gut, shortness of breath covered by a nervous yawn. He realized long ago the sensations were fear, although he hadn't recognized them at first. Fear was okay, as long as a soldier could keep it under control well enough to do his job. If a soldier felt no fear during combat, Nunez didn't want to be around him. He'd do something stupid and get people killed.

In the side mirror, Nunez caught movement. The backup company's vehicles were lining up behind them. Second platoon's Humvees formed up on the right side of the street.

"Red 4 Red 1, let's get going."

Nunez closed his eyes, imagined his wife and children for a moment, and thought, *Forgive me for putting you out of my mind. I have to focus on the mission.* Then he answered, "Roger that, moving." He handed the handset to his driver and said, "You and Barnes know what to do. Hooah."

His men hooahed back. Nunez popped his door and struggled out. His gear felt like it weighed a ton and he almost fell getting out of the Humvee. That was from fatigue, and he knew it. Corley and D'Angelo followed. Up and down the line of vehicles, soldiers clambered onto the street. Nunez looked back and saw third platoon's Humvees push up behind them. Third's men got out and lined both sides of the street.

"Reds this is Red 1, we're moving."

Sergeant Cuevas' Humvee pulled out of line and headed south. Quincy and Nunez had decided to keep Cuevas in his vehicle and have him lead the Humvees. Quincy would stay with the dismounted troops on the left side of the street, Nunez on the right side.

Nunez fell in with the platoon as it curved left. Two columns of soldiers huffed down Center street toward the intersection with Morgan. Nunez looked down blocks of run-down houses, some with front doors standing open, a scattering of cars in the street and driveways. No movement, no life.

Nunez cleared the first intersection. The wind shifted, carrying a familiar, faint scent of disintegrating bodies. He wondered how many dead were left in town, dissolving into stinking, gelatinous masses of skin, fat, muscle and body fluids. Entering the houses of the dead would not be pleasant.

Cuevas' Humvee pushed into the intersection and set security. Soldiers jogged toward the intersection with Fannin. Just as they had at the previous intersection, soldiers dropped onto their stomachs to cover every direction. Ahead, squads turned onto Fannin and began their move south. Nunez hooked around the corner of a house and saw his soldiers moving slower, paying attention to everything. Behind him, the Humvees took security positions in the intersection.

Loud barks sounded down the street. Two doors from the intersection, a dog yipped and whimpered inside a small wood-frame house. Nunez passed close to the front of the house and ran into a solid wall of death stench. He slapped his hand over his mouth and veered away. A loud buzz caught his ear as a swarm of flies exploded off a front window. He looked back. D'Angelo charged through the black cloud with his forearm over his mouth and nose.

Dumpy houses were left in the platoon's wake. No radio traffic, not a word spoken among the soldiers. No shots fired and no orders from Harcrow. Men weaved through front yards and raised their muzzles to cover empty spaces between houses. Nothing caught their attention either. Nunez wondered what the chances were the company would move all the way through town without finding a single living American. Ahead of Nunez, soldiers hit the first intersection since making the turn south.

"Red 4 this is Rapido 6."

Nunez keyed up. "Go ahead, 6."

"White platoon just reported what looked like a civilian about two blocks south of their position. One male, looked like a teenager. He ran east when he saw them."

"Roger that 6, any description?"

"Looked Hispanic, no weapon, dark colored clothing. That's all."

Nunez passed the information to the platoon. He wondered, *Why would an American teenager in this town run from us? Wouldn't he run to us? Or did he not recognize American soldiers?*

The men on point crossed the intersection to the next block south. Nunez turned the report about the teenager over in his head. One empty street was between his men and second platoon. The teenager had room to move parallel to each platoon's line of march. He could pop out between houses anywhere to scare the shit out of one of his troops. If they weren't careful, they might accidentally shoot some terrified kid looking for help.

The point man on Nunez's side of the street climbed a chain link fence around a brick house. Nunez watched each soldier ahead hop the fence. He waited for a Pit Bull or Rottweiler to charge out from behind the house and attack them. Nothing happened. Nunez hit the fence and hooked his waist to flip over it, low profile. The brick house was easily the nicest house on the block, although that wasn't saying much. Burglar bars covered the windows and the metal front door had three deadbolts. On the far side of the house a huge dead mutt was chained to a tree. The dog lay on his back with a chain wrapped around his torso and fangs bared, looking like he died twisting in agony.

Nunez cleared the far side fence. Death smells hit him at random, but still no activity. The platoon hit the next intersection and one soldier pointed right, then held up two fingers as he crossed the street. He had just seen second platoon, they were still on line. Everyone kept moving.

Hands shot upward on both sides of the street, the signal to halt. Soldiers pushed closer to the houses and dropped to a knee. Nunez stayed in place until his soldiers took up positions covering the lanes between the houses, setting 360 security without being told. He tucked in beside a sagging front porch and grabbed his radio handset.

"Red 1 this is Red 4, what's going on?"

"4 this is 1, point just saw something, your side of the street. Move up to the front of your column."

Nunez rose from his knee and rushed forward. His men took quick glances back as he passed. He reached the lead soldier, Specialist Eldridge, and dropped prone next to him. Eldridge was solid, a veteran of several good fights during his one tour of Iraq in 2006. He had the bipod popped open on his weapon and scanned through his scope.

Nunez whispered, "What's up, what'd you see?"

"Didn't see shit, Sergeant. Lyall saw it from the other side of the street."

Nunez looked down the street. Nothing. He asked on the radio, "1, what'd y'all see? We don't see anything from here."

"Echo 4 Lima saw two males. Young looking. One was in dark clothing, the other just wearing shorts. No weapons. They came out from between two houses on the next block, then jumped back when they saw us. How copy, over."

"4 copies. What's your call, 1? Want to move to them?"

Quincy looked at him from across the street and shrugged. They hadn't made plans for an encounter with unknown, unarmed males in Arriago. "I guess we have to, 4. We can't just wait here and do nothing."

"Concur, 1," Nunez said. "They can probably give us some good intel."

Eldridge tensed up on his weapon. "Sarge! Someone just walked into a yard on the next block!"

Nunez raised his head to see a young Hispanic male, in his teens or early twenties, stumble into a front yard midway down the next block. He held his ribs with one hand and hunched over, like he had a wound to his torso. Nunez put his eye to his scope to look the man over. Baggy blue jeans, oversized black shirt with a rap group's symbol on the front, shaved hair, tattoos on both forearms. As he watched, the young man dropped to his knees.

Nunez asked Eldridge, "You see any blood on that guy? I can't tell how bad he's hurt."

"Can't tell either, Sarge. His clothes are too dark."

The young man looked toward the soldiers, shielded his eyes from the sun. "Hey!" he yelled. "Are y'all Americans?"

Nunez looked across the street to Quincy. Quincy looked back, indecision clear on his face. Nunez wasn't sure what to do either.

"Hey man, please, we need help! There's a bunch of people shot over here!"

Nunez put his eye back to his scope. The man had an expression of agony on his face, with beads of sweat running off his bare scalp. He looked hurt. Nunez took his eye from his scope and glanced at Quincy, who slowly raised one hand and waved it back and forth.

The man struggled to his feet. "Over here, man!" he yelled, pointing to a house on Nunez's side of the street. "This house here! We need help! Please, man!"

Quincy asked Nunez over the radio, "Well, I guess we need to move." Watching the young man standing on shaky legs ahead, Nunez answered, "Uh... roger, I guess so."

"Call it up."

Nunez called Harcrow and said, "Rapido 6 this is Red 4, we have a civilian ahead calling for help. He says there's a house full of wounded civilians on the next block. We're about to move to him."

"Roger that. Be careful and keep me advised, 4. The rest of the company is holding in place."

Nunez answered back and gave Quincy a thumbs up. Quincy rose to his feet and signaled for the rest of the platoon to follow. Nunez and Eldridge jumped up and began their move. The young man staggered toward a house, out of Nunez's view. Nunez wanted to yell at him to stay where he was so they could keep an eye on him, but he couldn't violate noise discipline.

That kid shouldn't have moved, though. It didn't make sense that he would walk away, after trying so hard to get their attention.

Shit, Nunez thought. *This doesn't feel right. Something's fucked up.*

CHAPTER 7

"Where did that kid go?" Nunez asked as he crept forward.

"Don't know, Sarge," Eldridge whispered. "To the right somewhere."

Nunez keyed the radio. "1, can you see where that kid went?"

"He went between two houses," Quincy said. "One house's door is open, I think that's where the kid was pointing."

"Shit," Nunez said. *Wouldn't that kid have come toward us if he wanted our help? Or did he go back inside a house where his parents, brothers and sisters, maybe even wife and kids are?*

Nunez whispered to Eldridge, "Brother, be ready for something bad to happen. This makes me nervous as fuck."

Eldridge nodded. The soldiers passed several more houses and reached the intersection. Eldridge dropped prone, facing west. Lyall covered the opposite direction from the left side of the street. Quincy and Nunez took the lead and crossed the intersection at a fast walk.

Across the street, Quincy dropped to a knee and raised his carbine. Nunez had cars in the way and couldn't see what Quincy was looking at. Quincy keyed up and said, "That guy came out for a second, then went back between the houses."

Quincy got up and moved again. Nunez guessed they were about five houses away from the spot where the man called for help. He looked right and saw the corner house's windows open. He expected another wave of decomposition smell, but nothing hit him.

Eldridge rushed past Nunez and took point. They moved to the next yard. The windows of that house were shattered. He tried to remember how many other houses had shattered windows; he couldn't recall seeing any. No blinds hung in the openings.

Eldridge squeezed between two cars in a driveway and moved into the next yard. When Nunez pushed past the cars he saw that this house's front windows were also broken. No blinds in the windows. Shattered glass sparkled in the sunlight under the window frames. He looked across the street. Quincy and his soldiers moved past houses with intact, closed windows.

Nunez went over the facts in his head. The kid in the dark clothes had run from second platoon, but when Nunez's platoon saw him he acted almost too injured to walk. Nunez wondered, *Maybe that was a different person?* He looked at the windows again. Several in a row with open or broken windows on his side, no open windows on Quincy's side.

Why would only those windows be open? And the kid was on the same side of the street as the houses with open windows.

Nunez looked back at one of the shattered windows. A second after he got his eyes onto it, one small piece of glass, no bigger than a playing card, fell onto the shards below. A tin *clink* rang out. Nunez turned away as he let the image of the fallen glass sink in, then looked back.

Why would glass fall out now, this long after the people who lived there got run out of town? Wasn't that window broken a long time ago?

Nunez blinked hard, trying to clear the exhaustion from his mind. He wasn't thinking as fast as he should. He took a close look at the house they were passing. Windows open, not a sound inside. Everything seemed alright, but something nagged at him, trying to work its way through the fatigue. The glass was outside the windows, like they had been broken from the inside. And if the glass was still falling…

Oh, shit.

"Eldridge, stop. Back up."

Eldridge jerked like he had hit a brick wall. He gave Nunez a puzzled look, then backed up a step.

"Red 1 this is Red 4, we need to back out of here. Now."

Across the street Quincy jerked his head toward Nunez. Nunez keyed up again and said one word.

"Ambush."

"Red 1 roger," Quincy said. No argument, no questioning, he had told Nunez he trusted his judgment and now was proving it. "Peel back one block."

Nunez dropped to one knee and whispered, "Eldridge, peel back!"

Eldridge didn't ask any questions either. He spun left and ran down the column, slapping Nunez on the shoulder as he passed. Nunez looked across the street and saw Lyall sprint north past Quincy.

Nunez jumped to his feet and hooked left, slapped the next soldier's shoulder and pointed to the houses as he passed. *Watch the fucking houses, don't just look forward.* As he ran down the line he repeated the signal, pointing two fingers to his eyes and then the houses on their side of the street. The men dropped to kneeling positions, eyes wide, and turned just enough to get their weapons on the houses. Nunez looked to Quincy's side of the street and saw Quincy and another soldier running to the rear of the column. The movement was smooth, no panic. Nunez wondered if he had overreacted, if he had called a retreat because of jumpy nerves.

Nunez ran past D'Angelo, who kept his eyes on his sector. Nunez looked back and saw Berisha, a small and thin young immigrant from Macedonia, fall in behind him. A house ahead, Eldridge reached the intersection.

Flashes and muzzle blast exploded from a window. Nunez dropped and aimed his carbine. In his peripheral vision he saw Eldridge fall hard onto the street. Another soldier, Specialist Eckert, knelt by the front porch of a house. He was a twenty eight-year-old veteran, but he still shot Nunez a look of terrified confusion. Rounds blasted out a window no more than ten feet from him.

Nunez flipped the safety off and fired a handful of rounds into the window. Then he realized he had a bad angle. That, and the house was wood, not brick. He shifted his muzzle and emptied a magazine through the wall. Behind him more gunfire exploded. Ahead, Eckert dumped rounds blind into the house.

Nunez's mag ran dry. He dropped the empty, slapped a fresh one into the mag well and hit the bolt release, then reached to his grenade pouch. It was empty. Nunez reached for his second pouch before realizing he didn't have any grenades.

Motherfucker. If there was ever a perfect time for a frag, this is it.

He looked across the street. Quincy's entire half of the platoon was on their feet, hauling ass out of the open. He heard Quincy yell "Red 1, contact contact contact!" over the radio.

Nunez flipped his weapon to safe and scuttled sideways, closer to the house.

Eckert fired the last rounds in his mag and yelled "Cover!" as he reloaded. Nunez didn't hear any more fire from the window. He looked back to see soldiers shooting into houses as they ran past. Berisha was first behind Nunez, and Nunez screamed to him, "Get Eldridge out of the fucking street!"

Berisha yelled back "Rojah!" in Albanian-accented English as he sprinted past. Nunez yelled the same order to the next soldier, Private Gorham, who was busy reloading his carbine on the move and didn't respond. Just as Berisha stopped to grab Eldridge, the platoon's eight Humvees charged forward. Nunez caught a quick sight of Sergeant Cuevas in the commander's seat of the lead vehicle, his window down and carbine pointed up. Cuevas' face was blank and serious. Nunez turned to Eckert and yelled, "Eckert, go!"

"Moving!"

Eckert jumped from his spot and charged north. Nunez ran forward and dumped ten more rounds into the house. Berisha and Eckert stooped to drag Eldridge out of the street. Gorham was ahead of them, still running north like he hadn't heard Nunez's order. Berisha and Eckert struggled to pull Eldridge's limp body to cover. Nunez saw a bright red drag mark in the street, leading back to a pool of blood where Eldridge had fallen.

Gunners in the lead Humvees opened up. Cuevas' gunner fired his M240 into the front wall of a house. The second Humvee's's gunner fired at the same area, but Nunez couldn't tell where the rounds were hitting. Soldiers sprinted past, he tried to make a count. Eleven soldiers had been on his side of the street, ten on Quincy's side, seventeen in the vehicles. Four more had crossed the intersection headed north, three more were about to get there. Nunez and three other soldiers were still in the kill zone.

Nunez looked south. Specialist Fernandez charged from behind a car, looking toward houses as he fired into them. He paid no attention to anything in front of him, and was about to run wide of Nunez. Nobody followed him.

Nunez realized he was about to get shot by one of his own men. He waved his arm and yelled, "Fernandez, cease fire! I'm in your way!"

Fernandez kept shooting as he ran into the yard with Nunez. Nunez jumped in front of him and fired another three rounds into the house, just to make noise. Fernandez jerked his carbine forward, finally saw Nunez and veered toward the house as he lowered his carbine. Nunez jumped in front of him again.

"Fernandez, stop! There should be two more soldiers behind you, where are they?"

Fernandez yelled, "Doc and Lenny are both down, Sarge! Two houses back, between the houses!"

"Fuck!" Nunez yelled back. "Why the hell didn't you stay with them?"

Fernandez's eyebrows rose and a look of confusion crossed his face. His expression said, *Gosh, that never occurred to me.* Fernandez came to the infantry after four years as an Air Force aerial refueler. He had flown missions over Afghanistan but never set foot on ground. He said once during a drill that he wanted to see war through a grunt's eyes. The thought occurred to Nunez that Fernandez was getting his chance.

"Stay here with me!" Nunez screamed. "Cover back that way!" He keyed his mike and called to Cuevas, "Red 7 this is Red 4! Do you see two soldiers down to your right?"

"4 this is 7, I see one down and one assisting. We're suppressing the houses south of them, you're clear to get them."

"Red Humvees this is Red 1, we're moving to the west side of the street!" Quincy screamed over the radio. "Watch your fire!"

Nunez looked back to see Quincy's men cross the street to his side in a mad sprint, gear and weapons bouncing as they charged out of the kill zone. He couldn't get a count as they weaved between Humvees. They cut through yards and stopped near the houses on Nunez's side of the street.

"Red 1 this is Red 4, I need a count of your guys. Me and one other soldier are moving south to recover a casualty, 7 is covering."

"Roger," Quincy said in a breathless rush. "Make your move."

Nunez paused to assess the situation. The gunfire from both sides had stopped.

"7 this is 4, we're moving. If you fire anywhere near us call out a warning first."

"7 roger."

Nunez slapped Fernandez and said, "Let's go." Fernandez moved out. Nunez gave him ten feet and followed. Humvee gunners raised their muzzles as the two soldiers walked in front of them, then lowered them to cover the houses. Two gunners covered the other side of the street.

"Fernandez," Nunez whispered. "Where at?"

Fernandez pointed. "Around that corner, last I saw."

They passed another silent house. The front wall was peppered with bullet impacts, especially around the windows. Nunez watched each window as Fernandez focused on the corner ahead. When Fernandez reached the middle of the front yard, he ran to the corner and raised his carbine. Then he swung his carbine down, and Nunez knew he had just spotted their casualties. Nunez ran to the corner as Fernandez disappeared behind it.

When Nunez made the turn he almost stepped on Corporal Leonard's feet. Leonard was laid out on his back with his body armor open, uniform top unzipped, t-shirt cut open and chest smeared with blood. His eyes were closed. Nunez took that as a good sign. Dead people's eyes were usually open. Doc Corley was flat on his stomach on Leonard's right side, head and arms raised just enough to press a bandage to Leonard's chest. Fernandez ran past Leonard and dropped prone to cover the space between the houses.

Nunez fell to his knees at Leonard's side, searching the narrow passage leading to the alley. The pathway between the two houses was about six feet wide, with a chain-link fence separating the two yards. The alley was crowded with bushes and tree branches. Nunez couldn't see into it.

"Red 4 this is Rapido 6, give me a SITREP."

Nunez grabbed his radio mike. "6 this is Red 4, we got hit in a near ambush but were able to pull most of the platoon back. We have at least two wounded, one still in the kill zone. We're recovering him now."

"Red 4, are there still enemy around? Over."

"6, I think they hauled ass. I'll give you more info once we've moved from this location. Over."

"Roger. I'm sending a QRF platoon to move one street west of you. Over."

"6 this is Red 4, that'll work." He knelt by Leonard's feet and asked Corley, "How bad is he, Doc?"

Corley looked up, eyes intense. "He's hit in the upper left chest, but it came out the right side of his back. It's bad, Sergeant. We need to evac him, like now."

Nunez turned Corley's words over in his head. The round came from the side, not straight ahead. A wound that bad would probably have dropped him the moment it struck. Which meant the shooter had fired the window a few feet to their left. Nunez looked at it and saw glass smashed from the windowpane.

He swung his weapon to cover the window. "Doc, drag him around the corner to the yard. Then we'll help you get him into a Humvee."

Corley said, "Okay. I have to be real careful though, I don't want to do any more dam-"

"Movement!" Fernandez yelled, way too loud. "Movement in the alley!"

Nunez hunched lower and looked into the alley. He couldn't see anything through the brush. "Fernandez! Keep quiet, Goddamn it!" Nunez said. "What do you see?"

"I saw a couple people run by," he said. Nunez could tell he was trying like hell to keep his shaky voice under control. "They went south."

Nunez grabbed his radio to ask Cuevas, "7, did you see movement in the alley to the west?"

Before Cuevas could answer, Fernandez yelled "Sarge!" Then he remembered and lowered his voice to whisper, "There's more of 'em! I can barely see through the brush, but I saw like four or five more."

Nunez squinted into the brush again but still saw nothing. He asked Fernandez, "Is it second platoon?"

Fernandez started to speak, then froze. Fire exploded from Fernandez's muzzle as he fired a long burst into the alley. Nunez dropped flat. He popped his head back up, straining to see over the soldiers in front of him.

Flames and smoke shot toward him through the brush ahead. He registered the flash passing overhead as he recoiled from the searing heat. By the time he heard the near-simultaneous detonations, the firing of an RPG in front and impact on the Humvee behind, AK rounds were snapping past his head.

Fuck me. I almost got hit by an RPG.

He forced his head up to order Doc and Fernandez to fall back. Fernandez kicked him in the face as he frantically tried to back up. Nunez's vision went black for a moment. He snapped his eyes left to see Doc face down in the dirt. The sound of Fernandez's weapon registered in Nunez's ears as Fernandez kicked him again, in the chest this time. Nunez lurched to his knees to get his muzzle over Fernandez and return fire.

Fernandez popped two rounds into the dirt as he desperately crawled backward. Nunez still couldn't see a thing except for shaking leaves and branches ahead. He took a microsecond to ensure Fernandez was clear, put his red dot onto the brush and pulled the trigger.

"Doc! Fernandez! Move, Goddamn it!"

Fernandez jammed his muzzle into the dirt, using it as leverage to push himself up. Nunez heard gunfire further to the south, and from the street behind him. Someone was engaging from the Humvees. He spun his head to check their rear.

The Humvee that had been covering them was on fire. It crept ahead with no gunner in the turret. The cab was full of smoke. He turned back to see Fernandez lurch halfway to his feet. Fernandez's head snapped backward, a cloud of smoke and impacted dirt burst from his muzzle as he jerked his trigger. He went limp and dropped onto Leonard. Nunez heard the sucking sound of rounds passing close by. He pulled the trigger again to suppress the alley and dropped lower. Bullets impacted the wall of the house in front and behind him. He emptied his magazine into the alley and fell forward onto his elbows.

More dual explosions echoed from the south, RPGs fired from the alley hitting something in the street. Nunez rolled to his side to grab a fresh magazine. Rounds zipped by his head. Frantic voices screamed on the radio, but he couldn't make out what anyone said. He reloaded, fired and screamed, "Doc, fall back!"

He took a quick sideways look and saw Doc Corley scuttle around the corner on his hands and knees. Nunez jumped to his feet and backed up, covering his move with semi-aimed gunfire. More rounds screamed past him and he thought *Fuck this* before turning to run around the corner. It was only three steps away, but Nunez felt sure he was going to take a round in the back of the head before he made it. The blurred vision of a burning Humvee flashed past just before he rounded the corner and threw himself onto the grass. The impact jarred his helmet over his eyes.

He pushed it up and saw Staff Sergeant Dixon's gunner, Sergeant Petri, lean back on the burning Humvee's's roof with his legs still inside the turret. Black smoke poured through the hatch. Petri braced one foot on the turret rim.

Nunez's breath froze as he watched Petri kick himself away from the turret. Small tongues of flame and gray smoke covered his legs. Petri sat up in slow motion and slapped at the flames. Machine gun fire rang, rounds splashed against the passenger doors. Petri rolled over sideways to fall off the opposite side of the Humvee.

Nunez tried to organize his thoughts. *Petri's down, Leonard's down, Fernandez is down, Eldridge is down. I have to do something.* He looked down the street to see two Humvees slow roll south, their gunners firing like mad into the houses on his side of the street. One Humvee had shredded right side tires and trailed smoke. He spun to look north. Half of his section and Quincy's entire section had been behind him. He didn't see a soul now. Three Humvees backed away to the north, a fourth pushed up behind Dixon's burning Humvee.

Movement in the street caught his eye. The M240 mounted on the burning Humvee spun right, rounds blasted from the barrel. Nunez looked south and his eyes met Doc Corley's, across the gap between the houses. Corley's eyes were wide with terror and he mouthed something Nunez couldn't hear. Nunez lip-read a few words: *get the casualties.*

"4 this is 1! Where the fuck are you?"

Nunez grabbed his radio mike. "1 this is 4, I'm, uh, I'm by the burning Humvee! We have two casualties down between the houses and can't get to them! Where are you?"

"Dammit 4, I've called you like ten fucking times! We're pushing east one block to get out of the kill zone! Get to the intersection to your north and cross the street!"

D'Angelo lifted the M240 off the burning Humvee and dropped to the safe side of the vehicle. Nunez screamed back into the radio, "Negative 1, we have casualties we need to recover!"

Quincy didn't answer. Nunez yelled to Corley to come to him. Corley shook his head and yelled something back. Nunez shouted again, "I said come to me, Goddamn it!"

Corley's eyes widened and he screamed, "I CAN'T, SERGEANT! There's rounds coming from between the fucking houses!"

Nunez stood still, not comprehending for a moment. To his left, the Humvee that had pushed up behind the one on fire backed away. D'Angelo fired the M240 over the Humvee's's hood as he walked next to it. Nunez's hearing opened up; he realized there was a lot of gunfire from his side of the street, more than he heard before.

"1 this is 4!" he screamed. "We can't back out yet, we still have casualties down! Do you copy?"

The punching sounds of twin explosions forced Nunez onto his face. He didn't know how he got there, he was on the grass before he knew he had dropped. He looked up to see one of the Humvees to the south ease to a stop. The gunner jumped up, yanked his SAW off the mount and leaped off the roof just as the driver bailed out. They hit the ground together in a jumble of flailing limbs and gear, bounded to their feet and hauled ass.

Corley charged across the gap between the houses, headed straight for Nunez. Nunez sprang to his knees just as small, jagged square of camouflage material exploded off Corley's chest in a shower of gray dust. Nunez was hit by another shock of adrenaline as he realized a round had skipped off Corley's armor plate. Corley didn't react, he kept going until he cleared the gap. Rounds punched through the wooden walls of the house, tracking his movement. Nunez and Corley backpedaled as fast as they could. Quincy yelled over the radio, "4, I understand there's casualties, there's going to be a lot fucking more if you don't move one block east!"

"Sergeant Nunez!" Corley screamed, inches from Nunez's face. "We need to get Lenny and Fernandez! I think they're both still alive!"

"4, did you hear me? Acknowledge!"

Nunez tried to clear his head. Too much was happening, he was being over-whelmed. He felt like there was something very wrong with Quincy's order, something beside the fact that they'd have to abandon their casualties to move east. He took a moment to think. In the chaos, one moment felt like ten minutes. He looked at Corley again, and when their eyes met he realized what was wrong.

"1 this is 4, we can't move east," Nunez said, trying to keep his voice calm. "We need to move west so we can maintain contact with the rest of the com-pany."

More rounds exploded through the wall of the house ahead of Nunez. He backed up again. There was no way he was getting into that gap to recover their casualties, not now. Too many guys were down already, adding two more wouldn't help. And his lieutenant had ordered him to leave them there. He had every reason to leave.

If you leave them there to die, it's your fault. They're your responsibility.

Another RPG round punched through the downed Humvee at the intersection. Nunez looked north again and saw four Humvees making the turn east, their gunners covering him and Corley. He had to do something now, either charge between the houses to Leonard and Fernandez or follow the Humvees. He knew there wasn't much to think about. You don't leave men behind, period.

Motherfucker. If we stay here we're going to die.

"4 this is 1, say again and speak the fuck up!"

Too late, Nunez thought. *You're out of options. Stay here and it won't just be you, you'll get Doc killed too.*

He turned to push Corley east. "Cross the fucking street, Doc! Hurry up!"

Corley threw Nunez's hand off his chest. "We need to pull the fucking casualties out first!"

Nunez pushed him again and yelled, "Doc! We have to move, now! We'll get the QRF platoon to them and circle back around!" He saw Corley's eyes widen as he considered that option. "We'll come back and get them! I promise!" He started his run across the street, dragging Corley with him. Then he said it again, to himself this time.

We'll come back for them. I fucking swear it.

CHAPTER 8

D'Angelo backed over something and fell on his ass. The barrel of the M240 banged against his shin and he jerked his leg away from the burning metal. He looked up to see a yard gnome next to the corner of the house. As he scrambled back to his feet, through the flurry of battle noise one thought went through his head:

Of all the damn places to put a yard gnome…

Lyall screamed, "Over here, Sarge! Hurry!" D'Angelo looked up to see Sergeant Nunez make a mad dash across the street, dragging Doc Corley with him. Nunez was running right at him, but didn't seem to register D'Angelo's presence.

D'Angelo waved Nunez to one side. "Sergeant Nunez! Move the fuck over!"

Nunez's eyes widened as he recognized D'Angelo and his machine gun. He and Doc Corley veered out of the way. Behind them, a cluster of men in black spilled out from between houses. They sprayed inaccurate fire in Nunez's direction.

Nunez ran clear. D'Angelo yanked the stock of the M240 machine gun against his shoulder, braced himself into a tight kneeling position and blazed a string of bullets between the houses. Two men in black jerked and flopped onto the grass, others sprinted left and right out of his line of fire. He followed one that ran left and hit him low, in the waist. The man collapsed and screamed incomprehensible Spanish.

"D'Angelo, stop! Cease fire!"

D'Angelo turned around. Nunez hooked behind him, eyes wide, face beet red and drenched in sweat. "Lenny and Fernandez are between those two houses! Don't fire there!"

D'Angelo's blood froze. *Oh fuck,* he thought. *I think I just shot our casualties.* Above him, Lyall braced his carbine against the corner and fired several bursts. D'Angelo reassured himself, *No, I didn't hit them. Casualties would be on the ground and I fired at waist level.* He swung the barrel of the 240 left and opened up, just to suppress. He didn't see anyone now, other than the three men in black he had shot. Nunez grabbed his shoulder and tugged hard, yelling "We're clear, fall back to the next block! Let's go!"

Lyall slapped D'Angelo on the back. "D, come on!" D'Angelo jumped to his feet and started to turn. AK rounds zipped through the air in front of him. He caught sight of the wounded enemy fighter across the street, on his side in a fetal position. The man wailed in agony, grabbed his abdomen and rocked back and forth. He still held an AK in one hand.

D'Angelo stopped turning. He backpedaled a step, ignored bullets slapping the house beside him and fired from the hip at the wounded man. The first rounds chewed dirt several feet in front of the man, the next burst walked into his upper chest and face. D'Angelo felt a surge of satisfaction as chunks of flesh and bone exploded from the man before he went limp.

Heavy automatic weapons fire sounded from the west, toward downtown. Someone else was in contact. D'Angelo took a quick look south as he turned to run. What he saw made his heart stop. Dozens of men in black broke cover down the street, poured out of front doors and charged from between houses. Most were in a dead sprint across the street. D'Angelo knew they were trying to cut off the platoon's escape.

He twisted away from the corner and ran. Nunez and Corley were just ahead, hop-skipping backward. D'Angelo sprinted toward them and yelled, "Sarge, there's shitloads of 'em! They're parallel to us, running toward the next street!"

Nunez's hand flew to his mike. He glanced back over his shoulder, looked like he was about to speak into the radio. Then his expression changed from intense concentration to overwhelming frustration.

Nunez let go of the mike and yelled, "*Fuuuuuck!*" as he ran. "Second platoon just got ambushed trying to get to us!"

Ahead of the small group, four Humvees rolled east at a snail's pace. No gunner stood in the turret of the last one. The first started to turn south at the next intersection. D'Angelo heard the gunner yelled "Oh shit!" before the driver jammed on the brakes. The gunner hunched down behind his shield and opened fire with his SAW. The second Humvee rushed past it and stopped at the intersection's far corner. Its gunner dumped rounds down the street as the vehicle rolled to a stop.

D'Angelo didn't realize he was passing an alley until AK rounds snapped through the air a few feet ahead. He spun sideways and opened fire into the alley. It was overgrown with weeds and brush, he couldn't see any enemy. He sidestepped away and fired the last rounds in the belt. When he heard the *thunk* of the bolt slamming into an empty chamber he hauled ass and yanked another belt from a cargo pocket.

Explosions rang out around the corner on the street ahead. Two RPGs zinged past the Humvees at the intersection. Neither hit. One went high, the other split the gap between the two vehicles and skidded down the street. The three men ahead of D'Angelo hit the brakes so they wouldn't break into the open. As D'Angelo caught up he finally saw the other soldiers, clustered around a corner house across the street.

The soldiers took turns poking their weapons around the corner to fire. Lieutenant Quincy waved frantically and yell, "Jerry, get the fuck over here, hurry! The Humvees are covering!"

Nunez didn't hesitate. He yelled, "Follow me!" and charged into the intersection. Doc Corley and Lyall ducked their heads and followed. D'Angelo popped the 240's feed tray cover, laid the end of the belt on the feed tray and slammed the cover closed. He yanked the charging handle back and ran into the intersection.

A few rounds zipped by. He ignored them. The two Humvee gunners kept their heads down and hosed houses down the street. D'Angelo had the presence of mind to realize both gunners had linked at least two belts together. If they hadn't, they would have run dry already. In spite of the madness of battle, he was impressed. These guys had their shit together.

He skirted the Humvees and followed Nunez to the side of the house. Nunez dropped to a knee and yelled "360 security!" D'Angelo spun around, dropped prone and faced the way they had come. Other men took up positions facing outward. The two Humvee gunners were performing a "talking guns" drill, taking turns firing short bursts to keep the enemies' heads down. D'Angelo looked over his shoulder.

Private Conway, the driver of the Humvee with no gunner, jumped out. "Doc!

Barnes is wounded, he took a round through the shoulder! C'mere, hurry!"

Doc Corley sprinted toward Conway's Humvee. D'Angelo took a quick look at Nunez. Barnes was Nunez's gunner, the two of them were close. Nunez shook his head and squeezed his eyes shut for a second, then turned to Quincy.

D'Angelo didn't hear any more fire from the enemy, but sporadic fire rang out downtown. He kept one ear cocked toward Quincy and Nunez's conversation. He couldn't make it out at first, but then Quincy yelled into the radio, "Red... uh, Red... Cuevas, this is Red 1! What's your status?"

The response blared, "This is Red 7, we're south of you and one more street east, I think! We took a bunch of hits but we're good. We have the driver and gunner from 3 with us."

"Roger that. Stay put."

Other, frenzied voices spoke out, soldiers trying to make sense of what just happened.

"Goddamn! Did you see all those fucking RPGs they shot at us?"

"What happened to Cuevas? Was it his Humvee that got whacked?"

"Hey assholes, we need to get back over there! Lenny and Fernandez are down, we fucking left them behind!"

Nunez yelled out, "Everyone shut the fuck up! We're going back for the casualties, give us a fucking minute to make a plan!" Then he said, "Everybody, breathe. Get your heart rate down, check your ammo status. We're good right here, everything's under control."

D'Angelo glanced back. Quincy was on his knees, taking a deep breath and wiping his face. Nunez held a notebook and was checking off a list.

Nunez said, "I'm coming up short. Where are Petri and Brandon?"

"Petri's in my Humvee, Jerry. He's dead, KIA. Don't know about Brandon."

D'Angelo called out, "Sergeant Nunez! If Brandon was Sergeant Petri's driver, he's KIA and still in that burning humvee. He was on fire and I couldn't get him out."

The two humvee gunners ceased fire, at the same time the firefight noise from downtown stopped. Nunez muttered, "God damn it." Then he asked, "What about Eldridge? How is he?"

"He was hurt bad, Jerry. He bled out, KIA. He's in Allenby's humvee."

"Jesus fucking Christ," Nunez said with a sigh. "Alright, that's two KIAs recovered, one KIA not recovered, two wounded not recovered. And my gunner being treated right now. Anyone else I need to know about?"

"Don't think so, Jerry," Quincy answered. "What's our plan now? You think we should charge back and get Lenny and Fernandez?"

There was a pause. D'Angelo was anxious to hear Nunez's answer. When Nunez spoke, the frustration was obvious.

"Lieutenant, I want us to pull back north so we can take a breath and get our shit together. But we can't, not with Cuevas and the other Humvee one block south. I think… I think maybe the best thing to do is push one more block east and link up with Cuevas' two Humvees on that street. That'll put us two blocks over from our missing guys. Once second platoon gets their situation under control, they can push toward us. If Harcrow gets some platoons from our support company north and south of us, we might get these fuckers boxed in and trapped in a hammer and anvil maneuver."

"Yeah," Quincy answered. "Yeah, that sounds good. Get in touch with Harcrow and find out when second platoon can move to us. I'll tell Cuevas what's up."

Behind his machine gun, D'Angelo almost smiled. These infantry guys he hooked up with had just been through a horrible ambush. Some of their men had been killed and they even had to abandon two of their wounded, but they just made a plan to attack the enemy. They weren't screaming for help, weren't running away. They wanted to take the fight right back to the bastards who ambushed them. That's what real grunts do. Staying with them had been the right decision.

Quincy and Nunez spoke into their radios. D'Angelo kept his eyes open, hoping some enemy would be stupid enough to step into his sights. He had killed a few of them, but still owed them for wiping out his company. Some of his guys had been shitty soldiers, but they were good people. He hated the enemy for what they had done to his unit. Just a few dead enemy wouldn't settle the debt. He wouldn't feel right until he had killed dozens of enemy, maybe hundreds.

He reached to his left cargo pocket. No more ammo there. He grabbed his right cargo pocket. A short belt was there, maybe fifty rounds. He had broken that belt when he yanked it from the burning Humvee. He only had time to grab a few belts, the Humvee had been burning pretty well and the ammo was about to cook off in his face. He reached up and squeezed the dump pouch on his left hip. Another belt of 100 rounds was still there, it hadn't fallen out during all the running around. The belt in the weapon held a hundred rounds. So 250 rounds or so on his body, then he'd have to get more from Lyall. He was alright for the moment.

Behind him, squad leaders checked their men to see how many magazines they had left. D'Angelo heard hurried requests from soldiers who were almost out.

"I got one full mag in my weapon and one in a pouch, that's it! Who can spare a mag?"

"I can give you one. That just leaves me with two spares, so don't fucking waste it!"

"I got a half full in my dump pouch, take it. Heads up."

Staff Sergeant Allenby ordered, "Everyone drink some fuckin' water. No heat casualties now, that's all we fuckin' need."

D'Angelo bit his Camelbak hose and took a sip. Not too much, he didn't want to weigh himself down. He looked over his right shoulder to see Lyall laying close by his right leg, panting behind his weapon. Lyall was thirty, a little heavy but not fat, his light skin bright red and covered in sweat.

"Hey Lyall," D'Angelo said.

Lyall twisted to look back at him, eyes squinted. "What's up, D?"

"You good, brother? You look a little rough."

Lyall wiped his eyebrows. "I'm fucking smoked, man. But I'm alright, I just drank half my water." He checked his sector again. When he looked back at D'Angelo he asked, "D, why do you think it got quiet so fast? They were all over us a couple minutes ago. It didn't make sense to back off. They were kicking our ass."

D'Angelo checked his sector again. Still nothing. He looked back at Lyall without answering. Lyall had a good question, it didn't make sense for the enemy to back off. They had destroyed two of the platoon's Humvees, killed three soldiers and wounded three more, then overrun the platoon's first position. Their attack had split the platoon into two elements separated by a block. The enemy was winning.

In Afghanistan, the Taliban used ambushes to break large units into smaller, easy-to-eat groups. His battalion never let it happen, but a few other units around had let the Taliban separate platoons from companies, squads from platoons, fire teams from squads. Those fire teams were sometimes found dead to the last man. He didn't understand why this enemy wasn't doing the same thing.

D'Angelo said, "Just because there's a little lull in the fight, that doesn't mean the enemy backed off. We're using this break to get our shit together, they might be doing the same thing."

"Is this normal?" Lyall asked. "Are there breaks like this in every firefight?"

D'Angelo gave him a look of surprise. "You've never deployed?"

Lyall shook his head. "Uh uh. Lots of training and schools, but never done this for real. Until today."

"Never would have guessed that, brother. You did badass during that ambush. But yeah, that's pretty much how firefights go. They're not always a million miles an hour, they get slow sometimes. They can even get boring."

Lyall gave a disbelieving laugh and shook his head. He looked over his rifle sights and said, "D, if you can be bored in the middle of that shit, you're fucking comatose. That was so crazy I thought my head was going to explode."

D'Angelo gave Lyall a friendly kick in the leg. "That fight wasn't boring, brother. That was a fucking nightmare."

"Everyone, listen up!" Quincy yelled.

Soldiers answered, "Hooah!", which can mean anything but no. In this case it meant, "I'm listening."

"Get ready to move. We're going to push one more block east to the next corner, turn south and meet Cuevas' two Humvees. Once we're together I want everyone to set 360 security, with most of the platoon facing west. I'll adjust you when we get there. Everyone got it?"

D'Angelo gave a "hooah" with everyone else, meaning "I understand".

"Alright, we move in two minutes," Quincy said. "Make sure you've got a fresh mag in your weapon, check your safeties. We're gonna punch back through these fuckers and kill them all."

"D!" Lyall said. "What was that?"

D'Angelo looked towards Lyall's pointed finger, to the north. D'Angelo didn't see anything at first. He got as far as "What did you –" before he saw it bounce across the street toward a front yard. It was small, black and round, with a thin, flat protrusion.

"D, is that –?"

BOOM!

Steel whirred through the air. D'Angelo smacked his face into the grass. He held it there a second and listened to screams of "Holy fuck!" and "What the fuck was that?" When he lifted his head he saw a dirty grey ball of smoke in the street.

"Enemy frag!" D'Angelo shouted. "Grenade detonation a hundred meters north!"

Quincy dropped prone next to D'Angelo. His angular black face was tight with rage. In a tense, quiet voice he said, "If second platoon just threw a grenade at us, I'm going to kill them all."

Before D'Angelo could say "We don't have any grenades," a few shots rang out to the north. The dull thump of an explosion reached out from a block south. Cuevas' frenzied voice came across the radio, "This is 7, somethin' just blew up next to us! We're moving north toward you!"

More shots, now coming from the blocks north and south. One Humvee gunner covering the intersection opened fire again. The other spun his turret to face north. D'Angelo looked over his weapon and still didn't see anything.

Bullets smashed the rotting wood of the house they were next to. Glass shattered. D'Angelo looked south and saw puffs of smoke and muzzle blast between houses. He looked toward his sector again. Still nothing.

"Everyone get the fuck up!" Quincy ordered. "Let's move! Hit the intersection and go south, meet with Cuevas!"

Gear rattled. The two Humvees covering the intersection stayed put, D'Angelo struggled to his feet and ran. A few more gunshots popped a block north. He heard another grenade explode, out of view. Ahead, Quincy led the charge toward the next intersection. Nunez ran backwards, making sure nobody was left behind. The Humvees covering the intersection moved but stayed just behind the running soldiers.

Gunfire rattled ahead, maybe two weapons firing short bursts. Everyone hunched lower. D'Angelo saw impacts in the crumbling asphalt almost a hundred meters ahead. Inaccurate fire, it didn't hit anywhere near them.

Lieutenant Quincy reached the intersection, held for a half second, then ran south around the corner house. The rest of the platoon filed after him. D'Angelo was twenty feet from the turn when he heard another *BOOM!* He ducked and saw a gray smoke circle to the north.

As he made the turn south he thought, *They're behind us, in front of us, and to our north and south. It's like this street is the only place we can go.*

He headed south with everyone else. The platoon split into two elements again, Lieutenant Quincy's men on the east side of the street and Nunez's on the west. D'Angelo followed Nunez, looked in each window and open door. He was almost positive they were about to get hit again.

Two Humvees raced toward them from the south. The rear Humvee gunner had his weapon over the Humvee's's back deck and fired short bursts. The gunner ignored his sights and swiveled his head everywhere as he fired.

D'Angelo walked past the second house from the corner. The soldiers ahead jammed up at a fence. He took a knee, rested his machine gun on his thigh and looked around. No sign of a threat on his side of the street. Nothing across the street either. All he saw was Quincy leading his handful of tense soldiers past rundown houses.

Shots rang out, way behind him. He and several other men spun around to look. Humvee gunners scanned desperately for a target. Nothing was hitting near the platoon, he wondered why the enemy was firing at all. He turned south again. Lyall had crossed the fence ahead of him. He ran to the fence, handed Lyall his machine gun, then flopped over the sagging chain link and took his weapon back.

BOOM! BOOM!

All the soldiers on D'Angelo's side of the street dropped onto grass or pavement. The explosions were a block south of the platoon. D'Angelo recognized the sound as a close range detonation of an RPG. D'Angelo couldn't see what the RPG hit, but smoke rose down the street.

What the fuck are they shooting at? They're wasting ammo on nothing north and south of us, but nobody's firing at us on this block.

Nunez rose to his feet and leaned left, looked down the street toward the smoke. He gave the signal to get up. D'Angelo pushed himself to his knees, waited for soldiers ahead to clear the fence, and moved forward. The two Humvees to the south pushed toward them. About a football field's length separated the two groups of soldiers.

Tracer rounds zipped two feet in front of D'Angelo's face. He dove to the grass before the sound of automatic weapons fire registered in his brain. When he hit the dirt he spun his head to look for the source of the rounds.

More tracers hissed over his head at a thousand miles an hour. Nothing caught his eye at first, all he saw were dumpy old homes and deteriorating cars. He pictured the tracers that had passed him, tried to determine what angle they had come from. Did the rounds fly straight past him, or had they come from an angle? All he remembered were glowing red streaks zipping past his face. He looked again and found it, smoke and bits of debris flying from the front window of a faded blue house across the street.

An enemy fighter inside the window fired in a wide arc. Some rounds hit dirt, some knocked divots of pavement from the street, others punctured cars and shattered glass. Another stream of tracers ripped from a second window and peppered the street around the approaching Humvees.

D'Angelo was amazed. It looked like these two dipshits had loaded all tracers in their magazines. They were like neon signs telling everyone exactly where they were.

D'Angelo muscled his machine gun hard left, put the house in his sights and started to squeeze the trigger. A Humvee backed into his line of fire. He jerked his hand from the machine gun's pistol grip like it was red hot. Above the hammers on steel noise of the gunfire he heard three sharp *ping!* sounds. Tracers bounced off the Humvee and zinged straight up.

D'Angelo looked to the Humvee's turret and didn't see the gunner, just an unmanned machine gun pointing skyward. His heart sank. Another gunner hit.

To D'Angelo's right someone screamed, "I'm stuck, get me off this thing!" D'Angelo looked over and saw Lyall hanging on the fence. The Camelbak on the back of his body armor was caught on a protruding metal point. Lyall's body bent left with one foot on the ground and one flailing against the fence. Both hands searched desperately, reaching nowhere near the trapped Camelbak. D'Angelo looked forward, the Humvee still blocked his shot.

D'Angelo put the stock of the machine gun back into his shoulder and screamed, "Sergeant Nunez! Lyall's stuck in the kill zone!"

Nunez rose from a hedge and rushed through a yard. The ground exploded into red flashes ahead of him. Nunez stutter-stepped to avoid running into the fire. Lyall screamed, "Get me the fuck out of here! Somebody fuckin' help!"

D'Angelo screamed, "Lyall, fucking shoot back!"

The tracer fire shifted. D'Angelo heard the sickening *whack!whack!whack!* of bullets striking gear and flesh. Lyall kicked the chain link with one leg, head turned away and hands held to the side as if his palms would stop bullets. His body convulsed with each round that punched through. Tracer rounds looked like lasers disappearing into his body and escaping in a spray of blood and tissue. He screamed like a child and went limp, arms and one leg swinging like pendulums.

Return fire punched toward the house. The missing Humvee gunner popped up with a belt of ammo in one hand and carbine in the other. He fired his carbine one handed as he tried to load the machine gun. The Humvee backed out of D'Angelo's line of fire. D'Angelo was so angry he didn't bother to aim, didn't think about conserving ammo, all he wanted was to kill enemy. He yanked hard on the trigger and walked a forty-round burst from empty flowerpots in the yard up porch stairs to the window where he had first seen muzzle blast. No tracers came from either window now, no sound or fire from the house. He pivoted his weapon on the bipod and punctured the wall around the second window with twenty rounds.

Fire from a dozen weapons hit the house. Wood splintered from hundreds of impacts. The glass screen door exploded. D'Angelo got back on his sights and put another long burst into the second window, then traversed left and finished his belt on the first one.

The 240's bolt closed on an empty chamber. He flipped the feed tray cover open and yanked another belt from his dump pouch. The Humvee that had blocked his shot changed direction and moved south again, the gunner on top riddled the house with SAW rounds. D'Angelo wiped the feed tray to clear the last belt link, pushed a new belt onto the tray and slammed the cover. Across the street Quincy yelled, "Gunners, check your fire! Dismounts, assault assault assault! Get up here with me!"

D'Angelo yanked on the charging handle and jumped to his feet. He felt no fatigue, no heat, no fear, nothing but raw energy fueled by hatred and a lust for killing. He rushed toward the street, aiming for the gap between the two closest Humvees. He shot a quick glance back toward Lyall.

Nunez was hunched under Lyall, trying to lift him off the fence. Nobody fired at him, even though he was exposed in the open. For an instant their eyes met as Nunez struggled to free Lyall's two-hundred-fifty-plus pounds of body and gear off the metal point. D'Angelo saw fury in the platoon sergeant's eyes. Nunez yelled over the gunfire, "D, kill those motherfuckers!"

D'Angelo bellowed and charged between the Humvees. The return fire dropped to almost nothing, only one Humvee still ripped out a few bursts. D'Angelo slowed, braced his weapon against his hip and opened fire again. He screamed, "Fuck you motherfuckers! Die, you pieces of shit!"

Quincy crouched against the house next to the target house, yelled at everyone to cease fire. D'Angelo let go of the trigger. Quincy waved his soldiers behind him. There were only six soldiers with Quincy, he didn't have many people to assault the house with. D'Angelo charged across the front yard and slammed his shoulder into the wall behind Quincy. The other five soldiers stacked along the front of the house.

The last Humvee gunner ceased fire. Quincy turned around, nostrils flared, black skin glowing with sweat. He screamed "Follow me!"

He sprinted toward the target house. D'Angelo followed without a second thought, focused on killing enemy and nothing else. As he passed the first window he heard glass shatter inside. Shredded venetian blinds sagged behind shattered windows, he couldn't see anything inside. He pulled his machine gun's trigger and blew ten rounds through the front wall. Another soldier behind D'Angelo fired a burst through the window.

Quincy reached the front door and yelled, "Quit fucking shooting, we're about to breach!" The soldiers held their fire as Quincy kicked the front door in. The frame was already smashed to pieces, the bullet-punctured door split down the middle like it was papier-mâché. Quincy rammed past the broken door. D'Angelo charged inside and raised his weapon so he could shred the enemy bodies he expected to see on the floor. Quincy froze and said, "Oh, fuck."

D'Angelo ran into Quincy's back. Quincy stumbled forward a few steps. D'Angelo fell to his knees and his machine gun hit the floor. He jerked it upward to cover the living room, then saw what had stopped Quincy in his tracks. He mumbled, "Oh my fucking God," as the other soldiers tumbled through the doorway behind him. Each one got a few steps inside, stopped and stared until the next man pushed him forward and did the same thing. Gorham, the last man in the stack, didn't even make it through the doorway. He stopped in the opening and said, "Holy fuck. Did we… ?"

D'Angelo started to shake. He stood up and took one step into the living room, realized he couldn't do it, and fell back to his knees. He felt overwhelming nausea. One of the men behind him asked, "Lieutenant… what the fuck… what did we do?"

D'Angelo looked again. What he saw beat down his last molecule of self-control. His stomach heaved a ball of greenish-black vomit onto the carpet. Someone grabbed his shoulder. He slapped their hand away and screamed "Don't fucking touch me!"

He pushed himself to his feet. His legs quivered so badly he thought he would keel over into his own puke. He felt his temperature and pulse rate skyrocket, his breath cut itself off. A wave of uncontrollable fury washed over his brain, kicking reason out of its path.

A voice yelled, "Check them, someone might still be alive!"

Two soldiers slung their weapons over their backs and rushed into the living room. Quincy ran his hands over his face, looking lost and confused.

Insane with anger and hatred, D'Angelo stepped toward the window and lifted his machine gun.

CHAPTER 9

Nunez popped the clasp on Lyall's helmet and started to take it off. He stopped when he saw dark red blood and tiny gray clumps stuck to the rim.

On top of all his other wounds, not a head wound too.

Across the street, Quincy had just led the charge into the house. Nunez looked but heard no gunfire. He decided to leave the helmet on Lyall's head. He looked over Lyall at all the bullet holes, blood and ripped skin. Lyall lay on his back, Nunez knelt with one knee jammed into a gaping tear in Lyall's right thigh. The spray of arterial blood from Lyall's thigh had stopped, but Nunez didn't think the pressure from his knee had stopped it. Lyall probably didn't have enough blood left in his body to shoot from his torn arteries.

"Carillo, give me Lyall's tourniquet!"

Sergeant Carillo gave Nunez a deadpan look, asking silently, *What do you think you're going to do with it?*

"Give me the Goddamn TQ! Hurry up!"

Carillo shook his head and reached to the combat tourniquet on Lyall's left shoulder. He pulled it from Lyall's body armor and held it out. Nunez snatched it from his hand, ripped the Velcro open and forced the end under Lyall's thigh. When the tip of the band poked free he tugged it upward, fed it through the buckle and twisted the plastic bar as hard as he could. After he secured the tourniquet he lifted his knee and looked at the wound. No blood shot onto the grass. He moved to two massive wounds on the other leg. They didn't bleed, but he was going to TQ the leg anyway.

Nunez tore his own tourniquet from his shoulder. Lyall's left thigh had a wound high up, near the hip. The damage was too high on his leg, a tourniquet was useless. Nunez stuck it into his cargo pocket and tore open Lyall's first aid pouch.

"Carillo, bandage the wound on his lower leg! I can't TQ the one on his thigh, I'm going to bandage it."

Carillo sighed, "Sarge, don't waste the bandage. He's gone."

Nunez gave Carillo a furious glare. "Carillo, he's not dead! Bandage him and we'll get Doc over here."

"He's shot through both legs, both arms, pelvis and head, Sarge. His pulse is gone. He's dead."

Nunez held Carillo's stare for a moment, then lowered his gaze to the blood-stained grass. He realized he was panting instead of breathing. He looked at Lyall again. Sleeves and pant legs soaked with blood, face smeared with it, eyes and mouth half open. No chest movement. Nunez felt for a pulse again. Nothing.

He put the bandage in his cargo pocket and said, "Get his weapon and ammo, Carillo."

Nunez stood up. When he looked at his soldiers he saw everyone watching the house Quincy had assaulted.

"Hey!" he shouted. "360 security, watch our fucking backs!"

A few men fought the urge to watch the target house and made slow turns to their rear. Nunez ran to the street and slammed his palm down on a Humvee hood. The driver and gunner jerked their heads in surprise.

"Spin your gun around and face west! Watch that way!"

The gunner rotated the machine gun west. Nunez looked north and south down the street. Humvees covered both ends of the street. It looked ugly, but they had security.

Nunez jogged to the house. Specialist Gorham stood in the doorway, weapon hanging at his side, one hand on the door frame and one on his face. Nunez didn't have a clue why he didn't have his weapon in his hands, or why he was standing in the door. Doorways were "fatal funnels", areas where enemy concentrated their fire. Nunez opened his mouth to order Gorham out of the doorway.

An M240 machine gun smashed through a window and tumbled to the grass. Ripped, tangled venetian blinds and shards of glass followed it. Nunez stopped, shocked at the sight. He heard unintelligible screaming in the house. Gorham blurted "Whoa!" and backed out of the doorway.

Just inside the door, someone screamed, "I didn't know! I didn't fuckin' know!"

Nunez recognized D'Angelo's voice. An arm swung into the doorway from inside and grabbed the edge of the frame. Someone else yelled, "D, calm the fuck down!"

Nunez ran into the yard as D'Angelo pulled himself out of the door. Two soldiers held D'Angelo's gear and tried to stop him, Gorham moved out of his way. D'Angelo's face was twisted in agony. He screamed, "I didn't know! Fuck, I didn't know they were in there!"

Two soldiers tackled D'Angelo and held him down on the grass. Nunez heard someone inside the house scream, "Medic! Get Doc in here!"

Nunez keyed his radio and said, "We need Doc in the house ASAP!" before pushing his way through the door.

He stopped two feet inside and just stared. His mouth didn't drop open, but he felt a look of frozen incomprehension overtake his face. Two soldiers had overcome the shock and inertia and rushed forward to do something, but everyone else just stood and looked. Nunez took five seconds to let the sight sink in, then shook his head and blinked.

He swallowed hard, turned to Quincy and said, "Lieutenant, have the guys clear the house. We can't just stand here."

Quincy looked back, hand covering his mouth, eyes wide. Nunez knew he was about to break.

Nunez repeated, "Lieutenant, have the platoon clear the house. We don't have security. Get the guys moving."

Quincy blinked hard. Then he dropped his hand, grabbed the nearest man and pushed him toward the hallway. "Drake and Cowan, take care of the casualties! Everyone else, clear the rest of the house! Let's go!"

Shocked soldiers were jolted to action. Nunez swung his carbine onto his back and rushed into the living room. There was almost no hope, but he pulled a bandage from his pocket anyway.

Three bodies, two female and one male, hung suspended from ropes in the living room. Their ankles were duct-taped together, ropes were tied around their duct-taped wrists. The ropes led upward through holes knocked in the ceiling, over exposed rafters and back to their wrists.

A fourth body, in Army camouflage, lay shredded on the floor. Its hands and ankles were bound with tape and tied. All the bodies had tape wrapped around their mouths. The three bodies still upright sagged on the ropes, dead weight straining the knots on their wrists.

The platoon's massed fire had torn them apart.

Nunez looked for someone to help. He checked the man hanging from the rafters, who might have been in his thirties or forties and wore pajamas. Nothing could be done. The man's skull hung backward between his shoulder blades and gaped wide open on one side. Most of his brain was on the floor and wall behind him. A family picture was covered with it.

The two women's bodies were punctured from calves to shoulders. One was about sixty, the other couldn't have been older than Laura, Nunez's thirty-seven year old wife. Nunez lifted the younger one's head from her chest. One round had blown open her cheek and smashed her teeth. Her eyes were dull, flat and half open. Nunez tore his gloves off, jammed them in a cargo pocket and wasted his time feeling for a pulse on her neck. He looked over her body and saw ribs and pelvis exposed beside ripped flesh and skin. Nunez closed his eyes and gently lowered her head to her chest.

Corporal Cowan stood beside the old woman, pushed her head to the side and checked for a pulse. He waited, searched the other side of her neck, then took his hand away. He reached down and lifted her ragged, bloody nightshirt. When he reached her stomach he stopped and stared at her ruptured abdomen. Nunez stared too. Cowan put the nightshirt back down.

"Goddamn it," Corporal Drake said as he knelt on the floor next to the man in uniform. Nunez dropped to a knee beside the man. Drake had straightened the man's legs and unzipped his uniform top, and they both saw the man was done. His right hand had been blown off, Nunez couldn't see where it was. He thought that was probably why the man fell, the rope couldn't hold him up by one wrist. The man's left collarbone had been blown out of the skin by a bullet impact and his throat was torn wide open. Nunez counted seven bullet holes in his t-shirt, more below his waist. Drake ripped the shirt open.

Nunez took one look and said, "Fuck... he's dead." He looked over the man and wondered if he was a soldier. The man was about forty with a short military haircut, a little overweight but not out of shape. A pile of dirty brownish AK-47 spent shells lay beside the dead soldier. Nunez grabbed the dead man's open uniform top and flipped it over to see the nametape and rank. The nametape was ripped by a bullet and soaked with blood, but still legible.

First Sergeant Olivares.

"Lieutenant!" Gorham screamed from the back of the house. "One of these motherfuckers is wounded and lying just outside the back door!"

Nunez and Drake sprang to their feet. Drake started toward the back but Nunez yelled, "Drake, stay here! Cut the bodies down!"

Drake turned back to the living room as Doc Corley ran in. Nunez charged past another pile of spent shells into the hallway, turned through the entrance into the kitchen and slipped on an empty AK magazine. As he regained his footing he noticed another one a few feet away. Quincy and Gorham stood at the kitchen door, Eckert and Mireles ran into the kitchen behind him. Quincy yelled, "Gorham and Eckert, you got security! The rest of us are gonna get this piece of shit to the front of the house!"

Quincy flung the door open and rushed outside. Gorham went out a half second later, Nunez was right on Gorham's ass. Nunez saw the man's raised hands.

The man yelled, *"Yo no hice nada! Por favor, yo no hice nada!"*

Nunez understood *I didn't do anything. Please, I didn't do anything.* Just like almost every piece of shit he had ever arrested, whether they had just robbed, raped or murdered someone, they always claimed they hadn't done anything. His denial threw Nunez into a rage.

Quincy stepped off the porch, pointed his weapon at the man and screamed, "Shut the fuck up, motherfucker!"

Nunez stepped off the porch by the man's head. The man lay on his back with bloody and torn hands high in the air. He had an AK slung across his chest over body armor. No mask covered his face, his black clothing was wet and dirty, and he wore blood soaked gray tennis shoes. Both ankles looked like they were shot through.

The man screamed again in Spanish, *"I didn't do anything!"*

Gorham and Eckert spread out in the small backyard, looking outward. Mireles stepped next to Nunez and pulled a set of zip-ties from a pouch. Nunez looked down at the maybe twenty-five year old man who was desperately pleading innocence to the people he had just tried to kill.

The man looked at Nunez and said, *"Señor! Por favor, ayudame!"*

"You want my help, motherfucker?" Nunez screamed back. "Here's how I'll help you!"

Nunez kicked the man hard in the head. The man's skull bounced off a concrete step and he screamed in terror. Nunez reached down, grabbed the AK and wrenched it upward. The sling held it in place. Nunez yanked on it until it cleared the man's head, then kicked him again. When the man tried to cover his head with his wounded hands. Nunez grabbed a sleeve and pulled his hand away. He tossed the AK to Gorham and yelled, "Gorham, clear this weapon!" Then he told Mireles, "Help me turn this piece of shit over so we can zip-tie him."

Mireles rolled the man over and twisted an injured arm as far as he could behind the man's back. The man screamed again and kicked his body sideways. Quincy stepped on one of the man's wounded ankles. The man shrieked and tried to pull his leg away. Quincy put all his weight on it and said, "Like that, motherfucker?"

Sergeant Suarez and Specialist Gordon, the two men who had to abandon their Humvee after an RPG disabled it, ran from the driveway into the backyard. They stopped short when they saw the prisoner on his back being zip-tied. Suarez dropped down to help Mireles tighten the zip-ties, Gordon kicked the man in the thigh. The man stifled a scream.

Nunez saw that Mireles and Suarez had tightened the zip-ties so far they would cut off the circulation to the man's hands. *Good for that motherfucker,* he thought. He yelled, "Mireles, Gordon, drag this asshole to the front yard! Let's get him searched! The rest of you, pull security!"

Gordon and Mireles dragged the man into the driveway. Suarez kicked him in the ankle as he passed. The man screamed again. Behind Nunez, Gorham yelled, "Hey, this asshole fired all his ammo at us! His fucking magazine is empty!"

Gordon jerked the man's sagging head up by his hair. Nunez and Quincy followed the soldiers and prisoner to the front yard. D'Angelo still lay on the grass, but he wasn't being held down anymore. When D'Angelo saw the captured enemy fighter his face contorted with rage.

Gordon and Mireles dropped the man onto his face in the grass. Nunez grabbed an arm and flipped him onto his back. The man's face erupted in agony when the full weight of his torso and gear smashed onto his ripped hands. His jerked his hips upward to get the pressure off. Nunez dropped his knee onto the man's stomach and forced him down again. The man screamed and tears welled in his eyes. Nunez checked the pouches on the man's body armor. He had nothing, no ammunition or grenades.

Nunez stood up. "This goddamn asshole burned all his ammo on us. Fucking piece of shit." He kicked the man again, in the ribs.

Several more soldiers ran into the yard. Someone stomped the man's groin. The man groaned and tried to sit upright. Someone else grabbed him by the hair and slammed his head to the ground.

Nunez turned around. Drake stepped out the front door of the house and ran to the soldiers clustered around the prisoner. Nunez stepped away to get on his radio. He heard Drake say, "This is for those people in that house, asshole!" and a loud *whack!* The man wailed again and Quincy yelled, "I said shut the fuck up! Nobody wants to hear it!"

More shouts sounded from the enraged soldiers. Nunez stepped further away, he didn't want Harcrow to hear the platoon beating the guy's ass when he keyed the radio. He said into his mike, "Rapido 6 this is Red 4."

Harcrow's response was anxious and rushed. "Red 4 Rapido 6, send it!"

"6 this is 4, we got ambushed again. One additional KIA, and we found three civilians and one of the maintenance company soldiers murdered inside a house. Plus we captured one enemy fighter in the backyard. You copy?"

Nunez heard another loud shriek behind him. He turned and saw at least ten soldiers huddled around the prisoner. They threw punches and kicks and seemed to have forgotten about security. All the Humvee gunners were watching the asskicking. He yelled, "Hey! Pay attention to your fucking sectors! There's still enemy around!"

The gunners turned to cover their areas. The soldiers beating the prisoner didn't respond. Nunez looked for Quincy and saw him in the pack around the wounded enemy fighter. He yelled, "Hey Lieutenant, how about some security?"

Quincy didn't respond either. Instead, he yelled "I told you to *shut the fuck up!*" and stomped on the man's face. Nunez couldn't see the impact, but he heard the man's scream abruptly change to a pathetic whimper. Another soldier steadied himself on someone else's shoulder and kicked the man several times.

Nunez thought, *Oh shit. I better do something, or this guy's going back to Edinburgh with a broken jaw.* He yelled, "Lieutenant, that's enough! Y'all back off!" and took a step toward the group.

A bayonet flashed in the air and disappeared among flailing limbs. Nunez yelled "Shit!" and ran toward the crowd. The man's voice rose to a squeal. Someone yelled, "Yeah! Cut his fucking throat out!"

Gordon pulled his knife and knelt by the man's legs. The bayonet flashed again, near the man's head. Arms and legs flew, pummeling the man. Nunez reached the crowd and shoved Gordon off balance. Mireles kicked the man's ribs and Nunez yanked him backward by the drag handle on the back of his gear. Nunez shoved Eckert backward just as he drew his bayonet from its sheath.

Then he saw D'Angelo, twisting a bayonet blade into the notch just below the man's Adam's apple. Quincy stood watching, blood lust on his face. When he saw Nunez his expression abruptly changed.

"D'Angelo, stop!" Nunez screamed. "What the fuck are you doing?"

D'Angelo looked up. His eyes were like black flames in a blood-smeared, dirty, sweaty face. He pursed his lips, tightened his grip on the bayonet and ripped it free. The man's scream had stopped, he didn't make a sound when the knife left his throat. Nunez saw bubbles of blood foam from multiple stab wounds.

The soldiers' shouts and curses evaporated. They backed away from the dying prisoner. Nunez knelt beside the man and felt for a pulse. It was there, fading fast. The man's eyes rolled back in his head. Quincy's eyes grew wide and he looked at Nunez with an expression that almost looked like fear. He stammered, "Uh, everybody, um… pull security. Hurry up, go pull security! Now!"

The men spread out. Most of them ran to the west side of the street, giving an occasional glance back at the man they had just helped murder. Nunez looked around. No shots were being fired, the enemy hadn't pushed onto this block. The platoon had been left alone for some reason.

Nunez looked back at the prisoner. D'Angelo put his hands on the grass beside the man and struggled to stand. He slid his bayonet into its sheath, wiped his hands on his pant legs and walked to his machine gun. Slowly he bent down to pick it up, tore away tangled venetian blinds, and looked at Quincy and Nunez. Nunez stared back, unsure what to say. D'Angelo looked down, took a deep breath, and shuffled across the street after the others.

A voice came across Nunez's radio. "Red 4 this is 6, what's the status on that prisoner?"

Nunez grabbed the mike and looked at Quincy. Quincy looked away for a moment, then asked, "Jerry, what do I do?"

Nunez keyed the radio. "6, uh, stand by a minute, I'm trying to confirm something."

He let go of the mike and wiped his face, gave himself a moment to think. He realized they had just done something monstrous, something that could destroy all their lives. It happened in the heat of battle, after the enemy committed a horrible crime. But that wouldn't make much difference. Soldiers were expected to handle that kind of stress.

Nunez felt for a pulse again. Nothing. Blood bubbled from the prisoner's throat, but he didn't move or make a sound. His eyes were swollen and bruised, his lower jaw crooked. One ear was torn and bloody. His pupils rolled down again, fixed on the sky. The bubbling stopped.

Nunez put a bloody hand to his face. "Shit." He knew that even if D'Angelo hadn't stabbed him, the platoon was on its way to beating the prisoner to death. Nunez and Quincy had thrown their shots, too. Almost everyone in the platoon had.

Doc Corley ran to the murdered man. He stopped and gave Nunez a sharp, questioning look. Then he knelt and checked for a pulse.

"Anything?" Nunez asked.

Corley tried several spots on the man's neck. He touched the stab wounds in the prisoner's throat with a gloved hand and mumbled, "Jesus Christ." Then he looked at Nunez and said, "He's dead. What the hell happened?"

"Doc, go back inside the house," Nunez said. "Help someone else. Leave this guy alone."

Corley stood up and wiped dirt from his knees. He took another look at the dead man, then said, "Barnes is okay. He needs to be evacuated, but the bleeding's under control and he's still on his feet. The people in the house are all dead."

Nunez nodded without looking up. Corley jogged to the other side of the street. Nunez and Quincy looked at each other again, and Quincy's expression left no question now. Hewas scared.

Nunez forced himself to think. He tried to convince himself that they could just be honest about what happened. After all the shit they had just gone through, people should get it. This was a war, a worse war than anything the platoon had experienced before. People would understand.

But if they didn't, D'Angelo would burn. He'd probably get life in prison. All the rest of them could get prison time too, even if they hadn't killed the guy. They had a responsibility to stop the beating. All the soldiers who had been in the mob would go down, one way or another. The only men who might be safe were the Humvee gunners and drivers. And if some military prosecutor wanted to make a name for himself, they might burn too, for not getting out of their vehicles to stop the murder.

No matter what, if anyone higher up found out what they had just done, almost the entire platoon was fucked.

"Red 4 this is 6, what's going on? Give me a SITREP. What's the status of your prisoner?"

Nunez looked at Quincy and keyed the mike. "6 this is Red 4, there's no prisoner. I misunderstood one of my soldiers. We have several friendly KIA's and one WIA we're about to evac. How copy, over."

"Roger that, I copied. I'm pushing a platoon to you, hold your position."

In a rush Nunez answered, "Negative, 6! Don't send anyone, have them hold off at least a block away. We think there's still a bunch of enemy between us and them. Stand by until we know it's clear."

Harcrow sounded confused by the response. "Uh, roger. I need to get those guys to you, so tell me as soon as you think it's clear. They're standing by."

Quincy asked, "So what do we do now? Should we take the guy's gear off and hide him in the house?"

Nunez considered that, then shook his head. Too much evidence would be left that way. Somebody would find the body and ask questions. If they wanted to lower the chances of being caught, there was only one thing they could do.

Nunez said, "Burn him. Have a couple of guys drag him to the backyard, pour diesel from a fuel can on him and burn him. We'll get the friendly KIAs out of the house and pull back. If anyone asks anything about the burned body, we'll say he was like that when we cleared the house."

Quincy swallowed. "Okay, Jerry. Okay. You get the KIAs, I'll take care of the prisoner's body. And spread the word to not say shit about this to anyone. Let's get moving."

The two men turned away from each other. One went to his task of recovering murdered Americans, the other to hide evidence of a war crime.

CHAPTER 10

"You look like you're fucking a hole in the wall, Jerry."

Nunez gently pushed off the shower wall with his forehead again, swayed a few inches, and eased forward. When his head touched the wall he rocked his hips softly and pushed away, then repeated the motion. Quincy had watched Nunez rock like that for several minutes, silent and alone, fully dressed in the shower with no water running.

"I wish I was," Nunez said.

"If the kids see you like this, they're going to think you've lost it."

Nunez pushed off the wall with his head, swayed back, rocked forward and tapped the wall with his forehead again. His eyes stayed closed. He said, "I wish I had lost it. Then they'd take me out of here and say I'm not responsible for my actions."

Quincy didn't respond. Nunez kept rocking, eyes closed, trying to force the storm of worries and guilt from his mind. Back home he would have put his music on and gone for a run. That wouldn't have worked either, but at least it was a comfortable, familiar feeling.

"Jerry, everything'll be fine," Quincy said. "That body is long gone already. We can trust the guys, they won't talk about it. We got plenty of other shit to worry about, let's forget about that asshole."

Nunez rocked forward, let his forehead touch the wall and stopped moving. "Rod, we don't know that everything's going to be okay. We just lost seven fucking guys in one fight. Seven guys. We barely cleared any of this damn town, we still can't get air support because of the missile threat, and now the fucking regular Army troops are being committed to other towns instead of this one."

Quincy didn't say anything. Nunez kept his eyes closed and head down, analyzing his actions during the fight. The action that bothered him the most was that he left Leonard and Fernandez on the battlefield, wounded and dying. At least, Leonard had been dying. Nunez almost hoped Fernandez was dying too. Second platoon had found Leonard dead and Fernandez gone. Nunez knew Fernandez hadn't walked away on his own.

The action that bothered him second most was what the platoon had done to the prisoner. He knew that at some point, the murder and all the issues associated with it would become the most prominent worry.

"Jerry," Quincy said, "we had the deck stacked against us from the moment we stepped off. We're limited on what we can do and what weapons we can use, we have to follow rules, but they can do whatever they want. How were we supposed to get out of that shitstorm without casualties? Don't act like we fucked up, Jerry. We got dealt a shitty hand, that's all."

Nunez turned his head and opened his eyes. "We didn't fuck up, Rod? We murdered a prisoner. How's that for fucking up?"

Quincy looked away. "Jerry, I already told you, don't worry about it. It's over with, let it go."

Nunez gave a sarcastic laugh. "Oh, it's over? Yeah, that makes me feel better. Well, Rodger, let's assume we survive this shit. If we make it back home, all it'll take is one of these guys to get drunk in a bar and brag to some college chick about the captured prisoner we killed, and we're all fucked. Or some astute investigator gets curious about this dead, stabbed, burned guy wearing gear, and starts asking questions that we can't answer. Or someone has a crisis of conscience and decides he has to say something. Or there's some kid who was hidden in one of these houses, watched the whole thing and tells a reporter, 'Yeah, they killed that bitch!' But other than that, what could go wrong?"

Quincy's face tensed. Nunez knew when Quincy insisted there was nothing to worry about, he was trying to convince himself.

Quincy said, "Well Jerry, I guess we just have to trust in God then, don't we?"

Nunez rolled his eyes. "Oh, shit. For real, Rodger? God will cover us for murdering someone? Even if I was religious, that bullshit wouldn't work. I don't think God's job is to make sure guys who commit murder get away with it."

Quincy gave a sarcastic smirk. "What the fuck, Jerry? You ate up with guilt about that sorryass piece of human shit we killed? The guy who tied up two terrified women and some poor guy in his pajamas, and an American fucking soldier, so we'd kill them when he shot at us? The guy who fired every last round he had at us, who maybe killed Ben Lyall, Eldridge, Brandon, Mikey Fernandez, and all the other guys? The guy who executed American prisoners? You feel guilty about killing him, Jerry? You think we done wrong?"

Nunez turned from the wall. "Don't ask stupid fucking questions, Rodger. You know me better than that. That asshole deserved what he got. I couldn't feel guilty about that guy if I tried. If anything, I feel guilty that he didn't suffer worse before he died. That he didn't suffer like those people in the house did."

Nunez took a step back, rested against the back wall of the shower and blew out a long breath. "I don't feel guilty that we killed that shithead. I'm mad because we lost control of the platoon and did something stupid that might have fucked us all. We were pissed, we didn't think, and we fucked up. It's our job to not let things like that happen. We have a responsibility to the men, and we failed. That bothers me."

Quincy looked at Nunez's feet for a few moments. Nunez let him think for a while before saying, "Your voice goes all ghetto when you're pissed off."

Quincy's head came up. "What?"

"Your voice," Nunez said. "When you get pissed, your voice changes. You just asked me, 'you think we done wrong?' It's funny when you do that. It happened in Afghanistan once or twice."

Quincy frowned. "Well, eat a dick, Jerry. How was that, proper enough for you?"

"Yeah, that sounded good," Nunez said. "Thanks."

Quincy laughed softly. "Jerry, you're such an asshole."

"I'm just following my leader," Nunez said.

Silence followed. Nunez put his forehead to the wall and closed his eyes. After a full minute, Quincy asked, "What's on your mind now, Jerry?"

"I'm worried about Barney. He better be okay."

Quincy gave a nod. After the ambushes, Conway drove Sergeant Barnes downtown where medics put him in a Humvee with a badly wounded second platoon soldier. That Humvee and one other drove them back to Edinburgh for evacuation by air. Barnes was in good shape and would pull through; Nunez didn't think the second platoon soldier made it to Edinburgh alive.

"He'll be okay, Jerry. Doc said he was alright."

"He might talk about what happened with the prisoner."

"He was wounded and down when that happened. He never saw the prisoner," Quincy said. "So stop talking about that shit."

"We have to talk about it. We have to talk about all of it. And I mean, we have to get everyone together and decide what we're going to say and do about it."

Another minute of silence followed. Quincy broke it by saying, "Yeah. You're right, we do need to talk about that with everyone. Get everyone on the same page."

"Get everyone on the same page," Nunez mumbled. "Meaning, 'tell everyone to lie their ass off.'"

Quincy started to speak up and Nunez cut him off by saying, "We should do it now, before everyone falls asleep. Once we're awake again and step off to clear the rest of the town, there won't be time."

Quincy nodded. The mission was on an "operational pause" to let the company get some sleep and recover from their losses. Captain Harcrow had ordered second platoon to clear a two-story brick house and put all of Nunez's soldiers on break inside until nightfall. The support company used the platoon's six remaining Humvees to set up a perimeter around the house. The entire force in Arriago would stay put for at least six hours, until more resources arrived and the men were ready to advance again.

Quincy asked, "You have anything special you want to tell the kids, anything I should know about?"

Nunez thought a moment. "We have to ask if anyone feels like they have to report this. If even one guy says he's morally compelled to say something, then that's it. We have no choice but to come clean about everything."

Quincy took that in. "Are you sure, Jerry? Don't you think we could overrule one guy and make him go along with everyone else?"

"No," Nunez said. "Even if he says he'll stay quiet about it, he'd just wait until this is over and then report it. So if anyone at all says they have to talk about it, either for moral reasons or because they'd rather admit to it than wait to get caught, we have to 'fess up. If we overrule the guy, we'll spend the rest of our lives waiting for the hammer to fall."

Quincy rubbed his face with both hands. "Fuuuck," he said. "Yeah, I guess that's true. We'll tell everyone that, if you think that's the right way to handle it."

"I don't think we have a choice," Nunez said. "And whatever happens, we have to make sure D'Angelo is taken care of. If we have to turn ourselves in, we don't blame it all on him."

Quincy nodded. "Yeah. I thought he had gone nuts for a while there. He's okay now, I think. We won't let anyone throw him under the bus."

Nunez nodded and rubbed his temples. He didn't want to stand in front of his troops and talk about the worst thing any of them had ever done.

"Alright," Quincy responded. "You ready?"

"No," Nunez answered. "You?"

"No."

"Well, fuck it," Nunez said as he stepped out of the shower. "Let's get it done."

They walked out of the bathroom, down the stairs and into the living room. Their soldiers were spread out on the first floor, nodding off as they waited for orders. The men had removed their chest rigs and body armor but nothing else, not getting too comfortable until they knew it was safe to fall asleep. Nunez walked to Allenby and whispered, "Bring everyone into the living room. We need to have a talk."

Allenby nodded and announced "Rally up, platoon meeting!" Nunez waved Corley over from a sofa and asked, "Doc, how's everyone doing?"

Corley shrugged. "Okay, I think. Lots of minor injuries, small cuts and shit. Cowan hit his face on a curb and chipped a tooth. He's alright, just going to look goofy for a while. Gorham's been complaining about a bad headache, I think maybe he banged his head on something during the fight and doesn't remember it. I gave him some Motrin, he's in the bathroom now."

Nunez stepped in and whispered, "D'Angelo?"

Corley looked around. D'Angelo wasn't in the room yet. Corley whispered back, "Hasn't said a word about anything. I think he's okay, but he hasn't been talking. Just cleaning his weapon and loading up on ammo."

"Huh," Nunez said. "We have to watch him, I'm not sure how much more he can take. Thanks Doc."

Corley nodded and gave Nunez's arm a squeeze. Allenby walked back into the living room, followed by a cluster of soldiers. D'Angelo filed into the room in the middle of the pack, anonymous. He didn't look at Nunez.

A toilet flushed down the hall. Allenby gave quiet orders for everyone to have a seat, drink water, and stay awake. As the men settled into sofas, chairs and spaces on the floor Gorham walked down the hall into the living room. He rubbed his head, looked over the assembled platoon and asked, "Soooo, I guess we're having a meeting or something?"

Drake answered, "No, dipshit. We decided to sit in one room facing Sergeant Nunez and the Lieutenant for no reason."

Gorham said, "Oh, okay. That makes sense." Then he announced, "Dude, I figured out why I had such a bad headache. I just dropped like a four-foot turd, I think it was stabbing me in the brain."

Hushed laughter rippled through the room. Nunez covered his face and laughed with everyone else, thinking back to his deployments in the war on terror. In Iraq and Afghanistan, on every mission, even when the shit had hit the fan and good guys had gone down, someone always had a joke handy. Until Gorham decided to tell everyone about the size of his feces, there hadn't been anything in this war worth laughing about.

Quincy shook his head and said with a smile, "Gorham, sit your stupid ass down."

Gorham sat down next to his best friend Drake. Quincy looked at Nunez and asked, "You wanna drive, Sergeant Nunez?"

"Yes sir, I guess so," Nunez said, thinking *Holy shit I don't want to talk about this.* He looked around at his men, took in all the dirty faces, bloodstained uniforms, battered weapons and gear. Every face held a story, each man's personal perspective of the horror he had endured since jogging into Arriago one night earlier. He looked at D'Angelo, who sat against an old TV with his machine gun propped on its bipod beside him, muzzle pointed to the wall. D'Angelo met Nunez's gaze for a moment, then looked away.

Nunez leaned forward and said, "Alright guys, rule number one. Nothing anyone says in this house leaves this fucking house. Can we agree to that?"

Heads nodded and voices murmured, "Hooah," and "Roger, Sergeant." Nunez waited to make sure there were no dissenting voices, then said, "Here's what's up. There's no use in keeping our mouths shut around each other, we have to talk about what happened this morning after we assaulted the house. Shit went crazy, we went crazy, and something happened that none of us expected."

He looked around again. Eyes that had been heavy with fatigue were wide open. He said, "Every last one of us knows why we did what we did. Every one of us. We understand it. Other people who don't know what the fuck is going on in this town won't. Some of them are going to blame us for the deaths of the people in the house, they're going to say stupid shit like 'why didn't you go inside the house and make sure there weren't any civilians inside before you fired?' And some are going to call us murderers for what we did to the prisoner. If they ever find out about him."

A few eyebrows went up. D'Angelo's expression didn't change. Nunez said, "I want everyone to understand this. I don't speak for anyone but myself, but the only people I blame are me and the lieutenant. It was our job to keep everyone under control, and we didn't. So I don't want anyone thinking we're standing up here saying 'you guys fucked up.' You didn't fuck up any worse than we did."

Heads nodded. Nunez looked at D'Angelo and saw the same blank stare. He continued, "Guys, all we're doing now is deciding between two choices. We're either going to report what we did, or we're going to keep it quiet. We're not arguing about who did what or what should have happened. It already happened, it can't be changed, we're not going to waste time talking about that. All we're deciding is what we're doing from this point forward."

Carillo raised his hand. "Sergeant Nunez, are we talking about killing the civilians and that First Sergeant plus the prisoner, or just killing the prisoner?"

"Just the prisoner," Quincy answered before Nunez could speak. "I already told Harcrow about the civilians and First Sergeant."

Nunez added, "Guys, we were tricked into killing those hostages, and everyone knows that. So there's no reason to lie about anything up to the point Gorham looked out the back window and saw the wounded enemy fighter. We're starting from there. Everyone clear?"

More nods. Carillo spoke up again. "Sarge, I figured we had already decided to keep it quiet. You and the lieutenant went around telling everyone not to say anything about the prisoner, so I thought it was a secret already. I know a few other guys thought the same thing."

"I thought that too," Allenby added. "I think it hit me right around the time me and Mireles set the dead guy on fire."

A few other soldiers quietly agreed. Nunez said, "Yeah, I understand that. But that was just a snap judgment, something we decided under stress. Now that shit's calmed down, we can step back, take our time and make a better decision. Anyone have issues with that?"

Nobody spoke. Nunez said, "Good. So now we're on to rule number two. We know there are only two choices, either report what we did or stay quiet. So the rule is, if even one guy in this room thinks we have to report this, then we stand together and report it. If we decide we're going to keep it quiet, then every last motherfucker in this room has to agree to keep it quiet."

A few faces registered confusion. Berisha asked in his odd Balkan accent, "Sarjant, why must everyone admit this if just one man thinks we must? I do not understand this."

D'Angelo spoke up first. "Because all it takes is one guy to talk, and everyone gets dragged down. It doesn't make sense for us to agree to stay quiet if one guy runs his mouth about it."

Heads turned. D'Angelo looked Nunez square in the eye. Nunez nodded and said, "That's right, D. This is an all or nothing deal." Then to everyone else, Nunez said, "Guys, don't take this the wrong way. You have to decide on your own what you think is best. If you honestly think you have to report this, for moral reasons or whatever, be honest about it and we'll all stand with you in front of Harcrow."

There were a few snickers, and Sergeant Liu stifled a full-blown laugh. Corporal Mireles asked, "Come on Sarge, are we supposed to take a trip to prison just because one guy thinks he's been ordered by God or someone to tell the truth? If someone thinks that shit we can take him upstairs for a few minutes and straighten him out."

Someone added, "Damn right." A few more voices spoke up in agreement. Nunez yelled over them, "Hey! Cut that shit out, now! We're not going to bulldoze anyone into going with the crowd. That wouldn't work anyway, all they'd do is wait til this is over and report it when they're home. If someone thinks we have to report it, we have to report it. I'm no fucking expert on what to do after committing a murder, so I'm not about to talk shit if someone thinks we should admit what happened. I don't know what the right thing to do is, and neither do you, Mireles. So let's talk it out."

Nobody spoke up this time. Except Mireles, who said, "Sorry, Sarge."

Nunez said, "Let's take a vote. If someone needs to change their vote later they can, I just want to get an idea of what you guys think we should do. Before we vote, does anyone have anything to say?"

Nobody answered. Nunez said, "Alright. Who says we should keep it quiet?"

A sea of hands shot into the air. Nunez gave a quick glance around the room and said, "That looks pretty much unanimous. Now, does anyone think we should report it?"

The multitude of hands dropped. It was replaced by one single hand, rising above the old television on the floor. Heads turned and voices murmured surprise. Nunez was shocked to see D'Angelo holding one arm high above his head. D'Angelo, the man whose actions had been the most damning and who stood to suffer the worst punishment if the murder was exposed.

Nunez stared hard at D'Angelo. D'Angelo kept his arm up and stared straight back. Nunez asked, "D, are you sure you want to do that?"

D'Angelo lowered his arm and nodded. "Yes, Sergeant Nunez. I'm sure. I've been thinking about it for the last couple hours, and I've decided."

Nunez and Quincy exchanged a look. Nunez asked D'Angelo, "D, why do you think you should report it? Don't take this the wrong way, but you're the last guy I thought would want to tell anyone about this."

D'Angelo answered, "Sergeant, it's not about whether I 'want' to report it or not. Trust me, I don't. But if I don't, you guys might suffer because of what I did. And there's no reason to bullshit anyone about it, I'm the one who killed the guy. You guys rescued me and took care of the guys from my old unit, you accepted me into your platoon, and then I went and did that shit to you. I don't want any of you guys to pay for what I did. So I should report it, to make sure you guys are in the clear."

All eyes were on D'Angelo. He turned his face to the rest of the men, sighed and said, "Guys, I'm sorry. Y'all treated me like I'm one of you, not like an outsider. Being with this platoon has been like being back with my old First Infantry platoon in Iraq and Afghanistan. The last thing I want to do is cause you guys problems. But... I just lost it for a minute. First they wiped out my company, then they killed some of you guys, then Lyall, then when I saw what I had done to those civilians and my First Sergeant... I just lost it. I went crazy. I didn't mean to do anything to get you guys in trouble, and I'm sorry. Let me talk to Harcrow, I'll tell him it was my fault. Y'all will be safe then."

The rest of the platoon stayed silent. Nunez and Quincy looked at each other again. Quincy cocked one eyebrow as if to ask, *Well? What do you think?*

Nunez asked, "D, are you just saying this because you feel guilty about what happened to those hostages? That wasn't your fault. I know it's tough knowing you might have shot your own First Sergeant, but don't let that drive this decision."

D'Angelo surprised Nunez by saying, "Top Olivares was a piece of shit. I hated that motherfucker, Sergeant Nunez. I hated his fucking guts. If there's one guy to blame for what happened to my company, it's him. If we had found him alive I would have knocked his fucking teeth out. He was one of our guys though, and yeah I feel guilty that I might have shot him. But that's not why I want to turn myself in. More than anything else, I feel guilty for putting you guys in danger. So let me take the blame for what I did."

Nunez considered it. D'Angelo's offer was tempting, there was no question about it. If just one person took all the blame, Nunez could stop worrying about the entire platoon going to prison. And maybe D'Angelo would get off easy. He had been through hell when his company was ambushed, and he knew his machine gun fire had hit at least some of the hostages in the house. D'Angelo had more reason than anyone else to do something crazy. He might be able to get away with it. Then everyone would come through this whole shitty thing okay, nobody would spend the rest of their life in a military prison. The problem would be solved.

But if D'Angelo didn't get off, then what? If someone in the chain of command with high morals and low exposure to reality decided to make an example of D'Angelo, what would the rest of the platoon do? Stay silent and let him burn, for doing what they had all wanted to do? Nunez didn't think the soldiers who had fought alongside D'Angelo could do that if they tried. He knew he couldn't.

Nunez shook his head at Quincy. Then he looked at D'Angelo and said, "D, I get what you're saying. But it wasn't just you. Except for the guys in the Humvees, we all got punches and kicks in. Even if you hadn't been there, we were on our way to beating that guy to death. For us to dump this on you, that would be fucked up. I'm not willing to throw you under the bus so the rest of us will be safe."

D'Angelo held his palm out. "Sergeant Nunez, I'm not asking you to throw me under the bus. All I'm asking is that you let me admit to what I did. Like I said, I've been thinking about this for a couple hours, and I'm pretty sure I'll skate on it. I already got diagnosed with PTSD after my first deployment, and after all the shit that happened yesterday and today I bet some doctor will say I had temporary insanity or something. Worst case, I'll be in jail a couple of months, then they'll let me out with a bad conduct discharge."

"Worst case is a lot worse than that," Nunez said. "We're supposed to be able to handle anything, no matter how bad it is, and still follow the rules. I think the worst case is life in prison for you, and the rest of us would still go down for our part of it."

D'Angelo looked a little offended. He retorted, "Sarge, you guys don't have to go down for anything. I'll tell them that I beat the guy's ass, I killed him and I burned him. You guys don't have to admit to anything. Just let me take the heat for it, Sarge. I won't let y'all take any blame. It'll be okay for everyone."

"D," Nunez said, "and what are you going to say the rest of us were doing while you were allegedly kicking this guy's ass, killing him and burning him? You think the investigators are going to say, 'Oh sure, you did all this and nobody else noticed?' You think nobody's going to ask, 'Why didn't the other guys stop you?' Come on, D. It ain't gonna be that easy."

D'Angelo looked down, concentration obvious on his face. When he looked back up he said, "Everyone else was busy helping the friendly casualties in the house. I volunteered to watch the prisoner. When nobody was looking I walked him behind the house, beat his ass, stabbed him and set him on fire. You guys didn't know shit about it until it was too late. So none of you did anything wrong, it was just me."

Nunez closed his eyes and thought about the murder scenes he had been on. He tried to look at this situation like a homicide investigator would. Within seconds, two huge issues came to mind.

He opened his eyes. "D, first of all, if you were sharp enough to wait until we were too busy to notice what you were doing, you weren't nuts when you did it. You planned the murder, it was premeditated. That takes away your temporary insanity defense. Second," he continued, "after we found out what you did, we still had a responsibility to report it. So why didn't we tell anyone about it?"

D'Angelo looked down again. When he looked up, his face was hopeful. "What if I say you guys didn't even know about the prisoner? I could say I'm the only one that went into the backyard, I found the guy and I killed him. I didn't even tell you about it. You still don't know."

For a few seconds, Nunez thought this version of the story might work. He had another tug of war with his conscience, a fight pitting his desire to be free of this problem with his duty to protect a soldier who had become one of his own. But apart from principles and loyalty, there was something else ready to defeat D'Angelo's story. Nunez had to think hard through the fatigue, but he was almost sure he remembered his radio traffic with Harcrow, after the capture of the prisoner.

"That won't work, D'Angelo," Nunez said. "I'm pretty sure I said something about finding a prisoner in the backyard when I gave Harcrow a situation report. Afterward I told him I had misunderstood one of you guys, that there was no prisoner. I seriously doubt anyone would believe we didn't know about the prisoner in the backyard, if I said it on the radio and you say you killed the guy back there. I think they'd see through that lie."

D'Angelo asked, "But Sarge, didn't you say you just think you said something on the radio about the prisoner in the backyard? Like, you're not sure if you said it or not?"

"I said... something," Nunez said. "I'm almost positive I said we captured a prisoner behind the house."

"But you're not sure," D'Angelo said.

"I'm sure enough that I know your plan wouldn't work."

D'Angelo gave a frustrated grimace and didn't respond. After a few seconds Staff Sergeant Cuevas said from the sofa, "Sarge, you sure are a fucking buzz kill."

Nunez was surprised to find himself pissed off at Cuevas' comment. "What was your buzz about, Cuevas? Were you buzzed about D'Angelo throwing himself on his sword so we go free? What fucking buzz did I kill?"

Cuevas threw his hands up. "Fuck no Sarge, come on! You know that's not what I meant. I'm trying to figure some easy way out of this, just like everyone else. And every time D throws out an alternative, you shoot it down. I ain't saying you're wrong, but damn, it sucks to see you beat down every possibility with facts and logic."

Corley spoke up. "Sarge, what's your opinion? You've obviously thought this through, so what do you think we should do?"

Nunez said, "My opinion is that we'd all be pieces of shit for letting D take all the blame for what almost all of us took part in. I couldn't live with myself for doing that. And I'm almost positive we can get away with what we did. As far as we know, the only people in the entire world who know what we did are in this room. If someone does find that guy burned in the backyard, we can give a believable story that he was already there. We saw something on fire behind the house but didn't check to see what it was. I was the only one who said anything about the backyard over the radio. If anyone asks me why I said that, I'll say Gorham or someone said 'We found something on fire in the backyard' and I thought he said 'We caught someone in the backyard.' I mean, I'll figure out some reason I misunderstood him. Fuck, I'll even claim hearing damage after this is over to make it more believable."

"So your answer is that we keep this quiet?" Corley asked.

Nunez nodded. "Yes. We keep this a secret, wait for this shit to die down and see if anyone asks questions. If there's some secret witness, well, we'll deal with that later. But my gut feeling is that nobody's going to say a word about that guy. Maybe his people recovered his body already. If we don't run our mouths and screw ourselves, I think we'll be fine."

Nunez looked across the room, meeting each man's eyes. "Guys, almost every turd who commits the perfect crime winds up fucking himself over by bragging about it. There have been plenty of cases where we had zero evidence, no witnesses, no video, nothing at all to go on. And then someone calls and says, 'Hey, I was at a party and this guy I know got drunk and told me he murdered someone for their car.' If we don't do anything stupid like that, we'll make it past this. But we have to keep it secret, even from our families."

Most of the soldiers nodded and said, "Roger that," or "Hooah." D'Angelo didn't say anything at first, instead he looked down at the floor. Then he looked up and said, "Sarge, I can't let y'all get screwed because of me. I mean, I'm not even one of your guys. Don't risk your platoon for me."

Nunez pointed directly at D'Angelo and said, "D, shut the fuck up. I don't give a rat's ass what unit you belong to on paper or what unit you used to be in. You saved my life and Doc's life this morning, you recovered Petri's body, and you tried like hell to save Lyall. As of today you're first platoon, Alpha company, fourth of the one twelfth infantry. You fucking got that?"

D'Angelo looked shocked. Several soldiers said, "That's right, D," and "Roger that." Quincy said, "We'll make that official today, even if it's just while this war is on. I'll tell Harcrow to put you on our platoon roster, D."

D'Angelo looked close to tears. He gave a silent nod. Nunez added, "One last thing guys, we have to swear that we won't do anything like this again. If we wind up in the same situation tomorrow, we take the guy prisoner, search him, throw him in a Humvee and run him back to Harcrow like we're supposed to. This morning we got all the revenge we're going to get. From now on, it's all professional."

Soldiers nodded again. Sergeant Carillo didn't. He said, "Sarge, if we find Fernandez tied up dead in one of these houses and we capture someone afterward, I'll gut the motherfucker. I'll do it in front of you, the lieutenant, Captain Harcrow, whoever. I'd do it in front of God. Just so everyone knows, if this shit does happen again, someone better restrain me real fucking quick."

"Fair enough," Nunez said. "Thanks for the heads up."

Carillo nodded. Nunez said, "Alright, another vote. Who thinks we should report what we did?"

Nobody raised their hands. D'Angelo kept his eyes on the floor. Nunez waited several seconds before asking, "Now, who votes we keep it quiet?"

Everyone raised their hands. Even D'Angelo, although he didn't lift his eyes to look at Nunez. Nunez nodded, made a vertical cutting motion with his open hand and said, "That's it then. It's decided. What happened this morning is our secret, for the rest of our lives. Meeting adjourned. Everyone get some sleep, we can expect to be back on the offensive sometime tonight or tomorrow morning. Refill your Camelbaks, clean weapons, check your gear. Squad leaders, I want everyone up by 1800 and all precombat checks done. We'll have a plan for clearing this town by then." He turned to Quincy and said, "Lieutenant, you got anything to add?"

Quincy shook his head. "No. Everyone get your ass to sleep."

The men rose. Carillo helped D'Angelo to his feet, then surprised him by giving him a strong embrace. Nunez heard Carillo say, "Hey motherfucker, you're one of us now. After this, you transfer to our unit. You don't have a choice, you're coming to Alpha in Round Rock. Got it?"

Other soldiers stepped in and wrapped their arms around both men. D'Angelo stood in the center of a circle of brothers, warriors who had fought and bled beside him and who had now sworn to risk their freedom for him. D'Angelo nodded and said, "Okay, I'll transfer to Round Rock. Thanks, guys. I mean it."

The soldiers released D'Angelo, patting him on the back as they walked away. Cowan slapped his ass and said, "Good game!" D'Angelo bent down to pick up his machine gun, and as he stood Nunez saw that D'Angelo wasn't holding back anymore. The young soldier walked out of the room wiping tears from his eyes.

CHAPTER 11

"Sergeant Nunez, wake up. Captain Harcrow and some other dude are here to talk to you and the lieutenant."

Nunez opened one eye and peered into the darkness. All he saw was a dim red light, a few inches from his face. He still felt exhausted, as if however many hours he had just slept hadn't been enough. He moaned, rolled to his side and brought his watch to his face. 2151 hours. He yawned and stretched, started to ask Gorham where Harcrow was and then realized it was fully dark. He had slept past the time the platoon was supposed to be ready.

He rolled upright in a rush and said, "Motherfucker! I was supposed to have been woken up like four hours ago! What the fuck?"

Chill, Sarge," Gorham whispered. "They pushed the start time back, Harcrow came by and told us to crash out until three. Everything's cool."

Nunez wiped his face and forced himself to relax. He realized he had been out for almost ten hours. There was no question about it, he needed the sleep. He asked, "Did anyone wake up Quincy?"

"Berisha's taking care of it, Sarge. Harcrow wants y'all to meet him and the other guy in the garage."

Nunez felt a twinge of worry about the "other guy." He asked, "Who's the guy with Harcrow?"

"Don't know, Sarge. I didn't see him. Berisha didn't know who he was."

Oh, crap, Nunez thought. *Don't tell me it's some investigator, asking questions already.*

"Alright Gorham, I'm up. Go back to sleep, I'll head to the garage in a minute."

"Roger, Sarge. Toodles."

Gorham walked out of the room. Nunez forced himself from the pile of sheets and blankets he had slept on, stood up and groped in the dark for his carbine. He pulled out his small red flashlight and lit the way around other soldiers sleeping on the floor, out of the bedroom and down the stairs into the kitchen. When he reached the door to the attached garage he stopped and braced himself, just in case someone was waiting inside to interrogate him.

He went over the story again. They had agreed on this version: after Quincy led the charge into the house and found the dead civilians, the platoon cleared the rest of the house and found nothing. Gorham saw something burning in the backyard and told Nunez, who misunderstood and thought Gorham said something about a prisoner. Gorham corrected him a few minutes later. Nobody went into the backyard. All good, no problems with the story. As long as they all stuck to it, it would work.

Nunez opened the door. Another small red LED light lit up a space at the back of the garage, beside a washer and dryer. Quincy, Harcrow and a soldier Nunez didn't recognize stood over the light. Nunez walked up and saw the unknown soldier had a clean uniform with Sergeant First Class rank and the name Lacey above one pocket. He looked at Lacey's face, distorted in the dim light, and barely remembered him from the intel briefing he gave at the Apple store in the Edinburgh mall just one day earlier. That one day seemed like years ago.

Harcrow shook Nunez's hand and asked, "How you holding up, Jerry? You get enough sleep?"

"I'm good, sir," Nunez said. "I could sleep for another ten days and still not get caught up, but I got enough to keep going. Thanks for giving us those extra few hours."

"No problem Jerry, you needed it. You remember Sergeant Lacey, the intel guy from brigade?"

"Yes sir, I do," Nunez said, holding his hand out. "What's up, Lacey?"

Lacey shook Nunez's hand as well. "Sergeant Nunez, a whole lot of stuff is up. I wanted to come out here and tell you about it face to face, and I need to ask you and Lieutenant Quincy some questions about what happened today. If that's okay."

Nunez and Quincy nodded and said, "Sure, no problem." Lacey said, "Hey, the first thing I want to say is, I'm sorry about your losses. Six KIAs in one platoon in one fight is rough, and everyone back in Edinburgh knows how bad you guys got hit. I just wanted y'all to know you've got a lot of support and sympathy back there."

"Five KIAs," Quincy said. "Five KIAs, one wounded and one missing. I know there isn't much chance, but we might find Fernandez alive. I'm not ready to write him off."

Lacey gave Harcrow a sharp, questioning look. Harcrow sighed and said, "Rodger, a scout platoon found Fernandez's body inside a house several hours ago. He hadn't been moved far from where he was hit. I didn't want to wake you guys up to tell you, I figured it could wait."

Quincy said "Motherfucker" under his breath and looked away. Nunez thought of the last time he saw Fernandez. He remembered Fernandez's panic, the wild, unaimed shots he fired as he desperately tried to crawl backward over Leonard. Fernandez, who wanted to see war through a grunt's eyes, shot through the head minutes into his first firefight.

Nunez said, "I saw Fernandez get hit one time, in the head. How much damage was on his body when they found him?"

A pained expression crossed Harcrow's face. He answered, "Their medic said it looks like he was dead before his throat was slashed and fingers cut off." He let a few seconds of silence pass, then added, "I'm sorry, Jerry."

Nunez shook his head slowly and said, "We're going to get those motherfuckers for that."

Harcrow nodded. Lacey gave a respectful pause, then said, "Captain, I'm sorry. I thought they knew."

"Don't worry about it," Nunez said. "We're not surprised."

Lacey looked around and said in a nervous voice, "So, guys, I'm here because I know y'all aren't getting shit for information up here at the front line. Back in Edinburgh we're getting tons of it, so much that we really can't sort it all out. I want to tell you guys about some new stuff we've learned. And to ask you questions that might fill in the gaps we still have."

Lacey pulled a folded highway map from a patrol pack on the floor and spread it out. The four of them knelt around the map and Lacey said, "Okay, here's the short version. Of the eight towns affected, our troops have pushed all the way south through two of them. In Corliss, the furthest east, an artillery battalion made it to the border with light resistance and a few wounded, no KIAs.

The troops pushing through Curran's Pass didn't hit any resistance at all. Both those towns are being cleared house by house as we speak, but all indications so far are that enemy forces are gone. In three other towns, there's been enough resistance to stop our forces well north the border. In Morenitos we lost five guys in one Humvee to a car bomb. The clearing operation in that town came to a screeching halt."

Nunez asked, "A car bomb? No shit? Was it a suicide car bomb, or parked and unoccupied?"

"Parked and unoccupied, we think. A platoon was passing it when it detonated, and it wasted a soft-skin Humvee. I don't think it was that big of a car bomb, if those guys had been in an armored Humvee I'm pretty sure they would have been fine. That's been the only incident involving a car bomb so far, and I fucking hope it's the only one we see."

"No shit," Quincy said.

"Yeah," Lacey agreed. "No shit. Last thing, we haven't had soldier number one set foot into the last two towns. Every time any unit tries to move past the checkpoints, they take fire and someone calls the advance off. Most of the regular Army units that have arrived so far have been committed to those two towns in anticipation of heavy resistance."

"Oh really?" Quincy asked. "Do those dickheads think it'll be heavier than here? Do they think they'll lose a whole support company and a helicopter, and eight grunts? Why the fuck haven't they committed anyone to support us?"

Harcrow spoke up. "Rodger, don't blow up at Lacey about that, it's not his fault. Trust me, I've gone round and round with Colonel Ybarra about it, and he can't do shit about it either. First Cavalry and 4th ID sent a combined brigade to the border and it's being parted out as each company arrives. When their commander looked at our disposition of forces he said, 'There's already three companies in Arriago, and only one company in other towns, so we'll reinforce the other towns first.' Everyone up the chain argued for more troops here because resistance has been strongest here, but we lost that fight."

Nunez asked, "Since when do we have three companies here, sir?"

"Since about eight hours ago," Harcrow said. "We finally got the third one after I told you guys to crash out. They're a reflagged scout troop, used to be tankers until the Texas Guard got rid of all our tanks. Not sure how good of a unit they are, but they don't seem to be super fucked up or anything."

"Where are they, sir?" Quincy asked.

"Downtown, with everyone else. We've been expanding our perimeter around the maintenance company convoy all day, just pushing squads door to door around the business district. We're not trying to do too much, just give ourselves a bigger base to operate from."

"So we have three companies in town, the regular Army is pushing troops to other towns first, and we're doing what?" Nunez asked. "Are we just standing by until reinforcements show up?"

"I wish," Harcrow sighed. "No, we're pushing south again in the morning. And at the company level, we're not doing anything different. We don't have the people or supporting arms we need to make any significant changes. We're sending three platoons south, advancing on the same streets as today. At the platoon level you guys need to go slower, apply the lessons you've learned about cover and movement. But basically it's going to be a repeat of this morning's plan. If we run into heavy resistance, we're supposed to hold our ground and wait for armor to get here. First Cav is sending Abrams tanks and Bradleys down, but it's going to take another day before they're here. So it's just us and our two support companies tomorrow, and I need to decide who to put in the lead. Considering your losses, I think it'd be a good idea to use one of the other companies as the point element and keep you in trail as reserve."

Nunez and Quincy exchanged a glance. Nunez saw his own thoughts in Quincy's eyes: *Please, put someone else in the lead.* For a second, Nunez considered letting Harcrow go on with that thought. But he couldn't.

Nunez looked away into the darkness, his heart sinking. He didn't wish more danger on anyone else. And the last thing he wanted was a replay of the horror he had experienced earlier. The platoon had almost broken after the assault on the house, and he knew the only reason most of his men were alive was that the enemy had chosen not to press the attack. He didn't want to be in that situation again.

But putting a new unit in the lead didn't make sense. That truth was unavoidable. Nunez's platoon knew the route, knew some of the enemy's tactics, had learned hard lessons that can't be learned an easy way. Sending inexperienced soldiers into the same ordeal Nunez's men had gone through wasn't the best choice.

Nunez thought back to the words of an instructor at infantry school, a combat veteran who told him "Anyone can handle one good fight. But only a real soldier can make himself go back and do it twice." Now, after going to war twice and thinking he had done everything necessary to be a real soldier, Nunez was finally going to prove that he was.

Nunez waited for Quincy to speak. Quincy looked away and said nothing. Nunez gave him a few extra moments, then said, "Sir, you need to keep us in the lead. If you put someone else up front, they'll make the same mistakes we did and lose guys they don't have to. We know what we're doing, we should stay on point."

Harcrow pursed his lips and considered it. Quincy gave Nunez a quick, angry glare.

"Rod, what do you think?" Harcrow asked.

Quincy let the dirty look linger on Nunez for a moment, then turned to Harcrow. "Sir, he's right. There's no need for another unit to reinvent the wheel. We know what the enemy does, we should stay on point. I don't like it, but it makes sense."

"Alright, done deal. I hope your Joes don't freak when you tell them they'll stay up front."

"I'm not the one who has to tell them," Quincy said, looking at Nunez.

Nunez gave a guilty shrug. "They'll be alright. But I won't tell them there was an option until everything's over."

A few moments of silence passed. Nunez saw an unspoken apology in Captain Harcrow's eyes. There was nothing to apologize for, the situation was what it was and Nunez would have blamed Harcrow if he had made any other choice.

Lacey broke the silence by asking, "You guys heard about the prisoner we captured in Curran's Pass, right?"

Nunez's eyes lit up. "No, we didn't," he said. "I remember you saying there was a firefight in Curran's Pass, but that's it."

Lacey nodded. "Yup, there was. And it turns out it was cartel guys fighting themselves."

Nunez frowned. "So we know these are cartel guys now? Why were they fighting each other?"

Lacey answered, "Earlier today a company got into Curran's Pass without a fight and found a mass murder site. I saw it later, it was fucking horrible. Sixty-seven civilians murdered in and around a church, plus sixteen confirmed dead bad guys. They caught a wounded enemy fighter inside the church. He told us what cartel these guys work for. We're getting a shitload of good information from him."

"He's talking?" Quincy asked in surprise.

"Sir, he's not just talking, he's begging everyone to listen to him. He's been spilling his guts to our interrogators for hours and won't shut the fuck up. He said they fought each other because of the massacre in the church. Our prisoner said his guys didn't know that was going to happen, and when it started they fought the guys doing it."

Nunez thought that over. "Sounds like self-serving bullshit to me. Sure, he was just trying to save the people in the church. Whatever. And I'm sure he's told everyone how he's innocent and isn't responsible for any bad things that happened anywhere on the border," Nunez said.

"No," Lacey said. "No, he hasn't. This is the weird thing, we think he's telling the truth. He admitted to helping murder some police and firefighters. One thing he keeps telling us is, 'I know I'll get the death penalty for killing the police, and that's okay, that was just business. But I would have gone to hell if I hadn't tried to stop those other guys from killing women and children in the church,' or something like that."

"That still sounds like bullshit," Nunez said. "So these fucking guys had an attack of high morals after murdering all these other innocent people? And how the hell do they figure all this shit will help their business?"

Lacey shrugged. "It doesn't make a whole lot of sense to us either. I mean, I understand the concept. You know, kill a bunch of cops and other city officials, wipe out some civilians just to show everyone how ruthless you are, make people too scared to stand up to you. What doesn't make sense to me is the overkill. I don't see how it benefits them to wipe out a company of American soldiers, and

I sure as hell don't get why they murdered out all those people in the church in Curran's Pass. Those things can only work against them."

Nunez asked, "Were the people in the church cops or city officials and their families or something?"

"They weren't city officials, as far as we know they were all just regular civilians. Most were women and children. The prisoner says he doesn't understand it either. He swears that wasn't part of the plan, as far as he knew they were just supposed to kill the police and leave. You know, these cartel dudes are all Mexican and devout Catholics. It doesn't follow that they'd heard a bunch of Mexican-Americans into a Catholic church and murder them. According to our prisoner, a few cartel fighters forced people into that church and started shooting them. The other cartel dudes freaked the fuck out and attacked the guys killing people in the church. That started a full-blown shitstorm of a firefight among the cartel people. It was bad enough the entire force in Curran's Pass just dissolved and trickled back across the border over the next two days. After the firefight our prisoner waited in the church with all the bodies because he thought we'd treat it as sacred ground. You know, we wouldn't kill him there."

Good call, Nunez thought.

"Hey, before I forget, did he tell you how he got here?" Quincy asked. "How did all these guys move across the border with all their gear without being noticed?"

"I don't know," Lacey said. "He says he and several others from his group came across legally the week before the attacks. They stayed at a safe house with a bunch of illegal aliens and were met the day of the attacks by the main body of the assault force. The main body had all the uniforms and weapons. Our prisoner doesn't know how the main body got into the country, and was ordered not to ask. Oh, and get this. You know how they knew where all the cops, firefighters and everyone else they killed lived?"

Quincy and Nunez shook their heads. Lacey said, "American gang members acted as guides. Can you believe that shit? Fucking so-called Americans met these guys before the attacks and led them to their target houses. So what you guys reported about that thug-life looking asshole who claimed to be wounded and asked for help, it fits right in. He was a gangster, trying to lure you into an ambush."

Nunez bit his lip and thought, *Just wait til I'm back on the streets as a cop. I'll kill every last gangster shitbag I see.*

"Jesus Christ," Quincy said, shaking his head. "So cartel guys and American gangsters are working together to murder shitloads of Americans on our own soil. Why are they doing all this bullshit? Just to sell more drugs?"

"Yes sir," Lacey answered. "I guess the hundred billion they were making every year wasn't enough to live on."

Nunez and Quincy were silent a few seconds as the information sunk in. Nunez finally said, "But some of these dudes aren't on the same page. Their plans might not work. Did your guy say we can expect more of these groups to fall apart like the one in Curran's Pass?"

"No, he didn't say that. But he did say that about a week before this operation kicked off, several of the small unit leaders were abruptly replaced. These guys trained for months to do this, they had set leaders for each city's assault force, and ten or so days ago some leaders got switched out with new people. The new leaders brought their own small entourages, too. That pissed off a lot of people, because most of the new leaders weren't as good as the old ones. There was some complaining, but the bosses told everyone to shut up and get back in line. That caused a lot of friction within the assault teams, but our prisoner didn't think the teams would break down because of it."

"So the leader in Curran's Pass was one of the new guys?" Quincy asked.

"Yes sir, he was. Our prisoner is sure the new leader was killed in the fire-fight."

"What about here in Arriago?" Quincy asked. "Did this force get a new leader too?"

Lacey shook his head. "He didn't know about the Arriago force. He did say the force here was the biggest and most heavily armed, but he didn't know about the leader."

"Fuck. Great," Nunez said.

Lacey continued, "Sorry, man. We pushed the guy for more information about the force here, but he didn't have much. We want to know why the guys here have surface to air missiles, and why they're being so aggressive. The prisoner knew a lot about the new leaders and the assault forces, but not much about this one. He said the Arriago force was more secretive."

"Did he give you names of the new leaders?" Quincy asked. "Did he give you enough to maybe track down their usual locations in Mexico?"

"He gave some names and descriptions, sir," Lacey said. "He doesn't know where any of these guys live. But he gave us a starting point, and we're searching every database we have." He looked at his notebook again. "Omar Alderete, Miguel Medina, Ramiro Almaraz, Hector Alaniz, Humberto Alvarado. About the only thing that stands out is most of these names start with 'A.' We thought that was strange, like maybe the guy was wrong about the names, but when we pushed him he stood firm that these are the names of some of the new leaders. The ones he met and remembered."

Nunez squinted and searched his memory. Something was significant about those names. Almaraz was new to him, the others he had heard a million times. They were typical Spanish names, but different also. Maybe it was something his mother told him, when he was a kid? There were Alvarados on his mother's side, she must have said something about that name.

"Hey Nunez, just making sure about something," Lacey said. "You guys never had a prisoner, right?"

Nunez froze for a half second. It felt like an eternity before he managed to look at Quincy, who was motionless with his eyes on the floor, scared shitless. When Nunez moved his gaze back to Lacey and Harcrow he saw them staring at him with what looked like simple curiosity, not sinister knowledge of his guilt. He pulse-checked himself before answering, to ensure he wouldn't stammer when he spoke.

"No, the only time we saw any enemy was when we broke contact to the east. Even then, it was just for a few seconds. Why do you ask?"

Nunez saw Quincy's eyes move from the floor to Lacey, who still didn't seem to be holding any information back. Lacey nodded and said, "That's what I reported to brigade. But a few hours back the prisoner said something that made my commander curious, so he told me to ask you again."

Nunez glanced at Quincy again, who looked like he was calming down. Nunez asked, "What did he say? What got you curious?"

Lacey frowned. "Well, he said that late last night, before all the fighters hauled ass from Curran's Pass, a rumor went around that a cartel fighter had been captured and tortured by American soldiers in Arriago. Captured after American troops killed American civilians. And it was about Arriago, not some unnamed town. It just caught our attention that the rumor was so specific. Since you guys first reported you had captured a prisoner, it made people curious. I know the report was just a misunderstanding, but they still wanted me to ask about it."

There's no Goddamn way, Nunez thought. *They're off by hours. They couldn't know.*

"Uh," Nunez said, making sure he didn't let anything slip and give him away, "that doesn't make sense. We didn't get into Arriago until almost two in the morning. So this rumor went out before we even got into town."

"True, we realize that, but it still caught our attention. I was just trying to find out if there was any kernel of truth to that rumor. You know, anything at all."

"There's nothing," Nunez said. "I mean, other than the part where we killed American civilians. And that didn't happen until well after sunrise, so they couldn't have known about it last night."

"Yeah," Lacey said. "Yeah, that's right. They're full of shit. I think they had a little propaganda piece ready when they came across the border, a bullshit story about us committing atrocities against them. That's something they could use to keep their own people from surrendering and giving up critical information, like our prisoner is doing. When I get back to Edinburgh I'll tell my commander to shitcan any questions he has about that rumor."

Quincy looked to the floor again. Nunez made an effort to sound nonchalant, saying, "Yeah, that's cool. You have any other questions?"

Just before Lacey answered, Nunez saw Harcrow give Quincy a brief, curious look. Quincy was still looking at the floor and hadn't said a word since Lacey asked about the rumor. Harcrow moved his gaze to Nunez, who did his best to put an open, honest expression on his face,

"Nah, I already got most of what I needed from Captain Harcrow," Lacey said. "I'm sure other questions will pop up, so you can expect me to bug you for intel over the radio from time to time. If this war lasts long enough, I'll come back here for another face-to-face brief. Maybe it'll be over before I have to make a second trip."

"In that case," Nunez said, "I hope like hell I don't see you again."

The men stood up and shook hands. As they walked toward the door to the house Nunez noticed that Lacey hung back. When they opened the door he heard Lacey mumble, "Goddamn." Nunez turned around and saw Lacey holding his hand over his nose and mouth. Nunez smiled and asked, "Having a little problem, Lacey?"

Lacey nodded. "Don't take this the wrong way," he whispered. "But this place smells like a slaughterhouse. I guess you guys don't get to shower often."

"Not lately. Don't judge, you'll lower my self esteem."

The four soldiers wound their way to the front door. Before leaving, Harcrow whispered, "I'll see you two at 0400. Have your men ready to step off right that minute. I hope to have a better plan by then, but be ready for the same deal as this morning, except all your guys will be dismounted. The other two companies will trail in Humvees."

Yes sir," Quincy said. "See you in the morning."

Harcrow cracked the door a bit, whispered, "Coming out, coming out," and opened it all the way. Two soldiers on guard who Nunez didn't recognize waved them out. Lacey and Harcrow walked outside into the darkness, and Quincy closed the door softly behind them. As soon as the lock clicked, Quincy grabbed Nunez's shoulder.

"Back to the garage," he whispered. "I think I'm having a heart attack."

They threaded their way to the garage. Once they were safely inside, Quincy exhaled in relief.

"Holy fuck. When Lacey asked if we captured a prisoner I just about shit my pants. Damn, Jerry, I think I froze up worse then than I did when we charged the house and found the dead civilians. I hope they didn't see me freak out."

"Harcrow did," Nunez said. "He gave you a weird look while you were staring at the floor. I did my best to play it off, but I know I looked nervous as hell too. I don't think they picked up on it, though. I think we're okay."

"I hope so, man. Damn, Lacey blindsided me with that one. That question just came out of nowhere."

"No shit," Nunez said. "I was distracted with the names of the cartel leaders, and when he came out of the blue with… "

Nunez trailed off. He squinted again. Connections clicked, memories he tried to recall earlier came through in a rush. Names and histories linked. Without putting clear thought to it, Nunez suddenly understood why cartel fighters would massacre civilians in a church, wipe out an entire company of American soldiers, mutilate the bodies of the dead. He knew why poor leaders had replaced good leaders. He understood.

"You okay, Jerry?"

Nunez snapped out of it. He blurted, "Rodger, I gotta go! I'll be back!" and jerked the garage door open. He fumbled with his red flashlight, lit the kitchen and ran for the front door. When he opened it, the two soldiers on guard outside spun toward him in alarm. He asked in a rush, "Which way did the captain go?"

"Downtown, I think," one answered in confusion.

"I'm heading downtown then! Don't shoot me when I come back!"

Nunez ran through the doorway and jumped off the porch. He ignored Quincy's hoarse whisper, "Jerry! Where the fuck you going?" and sprinted through the front yard to the street. He had no night vision goggles, and had to stop and peer into the darkness, trying to remember which way downtown was.

Where the fuck am I? he thought. *The house we're in is two blocks east of downtown and one block north, I think. Which way am I facing?*

A partial moon obscured by passing clouds barely lit the streets. Nunez had to orient himself, work through the crush of thoughts in his head and figure out the answer to the simple question of how to get downtown. He started to make a turn, realized that was the wrong way and spun around to head south. A mental street map worked its way to the surface, he remembered where he was. He sprinted for the corner where the Harcrow and Lacey had to have made a right turn.

A voice ahead whisper-yelled, "Halt! Who the fuck are you?"

The hazy silhouette of a Humvee materialized ahead of Nunez. He sidestepped, jerked his hands up and answered in a hushed tone, "I'm a friendly, don't shoot! Alpha company!"

"Don't run up on me, dickhead! I almost shot you!"

Nunez ignored the warning and kept running. He made the corner, swung right and dodged another Humvee. He was already whispering "Friendly! Friendly!" when the gunner mumbled a scared curse and warning. A red light lit him up from behind for a second, then shut off. He kept running.

A faint flicker of movement caught his eyes, one block ahead. Clouds unmasked the moon for an instant, just long enough for him to recognize Harcrow's gait. He sped up, past another Humvee at the next corner. The gunner was already looking at him, Nunez waved both arms in the air as he passed. The gunner left him alone.

"Lacey!" he whispered. "Captain! Hold up!"

The two men spun around. Nunez waved his arms again as he closed the distance. He reached them and panted, "I just figured something out! I need to talk to you!"

"Sergeant Nunez, are you nuts?" Harcrow asked. "You're gonna get shot running around out here in the dark by yourself. What the hell's your problem?"

"Take a knee, sir," Nunez said. "This is important."

The three soldiers moved to the side of the street and knelt in a tight triangle. Nunez inhaled deeply twice, practicing "combat breathing" to get his heart rate down. Then he leaned in and said, "Lacey, remember what you said about the new cartel leaders having names that start with 'A'? I think I figured out what that's about."

In the moonlight, Nunez saw confusion on Lacey's face. Lacey said, "Yeah, what about it?"

"Those names," Nunez said. "They're Arab."

The confused expression on Lacey's face intensified. Harcrow's face almost matched it. "Jerry, you just lost me," Lacey said. "Those names are Mexican."

"Yeah yeah, I know they are," Nunez said. "What I mean is, they're Arab-based. You know, Arab origin."

Puzzled silence followed. Nunez rushed to say, "Look, what I'm telling you is that all the names you mentioned are Mexican, or Spanish, whatever. But the background of the names is Arab. They're names from the Muslim occupation of Spain."

Lacey asked slowly, "Nunez, where the hell do you get that from? Except for Almaraz, we've heard those names plenty of times. They're regular Mexican names. I'm not following you."

"Dammit," Nunez said. "It's a history thing. You know the whole story about the Moors invading Spain, before the Crusades?"

"I do," Harcrow said. "The Moors held most of Spain for hundreds of years. But what's the connection?"

"Sir, I'm pulling this out of my ass, but it's something I remember my mom talking about when I was a kid. Her mom's mom was an Alvarado. She told me we probably have some Arab blood, because Alvarado is an Arab-origin name. You know, Al-anything is probably Arab. Al Anbar province, Al Kut city, Al Jazeera, Al Basra and so on. The names of those new leaders are originally Arab, I think. Or they're a mix of Spanish and Arab. Al Maraz, Al Derete, Al Aniz, Al Varado. You get me?"

Lacey didn't answer. Harcrow said, "Whoa… okay, I understand. Are you sure these are Arab names?"

"I'm almost positive," Nunez said. "I mean, I think so. I'm not a college guy or anything, but my mom told me something about it and I've read some references to it. I know some of those names have to be Arab."

"What about Medina?" Lacey asked, sounding unconvinced. "That's not an Arab name, it's just regular Mexican."

Nunez frowned. "Lacey, you dumbass. Medina is the second holiest fucking city in Islam. You know, Mecca and Medina? Heard of those places?"

Lacey's face suddenly seemed to pop open. He said, "Holy shit. You're right, that never occurred to me." He shook his head and mumbled, "I'm intel. Nothing gets by me."

"Jerry, assuming you're right, what exactly does that prove? Even if the names are Arab, they don't stand out from all the other people with Arab-origin names. Even your family had some. So would this make any difference?"

"Sir, by itself it might not mean shit," Nunez said. "But remember everything we said we couldn't understand? Like, why would Mexican Catholic cartel members murder a bunch of Mexican American Catholics in a Catholic church? Or why did the assault force leaders get replaced with less proficient guys with funny names? Or why are these guys in Arriago attacking everything in sight, even though it can only hurt their own business? Well, what if all of that happened because there's some Muslim extremist influence within these assault teams? Do you get me, does that make sense?"

"It just might," Lacey answered. "So, are you thinking these assault force leaders are Arabs?"

"No, I don't think so," Nunez said. "I'm pulling this out of my ass too, but I think modern Arab names are different. I mean, the leaders could be Arab. Millions of Lebanese live in Mexico, and we know other Arabs have come into the U.S. through Mexico. But these guys are regular old Mexicans, and my gut feeling is that they were chosen to lead the assault teams because of their names."

"If they are regular Mexicans, why would they do the crap we talked about?" Lacey asked. "Why murder people in a church and all that stuff?"

"I don't know," Nunez said. "I haven't thought that far into it. The thing about their names just hit me, the murders and other stuff suddenly made sense and I hauled ass out here to tell you. Maybe some of these guys are Mexicans with old Arab names, and others are Arab Muslim fighters?"

"That would explain why some forces went in, killed their targets and left, but other forces stuck around and kept killing people," Harcrow said. "That sounds plausible to me."

Nunez had another sudden realization. He spoke before he fully remembered it, stammering, "Dude! One more thing! Uh... shit... didn't D'Angelo say something about the leader of the Arriago force making religious references after the maintenance company ambush?" Lacey looked up for a moment, then looked back at Nunez and exclaimed, "Fuck yes he did. The leader said something like 'God will be happy with our work,' and they'd be successful if it was God's will."

Lacey looked up again for several seconds, shook his head, and mumbled "Goddamn, I'm a dumbass." He looked at Nunez and said, "You know what else? D'Angelo said the leader was dark and had a full beard and mustache. At the time that sounded like an average Mexican. Now it sounds... different."

The three soldiers knelt in silence. Nunez thought, *I hope I'm wrong. I fought these guys in Iraq, Afghanistan, and in Houston. Not again.*

"Lacey, get your ass back to Edinburgh and push this up," Harcrow ordered. "See what they think. And keep us in the loop."

"Roger that sir. I'm gone." Lacey stood up and said, "Sir, Nunez, best of luck to you and all your guys. I know it doesn't mean much, but me and everyone back in Edinburgh are praying you don't lose anyone else. God bless you." Then he turned and jogged toward the mass of military vehicles downtown.

CHAPTER 12

Nunez lifted his head and forced his eyes open. At least half the platoon was as tired as he was, with eyes closed and heads hanging. The men were lined up the same way they as the day before, Nunez's half on the right side of the street, Quincy's on the left. The captain's decision to dismount the entire platoon created the illusion of more soldiers on the ground; in reality, the platoon had thirty-one, down from thirty-eight one day earlier.

Most of the soldiers had slept over twelve hours, but were still tired. Nunez knew why. Most of his "sleep" had consisted of a prolonged replay of the day's events, a mix of horrific images narrated by the voice of his own guilt. Fernandez's panicked backwards scramble before his head jerked from the round's impact, Petri's slow motion attempt to smother the flames on his legs before a burst of gunfire sent him tumbling off the roof of his Humvee, Lyall turning his head and holding his hands out in a pathetic attempt to stop bullets from tearing him apart. For every loss the platoon suffered, Nunez's subconscious offered ten ways he could have prevented it.

Nunez's rest ended around ten p.m. when Harcrow and Lacey showed up. After they left, his mind was racing too fast to allow more sleep. As he analyzed the possible new dimension to the border attacks, he heard soldiers mumble softly in their sleep, jerk awake from nightmares, or throw knees and elbows into anyone sleeping too close. He knew they were reliving the fight just as he had.

D'Angelo, on his knee just behind Nunez, tapped him on the shoulder and brought him back to reality. "Hey, Sergeant Nunez," D'Angelo whispered, a grin on his face. "Are we going to start this thing sometime today?"

Nunez shook his head. "You in some kinda hurry, D? I don't mind if we sit here all week. We'll just take a nap, someone else can do this shit. I'm not in the mood."

"Aww, come on, Sarge. Today's another chance to make this right. To get those fuckers for what they've done." D'Angelo smiled again. "We know the rest of the day is going to suck, so might as well be happy now, while we can. Hey Sarge, you remember mornings in Afghanistan, how beautiful it was over there? Doesn't today remind you of that?"

Nunez was surprised by the question. He had so many bad memories of Afghanistan. Whenever his mind drifted to that country his first thought was of his lost friend Eli Gore. Eli, laughing and dancing like a moron on an outpost perimeter, hours before his death. And that was on top of all the other pain, anger and frustration that was a part of every combat deployment.

But D'Angelo was right, Afghanistan was the most beautiful country Nunez had ever seen. He thought back to sunrise over Kapisa province, rays of light bathing mountains and valleys, sparkling off rushing creeks. Nunez never understood how so much hatred and violence could flourish against that amazing backdrop. If he tried, maybe he could see sunrise in Arriago the same way he saw sunrise in Afghanistan.

"Yeah, I remember," Nunez said. "Afghanistan was gorgeous. Prettier than Arriago, that's for sure."

"And way prettier than Iraq," D'Angelo said. "That place was a shithole."

Nunez nodded, "No joke. But you know what, D? I'd rather fight in those places than this one."

"True, but this is where the fight's at," D'Angelo said. "So let's be in a good mood about it."

Nunez gave D'Angelo a curious look. D'Angelo had suffered worse than the rest of the platoon, at least worse than those still alive. He lost his entire company in a horrific ambush, unwittingly killed innocent civilians and his own first sergeant, lost his mind and murdered a prisoner. His home, where his wife and daughter lived, was just twenty miles away. Yet there he was, smiling and happy, just before they stepped off into what would likely be a brutal, close-range fight.

Maybe that's the difference between a young, hopeful man and a middle-aged, burned-out soldier and cop on the verge of divorce, Nunez thought. *He can look on the bright side of everything, all I see is shit.*

"Okay, D. It's a deal." Nunez smiled and held out his fist. "From now on I'm just here to have a good time."

"There you go, Sarge," D'Angelo said, bumping fists. "Someday we'll have a good laugh about this whole thing while we're fucked up drunk in a bar in Round Rock."

Harcrow called over the radio, "Red 1 and Red 4 this is Rapido 6."

Nunez squeezed D'Angelo's arm, then keyed up. "Go ahead, 6."

"Be advised, the scouts put Designated Marksmen on the roof of a building downtown. We'll have overwatch for the first five hundred meters or so, then they're going to reposition and find a new roof. Expect me to stop the advance every few hundred meters so they can keep us covered. How copy."

"Red 4 copies."

Quincy answered, "1 copies."

Silence followed. Nunez put his head down and closed his eyes, enjoying the last few seconds of peace before the order to advance. He wondered how many of his men would be alive and on their feet when the sun set. If they kept losing people at the rate they had been, in less than a week the entire platoon would be dead or wounded.

Nunez heard the quiet rustle of leaves shaking in the wind. No gunshots, no screams. He knew those sounds would come. A single shot might set everything in motion, or the near-simultaneous explosions of an RPG attack, maybe a car bomb detonation. Then the symphony would begin. The hammering of machine guns, whine of straining engines, screamed orders of leaders trying to bring order from chaos, panicked shrieks of men with rips, tears, punctures and life-sustaining fluid spraying onto soil.

Nunez looked at his men ahead, the men behind, Quincy's soldiers across the street. Some of them, maybe even Nunez, were sure to die within the next few hours. Others might be maimed for life. Whatever happened, everyone who survived would be forever changed. At best, Nunez would go home after the war to a divorce, nightmares and a lifetime of worry about the murder of the prisoner coming to light. At worst, he'd be a wounded vegetable, kept alive by people without enough courage to pull the plug. Death was somewhere between those two extremes.

But no matter what, he was a soldier. The threat of sudden death was what brought him to life. Now, in the moments before battle, he realized there was nowhere he would rather be.

"All Rapido elements this is Rapido 6. Start your move."

Nunez rolled his head back, pointed his face at the sky, and opened his eyes. The sun was still in the east, sparse white clouds floated over the town. A beautiful morning, just like D'Angelo said.

"Rapido 6 Red 1, moving."

Nunez stood and gave the signal for everyone to rise. D'Angelo passed the signal back, Soldiers roused from uncomfortable half-sleep and pushed themselves to their feet. Across the street, Quincy's men did the same.

"4 this is 1, let's go."

Across the street, Quincy's men moved out. Nunez waved his men forward, waited until half of them passed and fell into the middle of the column. D'Angelo fell in behind Nunez, his new assistant gunner Drake at his side. Nunez watched the two point men, making sure they were awake and alert. They were wired, ready for a fight.

The familiar smells of post-attack Arriago wafted through the air. Rotten bodies, decaying trash, Humvee exhaust, burned cars, houses and corpses. Dogs barked in the distance. Soldiers walked through front yards, scanning everywhere, ready for the fight they knew was coming. Nobody spoke.

The point men crossed the first intersection. Berisha, on Nunez's side, looked west, gave a brief thumbs up to Nunez and kept going. That meant they were on line with the rest of the company. Nunez looked south again. Two more blocks and they'd reach the spot where they were ambushed the day before.

"Red 1 this is Rapido 6, the scouts report no activity ahead. I'm going to let you advance another three blocks, then we'll short halt so they can find a new hide."

"Red 1 roger."

The platoon kept going. A block of familiar houses floated past. Nunez flipped over a fence into a yard he remembered. Burglar bars on the windows, several deadbolts on the door. The dead dog still lay chained to its tree, tongue blackened and protruding from an agonized face, stomach distended. Nunez looked into its eyes as he passed. They were the same eyes he had seen in the faces of his dead soldiers.

He cleared the fence on the yard's south side, leaving the dog to rot in peace.

His men kept moving. Nothing out of the ordinary, no radio traffic. Berisha reached the next intersection. Once he crossed it, he'd be on the block where the platoon was ambushed the day before. Nunez saw Berisha look back before he stepped into the street, then sidestep around something. Nunez was puzzled until he got closer and saw a large, dark red stain, and a streak leading to the curb. Eldridge's blood, from when he was hit the day before.

The platoon moved onto the next block. Every soldier ahead of Nunez walked wide of the bloodstain, Nunez did the same. He guessed nobody wanted to feel like they were walking on Eldridge's grave.

The men had already been tense with anticipation, now that tension doubled. Berisha, on Nunez's side of the street, and Gorham, on the other side, scanned the area like mad. Everyone's head whipped in all directions, making Nunez think his platoon looked like a bunch of demonically possessed teenage girls, able to turn their heads all the way around.

Shattered windows and punctured walls marked every house on Nunez's side of the street. Spent shells littered the yards. Nunez saw a dark smudge in the street, next to an old Cadillac. The scar left by Brandon and Petri's burning Humvee, an unintentional grave marker. He saw everyone ahead slow at a gap between two houses, peering into the empty space. Nunez knew what they were looking at before he got there. When his turn came he looked toward the alley, tried to ignore what he knew would be there. He saw it anyway. A blood-soaked Israeli bandage, grass stained dark red, his and Fernandez's spent shells. He turned his head and kept going.

One more block and they'd hold up so the designated marksmen could move. Berisha and Gorham reached the next intersection, past the ambush site. The morning remained quiet. Berisha checked the progress of the rest of the company, stuck his arm up and gave a thumbs up without looking back. The platoon moved on to the next block.

"Red 1 this is Rapido 6, halt your move. The DM's just saw something ahead of you, stand by."

Nunez jerked to a stop and threw an open palm up. The soldiers behind him stopped, those ahead kept moving until the message reached the men on point. The platoon was spread out, most of the men on one block, two men just across the intersection on the next. Just like the day before, the men dropped to a knee and tucked in against the houses, kept weapons pointed into the gaps between them. Nunez felt a tremor of fear roll down his spine. Most of the platoon was stopped in the open, in a kill zone where they lost five men the day before.

"Red 1, watch your front. The scouts see a male walking on a side street, about to hit a corner a block ahead of you. It looks like he's in uniform. An Army uniform."

Oh shit, Nunez thought. *What the fuck is going on now?*

"Rapido 6 this is Red 1, are they sure?"

Across the street, Nunez saw Gorham's carbine fly to his shoulder, his eyes slam to his optic. Then a hand shot up ahead, pointing south. Nunez keyed his radio.

"Red 1 this is Red 4, point sees something. I'm moving up."

"Roger that, me too."

Nunez rushed forward at a crouch, Quincy did the same on his side of the street. The soldiers near the front frantically pointed south. Nunez didn't see anything until he was almost to the intersection. There the man was, almost a block away. Nunez stopped, brought his carbine to his shoulder and looked through the scope.

A young Hispanic man in an Army camouflage uniform staggered toward the platoon. Nunez couldn't make out the details of his face, but even from a distance it was obvious the man was badly hurt. His ragged, stained uniform hung off his hips, his head hung toward his chest. He took almost as many shaky steps sideways as he did forward. Nunez thought the man had a weird build, heavy on top with skinny legs, until he realized the man's arms were behind his back. Nunez took a closer look. Something was wrong with the man's upper body, but Nunez couldn't make out what it was.

Nunez sprinted across the intersection and dropped to the grass beside Berisha. Quincy keyed his radio and said, "Rapido 6 this is Red 1, we have a visual on a male in uniform less than a block ahead, walking this way."

"Red 1, don't let him walk up to you. Stop him however you have to."

The man weaved closer to the platoon. Nunez asked, "Berisha, is something under that guy's uniform? Can you tell?"

"I cannot say, Sarjant," Berisha answered. "Did you see that his hands are tied?"

"Yeah, I did. This is fucked up."

"Red 4 this is 1, if he gets close enough give him an order to halt."

Nunez acknowledged and looked through his scope again. The man was close enough that Nunez could make out his expression. The man's eyes were downcast, his face bloody and swollen. He looked pained, and not just in physical pain. Nunez examined the man's uniform top again. It was unzipped and pulled tight over something black underneath. Nunez squinted and was able to discern a single strip of duct tape wrapped around the man's stomach.

"Shit," Nunez said. "Something's under his uniform. I hope it's not what I think it is."

The man was about a hundred and fifty meters away now, too close if he was wearing a bomb vest with shrapnel. A bomb vest could hold over twenty pounds of explosives, enough to kill from hundreds of meters away. Nunez rose to his knees, cupped his hand beside his mouth and yelled, "Stop! Stop right there, don't come any closer!"

The man wailed something in response, but Nunez couldn't make it out. He kept staggering toward the platoon. Nunez swore under his breath and yelled again, "I said stop! *Alto!* Don't approach us!"

The man didn't answer. Quincy said over the radio, "4, if he gets within a hundred meters, shoot him. Try to hit him in the leg or something. We'll shoot too."

"4 copies," Nunez said. He looked through his scope again and got a good look at the man. His uniform and face were bloody, one eye was swollen shut. The man held his head sideways, looking through his open eye. His arms looked like they were pulled tight behind his back, not like he was holding them there himself. Nunez tried to read his nametape but the man was still too far away.

He slowly closed the distance. Nunez picked a spot in the road he thought was about a hundred meters away and said, "Stand by, Berisha. If this guy passes that brick mailbox on the left side of the road I'll give you the order to shoot. Aim low, go for his lower legs. Don't shoot unless I tell you to."

"Yes, Sarjant."

"1 this is 4, if he reaches that brick mailbox we're going to engage."

"Roger."

The man yelled something. His voice was so weak Nunez barely heard it. Nunez yelled another order to stop. The man ignored the order. After several minutes and two sideways stumbles, the man was almost to the mailbox. Nunez yelled another warning, the man responded with another unintelligible wail and kept coming.

D'Angelo saw one soldier captured and heard enemy fighters say they captured two, Nunez thought. *The First Sergeant we killed inside the house was one of them, this might be the other one. Or it could be another gangster, luring us into an ambush.*

The man was steps away from the mailbox. Nunez cursed again, Berisha steadied his weapon and prepared to fire. Nunez looked across the street to see Quincy and Gorham braced against their weapons, ready to shoot.

The man reached the mailbox. Nunez sucked in air and prepared himself to give the order to fire. Seconds passed. The man stumbled forward.

Fuck. I don't want to kill another American.

Berisha looked up and said, "Sarjant Nunez? Shall I fire?"

Quincy's voice answered instead. "Red 4 this is Red 1. You didn't shoot."

Nunez keyed his radio and said, "Neither did you."

Quincy responded, "Well? Should we?"

Nunez shook his head. Then he yelled again, "Stop where you are! If you come any closer, we have to shoot you!"

The man stopped, then staggered two steps sideways and almost fell to his knees. After a few seconds of struggling to stay on his feet, he steadied himself, raised his head and yelled, "I'm… I'm an American soldier!"

Nunez answered, "What unit are you with?"

The man started to answer, but broke into a coughing fit. Nunez waited until he recovered enough to yell, "336th Maintenance Company!"

Nunez turned around and ordered, "Get D'Angelo up here! Hurry up!"

The man in the street started walking forward again. Nunez yelled at him to stop. He yelled back, "I can barely hear you!"

Nunez yelled, "Alright, just take ten steps closer!"

Across the street Quincy's head popped up, a *What the hell?* expression on his face. Nunez looked at him with raised eyebrows and turned away.

The man took another ten steps and stopped. D'Angelo sprinted forward and dropped beside Nunez, Drake fell prone next to him. Nunez handed D'Angelo his carbine and said, "Take a look. He says he's from the maintenance company."

D'Angelo took the carbine and squinted through the scope. After several seconds he turned toward Nunez and said, "I think that's Specialist Ortega. He's real beat up, it's hard to tell. What's he got under his shirt?"

"I'm pretty sure it's a bomb, D."

D'Angelo's eyes widened and he said, "Then he's too fucking close already."

Nunez said, "Yeah, I know." Then he yelled, "What's your name, soldier?"

The man raised his head and yelled back, "Gabriel Ortega!"

D'Angelo handed Nunez his carbine and said, "That's him. He must have been the one I saw them capture. I didn't recognize him then."

Nunez yelled, "What's under your uniform shirt?"

The man shook his head. "I… I don't know! I was blindfolded when they put it on!"

Nunez keyed his radio. "1, Echo 4 Delta confirms this is a captured soldier from the maintenance company. If he's got a good-sized bomb vest on, we're already inside the kill zone. You have any ideas?"

Quincy didn't answer. Instead, he keyed the radio and asked, "Rapido 6 Red 1, do we have any engineer assets in town?"

"Negative, 1. We got nothing."

Ortega yelled, "Hey! Please, man! They told me to walk toward y'all or they'd kill me! I don't know what to do!"

"Fuck," Nunez muttered. Then he said, "D, talk to him. See if you can get any more information. Ask him how many enemy are in town and where they are."

D'Angelo nodded. He yelled, "Ortega! It's D'Angelo! How you doing, brother?"

Ortega brighten. He answered, "D? You made it through the ambush?"

"Yeah, I did! Are you okay, man?"

Ortega shook his head. "I'm fucked up, D! I need help!"

"Get off your feet, Ortega! Take a rest!"

Ortega fell to his knees. D'Angelo asked, "Ortega, what'd they put under your shirt?"

"I don't know, D! I didn't see it!"

D'Angelo answered, "Ortega, you know what it is."

Ortega deflated. His head fell forward, his upper body sagged toward the street. Then he nodded and Nunez barely heard him respond, "Yeah, I know what it is."

"Where are the guys who put it on you?" D'Angelo asked.

Ortega motioned with his head. "Back there, around the corner. In the alley."

"How many were there?"

"Just two. They told me they captured my parents and my girlfriend when they attacked Brownsville, D. They'll kill them if I don't walk toward you guys."

"Ortega, the cartel guys didn't hit Brownsville! Everything's okay there!"

Ortega sagged again, shaking his head. Nunez couldn't hear what he said. Then he raised his head and said, "D, I don't know what to do. Can you guys get this fucking thing off me?"

D'Angelo looked at Nunez. Nunez shook his head and said, "We don't have any engineers. And if we did, I don't think they'd risk it. That has to be a remote control device, whoever put it on him is watching."

D'Angelo frowned in frustration. "Well, what do I tell him then?"

"Uh... fuck, I don't know. Tell him to go sit on someone's porch or something. Maybe the situation will change, the guys with the remote might have to pull back out of range so the signal can't reach. We'll ask Harcrow to call for engineers from Edinburgh. Just tell him not to give up."

D'Angelo hesitated, and Nunez watched him search for the right words. Then he yelled, "Ortega, we can't do anything for you right this second! But we're calling engineers for you, brother! Find a porch and sit tight!"

Ortega gave another sad, slow shake of his head. He answered, "D, if I do that, they'll just kill me. I watched them kill our wounded guys. They'll blow me up."

"Ortega, you don't know that!" D'Angelo said. "Don't give up, man. You're alive and on your feet, so this ain't over."

"It's over, D. It's over. If I walk toward you guys, you have to shoot me. If I sit still, they'll blow me up. If I go back… maybe I can get close enough to take one of them with me."

"Ortega, shut the fuck up! Just lie down right where you are, we'll get the engineers out to take care of you!"

Ortega shook his head. "These guys won't wait that long, D."

Ortega almost fell over as he struggled to get back on his feet. He swayed, tested his balance, then yelled, "D, I think there's like fifty or sixty of these guys. That's how many I saw before they blindfolded me, beat my ass and put me in a house somewhere. I don't know where the rest of them are. If I make it back without getting blown up, I'll point out where the two bomb guys are."

Nunez said, "Oh, shit. Is he going to walk back?"

D'Angelo didn't answer. Quincy keyed up and asked, "4, is he going back?"

"I think so, 1."

"Uh… what do we do? Should we shoot him in the leg to stop him?"

Nunez thought about it, and came up with a shitty answer. "1, if we shoot him, then what do we do? We can't approach him to stop the bleeding. We might kill him anyway, and we'd still have the bomb to deal with."

Ortega yelled, "Hey, D!"

D'Angelo answered, "Go ahead, Ortega. I'm here."

"I shouldn't have surrendered. I fucked up, man."

"You didn't have a choice, Ortega. Don't worry about it."

"You didn't surrender. You got out."

"I fuckin' played dead and they left me alone, Ortega!" D'Angelo yelled. "You didn't fuck up, man! Stop telling yourself that shit."

"I fucked up, D," Ortega said. "Tell my mom and dad I'm sorry. I shouldn't have surrendered after the ambush. My dad's gonna be mad at me for that. But tell them I made up for it, okay? And tell my girl I wish she had been pregnant after all."

D'Angelo muttered, "Goddamn it." Then he yelled, "Alright, Ortega. I'll tell them."

Ortega swayed again. "D, kill these motherfuckers for me. Kill all of them."

D'Angelo answered, "We will, Ortega. You take it easy, brother."

Ortega nodded. Nunez said, "D, tell him to knock that shit off and stay where he's at!"

D'Angelo mumbled, "He's a grown man, Sarge. He made his decision. Let him go."

Nunez yelled, "Ortega! Sit your ass down!"

Ortega turned around, gave one more glance backward, and started walking south. D'Angelo watched Ortega for a few seconds, then put his face down into the grass.

Nunez radioed Harcrow, "6 this is Red 4, the captured soldier turned around and is walking back toward the enemy fighters."

"Can you stop him, 4? I already called for engineers."

"We can't stop him, 6. He made up his mind."

Down the block, Ortega yelled a long, rambling sentence. Nunez couldn't make out anything except "Fuck you" at the end. Ortega sped up his shuffle, then broke into an awkward, limping, lopsided jog. He was so badly injured his run was slower than a healthy man's walk.

Nunez ducked closer to the grass and kept watching. Nobody spoke. Ortega still yelled something unintelligible as he angled toward a house ahead. Drake said, "Sarge, you might want to put your head down."

An orange flash ripped the block ahead. Grey and black smoke blotted the street as the shattered glass sound of detonation and *Whump!* of the shock wave rolled over Nunez. Shrapnel whirred overhead. Car alarms went off up and down the block. Nunez watched tiny pieces of Ortega's body rain down. One large, round piece fell onto a car's hood, bounced onto the street and rolled to a stop against a curb. Nunez didn't have to look through his scope to know what it was.

Nunez looked over his men, making sure nobody had been hit. Heads rose on both sides of the street, he didn't see anyone clutch injuries or hear any screaming. D'Angelo still had his face down in the grass, but Nunez saw him breathe. Nunez reached for his radio.

Two explosions rang out to Nunez's right, a street or two over and a block south. The noise shocked him. Everyone ducked, D'Angelo jerked his head up and right. Ten or more automatic weapons opened up at once. Nunez heard faint, frantic shouts over the gunfire. More guns joined in. Nunez saw two tracer rounds sail over rooftops, arc south and burn out.

Quincy's voice rang out over the radio, "Rapido 6 this is Red 1! What's your situation, do you need us over there?"

Harcrow didn't answer. Nunez keyed his radio and said, "1, I'm switching to second platoon's net. Stand by."

He reached down and turned the knob on the radio. There was no traffic at first, until a voice he didn't recognize screamed, "My gunner's down and the fucking Humvee's smoking! Somebody get the fuck up here!"

Heavy gunfire sounded in the background. Another frantic voice screamed, "Two of my guys are down! Two of my guys are down! East side of the –"

The transmission cut off. Nunez hoped somebody from second platoon would key up, speak in a calm voice and take control of the situation. Lieutenant Campbell or Sergeant First Class Beall should have been all over the net, telling scared soldiers what to do. If not them, then a strong, experienced NCO needed to take over. Even if the order they gave was wrong, at least it was some kind of direction. Without orders, paralysis and inertia took hold.

Harcrow's calm voice came across the radio. "White 1 this is Rapido 6, I'm pushing up to you with an infantry platoon. Tell me where you need them."

Nobody answered. Harcrow keyed up again and said, "White 1, give me a SITREP."

Someone screamed back, "We're in a near ambush! Contact left, contact left! There's like a hundred of 'em!"

Harcrow answered, "Okay, whoever just answered me, tell me who you are and what you need."

No response. Harcrow tried one last time, saying, "Lieutenant Campbell or Sergeant Beall, talk to me. Say something."

Nunez heard a single gunshot over the torrent of machine gunfire, coming from high in the air downtown. The designated marksmen had engaged from their rooftop. A second shot followed it, then another. Nunez hoped they were hitting their targets.

An explosion rang out, followed two seconds later by another, coming from the same place as the single shots. Nunez saw smoke and dust in the air to his right rear. He knew what had happened; the enemy had hit the marksmen's hide with an RPG. He started to curse and then heard another single shot. He brightened for a moment. The marksmen were still in the fight.

He switched his radio back to his platoon's frequency. "1 this is 4, you there?"

Quincy smirked at him from across the street as if to say, *Yes I'm here, you're looking right at me.* "Go ahead, 4."

"Shit's hitting the fan on Nogales. Sounds like second platoon's getting nailed hard. Their leaders aren't answering the radio, 6 is pushing a grunt platoon to them. The enemy's on the east side of Nogales, between us and second platoon. One of their guys said it looked like a hundred enemy, but I think he's scared shitless and seeing things. How copy, over."

"I copy," Quincy answered. "4, I want you to take your guys and move west one street. Don't move any farther than the intersection. Just hold the east side of it, maintain security and waste any enemy you see moving east toward us. Don't forget to cover the alley. You copy?"

"Copy and moving." Nunez jumped up and signaled his soldiers to follow. The men on his side of the street vaulted to their feet and ran forward. Nunez turned right and sprinted as fast as he could to the alley, then stopped and grabbed the first two riflemen he could.

"You two keep this alley covered to the south. Get positive ID before you shoot anything. Hooah?"

The two soldiers answered, "Hooah!" Nunez grabbed the next two and set them facing north down the alley, then placed individual soldiers in a loose perimeter around the intersection. He grabbed D'Angelo and said, "D, you and Drake drop next to the corner of the house and face south. These fuckers might break contact toward us."

The two soldiers hustled to the edge of the corner house and dropped prone. Drake scooted as close as possible to D'Angelo's left side and threw his right leg over D'Angelo's left. He pulled a belt of a hundred rounds out of his left cargo pocket and connected it to the belt already in the gun. Then he pulled another belt from a pouch on his body armor and laid it in the grass beside him. Three hundred rounds, ready to go. Nunez stepped to the corner and knelt beside Drake. He braced his carbine against the corner of the house, then keyed his radio.

170

"1 this is 4, we're set. I'm switching back to second platoon's net to see what's up."

"Red 1 roger."

Nunez switched to second's frequency just as someone screamed into the radio, "This is White 1 Golf! 1 is KIA!"

Oh shit, Nunez thought. *Lieutenant Cambell's dead.*

"1 Golf this is Rapido 6. Calm down, keep security and watch for me and the scouts coming in. We'll be on your right."

Movement further west caught Nunez's eye. He looked to Nogales street and saw five Humvees speed south. Rapid shots rang out from the marksmen's hide. Ten seconds after the last Humvee cleared the intersection the volume of gunfire doubled. Gunners from the reinforcement platoon were suppressing the enemy's positions.

"White elements this is White 4, fall back to the west side of the street! Use the Humvees for cover!"

Nunez recognized Sergeant Beall's voice, finally taking charge of second platoon. Nunez kept an eye south, hoping the enemy would fall back onto the street so he and D'Angelo could mow them down. But there was no movement, no targets.

A deep *crump!* rang out on Nogales. Nunez knew right away it wasn't an RPG, there was no secondary detonation. Another sounded, then three more in rapid succession.

"White elements fall back, they're throwin' grenades!"

"Sarge!" Drake said. "I got one dude between two houses, about ten houses away on the right side of the street! Far side of the brown house with the red truck in front. You see him?"

Nunez snapped his carbine to his shoulder and looked through the scope. He picked up the red truck first, shifted right, found the front door of the house, and followed the wall left to the corner. Nothing. He lifted his eye from the scope to get a broad view of the street. Still nothing. Drake might be seeing things. Nunez put his eye back to the scope.

A man in black stepped backward from the corner of the house. He had a paratrooper AK with a folded stock in his right hand and held a radio to his mouth with his left. Nunez's breath froze, his heart rate doubled. The man looked south, then moved out of sight between the houses again.

"Did you see him, Sarge? He keeps coming out from the corner."

"Yeah, I saw him," Nunez said.

D'Angelo muttered, "I think that's their fucking boss. We need to kill him. He needs to die."

Drake asked, "Should we pop him next time he comes out?"

Nunez considered it. It sure as hell would feel good to waste one of those motherfuckers. Especially one that wasn't captured, disarmed and zip-tied. Especially the boss. One good, clean kill would do wonders for everyone's morale. But maybe if they didn't shoot right away…

"No Drake, hold your fire. Let's see if more come out."

"Gotcha, Sarge."

Nunez looked over the top of his scope. Maybe thirty seconds passed before the man with the AK and radio stepped back into view. Nunez put his crosshairs on the man's rib cage. The man backed around the corner of the house and took a position at the corner. He looked like he was giving orders into the radio. Nunez flipped his safety off. The man looked toward Nogales street and waved frantically, signaling someone to come toward him.

"Sarge! Can we waste this motherfucker?"

"Not yet, Drake. Steady, don't fire till I tell you."

Drake stifled a curse. Nunez kept his crosshairs on the man, who was still waving. The volume of fire on Nogales dropped. The man reached over his head and pointed south.

Another man rushed past him. Nunez jerked his head up from the scope. Two more broke out from between houses, pulling another who was trying to hop on one foot. Groups of three or four spilled from the sides of other houses. Most of them hooked around corners to the front walls of the houses and stopped to reload weapons.

"Holy fuck Sarge!" Drake exclaimed. "Can we fuckin' shoot now?"

"Wait, Drake! When I shoot, you shoot!"

Drake muttered, "Come on, dammit." Nunez snuck a quick glance downward and saw Drake fidgeting with his weapon, D'Angelo still as a statue with eyes glued to the machine gun's sights. Nunez looked down the street again. About forty men in black milled around in front of several houses. The man with the radio yelled something in Spanish. Some of the fighters began to jog south.

Nunez put his eye to his scope and his crosshairs on the man with the radio. Two other men stepped in the way. Nunez looked up, saw two fighters kneeling beside another man laying on his back. They'd be his target.

He shifted his crosshairs as fast as he could to one of the kneeling men. He took a breath, let it halfway out and thought, *Burn in hell, motherfucker.*

He pulled the trigger. His weapon bucked and he lost sight of his target. D'Angelo's machine gun opened up, tearing off a long burst. Nunez forced his scope back to the enemy fighter he had just shot and saw him hold his side as he struggled to stand up. Tracers flashed close by him. Nunez put his crosshairs on the man's pelvis and fired again. He dropped. The wounded fighter lying on the ground frantically tried to get up. Nunez pulled the trigger, got lucky and hit him in the face. He didn't just feel satisfied, he was elated. He looked over his scope again.

A black mass of enemy fighters was hauling ass south. D'Angelo's bullets knocked some off their feet. Several bodies in black littered front yards. Nunez fired unaimed shots south, just suppressing. Some of the fighters peeled around corners, heading back toward Nogales. Others jumped behind cars. Nunez saw AKs drop onto hoods and trunks, pointed back at him with barely visible heads behind them.

Uh oh.

He picked a car shielding an enemy fighter and swung his carbine toward it. Fire exploded from the man's AK. Nunez ducked and heard the *zipzipzip* of the rounds passing high and right. He fumbled to get his crosshairs on the right spot. A round smacked a wall somewhere behind him just as he got his sights onto the front fender of the car. *Close enough,* he thought. He pulled the trigger and walked rounds from the fender, over the hood toward the man's head. The man dropped behind the car and his AK fell out of sight. Nunez didn't know if he hit him.

More rounds zinged by. Nunez heard slaps and glass shattering as bullets punched through the house he was using for cover. He ducked lower and reminded himself, *These houses aren't cover. They won't stop bullets.*

"Grey Explorer!" Drake screamed. "Shift right, shift right! Two motherfuckers are shooting over the hood!"

In his peripheral vision Nunez saw D'Angelo bounce his body left behind his gun. His tracers lanced toward a beat-up old Ford Explorer in a driveway, missing left by inches. D'Angelo shifted right again and tore apart the right fender and hood. Nunez just caught sight of an AK swinging off the hood. D'Angelo aimed low and put a long burst under the front of the Explorer. The front end dropped onto flattened tires and a man screamed.

More return fire tore the air around them. A voice on the radio screamed, "This is White 4, who the fuck is in contact east of Nogales?"

Nunez grabbed his radio. "White 4 this is Red 4, we're at the intersection just northeast of you! We're engaging the enemy falling back this way!"

"Roger. How many you got?"

"We saw about forty," Nunez said. If you have dismounts fire south down the alley you'll kill some of them. They're trying to head south, but they're stuck between us and you."

"I copy," Beall answered. "We're fucked up right now, I don't know if I can do it before they haul ass."

Puffs of grass kicked up, fifteen feet ahead of D'Angelo and Drake. Nunez searched for the source of the fire but didn't see anything. More dirt and grass flew from the yard, less than ten feet away. Nunez fired in the general direction of the enemy without aiming as he scanned the area. Two more puffs of grass flew up, an arm's length ahead of D'Angelo's weapon.

Nunez felt a hint of panic. His eyes flew like mad, looking for the shooter. Drake yelled "Oh fuck!" and started to get up. D'Angelo kept firing.

Nunez heard a *tink!* and a slap. Drake screamed "Motherfucker!" and rolled to his side. Nunez looked down and saw him clutch his left arm. No blood sprayed from the wound, it didn't look bad. If Drake was going to die, it would be from another bullet.

D'Angelo held down his trigger for what seemed like a twenty second burst. Nunez followed the tracers to a smashed picture window of an old house. D'Angelo hosed the window and area around it with a zigzag pattern of gunfire.

Nunez emptied his magazine into the window, reloaded and yelled, "Doc! Get over here!"

Drake forced himself to his knees and crawled backward. Carillo shot out from behind Nunez, grabbed Drake's drag handle and yanked him backward behind the house. Another man charged the other way and dropped beside D'Angelo. Nunez looked down the street. The enemy force had melted away, only the dead were visible. D'Angelo ceased fire. Nunez's ears rang, but the street was quiet. No more gunfire from the dozen or so enemy fighters on the ground down the block, no gunfire on Nogales. Nunez keyed his radio.

"Rapido 6 this is Red 4, you there?"

"This is 6, go ahead."

"6, we just wasted about ten enemy. I think the rest went back into the alley and hauled. If we cover the streets, put guys in the alley and rush south, I think we can trap these shitheads and kill them all. How copy?"

"Red 4, I copied. Standby."

Nunez bit his lip. If they were going after the enemy, they had to do it quick before the enemy got away or set up another ambush. Behind him, Doc said, "Quit being a bitch, Drake. You're fine."

He looked back to see Drake on his back, Corley and Carillo tightening bandages on Drake's arm. Drake's head was turned away from the wound, and his right hand covered his eyes. He didn't look bad.

"How is he, Doc?" Nunez asked.

Corley waved off the question. "He's alright, Sarge. His arm's fucked up, but no arterial bleeding. Looks like one round hit it while he had it bent."

Carillo looked up. "Hey, thanks for hogging the corner, Sarge. You know, I didn't want to shoot anyone, or anything like that."

"Yeah, no problem," Nunez said. "I have to keep your soul pure. You'll thank me someday."

Carillo muttered, "Bullshit."

"Sarge," D'Angelo called. "I got one wounded guy squirming around left of that Explorer I shot. You see him?"

Nunez looked through his scope. Motionless enemy fighters dotted the yards, but one man lay on his side with hands on his stomach, facing Nunez.

The wounded man's face showed agony. Nunez watched him reach out with one hand to dig his fingers into the grass over his head, then pull himself a few inches toward the street. He twisted one heel into the yard to push himself, the other leg hung limp. His AK dragged the ground beside him, attached to his chest by a sling.

"I see him, D. You fucked him up good."

"Think he's gonna live?" D'Angelo asked.

"I hope not. I mean, not for long. Maybe just long enough to give us some good intel."

Nunez looked at his watch. Critical minutes had passed, still no answer from Harcrow. The enemy had plenty of time to escape already, if the company didn't press the attack right now the opportunity would pass.

"Rapido 6 to all Rapido elements, hold your positions, do not advance on the enemy. Higher just ordered us to wait for support."

"Goddamn it," Nunez said, shaking his head. Why the hell weren't they chasing the enemy down and killing the rest of them? He keyed his radio and grumbled, "Red 4 copies."

"Red 4 this is 6, what's your SITREP?"

Nunez answered, "One friendly wounded and stable. Ten or so enemy KIA. One wounded enemy fighter is rolling around out there."

"Roger. Prep your casualty for evac and keep an eye on that wounded enemy until I can push a detainee team to him. We rolled up three wounded enemy on Nogales."

"Red 4 copies."

Nunez looked through the scope again. The wounded fighter gave up trying to push himself toward the street. He pulled his mask off and laid the side of his head on the ground. The man was Hispanic, about thirty, dark haired and dark-eyed, with clean-cut hair. He could have been one of Nunez's cousins. The man lay still for a while, just breathing. Then he dragged a bloody hand across the ground to his chest, searched his body armor, and struggled to open a pouch.

"What's he doing, Sarge?" D'Angelo asked.

"Digging for a bandage, I think," Nunez said.

"He could also be going for a grenade."

176

Nunez and D'Angelo looked at each other. Nunez read the thought D'Angelo was trying to send, the subliminal message. He turned back to his scope without responding.

The wounded fighter managed to pop the buckle on the pouch and dug his fingers into it. On the radio Harcrow said, "Red 4, watch your muzzles. The scouts are pushing into the alley."

"Red 4 roger."

The fighter grabbed something inside the pouch and tugged. Nunez saw the top of something dark protrude from the pouch, but it looked stuck. The man had an AK on his chest, if he wanted to fight all he had to do was pick it up and shoot. Chances were, whatever was in the pouch wasn't a grenade. Nunez thought it was a bandage.

The scouts would capture the man within minutes. He would hopefully give up valuable information about the enemy force in Arriago. That information could bring the war to a close sooner. And if the man survived his wounds, the best future he could hope for was to rot in a Texas prison for the rest of his life.

The man stopped to rest. He looked toward the corner, they had a moment of eye-to-eye contact through Nunez's scope. The man stuck his hand back to the pouch and gave another weak pull.

I'm not going to take the chance that he'll pull a frag and kill some scouts.

Nunez knelt lower, steadied his weapon against the corner and centered his sight on the man's head. The man was less than a hundred meters away and nobody was shooting at Nunez. It was an easy shot. Nunez gave the trigger a slow, gentle squeeze.

The man looked at Nunez again, just before the round exploded from the muzzle. The image in the scope dipped as the weapon recoiled. When Nunez centered the crosshairs on the man's head again he saw the man's face hanging slack, eyes and mouth open. The grass turned dark crimson under his skull.

Nunez flipped the safety on. Then he yelled, "Gabriel Ortega!", lowered his weapon and whispered, "You motherfuckers."

D'Angelo added, "Andy Kallinen!"

"Red 4 this is Rapido 6, what's going on? Who's engaging?"

"That was me, 6. The wounded fighter was going for a grenade, I think. He's

KIA."

"Roger that. Be advised, the scouts just caught another wounded enemy fighter."

Nunez took a deep breath and rolled his shoulders, trying to relax. He and the platoon had done well. They had gotten some revenge. Second platoon had lost a couple of soldiers, which sucked, but there was no question the good guys had won this fight.

Nunez said, "Everyone check your weapons, make sure you're on safe. The scouts are in the alley and they're about to push out from between houses to check the enemy casualties. No friendly fire, guys."

Faint shouts sounded from the alley. Nunez heard someone yell, "Pull back, pull back!" Other voices answered, "Moving!"

Nunez wondered, *What the hell's going on now?*

Several minutes passed before Harcrow called on the radio, "Red 4 this is 6."

Nunez answered, "Go ahead, 6."

"The scouts found an enemy body with a possible bomb vest in the alley. Don't go anywhere near it, we're going to wait for engineers."

Whoa, Nunez thought. *These fuckers were going to use a suicide bomber against us. We're fighting Jihadis for sure.*

"Red 4 copies, we'll stay away."

Harcrow asked, "Red 4, Did you see anything on fire over here during that engagement?"

Nunez's eyebrows rose in confusion. "Negative 6, nothing was on fire. What's up?"

There was a pause. Nunez looked for smoke but didn't see any. Nothing had burned during the fight that Nunez knew of. He felt nothing but harmless curiosity at the question. Until Captain Harcrow spoke again.

"Red 4, the enemy body is burned. He's wearing something that looks like body armor but could be a bomb vest. We think he's enemy, but his arms were tied behind his back. He might be another civilian hostage."

Nunez's heart rate shot up again. *Oh, shit,* he thought. *Tell me that's not our prisoner. Tell me they didn't drag that motherfucker over here and leave him for us to find.*

"Uh, roger that," Nunez answered. "I'll pass the word."

"Red 4, let 1 know we're going to be here a while. It'll take hours until the engineers get here from Edinburgh. We're also going to need intel to check something else out. Maintain security and keep your guys awake."

"Red 4 copies. Uh, what did intel need to check out?"

"The scouts who saw the body swear there's a note pinned to the guy's chest. Sounds like someone's imagining things, but we'll have to check anyway."

Nunez's legs almost went limp. He sagged against the corner, his helmet made a quiet thud against the siding as his head fell forward. "Oh, shit," he mumbled. "Oh no."

He heard Corley's voice. "You alright, sarge?"

Nunez didn't answer. He reached backward and waved Corley off without looking back. Then he realized how he must have looked to his men, and straightened up again.

We're fucked, he thought, as he tried to hide his fear. *If that's our prisoner, we're all fucked.*

CHAPTER 13

"Can you read what's on that paper, Sergeant Nunez?"

Yup, Nunez thought. *But I'm not about to tell you what it says.*

"No sir. My Spanish sucks."

The soldiers stared at the screen in the back of the Explosive Ordnance Disposal team's Humvee, sharing the view from a remote-control robot. The screen was black and white and a little fuzzy, but the image was clear enough. A charred corpse, dressed in tattered remnants of black fatigues and an armored vest. The man's face was a silent, eternal scream. Fire had caused his lips to curl back, exposing bright teeth protruding from split, blackened gums. The body lay on its back on a dingy white sheet. The man's abdomen jutted upward because of the arms and hands pinned behind his back, and from decomposition gases distending his intestines.

None of that was interesting to Nunez. The interesting thing was the dirty, smudged sheet of paper safety-pinned to the body armor, just below the base of the man's neck. The note read:

ASESINADO

por soldados americanos

A dark-skinned EOD technician said, "I can read it, sir. It says, 'Murdered by American soldiers.'"

Nunez held his breath and glanced at Quincy. Quincy returned the stare for a moment before looking away. Nunez thought, *Don't ask any questions, Captain. Just blow it off.*

Harcrow rolled his eyes. "Oh, brother. What a load of bullshit. These idiots murder our troops and civilians, then accuse *us* of murder? Fuck them. I wanted to butt stroke those prisoners we captured, they kept saying the same stupid bullshit. 'Don't kill us, don't kill us. Don't do what you did to the last prisoner.'

Fucking morons."

Nunez's breath quickened. He looked down at the ground instead of Lacey and Harcrow, hoping they wouldn't notice his reaction. This was the first time anyone told Nunez that prisoners were talking about the murder.

"We'll need to recover that note, sir," Lacey said. "Bullshit or not, we still need it. I think something's written on the back."

Crap, Nunez thought.

"Good luck with that," an EOD lieutenant said. "We're about to drop an initiating charge on his chest. If it sets off a bomb vest, that note is toast. If the vest isn't a bomb, that note is toast anyway."

Lacey asked, "You can't grab it with a robot claw or something, sir?"

"Not that kind of robot," the lieutenant answered. "We're not overseas, we don't get all the cool toys here. This robot has a camera and hook, but no claw."

Put the charge right on top of that note, Nunez thought. *Blow it into a million pieces. We don't need to know what's on the back.*

"Can't you put the charge on the guy's stomach instead of his chest?" Lacey asked.

The lieutenant looked upward and considered it. "I guess we could, but it'll probably still waste the note. And if the vest isn't a bomb, the charge'll leave a hell of a mess for you guys to clean up. Especially since homie's stomach is about to pop anyway."

"Understood, sir," Lacey said. "Put it on his stomach anyway, please. Maybe the note will magically survive."

"No problem. But don't get your hopes up."

The dark haired EOD tech turned the robot around and steered it back down the alley to the waiting soldiers. Nunez tried not to fidget, Quincy leaned against the engineer Humvee and looked into the brush toward the dead prisoner. The robot whirred into view, leaving a dust trail in the overgrown alley. The dark haired technician rolled the robot to the back of the Humvee and turned it around. Nunez feigned disinterest in the bomb disposal experts as they hung a small gray cylinder with a green nylon loop onto the robot's hook.

The EOD lieutenant looked at his watch and told Captain Harcrow, "Sir, you might want to let the guys on the perimeter know there'll be a controlled detonation in five minutes." Then he pulled a ring on a tiny green cylinder attached to the gray cylinder, and the dark haired technician whirred the robot down the alley again.

"All elements this is Rapido 6, controlled detonation in five minutes. I say again, controlled det in five mikes."

Less than two minutes later, Nunez heard the whirring again as the robot came back. He checked his watch. 1:54 p.m., the dead body would hopefully be blasted to shreds by 1:57. But Nunez knew there was no real chance of that. He recognized the dead man's vest from the day before, when they captured him. It was burned body armor, not a bomb. He hoped against hope anyway, maybe there was a bomb on the guy's back they couldn't see.

The seconds ticked down. Nunez, Quincy, Lacey, Harcrow and the EOD team moved behind the Humvee for cover. Nunez bumped Quincy with his elbow and mumbled, "It would be nice if this guy blew the fuck up."

Quincy nodded and muttered, "Yup."

Harcrow looked at them. "You want this guy to have a bomb? Why?"

Nunez faked an unconcerned look. "I don't want to carry another rotten body around, sir. I got enough of that the first night here. If this guy blows up into a million pieces, no need to recover him. Problem solved."

The EOD lieutenant said, "Thirty seconds."

The soldiers stopped speaking. Nunez began a mental countdown, backwards from thirty. He was on four when he heard *pop! Pop! BAM!*

Putrid gut stench washed over him, but no secondary explosion rocked the alley. The dead man didn't have a bomb on him. Nunez lowered his head and closed his eyes. He hadn't gotten lucky. The body would be recovered, and chances were the stab wounds would be recognized, maybe even bruises and broken bones. And if that fucking note survived, if it had any specific information written on the back...

"Well, that's that," the EOD lieutenant said. "No bomb vest. Let's take a look."

They walked up the alley to the corpse. Even though the houses on both sides of the alley had been cleared and the scouts held a perimeter around the block Nunez was still on edge, looking for another ambush. He saw that Quincy was also nervous, and moved down the alley like he was walking into an attack.

The stink intensified. The other men made faces and covered their mouths and noses. Nunez acted like it didn't bother him, but twenty feet later he couldn't hold out anymore and covered his face as well. No matter how many times he smelled a dead human, he would never get used to it.

They pushed through brush clogging the path and saw the body, thirty or so feet away. Still on his back, feet toward the soldiers, abdomen blown open. What looked like short, dark gray lengths of rope hung out left and right of a huge cavity where the man's stomach had been. The bottom of his rib cage showed dirty white against a mass of black and red. Something dark, black and square obscured the man's face. Nunez was puzzled, until he realized the front panel of the man's body armor had been blown over his head. Nunez gave a silent groan. The note on the front had probably survived the blast.

They reached the body. Nunez, Quincy, Harcrow and Lacey stopped by the dead man's legs. The two technicians walked to the man's head and knelt. The lieutenant grabbed the body armor and flipped it onto the man's chest. All four soldiers by his feet jumped back as fluid splattered onto their boots.

The note fluttered on the man's body armor. The Lieutenant asked, "Lacey, you want this?"

"Yeah," Lacey said, moving to the man's torso. He knelt, pulled his gloves tight onto his hands and undid the safety pin at the top of the note. As soon as he slid the note off the pin he flipped it around. Nunez held his breath, saw bright colors and dark outlines.

"Yup, there's something on the back of it," Lacey said. "It's a picture of a house colored with crayon. These dickheads wrote this bullshit note on a page from a kid's coloring book."

Thank fucking God, Nunez thought.

Lacey pulled a large Ziploc bag from his pocket and carefully slid the note into it. He set it aside and dug into the dead man's pockets and pouches on his body armor. All were empty.

"This guy doesn't have shit on him," Lacey said. "Unless there's something in his back pockets. Nunez, can you give me a hand?"

Nunez knelt by Lacey's side. The stench this close made him want to gag.

Lacey said, "You roll him over and I'll check his pockets, okay?"

"Sure," Nunez said, showing zero enthusiasm. He didn't want to handle any more dead bodies, especially this one. But he grabbed the man's upper arm, set his feet and pushed the corpse onto its side. Something in the man's open abdomen made a *plop* sound and the smell intensified. Nunez turned his head to the side and closed his eyes. He growled, "Hurry the fuck up, Lacey. This motherfucker stinks."

"Whoa," Lacey said. "Check that out. This dude's wrists are zip-tied."

Nunez opened his eyes and snapped his head forward. *Oh, shit,* Nunez thought. *Allenby didn't cut the fucking zip-ties off. Anyone who knows the Army knows we use zip-ties as handcuffs. Why the fuck didn't he cut them off before he burned the guy?*

Quincy knelt behind Nunez and Lacey. Nunez didn't turn to look at him, but could almost swear he heard Quincy's labored breathing. Quincy said, "So he's got zip-ties. What difference does that make?"

"Sir, I've seen quite a few bodies the last couple of days, and seen pictures of a lot more," Lacey answered. "All the bodies with bound hands were duct taped. All of them. Some of the dead cartel fighters had rolls of duct tape on them. But not a single body was zip-tied. That might not mean shit, but it's interesting."

Nunez turned his head and locked eyes with Quincy. The look on Quincy's face said, *We fucked up.* When Nunez turned back he felt eyes on him, and looked to his right. Harcrow stared back, with the same curious look he had given Quincy the night before when Lacey asked if they had captured a prisoner. Nunez turned away.

Lacey took a camera from a pouch and said, "Hold still, I'm gonna get a picture."

Fuck your picture. "Hurry up, Lacey," Nunez said again. "I don't wanna hold this idiot any longer."

Lacey snapped several shots, then put the camera away and searched the dead man's back pockets. "Nothing," he said. "He doesn't have anything at all."

Nunez released the dead man's arm and held his hands out, as if he was dropping a bag of trash. The dead man flopped onto his back with a thud. Nunez stood and wiped his hands on his pant legs. He was already turning away from the dead man when Lacey said, "I'm done here, but we'll need to send the body back to Edinburgh. You got someone to help with that, sir?"

"The scouts got this one," Harcrow answered. "We've done more than enough of this shit."

"Roger, sir. I'll get with the scout troop commander."

Quincy said, "Hey sir, we're going to head back to our platoon, to get ready in case we wind up pushing south again."

"Yeah, that's fine," Harcrow said. Nunez thought he looked distracted. "But don't get your heart set on pushing any more today. We've been promised a support company from the First Cav, they're supposed to have armored vehicles and a shitload of crew-served weapons. When they get here, they take the lead."

Quincy's and Nunez's eyebrows both rose. Nunez felt a faint sense of hope, maybe they wouldn't have to go deal with the worst of the fight anymore. But Quincy surprised him by saying, "Sir, I don't know how I feel about that. I mean, this is our town and our mission. Today we wiped the floor with those assholes, and it felt good. As a company we killed seventeen enemy, sir. I don't see why we have to turn this advance over to the regular Army troops."

An angry frown crossed Harcrow's face. "Rodger, we lost another three killed and three wounded today. Your platoon did well, but that wasn't the only Goddamn thing that happened. In the last two days ten of my guys have been killed and four wounded, and I don't want to lose any more. If someone else wants to take the lead, they can have this bitch. I'm not arguing with them about it."

"Ten, sir?" Quincy asked. "I thought it was nine."

"Barrow died this morning at Fort Sam. He's the second platoon soldier who was wounded yesterday. We're not taking the lead anymore."

Harcrow turned and walked back toward the EOD Humvee. Behind him, Quincy gave Nunez a shrug and said "Yes sir" to Harcrow's back. Lacey slapped Nunez on the back and said, "I gotta run, see you later," and hurried after Harcrow. The dark haired technician followed, but his lieutenant hung back.

When Harcrow was out of sight the EOD lieutenant said, "You two need to know something. This isn't the first we've heard about Americans supposedly killing a cartel prisoner. So far we've captured more than thirty prisoners from all the towns, and from what I hear almost all of them are telling stories about American soldiers killing a prisoner in Arriago. This shit here," he said, motioning toward the dead man, "isn't going to look good. So if you know someone who knows someone who did something that might get someone in trouble, you might want to have a little talk with them. But that's just what I would do. You guys do what you want."

Nunez tried again to appear unconcerned. Inside, his heart pounded. He gave a dismissive wave and said, "Roger that sir, if we hear that anyone did anything we'll tell them people are talking. I'm sure this is some enemy propaganda shit though, I doubt anyone's worried about it."

The lieutenant nodded and said, "Alright, fair enough. I'm just putting it out there." Then he turned and walked out of the alley.

Quincy waited until he was gone, turned to Nunez and grumbled, "Why the fuck didn't Allenby and Mireles cut the fucking zip ties off? That should have been obvious, they knew to do that. Now they might have fucked us all."

"Rodger, they didn't cut the zip ties off because we didn't tell them to. They didn't think about it and neither did we. Don't blame them. It's our fault."

Quincy turned away and sighed in exasperation. When he looked at Nunez he said quietly, "I know it's our fault. I've known that from the beginning. I'm just so damn tired of recognizing all my mistakes, I wanted to blame someone else for once. Humor me on this one, alright?"

Nunez forced a smile. "Alright, Rod. Allenby and Mireles are flaming morons. This is all their fault. They probably did it on purpose. Does that help, you good now?"

Quincy smirked and said, "I'm better. Not good, but better."

Nunez turned serious again. "The zip ties don't prove shit. Anyone can get zip ties anywhere. The cartel guys could have taken some from someone's garage, or even from one of our dead soldiers. Like Lacey said, it's interesting but doesn't prove anything. I don't think we have to worry about it. As far as anyone can tell, a bunch of cartel guys have been coached into repeating a bullshit story. If we don't say anything that confirms the story, we'll be fine."

"I fucking hope so, Jerry," Quincy whispered. Then he said, "Let's get the hell out of here before the scouts show up and ask us to help with the body."

"Good idea," Nunez agreed. The two men walked toward the north end of the alley. Before they got there a squad of scouts with an unrolled body bag passed them, heading south. The soldiers nodded to each other without saying a word.

"Did Harcrow seem a little off to you?" Quincy asked.

"Yup," Nunez said. "I think our losses have him shook up. Ybarra might be hammering on him for losing too many guys. But… it sucks to say this, but maybe he's so preoccupied with our casualties he won't worry about this dead prisoner. I mean, gotta look on the bright side, right?"

"Fuck you," Quincy said. "You're an asshole."

Nunez shrugged and nodded, "Yeah, I guess so. Hey, pass the word back to your side about the zip ties and the rumors going around. Everyone needs to keep their mouths shut, don't say shit to anyone about anything related to the prisoner. Hooah?"

"Yeah. Whatever."

They reached the corner and turned right, toward their platoon. Soldiers from the two support companies were everywhere, holding a perimeter for a block in every direction. Nunez's men had been sitting still for hours, in the same places Nunez and Quincy left them after the firefight. They were bored already and wouldn't be happy with the order they were about to receive.

Nunez and Quincy crossed the street to the corner where D'Angelo's M240 was still set up. Carillo lay behind the 240, taking a turn on the gun. The enemy fighters D'Angelo, Drake and Nunez killed had been recovered by the scouts hours earlier, the machine gun pointed south toward nothing in particular.

Quincy kept going, Nunez left Carillo on the gun and gathered the rest of his people to pass information. Once he had everyone tucked in close by the side of the house, he took a knee. His soldiers crowded in and did the same.

"Alright, listen up. First and most important, the prisoner we killed was dumped in that alley with a note pinned to his body armor that said 'Murdered by American soldiers' in Spanish."

Several men said, "Oh, shit," in unison. Nunez held his hand out and said, "Chill out, guys. Captain Harcrow and the intel guy both think it's bullshit. There's nothing tying that dead guy to us. And we already know the cartels were spreading stories about Americans torturing a prisoner here, before we even rolled into town. So this seems like it's just more of the same. But," he added, "we found something today that puts a little bit of ass behind those reports.

"It turns out," he said, looking at Mireles, "our dead guy still had zip ties on his wrists. The cartel guys haven't used zip ties on anyone, so that stands out."

Mireles' face tensed. He gritted his teeth and blurted, "Shit, Sarge, we didn't even fucking think about that. We were so jacked up worrying that we'd get shot while –"

"Ease up, Mireles," Nunez said. "It's under control. The bad guys could've gotten zip ties from anywhere, and there's no evidence saying we put them on him. Don't blame yourself. Me and the lieutenant didn't think of it either.

"Here's the last thing though, and it's a big deal. An EOD lieutenant told me more than thirty enemy fighters have been captured in the eight towns we're clearing, and almost all of them are saying they heard a prisoner was murdered in Arriago."

Heads shook and D'Angelo said, "Aw, crap."

Nunez threw a hand up again. "What we have on our side is that we know for a fact these bastards were lying about us torturing a prisoner here, before we even set one foot in the town. So this looks like a bullshit propaganda story. But we need to be real fucking careful about what we say, to anyone who asks. Do not say anything about capturing a prisoner. Do not say anything about zip-tying anyone. Just focus on winning the fight and don't say shit to anyone. We do that, and we'll be fine. Hooah?"

The soldiers gave quiet "hooahs" in response. Nunez waited until everyone acknowledged and then said, "Alright, next thing. We're going to hold in place right here, maybe all night. Sometime tonight or tomorrow a First Cav company with armored Humvees and more crew-serves is supposed to show up and take the lead. Chances are we won't move til morning, and we're tired already, so check your buddies and make sure you stay awake. It might be a long night."

Heads nodded in response. Nunez said, "Cool. Take up security again, I'll pass more information along as soon as I get it. D, let Carillo know what's up."

His soldiers spread out. Nunez looked across the street and saw Quincy move down the line, briefing each soldier individually. Nunez took a knee at the corner of the house, rested his carbine on his thigh and waited for orders.

Hours passed. Men shared rations from MRE packages and drank small sips of water. Quincy and Nunez moved soldiers into better positions, then had to check them constantly to make sure food and heat hadn't put them to sleep. Quincy checked in with Harcrow every hour, and every hour was told to hold in place. Nothing stirred around them except bored infantrymen and scouts.

At almost 4 p.m. Harcrow finally called Quincy. His voice was slow and a little slurred but still had an edge, like he was exhausted but too angry to sleep. Quincy acknowledged and Harcrow drawled, "Red 1, we just got an update. That First Cav company isn't coming here, they got diverted to Verdele because a fight's going on there right now. Plus Brownsville received a threat and several regular Army companies are being sent there."

You have got to be fucking kidding me, Nunez thought. *Shit's hitting the fan in all these towns, and they send the regular Army to Brownsville, where nothing is going on?*

"By morning we're supposed to have a thrown-together company of artillerymen and truck drivers as reinforcements," Harcrow said. "That's the best they could do for us. Break."

Nunez knew what was coming. He closed his eyes and waited for it. He shouldn't have been hopeful, there hadn't been any reason to believe his platoon would catch a break. He knew better.

"Tomorrow morning, first light, we move south again. Same order and routes as today. The only difference is that I'm going to put scouts in the streets between us and in the alleys, so the enemy won't have freedom to move between platoons. You copy, 1?"

"Roger that, I copied."

"Alright. Maintain security, but implement a sleep plan ASAP. Take a house to use as your platoon command post if you want. Only move your people as necessary to get them into better defensive positions. Tonight I'll call all the leadership to meet downtown for a face-to-face about tomorrow. Out."

"1 copied, out."

Fuck, Nunez thought. *I don't want to do this shit again tomorrow. I hope something major happens and the advance gets called off.*

Three minutes later Harcrow called over the radio, "Red 1 this is Rapido 6."

Nunez was surprised at hear Harcrow on the radio again. Usually when your commander said "out" on the radio he was done talking. Quincy answered, "Go ahead, 6."

"One last thing. Echo 7 Lima contacted me and says he has to speak to you and Red 4 about something important. He couldn't say what it was over the radio. Expect a visit from him sometime tonight."

Echo 7 Lima? Nunez wondered. *Who the fuck is that?*

Quincy came back on the radio, echoing Nunez's confusion. "Uh, 6, who's Echo 7 Lima?"

"Our Mike India asset. The one who was in the alley with us earlier."

Oh shit. Mike India. Military Intelligence. He's talking about Lacey.

"Red 1 roger, I copied."

That doesn't mean he's coming here because of the prisoner, Nunez reassured himself. *It could be anything. He probably wants to talk more about the whole Jihadist thing. Or to ask about the enemy's tactics.*

Nunez looked around at his troops. They looked calm, not worried about anything but the fight. Nunez focused on D'Angelo, laid out behind his machine gun again, propped on his elbows having a quiet conversation with Carillo. He looked like a high school kid lounging on a campus lawn somewhere.

It's nothing to worry about, Nunez thought. *Everything's okay.*

CHAPTER 14

Nunez heard the *crack!* of the round breaking the sound barrier before the scream or gunshot. He ducked before he realized what he was doing. Movement across the street caught his eye. He turned just in time to see a scout fall to his ass five feet from the corner of a faded green house. The scout almost dropped all the way onto his back, but caught himself with one hand. The other hand held his left thigh.

Nunez saw most of the other scouts disappear behind corners or cars. The wounded man lifted himself to a sitting position and tried to push himself backward with one leg. Nunez looked south for the sniper.

"D! Carillo! Y'all see anything?"

Both soldiers' eyes were glued to weapon sights. Carillo answered, "Don't see shit, Sarge. He might be on our side of the street."

Nunez heard yelling. Two scouts sprinted into the open and reached down to their wounded friend. Nunez cringed, waiting for what he knew would happen. Charging into the open to rescue a soldier hit by a sniper was hardcore and all, but was exactly the wrong thing to do. The other scouts needed to spot the sniper's hide or at least the area he fired from and put suppressive fire onto it. Otherwise, the rescuers would become sitting ducks along with the wounded man. Like they were right now.

"Hey!" Nunez yelled. "Get out of the open! Suppress the sniper first!"

*Crack!*BANG!

Nunez grimaced and spat "Fuck!" as a rescuer hit the dirt. No scream, no hands flying to spots of sudden pain, no attempt to break his fall. The sniper's second victim fell with the grace of a dropped anvil.

Nunez screamed at the other scout, "Get your fucking ass back to cover!"

The second rescuer looked at Nunez with wide eyes and an expression of terror. He loosened his grip on the wounded man's arm, changed his mind and gave him one pull, then dropped the arm and turned to run. The wounded man reached to the running soldier, made a desperate attempt to grab his leg. He missed. The sniper didn't.

*Crack!*BANG!

"Motherfucker!"

The second rescuer stumbled, his left hand flew to his lower back. But he kept running until he collapsed onto his face between houses. Other soldiers ran to his side.

Automatic gunfire blasted the glass from a window, two houses south of the wounded scouts. Nunez recognized the sound of a Squad Automatic Weapon. Some gunner had charged into a house and fired his weapon through the window. More guns joined in, glass exploded from two more houses. Tracers zipped from broken windows toward something unseen.

The scout who was first hit managed to force his weight onto one leg and stand up. He took one hop and crashed to the pavement. Two more scouts sprinted from a corner, grabbed the man by the arm and dragged him toward safety. Nunez waited, but didn't hear the distinct crack of the sniper rifle.

The two rescuers dropped the wounded scout behind cover and ran to the limp soldier on the grass. They each grabbed one arm, yanked upward and backpedaled like mad. The limp soldier's head hung all the way back, the top of his helmet dragged on grass. He was pure dead weight and hard to carry, but the men made it to safety.

"4 this is 1, what the fuck's going on?"

Nunez keyed his radio. "One the scouts got engaged by a sniper. Looks like two wounded and one KIA. Sniper's south of us on our side of the street."

"Roger. Anything we can do?"

"Don't think so, 1. He's not shooting right now, I think he displaced. The scouts recovered their casualties already."

"1 roger, I'm going to give 6 a SITREP."

The gunfire across the street slackened. Nunez listened closely; no sharp cracks answered the few American weapons still firing. The sniper had to have jumped on an easy opportunity, taken his shots and moved on. Nunez knew there was no point in even asking permission to go after the sniper, the order would be to hold in place.

The gunfire and shouts faded, calm returned to Arriago. Scouts across the street stayed way low behind cover. Time passed with no more sniper fire.

Nunez looked at his watch. 6:58 p.m., less than an hour of daylight left. They had put a few men down for rest already, if the situation stayed quiet Nunez might even get some sleep himself.

"Sergeant Nunez!"

Nunez's heard jerked up. Lacey and a scared-looking young soldier with an immaculate uniform and gear stood across the street, beside the corner house at the intersection. Lacey waved and yelled again.

"Sergeant Nunez! Is it clear to come across?"

Nunez looked around. Everything was dead calm. He asked, "For real?"

"Yeah!" Lacey yelled, cupping his hands around his mouth. "Is it clear?"

"Uh... I guess so," Nunez shrugged. "You might get shot, but sure, go ahead."

Lacey said something to the young soldier, who had an instant transformation from looking just scared to crap-your-pants terrified.

Lacey yelled, "Cover us!"

Nunez and D'Angelo exchanged a glance. D'Angelo rolled his eyes before returning to his machine gun sights. Lacey and the young soldier raised their fists like they were about to give a *seig heil* salute. Nunez wondered *What the hell?*, until he saw them drop the fists at the same time, raise and drop again, raise one more time.

Oh, it's a countdown, Nunez realized. *On three...*

Lacey took an athletic lunge forward and shot across the street. The young soldier followed a second later. Lacey sprinted with track star grace, the young soldier stomped and flapped through the intersection like a wounded wildebeest. Nunez almost burst out laughing when they reached him and he saw tears of fright welling in the young soldier's eyes.

"You guys are funny," Nunez said with a grin. "Stay on this side of the house and you'll be fine."

"Thanks," Lacey mumbled. The young soldier dropped to a knee next to Nunez and raised his carbine, pointing toward other soldiers' hidden positions. Nunez slapped the muzzle down and pried the young man's finger from the trigger.

"You're safe here," Nunez said. "Keep your weapon low and your fucking finger off the trigger. The most dangerous thing for you to worry about is what we'll do to you if you accidentally shoot one of my men."

The soldier gave a fast, nervous nod. "Okay Sergeant. Sorry Sergeant."

Nunez saw Private First Class rank on the young soldier's body armor. He asked Lacey, "Is it 'take your kid to work day' or something?"

"No," Lacey said. "He's my analyst. He wanted to see the fight up close to get better situational awareness."

"Oh yeah?" Nunez asked. "Leave him here til tomorrow, he'll see the fight real close."

The analyst blanched. Lacey didn't react to the humor. Instead he said, "You got someplace private where you, me and your lieutenant can talk?"

Oh, hell, Nunez thought, remembering that Lacey had something serious to meet with them about. "Yeah, we got a house, around the corner. I'll call Quincy."

"Lead the way."

Nunez started south and keyed his radio. "1 this is 4."

"Go ahead."

"We need to have a meeting with Echo 7 Lima in the crib. Headed there now."

"Saw that. Be there shortly."

Nunez skirted the first house and stuck close to the front of the second. When he reached the door he knocked softly and announced, "Nunez coming in."

A hushed voice answered, "Come in."

Nunez pushed the door open and walked inside. Eckert, Liu and Gordon stood in the front room, geared up and ready. Gordon asked, "What the fuck happened outside? We came out but the lieutenant signaled us to come back in."

Nunez whispered, "Go back to sleep, Gordo. Scouts took some sniper hits, it's under control now."

"How bad they get hit?"

"Bad. Looked like one KIA and two wounded."

Gordon shook his head. "Snipers. Like we didn't have enough problems

196

already."

Nunez led Lacey and the analyst into a bedroom. Lacey slipped his patrol back from his shoulders and laid it on the bed. "Quincy on the way in?"

"Yeah, he'll be here in a minute," Nunez answered.

Lacey didn't say anything, instead he looked around the room at the rap group posters on the wall and basketball shoes strewn on the floor. He met Nunez's eyes only once, then turned away a little too quickly. The analyst still looked scared and uncomfortable, but Nunez thought his demeanor came from fear at being in a combat zone for the first time. Lacey had made several trips into the affected towns and had been talkative during his last trip to Arriago. His discomfort must have come from something else.

Outside Nunez heard, "Quincy coming in."

"Come in."

The front door squeaked open and closed, no slamming. Nunez called out, "In here, sir." Heavy footsteps approached. The door eased open and Quincy slid sideways into the bedroom.

"Hey sir," Lacey said. "You got a few minutes?"

Quincy answered "Yeah" and put his hand out. Lacey gave Quincy an effeminate-looking half squeeze. Lacey's eyes were elsewhere, not on Quincy. Lacey couldn't be called a friend to anyone in the room, but he should be comfortable around them. Nunez thought the air in the room just didn't feel right.

"Sir, we got some important things to talk about," Lacey said. "You're getting the good news first."

"Who the fuck is he?" Quincy asked, pointing at the analyst.

"He's my analyst, sir. Private Larsen. Harmless intel weenie. We'll send him out of here when we need to."

"Alright," Quincy said. "Give us the good news."

"The good news, is that you were right," Lacey said, nodding his head toward Nunez. "We've confirmed a Muslim extremist element within the cartel organization. We don't know if they're a huge part of the cartel or a minor, irrelevant piece, but they're definitely there."

"How'd you confirm that?" Nunez asked.

"Pure, blind luck," Lacey said. "We had a detainee at Edinburgh PD, where all the captured cartel guys get taken first. He was stonewalling, refused to say a word to anyone. So this Military Police corporal is getting ID info from another detainee in the same room, and the silent guy says something in Arabic."

"Huh," Nunez said. "In police work that's what we call a clue."

Lacey shook his head. "No shit. But the blind luck part is that out of the ten or so soldiers in that room, there just happens to be this MP corporal who was born in Syria, of all places. Nobody else in the room understood what the fuck the guy said or even knew what language he was speaking. I doubt any of them thought it was anything but Spanish. But this Syrian corporal recognizes it's Arabic, and recognizes the accent. The guy was telling everyone in the room that they'd die like cowardly women, or some shit like that. The corporal gets in the detainee's face and starts yelling back at him in Arabic. Detainee clammed up until the corporal said something to the effect of 'Your mother sucks cock.' So the detainee jumped up screaming and tried to fight even though his hands and feet were bound. The corporal beat the guy's ass until other soldiers pulled him off. It turns out the detainee is a Lebanese Shia, the Syrian MP is Sunni, and they don't like each other to begin with."

"No shit," Quincy remarked. "So are they getting good info out of the detainee now?"

"Nope," Lacey said. "Nothing. He shut up again after that incident. But the point is, now we know they're part of this force. How this information will affect you guys at the tip of the spear, I don't know. It might not mean anything to y'all, but further up the chain it's a huge deal. I mean, we know that at least some Muslim extremists have invaded American cities and murdered American civilians. And if it turns out the extremists are calling the shots, they're deciding who goes where and who's in charge, then this is a widespread terrorist attack, not a drug-dealing operation. A lot of people are going crazy about that possibility."

"Holy shit," Nunez said. "Wow. I mean, like you said, I don't think it's going to change anything for us. But damn, dude... that's big news."

"Yeah, it is," Lacey agreed. "And that leads to the next bit of good news. You guys'll get the word from Captain Harcrow later, but there's been a big change in our plans. The attack you're launching tomorrow isn't going to be like the last two days. If you guys get hit, you're expected to push through it. The goal is to reach the border no matter what. The governor and president have lost patience with this shit, they want our cities back ASAP. And General Koba wants Texas troops, not regular Army troops, to take Texas back. Details are still being hammered out, but you guys can expect tomorrow to be a busy day."

"Great," Quincy said. "Sounds like fun."

"It's going to suck," Lacey said matter-of-factly. "Our guys in three more towns made it through easy and are already on the border. Arriago, Verdele and Morenitos have been the hardest fights, and this place is the worst. I wish that wasn't the case, but I'm not gonna lie to you. Tomorrow's gonna be a bad day."

"And this is the good news?" Nunez asked. "It doesn't sound like it to me."

Lacey muttered, "In a minute it'll seem like great news, in comparison."

Quincy frowned. "What the fuck does that mean?"

Lacey gave Quincy a sad look. Then he rubbed his eyes and mumbled, "Larsen, take off. Chill out in the front room. I'll get you in a minute."

Larsen looked alarmed, but said "Yes, Sergeant," and walked out of the room. Lacey pushed the door closed behind him. Nunez watched him go to his patrol pack, open the zipper and lift out a green military issue rugged laptop computer. He popped the latches and raised the screen, then waited in silence for the computer to boot up. Nunez and Quincy exchanged worried, curious looks and said nothing.

When the computer was powered Lacey took a thumb drive from his pocket and plugged it into a port. He opened the folder showing the drive's contents, and double clicked on a file. Then he stood back and said, "Guys, take a look."

Quincy and Nunez crowded in to watch. The movie player program opened, a blank blue screen showed. Then the title of the homemade movie faded in, and Nunez's heart stopped.

American Soldiers MURDER American citizens
and an Innocent Mexican Immigrant

The blue screen and words faded into white, which materialized into shaky footage of a quiet residential street. A faded blue house held the camera operator's focus. No traffic moved on the street past the house, no noise sounded from outside. A picture of normal, peaceful smalltown America. An aluminum brace from a window screen hovered at the top of the frame. The camera operator had to have been inside a house across the street from the blue house.

Nunez swallowed. The video had been taken from a different angle than he had seen the house from, but he recognized it anyway. He was looking at the same blue house that Lyall had been shot from, that his platoon tore apart with gunfire, where his men killed three American hostages and a captured soldier. Where they captured, murdered and burned a cartel prisoner.

Ten seconds into the scene of calm and quiet, the camera swung left and zoomed in on a Humvee cruising toward the house. Then the image flashed to something else. The hammering of machine guns rang out. The video showed the same street, same house. But now several Humvees crowded the street, tracers lashed out from their gunners into the blue house. The camera operator focused briefly on one window, showed the bullets tearing the wall to pieces around it.

The scene shifted again. A black soldier crept along the front of the house, a line of soldiers tucked in close behind. Nunez remembered the burst D'Angelo fired into the window a second before he did it on the video. The camera operator focused on the black soldier's face. The movement of the camera, distance to the house and low clarity made it difficult, but Nunez recognized Quincy anyway. He knew other people would recognize him too.

Quincy kicked the door in and charged into the house, the other soldiers followed. The video stopped before they all made it inside. The next image was of two soldiers carrying the dead elderly woman outside into the front yard and laying her in the grass. The scene jumped again, this time showing two soldiers carrying the other woman. Then another scene of First Sergeant Olivares' sagging corpse being dragged out. Then the man in his pajamas. The camera operator focused on the man's bouncing, shattered skull.

Quincy swallowed hard. Nunez didn't look at him. He felt frozen, barely able to breathe.

Don't show the prisoner. We didn't carry the dead people out of the house until after we killed the prisoner, maybe this video won't show him. This is bad enough, we don't need to see the damn prisoner.

The image made another abrupt shift. Dead civilians and the dead First Sergeant vanished. Corley dashed across the front yard and through the front door. Nunez recognized the aid bag on his back. For a brief instant nothing else happened. Nunez felt a brief, unreasonable tinge of hope. Maybe nothing else damaging was on the video.

A cluster of soldiers stampeded down the driveway from the backyard, carrying the prisoner like a trussed deer. Even from a distance, the camera captured punches and kicks pummeling the prisoner's head and upper body. Nunez saw himself walking alongside the prisoner. Just walking, doing nothing to stop the beating. Quincy walked on the other side, throwing punches and kicks himself.

That right there is enough. No need to show the murder. We'll burn just for beating a prisoner, they don't need to show us killing the guy.

The camera zoomed in on the prisoner's agonized expression just before the soldiers dropped him onto his face. Nunez watched himself flip the prisoner onto his back. The prisoner arched his back to get the weight off his hands, Nunez kneed him in the stomach and knocked him back down.

Nunez flinched. He had forgotten throwing his knee into the prisoner's stomach. And his face was almost recognizable on the video when he did it. He clenched his teeth.

It didn't happen in that order. We didn't bring out the civilians until afterward. This looks like we had time to calm down before we captured the prisoner.

The video jumped again. A crowd of soldiers huddled around the prisoner, punching and kicking. Quincy smashed his foot onto the helpless man's face. Nunez realized he wasn't in the picture anymore. He watched a few more strikes, then caught the briefest glimpse of D'Angelo's bayonet. For a millisecond the camera focused on D'Angelo's arm as it rose and fell.

Nunez saw himself on the screen, making a vain attempt to rush to the prisoner's rescue. Before he reached the group, the image shifted again. Now Nunez and Quincy stood by the prisoner's waist, D'Angelo knelt by his head. The camera zoomed in again on D'Angelo's hand, held in a fist at the base of the man's neck. When the hand jerked upward, the long blade of a bayonet was unmistakable.

Quincy whispered, "Oh, shit."

Another cut. Now Allenby and Mireles dragged the prisoner toward the backyard as Nunez looked on. Eckert rushed after them with a fuel can.

The video snapped to a different image. Trees, brush, garbage cans and a sagging chain-link fence obscured the view into what looked like a backyard of a rundown house. No people appeared on the video.

Nunez squinted at the screen. *What the fuck is this? I don't recognize it.*

Hunched figures stumbled into the left edge of the frame. Nunez didn't know they were soldiers until they stood up and their heads rose above the brush.

Is that Allenby? Who is that?

The heads ducked down again. The camera operator tried to focus through the vegetation. All Nunez saw were dark figures hover around something on the ground. The camera operator lowered his aim. Through the foliage Nunez saw something in black laid lengthwise.

Motherfucker. That's the backyard of the house. They had people hiding in two other houses, watching the one we were ambushed from. They were waiting for this.

Something tan and square moved over the prostrate body. Side to side first, then shaking up and down. Brush blocked most of the view, but Nunez knew what he was seeing. Eckert shaking the fuel can, getting every last drop of diesel onto the dead prisoner.

The video cut again. The three men backed away as the body in the ground erupted in flames. They watched the body burn for two seconds, then spun and ran out of the driveway.

It didn't happen that fast, Nunez remembered. *They told me it took several minutes to get the diesel to ignite.*

The camera zoomed in on the burning body. Nothing blocked the camera enough to hide what it was.

The screen grayed out. Moments later the vague outline of a face emerged from the gray, becoming clearer by the second. A full face shot of a smiling young Mexican man, dark and handsome. The face looked different from the last time Nunez saw it, but Nunez knew who it was.

Then the shot expanded, the man's face drew backward until his entire body was visible. An attractive, slightly overweight young Mexican woman stood beside him, holding a smiling baby. A boy of maybe five years stood by the man's side. A beautiful family photo.

That picture morphed into another, of the man wearing a hard hat, dirty jeans and torn t-shirt at a construction site. He leaned against a battered work pickup with two other men and held up a sandwich. A huge smile crossed his face. In front of the truck, a sign proclaimed:

FUTURE HOME OF BARRY'S BBQ
SOON TO BE THE BEST BBQ IN CORPUS CHRISTI

The words *Arturo Espinoza-Aleman, 26 years old* drifted across the screen and stopped in the center. Then another line of words drifted in and stopped underneath the man's name.

A legal immigrant, working to support his family… murdered by criminals in US Army uniforms.

In a flash, Quincy reached out and slammed the laptop closed. Nunez felt like he was about to vomit. He turned around, sat on the edge of the bed, pressed his palms together as though praying and rested his forehead against them. Quincy lowered himself to his knees and sat back against a wall. Neither spoke.

"Did that look familiar, sir?" Lacey asked in a hushed voice as he put the laptop back into his pack. "Nunez?"

Nunez closed his eyes and tried to think. Should he answer? If he had any suspicion at all that Lacey might be gathering evidence for prosecution, then Nunez shouldn't say a damn word. On the other hand, if he was trying to burn them, why would he come to Arriago and show them the video? Nunez could expect nothing less than immediate arrest if his chain of command knew what the platoon had done.

Quincy kept his mouth shut. Nunez looked at Lacey and asked, "Why do you ask?"

Lacey held out both palms. "Nunez, we're not friends. I don't know either of you that well. But if you think I'm trying to get you to say something that'll come back to bite you on the ass, I'm not. I'm just giving you a heads up on what's about to fall on you."

Quincy snapped, "Why would it fall on us? That video isn't clear, how does anyone know who's on it? How do they even know the video's real?"

"Sir, it's real. Nobody doubts that. So far no one's putting names to faces of the soldiers, but it wasn't hard to identify the dead civilians. We had several close up pictures of them, so we knew their clothes, injuries, everything. It all matches with the video."

"Son of a bitch," Quincy said. "But they haven't ID'd anyone?"

"No sir, they haven't," Lacey said. "But, to be honest, it's because nobody's tried to. Yet."

Quincy spat and mumbled, "Fuck me."

"Where did this Goddamn video come from?" Nunez asked.

A pained look crossed Lacey's face. "Do you remember when you guys first got to Edinburgh Sunday and came to my brief? Remember when I told you that we assigned soldiers to do nothing but watch the news?"

Both men nodded. Lacey continued, "One of them saw this video on Fox. It's been uploaded to several web sites from Mexico, we think. And it spread like crazy. That fucking video is everywhere. The Mexican government has supposedly already filed a protest. This is all over talk shows and radio."

"Oh, shit," Nunez said, his heart sinking. "That's bad."

"Yeah. General Koba's having a fucking cow. Governer Mathieu hasn't said anything publicly, but supposedly he's saying in private that he doesn't give a damn because he knows that video doesn't show the whole story."

"It doesn't!" Quincy exclaimed. "That isn't how it –"

He caught himself. His mouth slammed shut. Nunez gave him a hard glare. Quincy blinked and said, "That video's bullshit. That's all I'm saying."

"Yeah, I know," Lacey said. "At the least, we know the video's been heavily edited. And guys, we know what else there is to it. We know what happened before the prisoner was captured. And now we know the entire thing was a setup for you guys, a way for the cartels to get a good propaganda tool."

How the fuck did they know we'd catch that guy in the backyard? Nunez wondered. *How'd they know we'd wound him so bad he couldn't run away? Did they expect to only get the dead civilians on video, was the prisoner just a bonus?*

"So what's the rest of the chain of command saying?" Nunez demanded.

"Different things. Colonel Lidell says this is serious but it's a lower priority than the mission to take back American cities from hostile invaders. General Koba says it's a stain on the honor of the Texas National Guard and it *will* be dealt with as soon as possible after this operation. The thing they're most pissed about is the cover up after the murder. Koba's saying that's proof of guilt."

"And Harcrow? What does he say?"

"He doesn't know yet," Lacey said. "Colonel Ybarra said he doesn't want to distract him from his mission."

"Well, that's convenient," Nunez said. "Lidell and Ybarra will let us… let the guys under investigation stay in the fight and maybe get killed, instead of pulling them out and leaving the company even more shorthanded. Fucking douchebags."

"Nunez, cut them a break. What else can they say? They can't tell people they don't care. And they're not trying hard to find out who's responsible. Even though it's pretty damn obvious."

Nunez sat back. Lacey was right. There was no question who was on the video.

"Lacey, how the hell can they know who that dead prisoner is?" Quincy asked. "How can they have pictures that quick?"

"Sir, it was set up beforehand. They had to have picked this guy out before the ambush, and arranged it so that he'd be the guy who got caught. I don't know how else they could come up with video and pictures of the dead guy this fast. He may not even have been a cartel guy, he might be an innocent immigrant who got set up like you guys did."

Quincy's dark face tensed with anger. He jumped up, pointed his trigger finger straight into Lacey's eyes and exploded, "Don't you even tell me that shit, Lacey! Don't tell me for a fucking second that guy wasn't enemy! Him and another guy in that house killed one of my men. They tied up those hostages and tricked us into killing them. They dumped an entire mag each from that house. The fucking guy's weapon was empty when we caught him. He was the fucking enemy, Lacey. Don't tell me you believe that bullshit, that he was just some poor immigrant."

Lacey's eyes widened and his head rocked back at Quincy's words. Nunez groaned. If Lacey was looking for evidence, Quincy had just implicated them.

"Sir, is it possible he wasn't a cartel fighter?" Lacey asked. "Obviously I don't have any details on his capture other than what I've seen on the video. Is there any indication that that guy wasn't cartel?"

"Fuck no there's wasn't!" Quincy blurted. "He was enemy. No question about it."

Lacey turned his head. "Nunez?"

Fuck it. He knows, no reason to hide it now.

"He was cartel, Lacey. We got ambushed by this guy and one other that lit us up from the house. We returned fire, assaulted the house, found the dead hostages and then caught that guy wounded in the backyard. He shot at us."

"You know that for sure? You know this guy fired at you?"

"Yeah," Nunez said. "His weapon was still on him and his mag was empty. We know he and the other guy fired all the rounds in their mags because their empties were laying on the kitchen floor. I slipped on one of them. So I know that he…"

Nunez trailed off. Something wasn't right in his memory. He stared at Lacey in silence, then looked away, trying to force whatever it was to the forefront of his mind.

"Nunez?" Lacey asked. "What's up?"

The connection ends linked. Blankets of fatigue and stress parted to let the memory through. Nunez saw it, realized what was bothering him. He immediately wished he hadn't.

He lurched forward, dropped his forearms onto his knees and head into his hands. "Oh God," he groaned. "Oh my fucking God."

"What, Jerry?" Quincy asked in alarm. "What is it?"

Nunez didn't look up. He said, "Rodger, the two guys in the house emptied their mags at us, dropped the empties in the kitchen and ran out the back, right?"

"Yeah. Right."

"We captured this guy in the backyard, with an empty weapon, right?"

"Yes. What are you getting at, Jerry?"

"Rodger… this guy's weapon still had a magazine in it. He didn't shoot at us and drop his empty mag in the kitchen, the two guys who shot at us did. This guy didn't do anything."

"Bullshit!" Quincy spat. "He was one of the fucking guys who killed Lyall."

Nunez asked, "Then why did he have an empty mag in his weapon, when we know the guys who fired dropped their empties?"

Quincy breathed hard. Nunez felt his eyes staring a hole through Nunez's skull. "Was the guy's weapon warm?" Quincy demanded. "You grabbed it. You know it was fired."

Nunez thought back to the moment he grabbed the man's AK. Was it warm? He didn't remember. But if it had been, he should have felt it through his gloves.

Wait, Nunez thought. *I took my gloves off when I checked the hostages for a pulse. If that weapon had just been fired, I would have felt it.*

"Rodger, I didn't even have gloves on when I picked up the AK. I took them off before that. And I don't remember that weapon being hot. I would have noticed."

Quincy didn't respond. Nunez kept his face in his hands, waiting for Quincy to go through whatever mental gymnastics were necessary to convince himself the prisoner has been an enemy fighter.

"Jerry, so fucking what if his weapon had an empty mag in it? So what if he didn't shoot at us? There were three fighters in the house instead of two. He was enemy, Jerry."

"Rodger, we know for a fact that two fighters shot at us from the house. We saw the tracers. We even saw two piles of brass. It doesn't make any damn sense that there would be a third guy in there with an empty weapon."

Quincy spat back, "Why else would he have been in there with them, in their fucking uniform, Jerry? Tell me that."

Nunez looked up, frustration obvious on his face. "Maybe 'cause they put his ass there, Rodger? Did you ever think of that? Come on, man. You think we just got fucking lucky and hit him in both hands and ankles? And he just happened to have an empty weapon?"

"Bullshit!" Quincy exclaimed. "That motherfucker got shot when we tore that house up with return fire. He was enemy."

Nunez lowered his head again. "His magazine and chamber were empty. He didn't have any ammo on him. He had no other weapons, not even a knife. He was shot through both hands and ankles. He had no way to resist or run. And

Rod… we were herded toward that house. Remember there was fire north and south of that block, grenades exploding north and south, gunfire ahead of us but not at us? That block was the only place we could go. They ambushed us from that house so that we'd kill the hostages inside, and they put that guy there for us to capture so they could film it. They used all tracers so we'd know where they were shooting from. That guy even tried to tell me he didn't do anything, and I wouldn't listen. They left him there for us, like a fucking gift. And we took it."

"My ass," Quincy said. "That motherfucker wasn't innocent."

"I didn't say he was innocent. I just said he didn't shoot at us."

Quincy didn't reply. Nunez hadn't lifted his head from his hands, he didn't know what Quincy was doing. He didn't hear any sounds or movement.

When he looked up Quincy was squeezing the bridge of his nose, eyes closed. Nunez turned to Lacey, who gave him a sad, helpless look. Nunez waited through another uncomfortable silence. Wheels turned in his head. Even though he was calming, his heart still pounded. He laid back on the bed, stared upward and imagined the murder playing through on the ceiling, as if it were a TV screen.

I'm such a moron. I missed all the clues. I got so charged up I let everything go right over my head. And now I'm fucked. Fifteen years of being a cop, nineteen years in the Army. For nothing. What I did two years ago in Houston won't mean jack shit either. No more honor, no respect for anything I've ever done. I'm finished.

"I have to get back to Edinburgh," Lacey said quietly. "I'll try to be back here for the push tomorrow. Good luck to you guys."

Nunez shook off his thoughts. He sat up and pushed himself off the bed. "Yeah, see you later, Lacey. Let us know what develops, alright?"

"I will, brother. I'll do what I can to look out for you guys."

"Lacey," Quincy said in a stern voice. "Remember that we didn't admit to shit tonight. If you have to testify about this conversation, we didn't admit to a fucking thing. Got it?"

Lacey smiled. "Yes you did, sir. But I'm not about to tell anyone that." He stepped forward and put his hand out. "I'm not your enemy, sir. I'm on your side."

Quincy shook his hand. Lacey nodded and said, "Me and Larsen will find our way back. Peace out." He picked up his pack and walked out the door.

Quincy stepped backward and leaned against the wall. For a time neither man spoke. When Quincy did manage to say something, it was just one word.

"Well?"

Nunez took a couple of breaths before answering. "I don't know, Rodger. I think we're done. I don't see a way out."

"Me neither," Quincy muttered, shaking his head. He rubbed his temples and looked at the floor.

Nunez gave him a minute before saying, "That's it, then. We'll turn ourselves in after we get done clearing this town. Me and you have to take the brunt of this, Rodger."

"Fuck me," Quincy said. "Yeah. Whatever we gotta do."

"It's what we gotta do."

Quincy rubbed his eyes and mumbled, "Son of a bitch." Then he gave Nunez an evil look and said, "If only you hadn't come up with that bullshit plan to burn the guy, we'd be okay. We would have gotten out of this."

Nunez jumped to his feet. "Man, fuck you! Don't feed me that bullshit. You were right fucking there when D'Angelo stabbed the motherfucker, and you didn't do shit, did you? All I did was let our guys beat the prisoner's ass, Rodger. You let them murder him. So go fuck yourself."

Quincy took an aggressive step forward and started to speak. Nunez turned sideways into a fighting stance, ready to go. Quincy shut his mouth and backed away, biting his lip.

Good thing he backed off. He'd beat my ass bad. Nunez forced the muscles in his face to relax, trying to calm himself. He knew Quincy hadn't exactly meant what he said. Just like Nunez hadn't exactly meant what he said back to him.

Nunez took a breath and said, "Maybe we should tell Harcrow so he won't be blindsided when this thing comes down."

Quincy shook his head. "I don't think so, Jerry. He's overloaded already, and it sounds like tomorrow's going to be his hardest day. We can wait til the fight's over."

Nunez gave a slow nod of agreement. "Okay. So first thing, once we make it to the south end of town and the situation is calm enough, we go to Harcrow and tell him the whole story."

"We tell him just enough," Quincy said. "He doesn't need to know all the details."

"Fair enough."

"Jerry... don't say anything to the guys either." Quincy said. "They don't need to hear about it yet."

Nunez's nodded. "Yeah, you're right. I don't want them going into the fight tomorrow with anything else on their minds. I wish me and you didn't know, 'cause I know we'll be thinking about this shit tomorrow when we should be thinking about running the platoon. We'll tell the kids after the fight."

Quincy nodded, then his face scrunched up and he slid down the wall to a sitting position on the floor. He looked near tears.

"Rod, keep your head up," Nunez said. "We might be wrong. The whole country is pissed about what the enemy's done here. We'll get arrested and charged, but people will be on our side. We'll get good lawyers. Maybe this will slide off."

Quincy pinched the bridge of his nose again. "Jerry, my dad is gonna be so damn disappointed in me. After I got my Bronze Star and Purple Heart for that ambush in Afghanistan he put a big framed picture in the house, with him in Vietnam and me in Afghanistan side by side. He brags about me constantly. What's he gonna do if I go to prison, Jerry? That would kill him. And my mom."

Nunez sighed, "Rod, your dad believes in you. I know how proud he is of you, when I met him at our welcome home ceremony after Afghanistan I saw it in his eyes. He won't stop being proud just because of this. He'll fight for you. You know that."

Quincy shook his head. "This'll kill him. It will." Then he wiped his eyes and mumbled, "Maybe it would be better if I didn't make it through tomorrow. My dad could still be proud of me then. He wouldn't be ashamed."

Nunez recoiled like he had been kicked in the nuts. He replied, "Shut up, Rodger. Shut. The fuck. Up. Don't ever say any shit like that again."

"It's true, Jerry. I'd be better off dying in combat than spending the rest of my life in prison."

Quincy wiped his eyes again, then his nose. He sniffled. Nunez watched, knowing what was about to happen.

Quincy's upper body shuddered. He clasped his hand over his mouth and nose, looked at Nunez with watery eyes. He shook again. He squeezed his eyes closed, forcing tears down his face.

Here it comes, Nunez thought.

Quincy pulled his legs in Indian style and rested his elbows on them. Nunez heard his breathing speed up and go ragged. Quincy laid his face into his hands and fought the flood Nunez knew was coming.

Nunez sat on the carpet next to Quincy and wrapped his right arm around Quincy's shoulders. Quincy made a halfhearted attempt to shrug him off. Nunez said, "Don't fight it, brother. Just let it out."

Quincy stopped holding back. He exploded into a crying fit. His body shook, small pathetic squeaks escaped from his lips. Nunez pulled him close and squeezed his shoulders. Nunez's vision blurred, but he held his tears in.

The door creaked open. Specialist Gordon poked his head into the room. He looked around at eye level first, then a shocked look crossed his face as he saw Quincy on the floor crying and Nunez beside him, cradling Quincy's shoulders.

Quincy didn't look up. Gordon opened his mouth to speak and Nunez snapped his left index finger to his lips, signaling Gordon to stay quiet. Gordon froze, then nodded.

Nunez whispered, "Take off. Lock the door behind you."

Gordon reached to the doorknob and pressed the button. He started to close the door and Nunez added, "Hey. Everything's fine. The lieutenant's just upset about Lyall and the others. Don't say anything about it to anyone."

Gordon nodded again, backed out of the room and eased the door closed. Quincy lifted his head, breathed in and got himself halfway under control. He sobbed, "Who was that?"

"Just Gordon. Don't worry, it's cool."

Quincy shook his head. "That's enough of this shit, Jerry. I have to stop. I can't let the kids see me crying."

"We all have to cry sometimes, Rodger. I've done it as a cop more than once. Hell, I cried after I almost got you killed in Afghanistan."

Quincy looked at Nunez in surprise. He wiped his eyes and asked, "For real?

You cried about what happened to me?"

Nunez nodded. In reality he hadn't broken down, but he had felt like doing it. He didn't think the lie would hurt. "Yeah, I did. I felt like shit about that. I still do. So don't feel bad about crying. Even if we hadn't just found out about this video, you still have plenty to cry about. The last few days have been tough on all of us."

Quincy nodded and wiped his nose on his sleeve. "Alright. I needed to cry, but I'm done now. I think… I guess I have to accept that we're gonna get arrested and charged, but that doesn't mean we're going to prison. We can beat this."

There's no way in hell we can beat this. We're screwed. At best, we can hope for light sentences. But we're going to prison. If not for the murder, then for the cover up afterward.

"Fuck yes, Rodger. We can beat this." As he spoke the lie, Nunez felt guilt stab him through the gut. "Stay faithful, brother. You're a war hero with a Bronze Star and Purple Heart. Nobody wants to put you in jail."

"You either, Jerry. You killed two terrorists murdering people in Houston. They don't want you in jail either."

Nunez smiled. "I'm a cop. Everyone hates cops. People get a thrill when one of us goes to jail. So I have to stick close to you, absorb some of your magic. You'll protect me."

Quincy grabbed Nunez's shoulder. "Hell yes I'll protect you. We're in this together."

Nunez nodded. The two men sat beside each other in silence for a while, Quincy recovering from his crying spell, Nunez fighting one off. Then Quincy squeezed Nunez's hand, released it and stood up.

"Okay, that's enough gayness for one night. I'm alright now. We better check on the kids, and we'll have to meet with Harcrow sometime tonight. Let's get out of here."

"Go ahead, Rodger. I'll be out in a minute."

"Alright. Bump me when you're back with your people."

"Gotcha."

Quincy walked out of the room, leaving Nunez on the floor. Nunez sat back against the wall and took a long, slow breath.

Fuck all this prisoner bullshit. You're a soldier. Just worry about the fight. Do your best, win this war, take this city back. Anything they do to you after that doesn't matter.

Nunez closed his eyes, tapped the back of his head against the wall.

Whatever happens, happens. You're not a criminal. You're a warrior.

Nunez opened his eyes, rose to his feet and picked up his weapon and helmet. He looked into a mirror by the bed, made sure a soldier, not a criminal or victim, returned his stare. Then he nodded to himself and marched out of the room.

CHAPTER 15

"Lieutenant McCann, are all your people here?" Harcrow asked.

The blond artillery lieutenant looked around in confusion. He seemed lost. Being a lieutenant assigned to command a thrown together half-artillery half-transportation company must have been bad enough. But to then have the improvised unit sent into an offensive within two days of being formed, that would be murder even on a good officer. This lieutenant looked like a zero to begin with.

McCann said, "Uh, I think they are, sir. I don't know them all yet."

Harcrow rolled his eyes in disgust. "Get a count, McCann. If they're not here, pass this information to them before we step off." Then he asked, "Scouts, you here?"

"Hooah sir. We're up."

"Captain Crow's grunts?" Harcrow asked. "Y'all up?"

Crow nodded. "Got one platoon leader taking care of some tasks, but we'll fill him in."

"Okay. My guys are here, let's get started."

Harcrow stepped to a dry erase board in the tiny bank lobby. A hand-drawn, not to scale, kindergarten-style map of Arriago filled the board. In the dim red light of a tactical flashlight, Nunez could barely decipher where on the map they were. He recognized the northern city limits and Rio Grande, but that was it.

Harcrow rubbed his temples. "Alright guys, here's what's up. For some damn reason I've been placed in command of our four companies for this operation. I'm not going to lie to you, I was hoping Colonel Ybarra would come down here and take over. But it seems like everyone above the rank of captain has some urgent business in Edinburgh or Austin, so this battalion task force falls on me. I've never commanded anything this big before, so bear with me."

He turned and pointed at the map. "One of my Joes drew this awesome map. If you can't read it, don't worry, neither can I. It doesn't matter anyway. Specific locations or streets aren't that important. What's important is the commander's intent and our goal."

Harcrow stood on his tiptoes and pointed at a cluster of red squares near the top of the map. "See that? That's us, where we are now. By 1300 we need to be here," he said, pointing near the bottom. "On the south edge of town, just north of the river. Colonel Lidell wants us to punch all the way through town and make a perimeter. The idea is that we push south, bypass any resistance and set a cordon south of town. Our support platoons will stay here and hold downtown. Scouts are on the highway to the east, two platoons of infantry are on the highway to the west. Once we make it south of town, additional companies come from Edinburgh and start clearing it. And I mean, clearing everything. We're talking about every last house, store, building, dog kennel, whatever. The same way they cleared New Orleans after Katrina."

Nunez wondered what unit would clear the house where the civilians and prisoner were killed. He imagined the expressions on the faces of the men when they saw the punctured walls outside, spent shells, blood, bone and brain inside. He imagined state police, maybe FBI, taking control of the house and holding it as a crime scene. And the only crime they'd worry about would be the murder of the prisoner.

Stop that shit, Nunez ordered himself. *Listen to the captain.*

"So here's how we're working this. We're pushing south on the same streets we've been on. My platoons follow their same three routes. Captain Crow's infantry stays mounted in their Humvees and follows my platoons. The two streets between my platoons will be filled by dismounted scouts, followed by mounted scouts. Scouts also have the alleys, but their Humvees stay on the streets."

We get the lead again. Whoopee, Nunez thought. He and Quincy exchanged a resigned look.

"So Lieutenant Quincy, your platoon advances south on Fannin. Sergeant Beall, your platoon stays on Nogales. Lieutenant Belding, you stay on Crockett. Easy enough, right?"

The three platoon leaders nodded. Quincy looked distracted. Beall had a pissed-off look on his face and a bandage on his left temple. When second platoon was ambushed the day before, the RPG explosion that killed Lieutenant Campbell knocked Beall into a fire hydrant. He woke up drenched in blood with a smoking uniform, his platoon leader shredded a few feet away, his men screaming in near-panic, and enemy bullets tearing ragged holes through vehicles and men. Beall jumped right back into the fight, took charge and saved most of his platoon. Nunez didn't know him well, but had no doubt he was a good soldier.

Behind Beall, Lieutenant Belding and Sergeant First Class Quiran stared hard at the map. Their platoon hadn't lost a man, fired a shot or taken a single enemy round so far. Nunez didn't see how that luck could hold for one more day.

"And Captain Hollis," Harcrow said, motioning to the Scout Troop commander. "You'll have a section in the alley west of Fannin, another section on Travis between Fannin and Nogales, and another section in the alley between Travis and Nogales. Same thing in the alleys and on Seguin between Nogales and Crockett. I'm spreading your people pretty thin, but remember your mission. Your guys in the alleys are just there to spot, not to close and engage. I don't want a section getting bogged down with a contact in an alley, with good guys on both streets east and west. If you get engaged, identify a location, fix the enemy if possible, and report. Back off if you have to. Your scouts' entire job is to keep the forces on the streets from being hit by enemy fighters running around in the alleys. Your Humvees stay on Travis and Seguin streets, not in the alleys. Is that understood?"

Hollis nodded. He was young, muscular and wiry, with nothing on his face but intense concentration. He looked like a born leader, like he was already on the mission.

"Captain Crow, your primary job is to follow the dismounted elements on Fannin, Nogales and Crockett. All your men stay mounted, like before. Be prepared to provide rolling gun platforms for my platoons, or on order to take over the advance. If the enemy falls back faster than my dismounted troops can move forward, I may have you take the lead. Understood?"

Crow nodded and wrote something in his notebook. No worry showed on his face. Simple enough mission, no more potential for disaster than normal.

"Lieutenant McCann, you get the easy job. I want you to leave one platoon here, the rest of your people follow in a column straight down Nogales. Your mission is to provide an extra Quick Reaction Force. All your people stay mounted until I give you an order to reinforce one of the other companies. Write down which street is where so if I order you to reinforce a platoon, you're not fumbling around trying to figure out where the fuck they are. And, uh, I think we should number the alleys, left to right. 1 and 2 are east of Nogales, 3 and 4 west. If I tell you to send a platoon forward, the order will be 'Send your people to Fannin', 'Send people to Crockett,' 'Send people to alley 2,' or whatever. Just make sure you know where I'm talking about. Got it?"

McCann didn't just look lost now, he looked lost and scared. He stammered, "Uh, sir, what do I when I get wherever you send me?"

Harcrow gave McCann a look that said, *Are you serious?* A frustrated-looking Sergeant First Class stepped to McCann's side and whispered something in his ear. Nunez thought it was McCann's acting First Sergeant. McCann still looked scared shitless. He listened to the sergeant, then nodded weakly and mumbled, "Sorry, sir. I got it."

Harcrow gave McCann a lingering, dirty look. Then he said, "Alright men, here's the fucked up part of this mission. I don't have any leeway on this, it's what's been handed to me and what I have to pass on to you. The goal of this advance isn't to clear the town, or even to destroy the enemy. The mission is to get to the river. If necessary, the lead elements will bypass enemy forces and leave them for the mounted platoons to handle. The guidance from higher is, 'Don't stop moving until you reach the Rio Grande.' That means you are not to pause the advance if you have casualties. If one of your men is wounded but still able to fight, he keeps moving. If he's still on his feet but can't fight, get him to a Humvee. That Humvee has to get him to the support platoons downtown. If a man is too badly wounded to move on his own, give him first aid at the combat lifesaver level, report his location and move on."

Harcrow looked around. "Listen to me, men. I'm not telling you to abandon your wounded. What I'm saying is, don't let the advance bog down because of a casualty. I know you won't just walk away from one of your wounded friends anyway. But we have to keep moving south. So if someone goes down, put a tourniquet or bandage on them, make sure their airway's open, report their location, make sure the mounted elements are moving toward them, and keep going. Don't leave them unless the mounted elements have eyes on them. Same thing for our dead. If you take a KIA, recover his weapon and sensitive items, call the mounted guys for him and move on. Does everybody understand that?"

Voices murmured, "Yes sir."

"Good. Now here's the two things that are most likely to cause us problems. First, and most important, is the possibility of a friendly fire incident. We're advancing on five streets and four alleys, and most of the time we won't be in visual contact with one another. It'll be easy for us to get off line, then some scared point guy sees someone ahead where they don't expect friendlies, and we take a KIA from one of our own guys. People, you have to prevent that. If that means the platoon leaders have to be right up front with the point men, then that's where you go. If that means your point man has to get permission before firing, so be it. Do whatever's necessary to make sure we don't have friendly fire casualties."

Harcrow pointed at the map again, to the general area south of downtown. "The other big problem is that the roads south of here don't stay nice and straight like they are around downtown. About six blocks from here the streets curve, hit dead ends at ditches, run into T intersections and so on. That's going to fuck with our simple advance, and if we're not careful the roads might cause paths to cross, get one element in front of another. The only way to prevent that is to pay close attention to your radio and your surroundings. And to make sure your Joes aren't making any Banzai charges across roads, not paying attention to what's left and right."

Captain Crow asked, "Brad, can designated marksmen keep an eye on the elements and let you know if we get off line? That should help with our overall situational awareness and cut down on the chance of fratricide."

"I thought about that," Harcrow answered. "But I think the advance will move too fast for them to keep up. And I can't spare anyone to provide security for them. Hollis, there's what, two DMs?"

"Three."

"Three," Harcrow said, rubbing his chin. "Huh. Think they can move on their own and provide their own security?"

"I'll give them two more for security, Brad."

"Done deal. Make sure they travel light. They'll have to haul ass from one hide to the next if the advance moves as fast as I think it will. And they may not have a spot high enough once we're past downtown. If they can't keep up, throw them into McCann's Humvees. But if you think they can do it, use them."

"Roger that, Brad. Got it."

"Cool," Harcrow said. "And on that note, we may have more eyes on the battlefield than a DM team. Just before we step off at 0630, F16s from Ellington are going to make several passes over the town to assess the missile threat. They'll be hauling ass and won't see a damn thing, but if they don't detect a threat they pull off and two Apaches roll in from Brownsville. If we get them, the Apaches are our over watch."

"What are they loaded with, sir?" Quincy asked.

"They have some thirty millimeter and two point seven-five rockets, but the only two types of ordnance they have permission to use are jack and shit. Air strikes are still unauthorized. All the Apaches can do is act as our eyes and hopefully spot the enemy's movements. Don't count on them being here, though. I'm not making them part of the plan."

A few mumbled curses floated around the room and fizzled out. Nunez rolled his eyes. An Apache's 30mm gun was accurate, but 2.75 rockets were unguided. Even if they had permission to fire, the Apaches would be of limited use.

Harcrow smiled. "Yeah, I know it sucks. But Apaches look intimidating as hell. Hopefully the enemy won't take a chance with them."

"How about Kiowas, sir?" Nunez asked. "They see better than Apaches."

"No Kiowas. They don't have armor, so they're not being allowed into this area."

Nunez suppressed a curse. Kiowas have open doors and windows, their pilots have a better view of the battlefield than Apache pilots do. Harcrow gave Nunez a shrug and looked into his notebook.

"Guys, one big issue I haven't addressed is that nobody knows how these bastards got across the border in the first place. We don't know if they're reinforcing the fighters already here, evacuating casualties, getting resupplied or anything else. They might be using the same routes across the border over and over. When you get to the river, watch for that. Try to spot paths through the vegetation, tire tracks, blood trails, whatever."

The lieutenants and sergeants nodded and made notes. Harcrow gave them a few seconds and added, "Well, that's pretty much it. All the companies should be finished with their ammo resupply, correct?"

Everyone nodded and a few answered, "Yes sir."

"Good. Radio frequencies aren't changing, so the scouts and infantry should be set. McCann," Harcrow said, with a scowl, "have your First Sergeant take care of your commo. Each platoon has its own frequency, your company has its own freq, and you communicate with me on my freq. Clear?"

McCann's First Sergeant spoke up, "I got it sir. It'll be taken care of."

Harcrow looked at his watch. "0317 now, we step off at 0630. All the infantry are already on their routes, and McCann's people are on Nogales. The only unit that needs to shift routes is the scout troop, and that'll take, what, ten minutes, Hollis?"

"Less than that, Brad. They'll be set on their routes by 0530."

"No. Leave them where they are until 0620. I don't want the enemy to see them and know we're doing something different."

"Aha, being sneaky," Hollis said with a smile. "We can do that."

"Of course we can," Harcrow replied. "We can do anything. We're the Army National Guard, we do more before 9 a.m. than most people do before 10:00, 10:30-ish. You know, brunch time."

The soldiers laughed quietly. Nunez joined in the laughter, Quincy stayed silent.

"One last time, guys. The goal is to get to the river. Once we're there, the troops in Verdele and Morenitos get there, we'll join hands with all the other troops that have already pushed through their towns and make a line in the valley, facing north. When the additional forces start clearing from the north, they'll push the enemy right into us. And we kill them all. Hooah?"

"Hooah," the men answered in unison.

"Alright, let's do this shit. Radio checks at 06, ready to roll at 0620, jets fly at 0630 and we're off. See you guys on the Rio Grande."

The meeting broke up amid handshakes, backslaps and wishes for good luck. Nunez and Quincy turned to leave and Harcrow grabbed Quincy's shoulder. "Nunez, Quincy, hold up. I need to go over a couple more things with you."

Nunez looked at Quincy, who kept his face blank. Harcrow stepped away to say a few words to other leaders. Nunez and Quincy stood by a desk and waited in silence.

The other sergeants and lieutenants trickled out. Harcrow watched the last of them leave, then walked back to the desk. Nunez and Quincy watched him approach, uncomfortable and apprehensive.

Harcrow set his carbine on the desk, then turned and slid his ass onto it. He rubbed his scalp. Nunez thought he looked about forty, whereas before the operation he looked younger than his thirty-three years.

Harcrow sighed, "When were you two assholes going to tell me about the prisoner?"

Nunez's heart fluttered again. He turned away and said, "Ah, crap." Quincy lowered his head and leaned against the desk. He mumbled, "Sir, we were going to tell you after the advance. We talked about it last night. We thought it would be better to wait until the fight was over, instead of distracting you with this."

Harcrow rolled his eyes. "Bullshit. Bad news doesn't get better with age. Don't tell me you kept this secret to spare my feelings. I think it's more likely you thought you could get away with it."

Neither man said a word. Harcrow waited a few moments, then said, "Well? No answer?"

Nunez said, "I didn't know that was a question, sir."

Harcrow leaned back. "Jerry, I should punch you right in your fucking mouth. Don't be a smartass. I've known both of you a long time, and you know I'd have helped you if you'd have come to me first. Now this shit's broken loose back in the rear and it's way beyond my control."

"Sir, how much do you know?" Quincy asked. "And how'd you find out?"

"I know enough. I know you guys captured and killed a prisoner Monday when you were ambushed. I know there's a video that shows you killing the prisoner and burning the body. And it claims the prisoner was an innocent immigrant."

"Fuck me," Quincy muttered.

Harcrow squinted. "That's it? That's your reaction? You don't seem real surprised."

"We saw the video, sir. We know what's up."

"No shit. Should I ask how you know?"

Neither man answered. Harcrow sighed and said, "Fine, whatever. Anyway, First Sergeant Grant saw it in Edinburgh when he was checking on casualties. When the staff guys found out he was with a company in Arriago they wolf-packed him, showed him the video and tried to get him to say if he recognized anyone. He blew them off, claimed he didn't and didn't have time to watch it again. But when he got back he told me he recognized you two, Allenby and a couple of others."

Goddamn it, Nunez thought. *I have to quit hoping for a miracle. They're going to find out it was us. No question about it.*

"Son of a bitch," Quincy said. "So what do we do now? Any chance we'll slide out of this?"

"No. If you had come to me right after you killed the guy, then maybe. Probably. But you covered it up, then lied about it. I don't think I can help now. You're going to be arrested at some point after we finish this clearing operation."

Nunez felt his resignation turn to anger. He bit his lip, exhaled and asked, "Sir, what's the point of us continuing this mission then? We get to fight our way through this town, maybe get our balls blown off and watch all our friends get killed, and as a reward we go to fucking jail? So you tell me, why shouldn't we just turn ourselves in now and spare ourselves the shit that we're gonna see today?"

Harcrow pursed his lips and cocked his head. Then he said slowly, "Jerry, I'm going to be honest with you. If you guys murdered an actual cartel guy, I don't give a fuck. After what happened at that house, I understand why you did what you did. I'm not saying it was right, or that you don't have to pay for it. I'm saying, on a personal level, I don't fucking care. But if it actually was an innocent guy who got tricked, well… that's different. But it's still understandable."

Harcrow looked back and forth at the two men. "But to answer your question of why you shouldn't wuss out of this mission today, here's two reasons. First, the only thing you have going for you is that you've been in the worst of this shit since it started. This country is going to have a hell of a hard time throwing the guys who saved Texas into a Texas prison. Second, and more important, neither one of you is a coward. You're not going to back out. We both know that."

Nunez closed his eyes and covered his face with one hand. When he uncovered his face he said, "Sir, I think I'm gonna fucking puke." Then he stood up, tightened his carbine sling on his chest and said, "We'll see you on the Rio Grande, Captain. Lieutenant, let's get the fuck out of here."

CHAPTER 16

The company radio net buzzed in Nunez's ear. "Rapido 6 this is Hatchet 6. My scouts are in position."

"Rapido 6 roger. Twelve minutes until the fast movers roll in."

Nunez looked at his watch. 0618, they were ahead of schedule. Except for a bit of confusion on McCann's part, all the players were in their positions and ready to go.

He switched back to the platoon net. "1 this is 4, scouts are set. Fast movers in twelve minutes."

"Super. Plenty of time for a nap."

Nunez looked across the street at Quincy. The sun wasn't fully risen, but he could make out Quincy's face. He keyed up and said, "1, no motivation is better than false motivation. Now smile so I can see you in the dark."

Nunez saw a set of bright white teeth appear, in the middle of the black circle of Quincy's face. Quincy keyed up and said, "When we get to prison you're fucked. Me and my black power homics are gonna take you out "

"Looking forward to it, 1. Don't make me your bitch, though. I'll give you herpes. Over."

Quincy shook his head but didn't respond. Nunez knew Quincy was laughing. He smiled, happy that he and Quincy could find humor in the ton of shit that was waiting to fall on them after the operation.

He looked up and down the street, down both lines of soldiers. No bobbing heads or closed eyes this morning, everyone was up and ready. Anticipation had been killing them all night.

Nunez looked back at D'Angelo, who smiled and nodded. He seemed still in a good mood about the enemy he killed the day before. He and Berisha, his new assistant gunner, had 1200 rounds of ammo on them for the machine gun. Nunez hoped D'Angelo would have the chance to burn it all before they reached the river.

Nunez patted the magazine full of tracers in his left thigh pocket. Quincy, Nunez and all the staff sergeants and sergeants carried one, just in case they needed to mark targets for the helicopters. Apache support was still not much more than a wish, but they were prepared anyway.

He checked his watch again. Only one minute had passed. *Jesus, by the damn time...*

In the distance, two blocks away, a puff of smoke rose above the dim outline of residential roofs. Nunez looked at it with curiosity, not sure if he was seeing what he thought he was seeing. He peered through his scope.

Yeah, looks like smoke. Where the hell is that coming from?

Bright flames shot into the air above the roofs. Then another puff of smoke from further south. Then another, across the street from the first one. Each puff of smoke was followed within seconds by glaring orange and yellow flames.

"Oh, crap," Nunez mumbled to nobody. He keyed his radio and asked, "1, you seeing this?"

"I'm seeing it. What do you think?"

"I think they decided to fuck with our usual plan of advancing at first light. I'm going to switch to company freq and report it."

"Roger."

Nunez turned the knob. "Rapido 6 this is Red 4."

"Red 4 this is 6, if you're calling about the fires we see them too. They're on all our main routes. I think they're trying to obscure them with smoke. The DMs are set on a roof and see over a dozen fires so far. Cars and houses. They saw movement near some of the fires but couldn't identify any targets."

"Copy, 6. Are we changing anything?"

"No changes. Continue with the plan."

"Roger. Switching back to platoon net."

Nunez switched back and relayed the information to Quincy. Nunez checked his watch again. Seven minutes left.

More fires flared in the distance. Two blocks ahead, smoke blurred the open streets. *Shit,* Nunez thought. *This could cause serious problems. We might not be able to see each other at some points, and the fires will create choke points and funnel our movement.*

The soldiers stayed quiet and waited. Nunez looked at his watch again. Three minutes. Nunez counted seven fires on the road ahead now. He looked through his scope and identified three burning cars and four houses.

"Red 1 and 4, this is Rapido 6. Fast movers coming in in two mikes. Start your move."

"Red 1 copy and moving."

Nunez answered, "Red 4 hooah." He stood up and motioned to his soldiers to rise. The platoon was on its feet in seconds. Quincy looked at Nunez and waved his arm forward. The men began their slow walk into town.

0629. Nunez looked ahead to Eckert, the point man on his side of the street. He seemed more than just nervous, as did Gordon, on point on the other side of the street. They moved at half the speed of the day before. The two young men crossed the street to the next block, looked over their shoulders and kept moving.

Nunez peered into doors and windows as the platoon moved slowly past. No broken windows. The few open windows seemed random, not set for an ambush. Nothing interesting on the northern half of the block. On the southern half they'd see many smashed windows, blown apart by Ortega's bomb vest. Ortega's head was visible beside a curb half a block ahead. The platoon would hopefully ignore it and stay focused on their route.

A dark blur streaked over Nunez's head, well above the treetops. Everyone ducked. Nunez had time to wonder *What the fuck?* before the roar of the fighter jet's engines smashed down onto his ears like falling cement. Car alarms went off all over town. By the time he spotted the aircraft the pilot had it in a steep climb. The plane twisted and threw off flares and chaff, small strips of foil designed to confuse antiaircraft missiles. Nunez snapped out of the protective crouch he had hunched into and looked for missiles chasing the F16. Nothing followed it.

A second jet zipped over the platoon's heads. Nunez ducked again, then chided himself for being chickenshit. It was just noise. He looked up to see the second jet spiraling upward, shooting flares to its flanks. No missiles followed in its wake.

Nunez looked around. The platoon had stopped when they heard the noise, just as he had. He growled, "Hey you bunch of fags, move out! They're on our side."

Eckert looked back at Nunez, gave a sheepish grin and stepped off again. The roar of the two jets faded. Nunez took a last look at the sky, then went back to scanning the houses ahead. He caught a brief whiff of decomposition and dismissed it as unimportant. He barely noticed it anymore.

One by one, car alarms chirped into reset, the noise cut itself off. Nunez saw Ortega's head, charred black, a few feet from a ruined car. He waved at Quincy and pointed to the head. Quincy nodded.

The platoon passed Ortega's head and was near the end of the block before the last alarm stopped. Across the intersection, half a block away, a house burned on the right side of the street. The flames reached higher by the minute. More fires burned further down the block.

Nunez saw windows shattered on cars and houses. Two cars on Quincy's side of the street were punctured and pockmarked with dozens of shrapnel holes. Nunez had his eyes on the cars when D'Angelo whispered, "Sarge."

Nunez looked over his shoulder at D'Angelo. D'Angelo pointed to a mottled green and black, angular L-shaped object resting against a curb. Nunez focused hard on it, then realized what it was. Ortega's legs, one laid out lengthwise, the other bent and pointed ninety degrees from its partner. The pants that held them together were burned black and tattered. He looked away to the next block, flipped the knob on the radio and keyed up.

"Rapido 6 this is Red 4. We're passing remains of the maintenance company soldier who was blown up yesterday. The mounted grunts need to recover him."

"6 roger, I'll pass it on."

Eckert and Gordon reached the intersection. Eckert looked right, hesitated a moment, stuck a thumb up over his head and crossed the street. Nunez judged the distance to the first fire. Less than a hundred yards, then his soldiers would have to veer toward the street. Smoke clogged some of the street, but Nunez could still see through it. On the next block, where three cars burned, black smoke blocked the view south.

Nunez crossed the intersection. The soldiers ahead slowed their advance as they approached the first fire. Nunez didn't blame them. He was scared to get near the burning house himself. It was just Gordon and Eckert's luck that they would be on point the day the enemy set fire to houses in their path.

A dark streak flashed past, from right to left. Nunez ducked again. The noise crashed down, obliterating all other sound. Nunez saw the F16 ascend to the east, leaving a trail of flares and smoke. Car alarms kicked off again. Eckert looked back, made a *Holy shit* face and angled toward the street.

The second jet flashed by, its unbelievable roar a second behind. Nunez tried not to flinch, but did anyway. Eckert ducked hard, stumbled and fell forward. Nunez smirked a little. After the operation everyone would have a ball jacking with Eckert about faceplanting because of a little engine noise.

The roar dissipated, shifting into a *pop!pop!* sound. Nunez wondered, *What's that? The chaff dispensers? Are they that loud? I don't remember hearing them before.*

A bullet zinged past Nunez's head. He threw himself to the ground and yelled "Shit!" Behind Eckert, Sergeant Carillo dropped to a knee and searched through his scope. Then he jumped up, ran to Eckert, vaulted over him and dropped prone. Eckert didn't move. Carillo opened up with his carbine, hitting something across the street toward the end of the block.

Nunez jumped up, charged past Eckert and dove to the ground. He looked through the smoke but couldn't see what Carillo was shooting at.

"Carillo! What's your target?"

Carillo ceased fire. No enemy gunfire sounded from down the street. "I thought I saw muzzle flash! Across the street, three houses from the corner. Don't see shit now."

Nunez looked back. D'Angelo and Berisha rushed forward and took a position beside Carillo. Nunez turned around and high-crawled to Eckert, who was still on his face and hadn't moved an inch since he fell.

Doc Corley got there first. He rolled Eckert over just as Nunez reached him. Eckert flopped onto his back, his left arm splayed out beside him. His head sagged to one side. Corley pulled Eckert's helmet off and turned the injured man's head. Nunez winced when he saw the wound.

Eckert had been hit in the lower jaw. The round blew half his jaw off and continued through his throat. The bottom of his face and left side of his neck were a mass of torn, bloody flesh, but no blood sprayed from the wound. Corley said "Goddamn it," and popped Eckert's first aid kit open. He grabbed the bandage from the kit and ripped it open with his teeth while checking Eckert's pulse.

Nunez asked, "Is he alive?"

Corley unrolled the bandage and pressed it to Eckert's neck. "I wouldn't be wasting my time if he wasn't. He's bad, though. We need to get him out, fast."

Nunez keyed his radio. "1 this is 4, Echo 4 Echo is hurt bad. I'm switching to company so we can get the Humvees up here for him."

"Roger."

Nunez changed frequencies. "Rapido 6 this is Red 4. Contact report."

"Send it."

"Contact, small arms fire, south end of the block we're on. Possibly a sniper. The fire has stopped for the moment. We have one critically wounded who needs evac. How copy, over."

"Solid copy. I'm pushing Humvees to you for evac. Don't stop the advance, Red 4. Keep moving. Out."

Nunez cursed and shook his head. "Red 4 roger." He switched back to the platoon's frequency and said, "1 this is 4, the Humvees are coming for our casualty. We need to keep moving."

The morning was bright enough now that Nunez could see the anger on Quincy's face. Quincy answered back, "Whatever. Let's go."

Nunez told Corley, "The Humvees are coming up to get Eckert. Stay with him til they get here, but don't lose contact with us. Grab a private to stay with you. We'll move slow."

Corley grumbled but didn't answer. Nunez rose to his knee and scanned down the block. No activity. He turned back and asked, "Doc, what's his chances?"

Corley looked up, frowning, and said, "Not good."

Nunez nodded and stood up. *Less than two blocks into the advance, and we lost one already. Today is going to suck.*

"Let's go, people," he ordered. "Keep moving."

The soldiers stood, took a few seconds to fix their lines and moved south again. Carillo took over point, and kept his weapon pointed toward the suspect house across the street. He led the men toward the curb to avoid the burning house. The house was an inferno, flames reached thirty feet into the sky. Soldiers ahead turned their heads away from the intense heat.

Carillo led them past the house and arced back toward the front of the next house. Two doors ahead, another house burned. Smoke poured upward from the front of the house, but all the flame was in back. They wouldn't have to detour around that one. Across the street, the last house at the corner glowed orange and belched black smoke into the sky.

Nothing happened. Quincy's men slid past the house Eckert had been shot from, crossed the next yard and veered away from the burning corner house. They reached the next intersection, crossed it without incident and moved on.

"Red 1 this is Rapido 6."

"Go ahead, 6."

"Your casualty has been recovered, and the KIA from yesterday. The scout DMs still don't see anything. Charlie Mike and keep me informed."

Charlie Mike. Continue Mission. Quincy answered, "Red 1 roger."

Black smoke shrouded the street ahead. Two cars burned in the street, flames raged from a house on the right side of the block. Another car burned in a driveway on the left. Nunez swallowed, readied himself for the ambush he knew would happen ahead.

A shot rang out from above and behind them. Everyone dropped. Nunez couldn't see where the round came from, but he knew who had fired. He switched his radio to the company net and listened.

"Rapido 6 this is Phantom. We just popped one enemy on Travis, east side of the street a block ahead of the lead scout. Two others hauled ass toward the alley between Travis and Fannin. How copy."

"Rapido 6 copies. Good job and keep it up."

Nunez switched back and relayed the information. His men stood up and moved out. Nunez looked back, saw Corley where he was supposed to be, near the rear of the column. Captain Crow's Humvees followed at a distance.

The roar of engine noise punched through the air from the south. Nunez didn't see the airplane. This time the sound was far enough away that nobody ducked or hesitated. They kept moving, not reacting to the second jet's noise either. Nunez thought they must be testing the waters closer to the river.

The point men reached the first burning car. Gordon and Carillo looked like meth addicts as they passed it, going nuts looking for an ambush. Nothing happened, and nothing happened when they passed the second burning car either.

Harcrow bumped them on the radio. "Red 1 this is Rapido 6. That's it for the fast movers. Their spider sense never tingled, so we should have Apaches within minutes. How copy, over."

"Red 1 copies."

Several blocks west Nunez heard the *pop pop* of a light machine gun. His men hunched and slowed their movement but didn't stop. Nunez flipped his radio to the company freq, but there was no traffic. A longer burst of fire answered the first one, then more guns joined in. It sounded to Nunez like a small element was in a firefight, probably not at close range. The volume of fire was too low. Within a minute, the firing petered out.

"Rapido 6 this is Wolverine 6. My scouts just engaged enemy fighters in the alley between Seguin and Crockett. No casualties. The enemy withdrew south."

"Rapido 6 roger. Any word on enemy casualties or strength?"

"They haven't reported any enemy casualties, Rapido. They said they saw a few enemy, no hard numbers."

Nunez switched back and passed the word. He felt a little bit hopeful. Despite the fact the enemy had hit Eckert, they weren't putting up much of a fight so far. The platoon had already advanced farther than the previous two days. The enemy seemed worn out, delaying more than anything else.

Nunez crossed the intersection to the next block. Past the fire on the left side, the road curved left. The end of the block was out of view. Carillo turned around and pointed toward the curve. Nunez nodded and waved him forward.

Carillo and Gordon led the platoon down the block, peering into every house and vehicle they could. They reached the burning house on the left and Gordon skirted the yard. Nothing happened as they passed.

What the fuck? Nunez wondered. *They didn't set all these fires for fun, they had to have some plan. Why haven't they hit us harder yet?*

The soldiers made the curve left. At the end of the street was a T intersection, facing a solid wall of trees and brush.

"Motherfucker," he mumbled. He keyed up and said, "1, any special plans now? You want us to just punch through that brush?"

"Yeah, roger that. Everyone stays in column, point finds a path through it and then a street that leads south. Me and you move up to point if there's any confusion."

Nunez heard rotor blades. He searched the sky. Between two roofs he caught a brief glimpse of helicopters far to the west. Nunez smiled. The last two days without helicopters had been hell. He would never take air support for granted again.

"Red 1 this is Rapido 6."

"This is Red 1."

"Now that we have air cover, increase your speed. I think these guys may have just left behind a rearguard. Increase to a jog if you can, not faster than an airborne shuffle. How copy, over."

"Red 1 copies. Be advised, we're about to push through a dead end. We might have to wait for the Humvees to find a way around."

"Yeah, they just told me that. Don't worry about them, they'll catch up."

"Red 1 roger. We'll speed up."

Quincy looked at Nunez. Nunez gave him a thumbs up. They both pumped their right arms up and down, the signal to speed up. Their soldiers repeated the signal, and within seconds the entire platoon was jogging south.

They hit the woods and spread into a skirmish line. Nunez caught glimpses of them through the brush, more or less in the right places. He took several more steps before the leaves and branches thinned and he saw a ditch ahead. His soldiers were running down the slope toward the four foot wide stream of water at the bottom. On the other side of the ditch there was no road. An open field stretched a hundred meters to another east/west street. One side of the field was bordered by a wooden privacy fence, the other by a tall chain-link fence topped with razor wire. A junkyard occupied the open ground on the other side of the chain link. Houses lined a street at the far end of the field.

Nunez stepped over the lip of the ditch and slid to the bottom. Soldiers were already climbing the eight feet up the other side. Quincy yelled, "Hold up at the top! Set a defensive line at the top of the ditch!"

Nunez stopped at the bottom of the ditch to count his men. An Apache slid across the sky over the platoon. Nunez watched it bank left across the field. Then he climbed to the edge of the ditch, threw his carbine muzzle over the edge and peered over.

Nothing moved in the field, nothing stirred around the houses across the field, nothing caught his attention anywhere. He switched his radio to company and keyed up.

"Rapido 6 this is Red 4."

"Send it, Red."

"We're in a ditch on the north end of an open field, and I don't have a clue where the Humvees are. Over."

"Roger. The birds will direct the Humvees in. If you can, move out to the next road, set security and wait for the Humvees. Over."

"Red 4 roger."

Nunez switched back over and gave Quincy the information. Quincy acknowledged and yelled, "Everyone good? Any casualties?"

Nunez took a minute to check with the sergeants, then answered, "We're all good!"

"Get ready!" Quincy ordered. "We're going to cross this field and head to the next street! Stay in a skirmish line! Once we're there, we find a spot, hold security and wait for the Humvees!"

The men hooahed back. Quincy looked left and right, climbed out of the ditch, stood at full height and yelled, "Follow me!"

Nunez scrambled out of the ditch. The men climbed to the field as one, stood and moved out. An Apache swooped low over the houses across the field. Nunez didn't hear anyone fire at it. He hunched his shoulders and focused on the other end of the field, less than a hundred meters away.

To Nunez's left, Quincy began a medium speed jog. Nunez's gear bounced on his shoulders and chest, he huffed from heat and fatigue. The houses across the field bounced in his vision. Ahead, the Apaches cut a huge semicircle over the southern end of town.

Over the beat of helicopter blades he heard a sudden *crack POP!* Far to his left, someone yelled "Motherfucker!" Nunez looked that way but didn't see anyone down, the line still trotted forward.

Crack POP!

A voice cried out in pain. Nunez looked left again to see men dropping prone. He went down to his knees and fell forward to his chest. He searched the field's far side. Nothing.

Crack POP!

Dirt erupted from the ground a few feet forward of Nunez's head. He ducked and opened fire toward the houses. Other soldiers flipped off safeties and yanked triggers, sending rounds southward. Nunez searched across the field but he couldn't see anything to shoot.

Another *crack* penetrated the growing wall of noise. No scream followed it. Not until several seconds later, when a panicked voice screamed, "Casteneda just got hit! Medic!"

Nunez threw his eye to his weapon's scope, picked a house and fired into a window. He couldn't see anything inside it. After putting two rounds through the glass, he picked another window. Then another. Then the hedges at the left corner of the house.

Crack POP!

"Ow!"

Nunez turned left to see Specialist Robinson push himself off the ground. A hand grabbed his shoulder and yanked him down.

Shit, Nunez thought. *We've got two hit, fences on both sides, open ground in front and behind. We're in a shitty spot.*

"Lieutenant!" Nunez screamed. "We need to move!"

Quincy answered, "Where? Which way?"

Harcrow's voice came over the radio before Nunez could answer. "Red 1 or Red 4, give me a SITREP."

Quincy answered, "We're in contact! Sniper fire from an unknown location south, I've got two down and we're pinned down in the open! Over."

"Roger. Stay cool, I'm pushing the Apaches that way."

Great. Apaches that can't shoot, Nunez grumbled to himself.

The platoon kept up suppressive fire. Nunez listened closely, but didn't hear any enemy fire. Far south, the Apaches hooked east to circle back to Nunez's men.

CrackBOOM!

Everyone ducked lower. Nunez took a half second to realize the sound wasn't a sniper rifle. He saw a cloud of dust rise behind the houses ahead just as he heard the roar of a rocket motor.

He snapped his eyes to the sky. The Apaches dove in different directions as flares shot from their sides. Nunez barely caught the dark streak closing on one of them.

A black circle of smoke swallowed a momentary orange flash, just short of a diving Apache. The helicopter dipped to one side, the nose dropped. The tail boom made an arc around the fuselage, slowly at first, faster after the initial revolution. The helicopter fell toward the ground in a slow, flat spin.

"Missile launch!" Nunez screamed into his radio. "An Apache's been hit!"

His men doubled their volume of fire. The crippled helicopter sank below trees and roofs, out of Nunez's view. The second Apache made a drunken pattern as it fled eastward. Nunez waited to hear the thump of an explosion from the doomed Apache's impact.

He heard only gunfire and chopper blades. The wounded Apache rose above rooftops, no longer spinning. It flew north, trailing smoke.

Crap. They travel in pairs, his wingman is about to haul ass too.

"Red 1 this is Rapido 6, do you have eyes on the point of origin for that missile?"

"Roger! It's south of us about seventy-five meters!"

"Are any of your soldiers near it?"

"Negative, 6! We're still in a field to the north!"

"Roger. Standby and hold your position."

Corley, to Nunez's right, jumped up and ran down the line. Nunez heard another *crackPOP!*, but Corley kept running until he reached a wounded man.

"Reds this is 6, keep your heads down. Air cover is about to break the rules."

To the east, the remaining Apache circled back toward the town and skidded to a halt over a mile from the platoon. Black puffs of smoke drifted from the helicopter's nose. The noise was like dozens of cannonballs falling onto a sheet of steel.

Houses on the south end of the field erupted into white flashes and geysers of wood splinters. A chain of earsplitting crashes rang out as a stream of 30mm explosive rounds, each with the power of a hand grenade, detonated around the old houses. Tiny eruptions of dirt in the field marked the splash of stray shrapnel.

The fire let up for a moment, then another string of explosions erupted out of sight, behind the smashed, smoking houses. Faint screams filled the spaces between explosions. Nunez turned to Gordon. They both smiled.

A last few rounds shook trees and blasted fountains of dirt and rock into the air. The hammering noise abruptly disappeared, a silent shroud of dust and smoke hugged the houses. Nunez keyed his radio and asked, "1, who got hit?"

Quincy answered softly, "Robinson and Castaneda. Cass is KIA, Robinson looks okay but we need to get him out. Switch to company and get us some support."

"4 Roger." Nunez switched over. "6 this is Red 4."

"Send it."

"Enemy fire has stopped. We have one KIA and one wounded. We need Humvee support. Over."

"Roger. The Apache sees you and your support platoon, I'm pushing him down to their freq so he can direct them to you. Once they get there, keep pushing south. Over."

"Red 4 roger."

Nunez rose to his knees, backed up behind the prone men and scrambled toward Quincy at a crouch. Ahead, Robinson lay on his back with his hands on his stomach, eyes closed, body armor pulled open. His uniform top was bloody and had been cut open around the wound. Corley was tight against Robinson's ribs, pressing a bandage to the stricken soldier's right shoulder. Quincy lay on the other side, searching the other end of the field through binoculars.

Nunez dropped by their feet. Robinson forced one eye open and turned his head. He smiled a little and tapped Nunez with his boot.

"Hi, Sarge."

"Hey Robbie," Nunez said. "How you doing?"

"Unh. Not real good. Some asshole shot me."

"Yeah, I heard," Nunez answered. "But if it makes you feel better, I think we got him."

Robinson nodded and closed his eye. Nunez asked Corley, "Morphine already?"

Corley said "Yup" without looking up. Nunez crawled beside Quincy and asked, "You hear the captain's orders?"

Quincy handed Nunez the binoculars. "Yeah, I heard." He pointed toward the houses and said, "I can't see shit, but I know the bird took some of those assholes out. As soon as the Humvees get here for our casualties we're going to push through there and see what's left. Just the open spaces and the alley, we're not going to clear the houses."

Nunez looked through the binos at the smashed old houses. Eight homes faced them from the south end of the field, four of those were smoking, crushed shells.

"Damn." Nunez handed the binoculars back. "What happened to Castaneda?"

Quincy shook his head. "Fucking good shot is what happened. That sniper nailed him right here," he said, tapping his chest two inches below his jugular notch, "just above his armor plate. Bailey said the round actually skimmed the edge of the plate. It went through the Kevlar and right through his chest."

"Shit," Nunez muttered. "Alright, I'm gonna check on everyone else."

Quincy nodded. Nunez got up and ran left to the end of the line. Castaneda was second from the end, also on his back with his arms laid close along his sides. His body armor had been torn open just like Robinson's, exposing a not very large, dark circle of blood on his uniform below his neck. Two bloody bandages and empty bandage wrappers littered the ground beside him. His face was covered by a grey *shamagh,* a cloth wrap used by Arabs as protection against the sun and blowing sand. Many soldiers bought them in Iraq, and Nunez recognized this one. Staff Sergeant Allenby, at the end of the line beside Castaneda, always carried it in his cargo pocket.

Nunez knelt in the dirt. "Allenby, you good?"

Allenby shook his head, anger on his face. "No. But I'm not hit, if that's what you mean."

"I hear you. Stay loose."

Nunez ran all the way back down the line, checking everyone. Nobody else was hit. By the time he reached the end, soldiers from the support platoon were yelling from the wood line behind them.

"Friendlies coming out!"

"Come out!"

Ten infantrymen charged through the brush . Quincy waved and yelled, "Over here!"

Nunez got there the same time they did. Quincy told their squad leader, "You got our casualties, we're heading out."

The squad leader nodded. "We got them, and as soon as we figure out how to get our vehicles up there we'll be behind you, sir. Y'all can take off."

Quincy got up. "Thanks, brother. Jerry, let's go."

Nunez jumped to his feet. "Let's go!" he ordered, waving everyone up. "Skirmish line, move out!"

The soldiers strained to get to their feet and moved forward. Nunez hung back to make sure they were all moving, then trotted behind them. Quincy gave the speed up signal again and they broke into a slow jog.

"We're not gonna clear the houses!" Quincy yelled. "Just the gaps between them, and the alley! Hooah?"

Voices yelled back, "Hooah!"

Fifty meters remained between the platoon and houses. A few men threw out self-conscious, halfhearted war cries, seeming unsure of what the others would think of them. When Quincy bellowed "Here we come, motherfuckers!", the entire platoon sped up to almost a full print.

Twenty yards to go. A gust of wind from the south blew smoke toward the charging soldiers. Nunez smelled the blown cordite and blasted, charred wood. The lone Apache crossed the sky behind them.

Soldiers ahead stepped off the field and leapt over the curb into the street. When Nunez hit the curb they were crossing front yards, angling left and right to charge the gaps between houses. Nunez cut left and weaved around a car covered by a tarp in a driveway. The houses on both sides were blasted full of jagged, basketball-sized holes, doors blown open, windows smashed to pieces. Soldiers spontaneously split into short columns and sprinted into the gaps, headed toward the alley.

Pow! Pow! Pow!

Nunez felt a twinge of fear at the unseen gunfire. His men didn't slow down. When he heard Carillo yell "Take that, motherfucker!", the hint of panic blew away like smoke rising from the ruined old homes. He broke out from the driveway into the backyard. Scattered craters littered the tiny, weed-choked yard. Jutting from one crater Nunez spotted a single black tennis shoe, smeared red with charred strips of flesh and a short bone jutting from its mouth. He looked left to see a shredded rag doll dressed in torn black fatigues, face and both feet gone, one leg draped atop an overturned doghouse. Beside the corpse, Carillo skipped sideways as he draped a long-barreled Dragunov sniper rifle over his back.

Nunez spun around to watch their backs. In a back doorway a dead cartel fighter was laid out facedown, half on the steps, half in the house. The back of his body armor was blown away, upper spine and dirty white shoulder blades exposed.

Ahead of Nunez, Private McClendon kicked a battered wood fence down and charged over it. In the alley, Quincy yelled "Spread out, spread out! Hold up here!" Nunez threaded his way around the craters and jumped the fence. Men rushed into the alley on both sides and re-formed their skirmish line. Nunez looked left and right. Nothing stood out.

As he scanned the alley he caught sight of something long and straight jutting from brush, covered in dust and no more than eight feet away. A bulky rectangular block was attached to one end. After a few seconds of staring at it, he realized what it was.

A fucking antiaircraft missile launcher. I've never seen a real one before.

Nunez bent down to look into the tube. He could see all the way through it, it was empty. He stepped back and searched around the launcher. A few feet left at the end of the brush he spotted an oddly-shaped blob, coated with gray dust and flecked with dirty red dots. A wrist and hand, two fingers gone.

Nunez searched further. Nothing. He turned around. Directly behind him, just under the old fence McClendon kicked down, a mangled body lay on its back in a twisted heap, one arm and one leg ripped off. Its face was covered in dirt but otherwise untouched. Lips parted, eyes half open, pupils looking straight through Nunez.

"Hey Mac," Nunez said.

McClendon turned around. Nunez pointed at the body.

"Look what we almost stepped in."

McClendon's eyes went wide. He stepped toward the body and gave it a closer look, keeping his weapon pointed at the dead man's face. Without warning, he kicked the dead man in the head. The fighter's head rocked, the dead eyes moved away from Nunez. McClendon looked up at Nunez and said, "Just needed to make sure, Sarge."

"Of course. No worries, Mac."

"4 this is 1, send 6 a SITREP."

Nunez acknowledged and switched frequencies. "Rapido 6 this is Red 4, SITREP."

"Send it."

"We've pushed into the alley the SAM was fired from. Three enemy KIA, we've recovered a Dragunov and found the used SAM launcher. No further casualties. Over."

"Roger. Your support platoon is having trouble finding a route to you, but they're on the way. We're holding up in the middle, the platoons to the right have pushed way ahead. I want you to keep going, don't wait for support. Keep up the momentum. The Apache saw a few enemy retreating south. These fuckers are running scared. Over."

"Red 4 copies."

Nunez switched back. "1 this is 4, 6 wants us to keep going. Support will catch up."

"Okay, let's do it."

"Listen up!" Quincy shouted. "We're gonna keep pushing south. Bypass the houses in front of us, form into columns on the next street we find and keep moving. Let's go!"

Everyone moved forward. Soldiers kicked gates open or clambered over fences to drop into overgrown backyards, regained their footing and crept south. Nunez skirted a garage and followed McClendon through a wooden gate. The house before them was a wreck, with a sagging roof, rotting wood around doors and windows, and cracked panes of glass. And that was without any damage from the air strike.

Nunez passed between houses into a front yard. Ahead there wasn't a street; instead, he saw a wide lot, smaller than a football field, filled with red-brick, cookie-cutter duplexes. Narrow, potholed streets led north to each duplex. Gang graffiti covered almost every exterior wall. Beer cans and bottles littered every front porch he could see.

The projects, Nunez thought. *Good spot for an ambush.*

"Stay in a skirmish line!" Quincy ordered. "Push through this shit, then we'll find a street and get back in columns! Move out!"

Soldiers stepped off again, leaving crumbling houses behind. Nunez didn't care much for walking through housing projects as a cop and didn't like walking into them in a war. He held back long enough to make another count, then fell into the line and walked forward.

Soldiers split into small groups as they encountered each duplex, flowed around them and linked up on the other side. Nunez didn't see any damage to the duplexes. No bullet marks, no broken windows, no dead bodies around. He felt a little anger.

The cartels didn't fuck with this place because all their gangster helpers live here.

Nunez passed three duplexes and saw what was on the other side. Another open lot, about forty yards long, with a ditch at the end. One bridge crossed the ditch. Beyond the ditch, another east/west street, another row of crappy houses, and a north/south street. Once they got there, they could hopefully get on line with the rest of the advance.

Nunez looked left and right. The platoon flowed past the duplexes like water and formed into a skirmish line again. Nunez looked over the houses ahead. Open doors, clothes and trash in the front yards, two cars with doors hanging open parked on the street. Nothing stood out, but nothing about the last couple of places they were hit from had stood out either. And the Apache had seen enemy heading that way.

Quincy started jogging again. Everyone broke into a slow run. Nunez looked to the ditch at the end of the field, trying to gauge its depth. If it was deep or full of water, Quincy would have to hold everyone up and send soldiers across the bridge in small groups. If everyone tried to cross at once, they'd jam up and become a perfect target.

Ten more steps and Nunez's question was answered. The ditch was damn deep. The bridge was clear, with concrete barriers that rose to thigh height on both sides. Quincy slowed to a walk and closed to ten meters, then dropped prone. The platoon followed him down.

"Two men at a time, cross the bridge! From the left!"

Allenby and Suarez jumped up without hesitation and charged toward the bridge. They kept about ten feet from each other as they crossed. Nunez held his breath for the few seconds it took them to get to the other side. No shots rang out. They hooked left, sprinted to parked cars and took a knee.

Carillo and Liu jumped up and broke into a dead run. When they hit the bridge they spread out. Carillo held the lead and stayed left, Liu hugged the right barrier.

Deafening noise exploded from across the street. Windows exploded as automatic weapons fired from inside houses. Dirt and grass flew from dozens of points ahead of the platoon. Carillo stumbled at the far end of the bridge and landed on his hands and knees. He tried to force himself up. Concrete chips flew from the street as machine gun bullets impacted around him. He shuddered and dropped to his face.

Liu made a mistake and tried to backpedal instead of running forward. Red streaks shot from his left leg as a magazine full of tracers detonated. Liu screamed, hopped sideways on his right foot and flipped headfirst over the barrier into the ditch.

Soldiers on the right side of the bridge opened up. The soldiers on the left had friendlies in their line of fire and couldn't shoot. Across the ditch, Allenby and Suarez fired over hoods at unseen enemy in the houses. Nunez picked a window and fired into it.

"Left side, get into the ditch!" Quincy screamed over the gunfire. "Left of me, into the ditch!"

Half the platoon rose and sprinted the short distance to the ditch. Quincy went with them. Nunez looked left and saw one soldier still on his face, not moving.

Across the ditch movement caught Nunez's eye. Suarez fell backward as glass and metal exploded from the old Honda Civic he had been using for cover. He collapsed onto his back, his arms flopped straight to the sides. He didn't move.

To Nunez's right, D'Angelo dumped rounds through the front door of a deteriorating red-shingled house. Berisha yelled "Left! First window left!" and D'Angelo walked rounds into it.

Nunez heard splashing and cursing from the ditch. Allenby's car was ripped by a long burst of fire, but Allenby didn't look like he had been hit. He lifted his carbine and emptied a magazine over the hood as he shuffled backward toward the ditch. Rounds skipped off the street around him and he almost tripped over the curb, but he reached the edge of the ditch. He dropped backward to cover as others threw their muzzles over the edge and opened fire.

Two rounds zipped low over Nunez's head. He ducked and fired back at nothing in particular. Nothing looked like a target. To his right two soldiers yelled "Cover!" as they reloaded their weapons or cleared malfunctions. Berisha pulled open D'Angelo's patrol pack and yanked out a fresh belt of ammunition.

Heads popped up in the ditch, more weapons fired south. Quincy rose into view, turned backward and yelled "Right side, into the ditch!"

Nunez climbed to his feet and yelled, "Let's go, follow me!" When he reached the ditch he dropped to his knee and fired blind as he looked back to make sure his men were moving. They jumped into the ditch and slid to the bottom. Nunez made sure nobody else had been hit, then stepped into the ditch and slid downward. Soldiers around him hit the bottom, sloshed through the water and climbed the other side.

Liu lay on his back just out of the water under the bridge, tying his leg off with a tourniquet. He was covered in mud and green slime, his left leg jutted at the wrong angle from his knee. Nunez yelled "Doc!" and looked around for him. He caught sight of him a few seconds later, splashing along the bottom of the ditch, heading toward Liu.

Something exploded in the stream behind Doc Corley. He flung himself face-first into the water. Behind him, a soldier rolled down the ditch into the running stream. Corley sat up out of the water and spun around. Water flew off him like a dog drying itself off.

On the left, several men screamed "Grenade!" and "Oh shit!" Quincy and the other soldiers ducked below the edge of the ditch as something exploded in the street. Nunez watched a small black object bounce over the edge of the ditch, fly over Allenby and fall into the water. Two seconds later a loud *Wham!* rang out and a geyser of mud shot skyward. The concussion felt like a punch in the chest.

Nunez flipped his radio knob. "Rapido 6 this is Red 4!"

"Send it!"

"Contact contact contact! Another ambush, just south of the projects! We're spread out in a ditch, taking small arms fire and grenades! We have several men down! How copy, over!"

"Copy! Stand by, I'm pushing the Apache back to you!"

Corley jumped back to his feet and ran down the stream to Liu. The men at the top of the ditch raised their heads again and opened fire. The soldier who had rolled down the ditch after the grenade blast raise his head from the stream. He crawled forward until his upper body was over mud instead of water, then eased forward onto his chest and lay still.

Soldiers on the right yelled "Grenade, get down!" Nunez turned his head and saw everyone but Berisha jerk down below the edge of the ditch. Berisha lurched forward, his arms flailed as he pitched something away. An explosion caught him from the shoulders up and flipped him in an arc, head over heels. He slammed onto his back, head pointed downward toward the stream. He slid a foot down the ditch and didn't move.

"Red 4 this is 6, the Apache's got you but you're too close for him to fire rockets! He's almost out of 30mm and he says if he fires on the houses he'll hit you! Hold your position, I've got your support platoon headed to you! How copy?"

"Motherfucker!" Nunez spat. He keyed up and yelled, "Red 4 copies!" as he scuttled sideways to Berisha. Soldiers to his right jumped up and fired south. D'Angelo screamed "I need another A-gunner! Someone grab ammo from Berisha's patrol pack, I'm almost out!"

Another grenade exploded to the left, near Quincy. Nunez turned to see a cloud of dust spreading over several soldiers who were ducked below the edge of the ditch. Rocks and gravel rained down on them. Cuevas screamed and grabbed his face.

Gorham ran to Berisha, shoved him to his side and yanked a belt of machine gun ammunition from his pack. Berisha flopped around like a crash test dummy. He looked dead.

Oh fuck, Nunez thought. *We're in trouble. We need help, bad.*

CHAPTER 17

Nunez heard the Humvees before he saw them. They turned a corner to the platoon's left and punched it to reach Nunez's position. When the first Humvee was close enough the gunner opened up with his M240 and tore the front windows of a house apart.

"Cease fire!" Quincy yelled. "Cease fire and stay low!"

Nunez repeated the order to cease fire. The men around him took their fingers off triggers and flipped safeties on. The support platoon's four Humvees rolled past the bridge, their gunners dumped hundreds of rounds into the houses. Nunez felt relief surge through him like a tsunami.

Nunez rushed to Berisha and grabbed his shoulder. Berisha turned his head and moaned. His nose bled and his eyes were squeezed shut. Nunez was surprised he was alive. He expected to see blood spray from wounds on Berisha's face and neck, but there was nothing other than the nosebleed. Nunez pulled Berisha's uniform collar away from his throat and took a close look. Nothing, no injuries. Berisha had taken a hard hit from the grenade's concussion, but no fragmentation.

Nunez mumbled "Lucky motherfucker" and pushed Berisha up by the shoulders. Berisha moaned again and mumbled, "*Jam mire, nona. Jam mire.*"

"Berisha!" Nunez yelled. "Wake up! Speak fucking English!"

Berisha opened his eyes and looked into the sky for a moment. His gaze drifted past Nunez's face, stopped and drifted back. Then Berisha's eyes widened, recognition lit his face. He fumbled to get his legs under him and stammered, "I'm good, Sarjant. I am okay. Where is D'Angelo?"

"Right where you left him. His head would have probably been blown off if you hadn't tossed that grenade away. What language were you speaking just now?"

Berisha gave him a confused look. "I think English, Sarjant. What do I say?"

"Fuck, I don't know. Something about yams and mere."

"Oh," Berisha said. "I think I speak Albanian. But I am awake now, I speak English."

"Okay, brother." Nunez patted Berisha's shoulders. "Stay here a minute and get your head together. Things slowed down a little, take a break."

Berisha nodded and took a drink from his Camelbak. Nunez squeezed his arm and turned to check on Liu. By the time Nunez reached Liu and Corley, Berisha had already climbed up the ditch to D'Angelo's side. Nunez shook his head in wonder as he saw Berisha slap Gorham on the back and take his place.

Gunfire from the Humvees slowed to a burst every ten or so seconds. Fire from the enemy side had stopped. Nunez wondered if the enemy had hauled ass because they thought the Apache was about to light them up again.

Nunez knelt by Liu's side and asked, "Hey man, you good?"

Liu looked at Nunez with a face full of pure agony. His breath came in short gasps. "Sarge, this sucks," he wheezed. "This shit hurts worse than anything I've ever felt before."

"Hang in there, Liu. You'll be okay. Help is here."

Liu nodded and closed his eyes. Corley looked at Nunez and silently mouthed, *He needs evac, quick.* Nunez nodded and asked, "Who got hit by the grenade at the other end of the line?"

"Dixon. He took some shrapnel in his ass and legs, and almost drowned. He says he can go on, but he can't. Cuevas took a little piece of shrapnel in the face but he's fine."

"And who did we leave up there?" Nunez asked, pointing the way they had come.

Corley looked away. "Hendricks. I don't know if he's alive or dead."

"Alright. We'll get him."

Nunez looked around. "Gorham! Conway! Go get Hendricks and bring him here! He's back there behind us!"

The two soldiers yelled acknowledgement, slid to the bottom of the ditch, climbed up the other side and stepped over the top. Nunez lost sight of them as they sprinted to Hendricks. A minute later they struggled back into view, dragging Hendricks by his body armor.

Nunez yelled, "Gorham! Is he alive?"

Gorham shook his head. "He got hit through the helmet in the top of the head, Sarge."

"Leave him there. Go check on Carillo and Suarez."

They dropped Hendricks and ran to the bridge. Nunez climbed to the top of the ditch, stepped out and jogged to one of the Humvees. He saw Gorham and Conway stand up from Carillo's side and start toward Suarez. Nunez gave them a *What's up?* gesture. Conway shook his head and made a throat cutting motion.

Damn it. Carillo was one of our best. One of our brothers.

Nunez cursed and ran the last few steps to the closest Humvee. The vehicle commander opened his door before Nunez got there.

Nunez wheezed, "We got at least two KIA and maybe one more, plus two wounded. Can you break two Humvees off to get them downtown?"

The vehicle commander nodded and said, "Goddamn, Sarge, how many fucking guys do you have left? You're going to run out if this shit keeps up. Maybe we should take over."

Nunez asked himself, *Do we even* want *to stay in the lead?*

He snapped back, "You don't need to take over. We have, uh, twenty-two left. Plenty of strength to finish the advance."

"Alright, just asking. We see your KIAs, where's your wounded?"

"In the ditch."

Nunez started toward the ditch, then turned back to the humvee commander. "One of our KIAs has a Dragunov on his back. That rifle belongs to us. Tell your Joes not to steal it."

"Roger."

Nunez looked toward Suarez. Soldiers from the support platoon were already helping Conway and Gorham load Suarez's body into the back of a Humvee. Others bailed out of Humvees and charged across the bridge toward Hendricks. Nunez yelled, "Hey, we have two wounded in the ditch! Down there!"

Support soldiers ran down the ditch. Quincy climbed out and yelled, "Alpha first platoon, let's go! Let's get down the side road and cut these fuckers off!"

Nunez turned back and yelled, "You heard him! Let's go!"

The platoon climbed out of the ditch. Nunez switched to company freq and gave Harcrow a report.

"6 this is Red 4, the support platoon is here recovering our casualties. We're about to push south. Over."

"Red 4, what's your slant?"

Nunez wiped his face. Slant meant the number of soldiers in the unit. Nunez had a feeling that when he answered, his platoon would be pulled off the lead. He wasn't sure how he felt about that.

"Rapido 6, our slant is two-two."

There was a pause. When Harcrow spoke again, his voice was much slower and softer than normal.

"Roger that, Red 4. Charlie Mike, and don't lose anyone else."

Nunez sighed. The faint hope that Harcrow would pull them off the lead evaporated.

"Red 4 roger. We'll do our best."

Soldiers ran past Nunez to the T intersection to their right. The first men to reach the corner stopped and held security while the others formed into columns. No orders had to be given.

Nunez fell into the line on the far side of the intersection. He found himself looking down a long, more or less straight street. Three stop signs were visible, then tall grass and open space. The enemy had fallen back between houses and across streets to the platoon's left.

"Four this is 1, do you see what I see?"

Nunez looked around. "Uh, I don't think so, 1. What's up?"

"I'm looking through binos at the end of the street. I think that's open fields, woods and the river just past that last stop sign."

Nunez looked up but couldn't see it. *Holy shit. I hope he's right.*

"Hallelujah, 1. I'm going to give 6 a SITREP." Nunez switched frequencies. "Rapido 6 this is Red 4."

"Send it, 4."

Nunez looked at the nearest street signs. "6, we're at Hidalgo and Menefee. Are we close to the south end of town?"

"Red 4, my map doesn't have all the streets marked. But if you're past the projects, you should be within a few blocks of the last houses in town."

"Hot damn, 6. Okay, I'll keep you advised."

"Red 4, I have more info for you. A Marine company arrived downtown about thirty minutes back. I pushed their platoons south on the main three routes. First Cav tanks and Bradleys are supposed to be a few miles north of us. And higher is trying to get us more Apache support so the one we have isn't running around alone. Over."

"Copied. What kind of progress is everyone else making?"

"They're moving slow but have the end of town in sight. The only resistance any of them hit was the short firefight the scouts had. Mostly they've just been trying not to get lost."

Nunez thought it over. A plan took shape. "6, can you have the Marine platoon on our route shift east two blocks? If the Marines get east of the enemy we can hit them from two directions. How copy?"

"That sounds good, 4. Consider it done."

"Roger that, 6. Keep the good news coming."

Nunez switched back and gave Quincy an update. Quincy answered back, "Roger. Let's speed up and get the fuck out of this damn town."

Quincy pumped his arm up and down. The twenty-two men on the street repeated the signal and jogged south. Their speed was far from a sprint.

The Apache passed far overhead at high speed. Nunez figured the pilot wasn't about to risk taking a missile up the ass. The helicopter was still a deterrent, but the pilots wouldn't see anything flying that high and fast.

The point soldiers reached the first stop sign. Gordon, on the left side of the street, checked east down the side street and sprinted across the intersection. Gorham checked right and followed Gordon's move. The soldiers sprinted across one at a time. Nunez smelled death again as he approached the intersection. When he reached it he looked right.

In the middle of the street, a few houses from the corner, the body of what looked like a young girl in a stained white t-shirt lay face down. Her skin was almost black. Wind caught long hair and lifted it above her motionless body. To her side in a front yard a bloated corpse rotted on its back. A dead woman in a house dress lay in a pile on the front steps of the house. Nunez turned away and concentrated on the road ahead.

The soldiers kept running. Nunez looked back and saw two support humvees in the platoon's wake. Now that they were a block closer, Nunez was able to see past the end of the street. Just on the other side of the tall grass was an expanse of open ground, then a heavily wooded area. The woods had to be on the river.

Another two minutes passed, the soldiers on point reached the next stop sign. Gordon looked a little more relaxed as he crossed the second intersection. Nunez leaned out and saw Gorham cross the side street.

A burst of fire rang out from ahead. Nunez heard the rounds slap into brick ahead. Everyone dropped prone except Nunez. He didn't bother, instead he ran forward to make sure nobody had been hit. A second burst rang out about a block away. Bullets tore the air ahead. He changed his mind and dropped beside Conway. Single shots sounded from the front of the columns. He lifted his head and saw Gorham fire aimed rounds down the street.

Three men in black suddenly charged across the road at the end of the block, running left to right. Gorham and Gordon fired at once. One of the running men spun and flopped onto his back. Another staggered and dropped to his knees. The third man bounced to a stop, turned and ran back the way he had come. Rounds impacted the street around him, but he made it back to cover and disappeared. Gorham kept firing until the man on his knees collapsed like a falling tree. Nunez jumped up and ran to Gorham's side.

"Red 4 this is Rapido 6, what's going on? I hear firing on your route."

Nunez wondered, *Where are they trying to go? There are just more troops that way.* He saw nothing but more houses down his side of the street. There was one larger, two story brick house visible above the others, but why would they try to get there? They'd just be surrounded, hunted down and killed. And the fucking border was just south of them, if they hauled ass south they'd be at the river in minutes.

He answered, "6 this is 4, we took light fire and three idiots just ran across the street in front of us, heading west. We killed two. Not sure what the fuck's going on. Over."

"Roger. Hold up a second, I'm pushing second platoon and the scouts to you. Over."

Nunez rogered and yelled, "Lieutenant! 6 says to hold here, scouts and second platoon are coming!"

Quincy cupped his hands around his mouth to shout back a response. His words drowned in gunfire. Nunez ducked and looked down the street to see muzzle blasts from the corners of the houses on the left. The platoon dumped rounds back at them as individual soldiers scrambled to find cover. Bullets smacked into walls, concrete and grass. As the platoon tore up the attackers' positions with return fire, another group of eight or ten men in black ran sideways across the street, firing wild.

Nunez heard D'Angelo's M240 open up from the other side of Gorham. Tracers flew in a steady stream at thigh level down the right side of the street. D'Angelo knew what he was doing.

Several men went down in the street, four ran right into D'Angelo's bullets. The rounds blasted legs and femurs apart, knocking the men off their feet. Nunez watched one of them take a round through the head as he fell straight down through the torrent of gunfire. Another man turned back from the center of the street, dragging one leg. Gorham took careful aim and shot the man through the hips. The man fell to his stomach and wailed in agony. Nobody else fired at him.

Enemy cover fire stopped. Nunez flipped to his back and yelled, "Get those two fucking Humvees up here! Hurry up!"

Soldiers down the line frantically waved to the Humvees behind the platoon. They rushed forward until they were even with the last soldiers in line, then slowed. Nunez jumped up and directed them to the front of the columns. They parked side by side and the gunners hunched low in their turrets, ready to shoot. Nunez keyed his radio.

"1 this is 4, what you wanna do?"

"4, I'd kinda like to just sit here and let those dipshits keep crossing the street in front of us. Let's give them a few minutes, then we'll move out."

"Roger."

Nunez took his position beside Gorham again. He looked through his scope and counted the bodies clumped together in the street. It was hard to tell because some of them were tangled with others, but Nunez thought he counted eleven bodies. Actually, ten bodies and one skinny, masked man holding his stomach and groin, writhing in agony. Every few seconds he screamed in pain. Nunez hoped the man would last hours, maybe days before he died.

Gunfire rattled down the street again. Nunez heard slaps of steel on steel and the crack of breaking glass. The nearest Humvee gunner yelled "Oh shit!" and opened fire. Nunez looked over his scope and saw a man drop to his face beside a corner house.

"Red 1 this is Rapido 6."

Quincy answered up. Harcrow said, "The Apache confirms that you guys are almost to the south end of town. The enemy's clustered on the last street in town, I think they don't want to run south because of the helicopter. In five mikes I want you to move up and hammer those motherfuckers. Second platoon is taking a big brick house on the west side of the street and will put fire on the enemy from there. I'm about to push them and the Apache down to your frequency. Over."

"Red 1 copies."

Nunez passed the word, "We move in five minutes. Second platoon's about to take the big brick house up ahead on the right."

"Sarge!" Gorham yelled. "Someone's running down the street toward us with his hands up! Looks like a little kid!"

Nunez looked south. A child, maybe thirteen years old, with no shirt and sagging blue jeans, ran down the left side of the road with his arms held straight up. He screamed, "Don't shoot! Don't shoot!"

Through his scope, Nunez could see the kid had nothing on him, or at least didn't have a bomb. His pants sagged so far his underwear was almost completely exposed. The kid's head was shaved, he was skinny with a dark face that bounced with each step he took. He looked back over his shoulder, eyes wide with fear.

"Stop, motherfucker!" Quincy yelled. The kid jerked to a stop. Quincy ordered, "Take your fucking pants off and turn all the way around!"

The kid shoved his jeans down and stepped out of them, then spun in a circle. His white briefs were stained dark brown in back. He yelled back, "I ain't got nuthin', man! They're going to shoot me! Help me, man!"

"Get over here! Hurry up!"

The boy ran forward. Nunez jumped up and ran behind the Humvees to Quincy. The boy stopped in front of Gordon, who passed him back to Nunez.

The boy shook with fear, tears ran down his face. He smelled like crap. Nunez asked, "Where'd you just come from?"

The young boy motioned backward with his head. "From my house back there, man! I been hidin' since those guys got here! They was comin' in the house, so I ran!"

"How many were there?"

"Fuck, dog, I don't know! A hundred, maybe two hundred. They're all over the place."

Nunez went into cop mode and ordered, "Don't call me dog."

"Sorry, man."

Nunez looked at the kid's forearms and saw a 1 tattooed on his right arm, 3 on his left. Across his stomach another green, roughly done tattoo read *Los Nortenos.*

Nunez asked the kid, "What fucking gang are you with?"

The boy gave him an innocent look. "I ain't no gangster, dog. Why you ask me that?"

"Because of the fucking 13 and 'Los Nortenos' bullshit tattooed on you. Why the fuck would you get that shit if you're not in a gang?"

"Aw, dog, that's just neighborhood stuff. I don't run with no gang."

Nunez leaned forward. "Call me dog one more time, motherfucker. See what happens."

The kid leaned backward. Gordon held his arm tight. Quincy said, "Jerry, ease up. This is just a kid."

Nunez mumbled, "My ass he is." Quincy asked the boy, "What's your name?"

"Antonio Guevara, sir."

"You're safe, Antonio. Gordon, put him in a Humvee."

Gordon rushed the boy to a Humvee. The soldier in the back seat stepped out, shoved the kid into the center and got back in. Nunez saw a disgusted look come over his face as he caught the boy's stench.

"Red 4 this is White 4."

Nunez answered, "Go ahead, White."

"We just cleared the two story brick house on the west side of the street. You see it?"

Nunez looked down the street. Only one big brick house was there, that had to be it. "Roger that, White. I see it."

"Okay. We're looking east and don't see anything, but there's a shitload of brush all around these houses. We'll keep watch as you advance. Over."

"Red 4 roger." Nunez turned to Quincy. "Well, I guess we're ready."

"Let's do this shit, Jerry. Here's where we win the war."

Nunez bumped fists with Quincy and ran back across the street. He heard Quincy ask on the radio, "Rapido 6 this is Red 1, are you on this freq?"

"I'm here, Red."

"We're about to make our final advance. How copy, over."

"Good copy and good luck."

Nunez ordered everyone on his side of the street to stand up. They formed back into their column and got ready to move. Nunez wiped his face and thought, *One more block to go. It's almost over.*

On the other side of the street, Quincy waved his arm forward. Nunez did the same. The two columns began their march south. One of the Humvees crept forward, the second fell in behind it.

Shots rang out from the brick house. Nunez saw muzzle blast from a second floor window. There were only a few shots at first, then a SAW opened up. Tracers shot downward to a spot across the street. Nunez heard more, deeper gunshots answer back. Tiny clouds of dust erupted from the house's east wall.

"Red 4 this is White 4, they're coming this way!"

Nunez answered back "Roger!" and was about to yell across the street to Quincy when Gorham dropped to a knee and dumped rounds down the street. Men in black charged into the street, sprinting for the brick house. Everyone ducked as an RPG was fired from the corner. The round detonated harmlessly against a roof far behind Nunez.

The lead Humvee gunner raked enemy fighters with M240 fire. M4 rounds rained down on them from the brick house. Enemy fire trickled off. Soldiers on the second floor of the brick house fired at a slow and steady rate.

"Rapido 6 this is White 4. The enemy's trying to get to this house, I think. We saw a bunch about to cross the street. We killed a few. Over."

"Rapido 6 copies. Where is the enemy now, do you still see them?"

What the fuck? Nunez thought. *Those idiots have to know we have troops in that house. Why are they still trying to run that way?*

"Negative, 6. They backed off and I can't see where they went. Last I saw they were pulling back to the houses near the center of the block on the south side."

Pow!... Pow!... Pow!

Nunez looked left. These gunshots came from further east. No fire had come from there before.

AK fire erupted, with the buzzsaw sound of an RPK. Nunez heard screams in guttural Spanish. On top of all the confused shouts and gunfire, he heard the steady *Pow!... Pow!* of disciplined marksmanship.

Nunez keyed up. "6 this is Red 4, are the Marines engaging from the east?"

"Roger that, Red 4. Give me a minute, they're reporting right now."

Nunez looked across the street at Quincy. They locked eyes momentarily. They both knew the Marines were doing what they do best, killing enemy with accurate fire.

"This is Rapido 6, the Marines killed another six or seven around the houses near the center of the block, south side. They've lost sight of them now."

Nunez keyed up and asked, "6, can the Marines mark the last place they saw the enemy with tracers for the Apache?"

Beall spoke up, "6, we can mark with tracers if the Marines can't. It looked like —"

Gunfire and screams cut Beall off. Nunez's ears perked up. He stared at the house and heard a shitload of firing inside, but didn't see any muzzle blast from the windows. Beall keyed up again and Nunez heard more booms of gunfire, deeper and louder than an M4 or SAW. Deep and loud enough to come from AKs.

Just before the transmission cut off a second time, Nunez heard a shout in Spanish. The words weren't quite decipherable, but they were without question Spanish. Nunez swallowed and thought, *Oh, shit.*

"This is White 4, they're in the fucking house! We need support, fast!"

"This is Rapido 6, I copy! I'm pushing scouts to you!"

Nunez and Gorham looked at each other. Gorham asked, "How the fuck did they get in the house? Did Beall not put soldiers at the doors and windows for security?"

Nunez shook his head. "He's smarter than that."

Brush blocked his view, but Nunez caught movement on the side of the brick house. An arm thrust out from a ground floor window, an M4 dropped to the grass. A soldier's head and shoulders emerged from the window, he struggled to get his body armor past the edges. He was halfway out before shots rang out and glass exploded from the pane over his head. The soldier jerked and arched his back, his head snapped upward for a second. Then he collapsed, his upper body dropped vertical and he poured out of the window like molasses. When he hit the ground, puffs of dirt and grass sprang from a dozen points around the soldier. He didn't move.

"Jerry!" Quincy yelled. "Let's get up there!"

The men stood up again and started to jog toward the house, less than a block away. Nunez felt like a dog chasing a car, he didn't know what they'd do when they reached the house. Enemy fighters were inside, mixed with the good guys, and a whole lot more enemy were in houses and brush to the left. If Quincy wasn't careful he could lead his men to a spot where they'd be hit from both sides.

Beall keyed up again, his voice near panic and barely decipherable above the gunfire in the background. "Rapido 6 this is White 4! All my guys who are still alive are on the second floor! I don't know how many enemy are downstairs, but it's a shitload! Where are the fucking scouts? Tell them to hurry the fuck up, they're shooting at us through the floor!"

"White 4 this is Hatchet 6, my guys are about to assault the first floor! Can you confirm there are no living friendlies on the first floor? Over."

Beall didn't answer right away. Nunez knew he was conferring with his men, making sure there was no possibility any of his men were cut off and alive on the ground floor. If he was wrong, American soldiers were about to be killed by other American soldiers. Nunez was glad he didn't have to make that call.

"Hatchet 6 this is White 4, as far as I know all the men downstairs are dead. You're clear to assault the first floor."

"Roger. Hold your positions, don't let anyone go downstairs. We'll keep our rounds low."

The chatter of machine guns exploded around the house. It sounded like Captain Hollis' scouts were clearing the house by firing into every window. Nunez looked to Quincy with concern; he didn't want the platoon to walk into a raging firefight. Quincy walked forward with his head low and weapon ready. He didn't look at Nunez.

Ahead and left, several AKs opened up. Nunez couldn't see where the rounds were impacting, but they weren't coming toward his platoon. Tracers zipped across the street as Hollis' scouts fired back at cartel fighters. If Nunez's platoon moved another half a block south, they'd be in the middle of a crossfire.

"Hold up!" Quincy ordered. "Hold up here!"

The platoon stopped and took a knee. Bullets crossed the street ahead as the scouts and enemy shot it out.

"This is Hatchet 1-4, we're breaching the side door!"

Nunez heard glass shatter and sharp, guttural yells. Five minutes of sporadic fire followed, until a scout keyed up on the radio, breathless and excited.

"There's a fucking tunnel entrance inside the garage! They're comin' outta the fuckin' garage!"

Jesus Christ, Nunez thought. *I guess now we know why they kept trying to get to that house, and how they got back and forth across the border.*

"This is Hatchet 1-4, We've taken the bottom floor! There's like twenty enemy dead in here! We have several casualties, and I think there's more enemy fighters in the tunnel. Do we have any engineers? Over."

"This is Rapido 6, negative on the engineers. Can you seal the tunnel entrance?"

"Negative, 6! We don't have anything!"

Nunez keyed up. "Burn the house down, Hatchet! Get the friendlies out and burn the fucking house down!"

Several seconds passed. Nunez wondered if Harcrow was pissed at him for jumping in and giving orders.

"Hatchet this is Rapido 6. Red 4 has a good idea. Burn the house down. Any enemy in the tunnel will probably suffocate. Over."

"Roger. Standby, we're pulling the friendlies out."

Nunez tapped his fingers on his carbine. This was taking too long. If they hurried they could force the enemy into the open and mow them down. It would be fucking massacre. The good kind of massacre.

Several minutes passed. A few more shots rang out, no heavy gunfire. Beall's voice came over the radio, "Rapido 6 this is White 4, my platoon is clear of the house. We have seven KIAs and several more wounded."

"Goddamn it. Roger that. Find a place to set security and sit tight."

"This is Hatchet 1-4. We just set fire to the house and we're backing out."

As Nunez watched, wisps of smoke rose from the broken ground floor windows on the east side of the house. Within a minute heavier smoke trailed from the upper floor's windows. Two minutes later black smoke poured out like a flood.

Nunez heard screams. He searched for their source and saw nothing at first. Then a body flopped out a window, the same window the American soldier had crawled out of. This body was in flames from the waist down. The burning man jumped up and beat on his pant legs, stomped his feet frantically. It didn't put the fire out.

'Shit," Nunez said. "I hope that's an enemy."

He put his eye to the scope. The burning man was shrouded in smoke, but was dressed in black. The cartel fighter dropped to his ass and beat his legs, screamed and thrashed his head back and forth.

Gorham looked through his scope and asked, "Should I shoot him, Sarge?"

"Fuck him. I hope he burns for hours."

Another voice crossed the airwaves. Nunez didn't have to recognize the call sign to know it was the Apache pilot. His voice sounded tinny and artificial. Rhythmic noise thumped in the background.

"Rapido 6 this is Gremlin 08."

"This is Rapido 6."

"You want to have those Marines mark a target for me? I know you've been busy down there, but if the enemy is clustered up in one spot let's hit them before they move again."

"Roger. Stand by."

Thirty seconds later rapid fire sounded from the east. The Marines must have been waiting in eager anticipation for another opportunity to kill more enemy. The fire was more than twice as fast as it had been before. This time the Marines didn't have specific targets, instead they were marking an area.

Pow!Pow!Pow!Pow!Pow!Pow!Pow!

"Rapido 6 this is Gremlin 08, I'm about to engage. Are all your troops clear?"

"Affirmative, Gremlin. Hit those motherfuckers."

Nunez heard the Apache move north. He knew the pilot was positioning himself to ensure any rounds that went short or far wouldn't hit friendly troops. Nunez called out, "Apache's about to engage, watch for enemy running this way!"

Colossal explosions sounded from the air to the north. Nunez took in the sound of American air power. When the world was falling apart around our troops, no sound in the world was sweeter.

The burst from the Apache lasted less than two seconds, then the noise was replaced by an eruption of individual blasts from the last street in town. Smoke, sparks and debris shot skyward. Nunez heard screams. His heart lifted at the sound of enemy being blown to pieces.

"This is Gremlin, you've got about a hundred enemy running across the field to the south! They have about a hundred fifty meters before they hit the tree line."

"Roger! Can you engage?"

"6, I'm out of 30mm and all I have left are rockets. They're inaccurate as hell and I can't use them within three hundred meters of friendlies. Once the enemy reaches the tree line I can put some rockets in there, but I only have fifteen. More birds are on the way, if I can keep the enemy from getting across the river the other Apaches can tear them up. Over."

"Roger that, Gremlin. Red platoon, get the fuck up to the edge of town and kill some of those motherfuckers before they get away."

Nunez answered "Red is on the move," and jumped to his feet. "Listen up! The enemy's running across that field ahead of us! We need to move up, find a good position and wipe them out! Let's go!"

Soldiers yelled "Hooah!" and sprang to their feet. The platoon surged forward, alive and energized.

"This is Gremlin. Another group just broke from cover, maybe fifty more of them."

"Fuck!" Nunez yelled. "There's over a hundred of them in the field! Speed up, don't let them get away!"

The platoon broke into a full sprint. Nobody slowed as they reached the last intersection, even though bullets had been zipping back and forth across it just minutes earlier. The entire platoon made a decision to just risk it.

They reached the cluster of dead enemy fighters in the street. Quincy's column stayed clear to the left of them, Nunez's column had to run through them to stay away from the burning house. The man who had fallen out of the house on fire lay on his back at the edge of the cluster, moaning and still in flames below the belt. Gorham ran past the man as if he wasn't there. Nunez ignored him as well. He heard a weak scream as the soldiers behind him reached the man. He guessed one had given the dying man a kick.

Fuck him. He deserves it. For all the men we lost.

The lead men reached the high grass at the end of the street. Gordon slowed and looked back at Quincy.

"Push through, Gordo! Find us some cover!"

Gordon turned and ran through the grass. Gorham slowed to keep on line. The two young soldiers veered left as they broke into the field.

Nunez ran past the last houses and found himself in the open. He heard the Apache far to the right, looked across two hundred yards of open rolling ground between the houses and a belt of thick trees. Enemy fighters were disappearing into the trees. On the other side of those trees was the Rio Grande.

A few enemy turned and fired wildly toward Nunez's platoon. Nobody returned fire, nobody stopped or turned back.

"Skirmish line!" Quincy yelled. "Make a skirmish line! Machine gun, come to me!"

The two columns dissolved as the men made a long, single line parallel to the river. D'Angelo and Berisha charged sideways to Quincy. Once the line was even, a few soldiers fired at enemy fighters rushing into the woods almost two hundred yards ahead.

Nunez looked around. Charging across the open toward enemy hidden in woods wasn't a good idea. He didn't want to break the platoon's momentum, but they might have to turn back if there was no cover in the field. The field wasn't flat though, there should be something to take cover behind.

Ahead he saw what looked like a long bump going east to west across the field, thirty yards ahead. He focused on it and ignored the inaccurate fire zipping over his head. It was a berm alright, and it looked high enough for the soldiers to use as cover. Ahead he saw many more berms just like it. The field was full of them.

"Lieutenant! Let's get behind this berm and put some accurate fire on those assholes!"

"Roger! Do it!"

Nunez charged ahead of the platoon and threw himself down behind the berm. Soldiers dropped to his left and right, yanked their weapons into their shoulders and fired south. Nunez held his fire, checked his men to make sure nobody had been hit. Nobody was down behind them, but the two Humvees had fallen back as the platoon rushed into the field.

Nunez pointed at one Humvee and then the right end of the platoon. The driver nodded and headed that way. Nunez sent the second Humvee to the left end of the line.

When he looked toward the woods he saw six or seven dead or dying enemy fighters scattered in the grass just short of the tree line. He looked into the woods and caught brief flashes of movement but no clear targets.

He keyed his radio. "Rapido 6 this is Red 4, we're spread out in the field south of town! The enemy is in the woods just north of the river. We're holding here. How copy, over."

"6 copies. The Marines are almost to you, and we have two Apaches less than five minutes out. Hold your position, I might have you and the Marines assault through the woods."

"Red 4 roger."

Gunfire echoed from the woods. Rounds went high over Nunez and hit short in front of D'Angelo and Berisha, way to his left. Nunez looked through his scope at the woods and didn't see any movement. His men were firing so fast he couldn't tell if they were receiving return fire. He looked to the hovering Apache and keyed up.

"Gremlin 08 this is Red 4."

"Go ahead, Red 4."

"Can you see the enemy in the woods? We lost sight of them. Over."

"Red, I can't see a damn thing. There's too much vegetation, my thermals aren't picking up shit. Those woods are only a couple hundred meters deep and maybe half a kilometer east to west. They're in there somewhere."

"Understood. Can you engage yet? Over."

"Red, I'm going to throw a couple of rockets into the woods and see if it pushes them out. They'll probably break out across the river. Stand by."

Quincy yelled, "Cease fucking fire! Quit wasting your ammo! The Apache's about to engage!"

The platoon's fire stopped in seconds. Not a single shot was fired from the woods. Nunez figured the enemy had run all the way to the south end of the woods and were trying to figure out how to get across the river.

D'Angelo yelled, "There it goes! Waste 'em!"

Nunez looked to the Apache, almost a mile away, and saw smoke drift south as a single rocket blazed east toward the woods. He followed the rocket's trail until it crashed through the treetops and disappeared. Smoke and dust erupted high into the air. A second later the deep thud of the explosion rolled across the field. Nunez smiled, reassured by the sensation.

Another rocket whooshed from the Apache. It impacted over a hundred yards from the first one. Nunez wondered if the pilot did that intentionally, or if the rockets were just that inaccurate. Faint screams filtered through the trees to the berm. Nunez forgot about the accuracy of the rockets.

"Gremlin this is Red 4, those bitches are screaming in the woods. Hit them again, same area as the second rocket."

"I'll do my best, Red. The wind is blowing like crazy up here, the rockets are going off course."

Another rocket exploded from a launcher on one of the Apache's stubby wings. It landed far east of the second rocket's impact, barely inside the woods. Two more rockets landed close to the middle of the trees, fifty meters apart from each other. Louder screams rang out from deep in the woods, mixed with what sounded like orders in Spanish.

The Apache fired two more rockets. They punched into the woods almost two hundred yards apart and detonated out of sight near the river. A breeze carried a cordite scent to Nunez's nostrils. He breathed deeply and enjoyed it. Across the field more indecipherable orders were shouted, a few weak screams trailed off.

"Red this is Gremlin, I'm down to eight rockets. I'm holding my fire for now until I get some help up here."

"Red 4 roger. Did any of them break out across the river?"

"Negative. No movement."

"Reds this is Rapido 6, two more Apaches will be on station momentarily."

Nunez rolled to his back and scanned all directions. Within a minute he saw them, a pair of Apaches angling in from the northeast.

"Rapido 6 this is Red 4, if those birds are loaded have them hit the woods parallel to the river with 30mm fire. Once the enemy is away from the river they can tear up the woods with rockets. Over."

"Rapido 6 copies. Stand by."

Nunez watched the two Apaches grow larger on the horizon. As they approached they broke left and right. One slowed and took up a slow orbit to the west. The other swung east and began a low circle.

"Reds, the birds are ready to fire. Watch for squirters."

Nunez yelled a warning to his men. Soldiers on his sides got down on their sights and prepared to hit anyone stupid enough to break out of the woods.

The Apache east of the woods broke orbit and began a gun run. A string of intermittent smoke fell from its muzzle. Rounds were exploding by the time the noise of the gunfire reached the platoon. Smoke, leaves and branches flew into the air. Nunez watched a chain of explosions slowly advance along the south side of the woods.

The first Apache pulled away as the second charged in from the west. Gremlin slid sideways over the platoon, holding his fire. 30mm rounds from the second Apache arced into the woods. Nunez watched with satisfaction as they exploded in the trees. He hoped the airbursts were blowing the heads off enemy fighters. The second Apache began launching single rockets into the woods, then broke off and circled away as the other Apache rolled in from the east.

CrackBOOM!

"Oh shit!" Nunez yelled. By the time he keyed the radio, it was too late.

The Apache that had just finished its attack run dove left. A missile lanced out of the woods, curved right and exploded meters from its side. Cries of "Oh fuck!" rose from the platoon. The Apache that took the hit stopped its diving turn and hung in the air. It spun until its nose pointed toward the woods, and a shower of rockets exploded from its launchers. Nunez mumbled, "Oh, no," as the smoking helicopter shuddered, nosed up, and exploded into flaming chunks of debris that tumbled to earth like meteors.

The other Apache dumped all its ordnance into the woods. Nunez watched the pilot launch every rocket it had and fire a long string of 30mm rounds into the trees. Then it hauled ass away from the border.

"Rapido this is Red 4, we just lost another Apache!"

Nunez heard a few weapons fire single shots from the woods. The noise was to the left, at an angle from the platoon's position. Only a few rounds were fired at first, then the volume picked up as more weapons joined in. Bullets snapped over the soldiers' heads and plowed into the dirt ahead of them. Men ducked from reflex, lowered their eyes to their sights and returned fire.

Bright balls of fire flashed from the tree line. The booms of firing launchers were drowned out by the eardrum-shattering blasts of RPGs impacting all around the platoon. Nunez slammed his face into the grass and covered his ears. A metal clang penetrated the flesh of his palms. He snapped his head right. The Humvee at the right end of the platoon's line rocked backward, smoke and flame shooting upward from its hood, windshield white from shrapnel impacts on the bulletproof glass. The Humvee's's gunner launched a stream of tracers through the smoke toward the tree line.

Nunez saw the doors fly open and soldiers tumble out. The gunner frantically climbed out of the turret, yanked his gun off the mount and jumped off the side of the Humvee.

Nunez yelled, "Hey! Get the fuck over here with us!" The soldiers charged toward Nunez and dropped into the line with his men.

"Stop! Don't shoot! It's me!"

Nunez looked back to the Humvee. Antonio Guevara leaned out an open door, waving like a madman toward the woods. Nunez thought, *I fucking knew it. That little bastard's working for them.*

An RPG went over the Humvee. Antonio ducked back inside. Another RPG nailed the windshield, dead center. Flames and black smoke blasted out of the Humvee's's open doors. The explosion flung Antonio sideways onto the grass, limbs flying. He collapsed in a pile of red and brown, and didn't move again.

The second Humvee backed up. Nunez raised his head, fired his weapon and shouted "Pick your fucking heads up and shoot back!"

D'Angelo fired first. Others followed his lead in ones and twos. Compared to the rain of bullets and grenades coming from the enemy, the platoon's half-hearted scatter of return fire sounded like popcorn in a microwave.

Quincy shouted into his radio, "Gremlin, we're getting hammered by small arms and RPGs! Put rockets into the north edge of the tree line!"

A second volley of RPG rounds arced toward the platoon from the woods. Soldiers shouted warnings and ducked behind the berm. Nunez pushed his head down and made himself as small as possible. He heard the whoosh of the Apache's rockets between blasts. The enemy gunfire didn't let up.

"This is Gremlin, you guys on the ground get ready! They're in the open heading your way!"

Nunez's eyes popped open. *There's no Goddamn way,* he thought, and jerked his head up.

A flood of enemy fighters poured from the tree line at a dead run. Nunez froze for a second, dumbfounded. He couldn't believe what he was seeing.

The enemy was charging the platoon from straight ahead. The cover fire came from ahead and left. It took Nunez only an instant to understand what was happening.

They set a base of fire to cover the assault element. They're trying to get so close to us that we can't use air support. There's barely any of us left, over a hundred of them. Holy shit.

"They're comin' across the field! Get your heads up! Open fire!"

Heads popped up. Men left and right of Nunez yelled "Holy fuck!" Weapons fired toward the stream of black-clad fighters charging from the woods. Quincy screamed frenzied orders, "Aim, don't just shoot! Stay low!"

Nunez groped for his radio. "Rapido 6 this is Red 4, the enemy's charging at us from the woods! There's over a hundred! We need support platoons up here, now!"

Quincy keyed up and screamed, "Gremlin, hit the field, hit the fucking field!"

Nunez pushed his head down to his weapon, picked out a clump of running men and fired into the center. The image in his scope bucked and jarred with each shot. He couldn't see the impacts. On the fifth shot one man stumbled as if he had tripped over a rock. Other fighters trampled the man and kept coming. Nunez picked another man in the center of the clump and fired again. Tracers from D'Angelo's machine gun cut across Nunez's view and smashed three enemy fighters into the dirt. Two fell flat and didn't move, one rolled to his back and sat up as he clutched his torn stomach. Nunez saw agony on the man's face and heard his shriek from more than a football field away.

More explosions rocked the air. Nunez and other soldiers screamed "RPGs! Get the fuck down!" before Nunez slammed his head below the edge of the berm.

Rockets tore into earth. The detonations felt like kicks in the chest. Nunez heard screams and turned to see smoke and dirt spray into the air from the far left side of the line.

"Motherfucker! My leg!"

"Oh shit! We need to get the fuck out of here!"

Nunez screamed, "Hold your positions, there's too much fire to fall back!" The noise of battle was so loud he doubted anyone heard it. He got back on his sights to look for a target. The morning was hot as hell, bullets punched the life out of some enemy and crippled others. The cartel fighters were burdened with gear and ammo and had to be as exhausted as Nunez. They weren't running the sprint at Olympic speeds, but they were coming.

Nunez's magazine ran dry. He yelled "Cover!" as he simultaneously dropped the empty and pulled another from a mag pouch. By the time he slammed the fresh mag into the well, slapped the bolt release, hit the forward assist and got back on the sights, the lead enemy fighters were well within a hundred yards.

Gorham screamed, "I need a mag! Someone give me a fucking mag!"

Nunez opened up on the closest enemy at the same time he searched for a magazine. He shook so badly he couldn't tell if he hit anything. He tore out a spare mag, yelled "Heads up!" and launched it left without looking. Someone yelled "Ow!" A few seconds later Nunez heard the metal banging of a weapon being reloaded, then more gunshots.

"Gremlin this is Red 1, we need rockets in that field now! They're almost on us!"

The Apache pilot's voice was pure calm. "Red this is Gremlin, I hear you but you're too close. I might hit you."

"Gremlin this is Rapido 6! Red 1 has control, hit the Goddamn field!"

"Alright, Gremlin acknowledges. Stay low, rockets inbound."

D'Angelo's M240 machine gun abruptly quit firing. Berisha and D'Angelo both screamed "Reloading!" On Nunez's right Corley screamed for a magazine. Nunez wondered *Where's our Goddamn support platoon?* He whipped his head back to look for it. He saw smoke rising and heard screams and gunshots around the houses. A fight was going on behind them. He hadn't even heard it.

A tearing noise, incredibly loud, ripped the air. Nunez spun back around to look for the impact just as two rounds smacked into the dirt near the top of the berm in front of him. Pebbles bounced off his face and he jerked back. He heard the crash of a rocket exploding far across the field. Over the top of his carbine he saw the face of the nearest fighter, fifty yards away. The man's eyes and mouth were wide open, he looked terrified. Bullets spurted from D'Angelo's machine gun and raked the man across the thighs. He gasped and fell to his chest. Other men ran past him, screaming and shooting.

Nunez got his scope to his eye just as three men leading the charge went down in a hail of 5.56 and 7.62mm bullets. He fired past them at the men following a few feet behind. For every round he fired, two snapped past his head. He kept ducking, it was impossible to keep still and get a good shot off.

Another rocket slashed across the sky and plowed into the field near the woods. Too far away, no affect that Nunez could see. A second group of enemy, thirty or forty more men, broke cover from the woods and charged.

"Closer!" Quincy screamed. "Gremlin, bring them closer!"

Forty yards to go. The lead fighter hurled a grenade that bounced to the berm before a tracer punched through his head. Everyone near the grenade ducked. The explosion shook Nunez's teeth and launched a shower of dirt and rocks over him. By the time Nunez got his head back up the enemy was less than thirty yards away. He searched for the red aiming dot in the sight on top of his scope, didn't find it and fired anyway. An enemy fighter shook and grimaced, and kept coming. Another rocket exploded in the center of the field, halfway between the berm and woods. Nunez saw an AK spin out of the dust cloud.

Wind blew smoke into Nunez's face. He emptied his magazine into the scattered mass of men ahead, dug out a full one, reloaded and fired blind. Enemy fighters screamed curses in Spanish. Nunez heard his soldiers firing bursts instead of single aimed shots. Panic firing. He wasn't on burst, but he wasn't aiming either.

Another rocket blasted into the rushing enemy, fifty or so yards ahead of Nunez. A body flew sideways out of the dust cloud. Nunez felt a glimmer of hope. Some enemy fighters looked back in terror and sped up. Nunez aimed at waist level and fired across the nearest group. Twenty yards to go. His and other soldiers' rounds knocked three of them off their feet. Nunez heard another rocket launch in the sky.

Over the noise of his own gunfire, Nunez yelled, "Keep your rounds low! Rockets are –"

Charging fighters ahead of him vanished in red and black mist. His eyes slammed shut from a ripping roar and a crash like a brick smashing through a dozen windows. What felt like a baseball bat slammed into his helmet, the tremor rushed through his body to his feet. He tasted blood and steel. The noise of combat went dull and flat. He sucked in a breath and got two lungs full of dirt, smoke and cordite. He forced his eyes open and saw torn bodies in the dust cloud.

Holy fuck. That was too close.

He opened his mouth and worked his jaw, trying to clear his ears. He saw heads shaking on both sides, heard the faraway bangs of soldiers beside him firing into the smoke. Barely audible above those bangs was a different sound, like a monster tearing a giant sheet of paper down the middle. He knew what the sound was.

That Apache has to be almost out of rockets. There can't be more than one or two left.

Enemy bullets zinged through the smoke. To his right Nunez heard a wooden *thunk!* and agonized scream. Someone had taken a round in the helmet.

Oh shit. I hope that wasn't Doc Corley. Nunez jerked his head up and looked right to see who it was. Someone near him yelled "Rockets coming in close! Get down!"

"Dios ayudame!"

Nunez ducked as something crashed into his helmet and shoulder. A black mass of flailing arms and legs thudded into the dirt by his left side. Boots kicked dirt in front of his face. He shoved the boots away and looked toward his own feet. The bloody, torn face of an enemy fighter looked back at him in terror. Half the face was shredded and pulpy, one wide eye stood white against a brown and red background.

"Oh shit!"

Nunez yanked his carbine off the berm and swung the muzzle toward the man's head. The wounded fighter screamed *"No! Dios mio, no!"* and kicked his feet like a child throwing a tantrum. Nunez got his muzzle onto the man just as the man kicked him in the cheek. Nunez winced and tucked his head into his shoulders. The man fired his AK. Nunez couldn't see it, but he felt the muzzle blast on his feet and ankles.

He reflexively jerked his feet toward his ass and pulled the trigger. The man's shrill scream lasted just a second before it was buried under an unbelievably loud blast that felt close enough for Nunez to reach out and touch.

CHAPTER 18

"Ow!"

Berisha had just slammed the feed tray cover of the machine gun onto D'Angelo's fingers. The ammo belt fell out. D'Angelo yanked his hand away as Berisha jammed the belt back onto the tray and closed the cover. D'Angelo pulled the trigger before he even looked at his sights. Enemy fighters were less than twenty yards away, no need to aim. His bullets tore the ground ahead, he walked them into an enemy fighter hopping on one leg trying to reload his rifle. The man melted to the ground. He swung left and blasted another man across the shoulders. Berisha yelled something in another language and fired over the M240's barrel. D'Angelo jerked his head back from the blasts and kept shooting.

Rockets made a *crump!* sound as they blew gaps in the stream of rushing enemy. Great geysers of earth blasted skyward. Wounded and dying men cried out in Spanish over the chatter of gunfire. Smoke drifted over a breadcrumb trail of bodies that reached from the woods almost to the berm. Soldiers launched bursts of carbine rounds into thinning groups of enemy. Maybe half the attackers were down, sixty or seventy still coming.

Quincy slapped D'Angelo's right arm. "D! Shift right, they are closing on Nunez's side!"

D'Angelo shifted his fire just as a rocket blew a man apart sixty yards ahead. He thought, *That pilot's walking those rounds in way too fucking close.* His rounds cut a line across a half-dozen charging men. Four of the men kept running. One man firing a paratrooper AK went down with limbs flailing and fell flat on his face. He jerked upright and grabbed his waist.

D'Angelo began to look for another target and barely caught the movement of the man ripping his mask off. He took a microsecond glance at the man's face before turning to a different attacker. Then the flash image found the memory, and D'Angelo jerked his head back to the man.

The wounded fighter shook his head and screamed in pain. His medium dark skin was marred with sweat, beard matted and dirty. He looked older now, as if he had aged years in the two days since D'Angelo first saw him. Recognition dumped another rush of adrenaline through D'Angelo's veins.

That's the son of a bitch who was giving orders when my company was ambushed. That's the jefe.

D'Angelo gritted his teeth, mumbled "motherfucker" and traversed left toward the man. Two fighters grabbed the man at the armpits and tried to lift him. The man screamed and fought to pull his arms away. D'Angelo pulled the trigger and saw his tracers miss just right of the men. He leaned onto his elbow to adjust left and over the gunfire heard a growing roar from the sky. He put a line of bullets vertically through one of the *jefe's* helpers, from groin to face. The man's head snapped backward, a spray of blood threw a red arc over his falling corpse. D'Angelo pushed the sights left onto the *jefe.*

An orange flash burst a few yards ahead of the berm, near where D'Angelo had last seen Nunez. D'Angelo's head rocked sideways. A dark cloud blasted into the air, steel whirred in all directions. Three enemy fighters spun away from the blast, throwing chunks of tissue and globs of fluid outward in a circle until they crashed to earth. D'Angelo heard screams in English and Spanish from the right side of the line.

"Lieutenant!" D'Angelo screamed. "I think our guys just got hit!"

Quincy rose to his knees and scrambled sideways, shouting into his radio, "Gremlin, check your fire!"

Berisha slapped D'Angelo and yelled "D! Shift left, they are almost on us!"

D'Angelo yelled "In a fucking second!" He looked over the berm to his direct front and saw an enemy fighter go down as bullets smashed through his skull. He turned to find the *jefe,* lined up his barrel on the man and his helper. Another fighter ran right past D'Angelo's muzzle, screaming in terror. D'Angelo pulled the trigger but his bullets missed the man.

The monstrous roar of an incoming rocket was drowned out by the blast of D'Angelo's weapon. Bullets cut across the legs of the man helping the *jefe* and dropped him. The *jefe* fell back to his knees. D'Angelo let off the trigger, put the *jefe* in his sights and fired again. As rounds walked into the man D'Angelo thought, *Die, you fucking piece of shit.*

Flame flashed to his right. D'Angelo's breath disappeared, his heart felt like it froze mid-beat. Burning spikes of pain shot through the right side of his body, from ankle to head. Sky and earth traded places, the cloud of smoke swallowed him an instant after he saw the sun flash across his eyes. He realized he was airborne just before he crashed headfirst onto his back. His machine gun's red-hot barrel bounced into his cheek, adding another stab of burning pain. He felt his eyes water as if he had been punched in the nose.

D'Angelo opened his eyes and looked through brown dust and wisps of grey smoke into blue sky and sunlight. He opened his mouth like a fish and tried to breathe. Nothing entered his lungs. He threw his head back and fought harder. It didn't work.

A man in black vaulted over the berm and crashed to his knees by D'Angelo's feet. D'Angelo heard nothing, but felt the concussive waves of a weapon firing beside him. He struggled to turn his head but was barely able to move it. He saw Berisha lean backward against the berm, hold his carbine between his legs and fire into the enemy fighter's back.

Berisha threw the carbine aside and rolled to D'Angelo. Berisha's face was marred with blood. He knelt over D'Angelo, looked down with eyes wide. D'Angelo looked back at him, tried to speak through clenched teeth. Nothing came out. Berisha reached to D'Angelo's side, lifted the machine gun and pushed himself up. D'Angelo tried to grab Berisha's leg. His hand wouldn't move.

Berisha swung the machine gun in an arc, firing a long burst. Three more men in black rushed past him further down the line. Berisha paid no attention. D'Angelo tried to reach for Berisha's carbine. He couldn't make his arms work.

Another man in black flew over the berm. One of his boots came down on D'Angelo's chest. Pain tore through D'Angelo's body as the man ran north. Bullets blew the man's head apart.

Sharp burning inside D'Angelo's body faded from white-hot to warm. He felt the pain ease and spread. His eyes grew heavier. A deep throb thumped within him, getting slower with each beat. He knew bullets were hitting around him, he could see dirt fly into the air, but there was still no sound. He swallowed hard. His mouth was dry, the effort fatigued him worse.

His eyes closed. He left them that way a second, then decided to leave them a few more. He felt his head tip to the side. A blast that felt distant tugged at the fabric of his pants. He opened his eyes to see Berisha on his back, firing his carbine to the side with one hand. The M240 lay across his lap, barrel smoking, feed tray cover open. Red tracer rounds zipped through the air over D'Angelo's head, coming from Nunez's side of the line.

D'Angelo mouthed the words, *I've got more ammo in my pack.* No sound came out. He thought about trying again. Just thinking it made him tired.

Beyond Berisha several enemy fighters rushed over the berm, firing their AKs downward as they breached the platoon's line. Two dropped like rocks, the third was several steps past the line when he dropped his rifle and curved sideways until he hit the dirt. Bullets punched through his body and tore into the ground around him. He jerked twice and lay still.

D'Angelo's head rolled left on its own. He gazed up to see Berisha staring into his eyes and holding his chin. Berisha's lips moved but no sound came out. D'Angelo knew it wasn't worth trying to talk, it wouldn't work.

Berisha slapped his cheek. D'Angelo didn't understand why. His wife and daughter popped into his mind without warning. He wondered where they were, what they were doing. They couldn't know what had just happened to him. He hoped they didn't know.

Berisha dropped across D'Angelo's chest. It hurt, but the pain wasn't as bad as it was when the cartel fighter stepped on him. He tried to turn his head to see if Berisha was hit, but Berisha popped up and fired his carbine over the berm. He was still in the fight.

A slow, sleepy smile crossed D'Angelo's face. Whatever happened with him, Berisha and the other guys were going to win. They'd get revenge for all the guys in his company, for all the murdered civilians, for Ortega, even for that asshole First Sergeant Olivares. They wouldn't give up. He trusted them.

The throbs in D'Angelo's chest shut off like a light switch. His pain vanished. Spent shells from Berisha's weapon bounced off his face. He didn't care, but the pokes in the face made his eyes close. He left them closed, decided he deserved a break. He had fought hard, done a lot. More than he had to. He could rest now.

Corporal Marcello D'Angelo, twenty-four year old husband and father, veteran of three wars, faded away amid the chaos of the most critical, most desperate battle he had ever fought.

****

Nunez hit his bolt release and slammed a new round into the chamber. By the time his carbine was back into his shoulder everyone had stopped shooting. The only sound now came from the Apache circling overhead. Nunez scanned back and forth over his scope. Nobody moved. Not the enemy, not his men on Quincy's side of the berm, nobody.

Please, God. Please don't tell me that air strike and the enemy killed all our guys on that side.

Nunez, Gorham and Corley had turned left and shot the enemy fighters breaking through Quincy's half of the platoon. It had been a nightmare. After Nunez killed the fighter who ran into him, he had watched the enemy charge through the line shooting their men at point-blank range, heard the terrorized screams of his friends. As Quincy's side of the line was being overrun, Nunez's side was about to be overrun. They had barely survived the assault.

Nunez looked right. The enemy fighters in the field were all down. A few rolled back and forth in agony, but they were down. Most of the bodies were within fifty yards of the platoon. At least ten were mixed in with Quincy's men or had just passed them when they fell.

Nunez looked backward to see most of his soldiers searching for targets. Two were down, not moving. He knew they had already been checked. They were dead. He didn't know who they were yet. He didn't want to know.

Soldiers on Quincy's side of the line stirred. Heads shook, men pushed torn enemy bodies off and lifted their heads. Nunez felt a flutter of relief. They weren't all dead.

"Doc, Gorham, come with me."

Nunez started toward them, praying, *Please, let most of them be alive.* He kept a nervous eye right as he moved, making sure he wasn't going to be shot by one of the enemy in the field. All he heard was the faint sound of blowing wind and fainter moans of dying men. He kept moving.

A dead fighter lay sprawled on his stomach ten feet away, hands thrown over his head, smoke rising from his back. Just past him, close enough for the dead fighter to reach out and touch, was a motionless man in a dirt-coated Army Combat Uniform. His head was down beside the stock of his weapon, one hand on the pistol grip, finger still on the trigger.

Nunez kicked the fighter in the head. The man rocked, no response. Nunez stepped over the dead enemy and grabbed his soldier's shoulder to turn him over.

Corporal Mireles. Shot in the face and back, tongue hanging out, a mass of thick blood caked with dirt soaking the berm below his body. Nunez didn't have to check his pulse, there was no question. He squeezed Mireles' shoulder and eased him down.

"Sarge! It's the lieutenant!"

Nunez jumped to his feet and ran the few steps to Gorham and Corley. They knelt over two bodies, one enemy, one friendly. Half the enemy fighter's head was gone, his legs rested on Quincy's legs. Nunez took one look at Quincy and his knees almost buckled.

Quincy's left arm was missing at the elbow. A bloody rag that used to be a uniform sleeve covered the stump. Quincy was on his back, helmet gone, face swollen. His mouth was open, eyes closed. Both pant legs were punctured and bloody. Corley tightened a tourniquet on Quincy's arm and grumbled, "Gorham, go check on everyone else. Hurry the fuck up."

Gorham hurried away. Nunez knelt in silence as Corley took a pair of medical shears and slashed Quincy's pant legs open.

"Sarge, you're not doing any good here. Go check the other guys for me."

"Leave me alone, Doc."

Corley gave Nunez a momentary evil glare. Nunez saw bloody holes in Quincy's muscular legs, but no spurts from punctured arteries. Corley took a quick look and moved to tear open Quincy's body armor. No blood, no wounds. Corley unzipped Quincy's sweat-soaked uniform top, put his hand on Quincy's heart and his ear to Quincy's mouth.

"He's got a good heartbeat and he's breathing. Go on, Sarge. I got him."

"Okay, Doc. Thanks."

Nunez stood up and turned away. Gorham knelt on the other side of a smoking, blackened three-foot crater, talking quietly to someone in the dirt. Nunez looked down to see Berisha nod and tremble, prone with the M240 over the berm, ready to defend his position. A black-faced body in an American uniform lay on its back beside him. Nunez closed his eyes. He knew who the body next to Berisha was. He walked over a dead enemy and stood helpless, looking down at another of his fallen brothers.

"Aww, D," Nunez whispered. "Don't be gone, man."

D'Angelo, almost unrecognizable, stared through Nunez into the sky. The right side of his face was blown open, teeth showed through a torn cheek. Pelvic bone glistened through shredded uniform pants. His right foot was nowhere in sight. Nunez stepped over the body, one foot on each side. He dropped one knee to the blood-saturated dirt, popped the clips on D'Angelo's chest rig and pulled the Velcro of his body armor apart. He put his hand on his friend's chest, knowing what he'd feel.

No heartbeat. Nothing.

His head sagged. He reached up and closed D'Angelo's eyes with his fingertips. Words from a childhood prayer wandered into his mind. He chased them out. They sounded too flat, too wooden. If he was going to say last words over D'Angelo's corpse, they had to come from his heart, not his memory. After a quiet struggle, he settled on the only thing that felt right.

"You did good, brother. You were a warrior. Go to sleep, D."

He stood up, blew out a breath and stepped to Berisha. Berisha looked up at him, face smeared with blood, helmet cover torn, eyes red. A grimace of pain was on his face and he shook as though freezing.

Nunez knelt and asked softly, "You okay, Berisha?"

Berisha gave a shaky nod. Nunez heard his breathing, he was almost hyperventilating. Nunez reached across and put both hands on Berisha's shoulders. Now he felt it, Berisha's trembling was so bad Nunez thought he was about to have a seizure.

"Breathe, Berisha. Take a breath, hold it, let it out slow. Get your heart rate down. You're okay."

Berisha nodded again, took a deep breath and tried to exhale slowly. He stammered, "S-Sarjant, how... how is the l-lieutenant?"

"He's hurt, but he's alive. I think he'll be okay."

"Okay, Sarjant. Th-that is good."

Berisha breathed in and out. Nunez whispered to Gorham, "Go check on the others." When Gorham left, Berisha said, "S-Sarjant... D'Angelo is dead."

"I know he is, Berisha. Don't worry about him. You just take care of yourself now."

"Y-yes, Sarjant. I will."

A voice called out from behind, "Marines, coming out!"

Nunez looked back. Angry-looking men in green digital camouflage knelt in the brush behind the last houses, weapons at the ready. Nunez forced a response, "Come out!"

The Marines stood up. Twenty or so walked out of the brush in a skirmish line, others streamed out behind those. Dozens of men stalked into the field, faces tight, gloved hands wrapped around carbines and machine guns.

Nunez wondered, *Where the fuck were you guys five minutes ago?* But he still felt his pulse slow a little in relief. In a hoarse voice he wheezed, "We need medics up here!"

Several Marines called out, "Corpsman up!" Nunez watched several heavily laden men run forward through the skirmish line and drop their packs along the platoon's line. Behind them, a tall red-haired Marine with a radioman in tow ordered, "Listen up! First and Second platoons, advance on line through the field! Flex cuff every enemy body, even if the son of a bitch is blown in half and headless! If any one of these motherfuckers even looks like he wants to resist, waste him! Lieutenant Carahan, your platoon stays here to help these soldiers! Move the fuck out!"

Marines gave guttural yelps and oohrahs and moved forward. Nunez mustered the strength to order his men, "Alpha first platoon, weapons on safe and lay them down."

Nunez's men slowly laid their weapons aside so they wouldn't point them at the Marines' backs. More men moved than Nunez expected, but it still wasn't many. Nunez turned on his knee to face the Marines as they advanced. They stepped gingerly around bodies and passed through the platoon's lines without looking at Nunez. He watched the first line step over the berm into the field, a second line go straight to his men. On both sides of him Marines knelt beside his men and asked, "You alright, brother? You hurt?"

Nunez bent at the waist, rested his elbows on his knees. He forced himself to follow his own advice. *Breathe deep, hold it and let it out. Calm down. Your men are being taken care of.*

The fight was over. He still had to get a count of who was dead or wounded, who was on their feet. He had to make a report to Harcrow about the platoon's status. But that could wait a minute. First he needed to take a breath.

"Who's in command here?"

Nunez opened his eyes. A young Marine with the mannerisms of an officer stood by the right side of the platoon's line. Nunez waved his hand and answered, "Me. I'm in charge."

The Marine walked to Nunez. "Who are you?"

"Sergeant First Class Jerry Nunez, the platoon sergeant. And you?"

"Lieutenant Brian Carahan, Charlie company Fourth Recon Battalion. What unit are you guys with?"

Nunez swallowed and answered wearily, "First platoon, Alpha company, Fourth of the One-Twelfth Infantry, sir."

The Lieutenant gave Nunez an odd, puzzled expression. "Alpha Fourth of the One-Twelfth? Aren't you the guys who killed that prisoner? I thought y'all got arrested already."

Nunez dropped his weapon. He felt his mouth fall open. His body sagged and he fell to his knees. He felt dizzy and exhausted, as if all the fatigue he fought off the last five days suddenly caught up. For a moment he thought he was going to puke. His hands covered his face and he thought, *No, no, no.*

"Everything we just did," he whispered. "All the shit we went through, and that's all you ask about."

"What? Speak up, Sergeant."

Nunez took his helmet off and let it fall to the side. In the field behind him, Marines shouted orders and warnings to one another. One man yelled, "If you think he's still alive, stick your muzzle into his eyeball! He can't play dead if you do that shit!"

Above them, rotors beat the air. Nunez glanced up to see three Apaches crisscross the sky and a lone Apache fly north. Probably the Apache that killed D'Angelo and almost killed Quincy, even as it saved the platoon from being overrun.

Nunez looked at D'Angelo and thought, *You beat this, D. You died a hero, not a criminal. Good for you.*

Nunez closed his eyes and tried to force the pain and anger from his mind. During the fight, he had forgotten the prisoner's murder. He had forgotten that to some people, he wasn't a soldier who had helped lead his men through a horrible fight inside their own country. Instead, he was just a criminal who belonged in prison.

"Goddamn it," he mumbled.

"Sergeant Nunez?" the lieutenant asked. "What did you say?"

Nunez answered with angry, defeated silence.

EPILOGUE

"So that's it?" Gorham asked. "We're fucked and we can't do anything about it? It's a done deal?"

Nunez shook his head. "Not exactly. It's more complicated than that."

Nunez looked around at the soldiers in the back of the five-ton truck. Eleven men, including him. All that was left of thirty-eight who had started the advance into Arriago two mornings earlier. Not all the others were dead, but many were. Nunez didn't know yet how many of the badly wounded from the last fight would survive. Three of the eleven in the truck were slightly wounded and should have been evacuated, but wanted to stay with the platoon.

All the soldiers who had first moved into the towns were being pulled out and sent back to Edinburgh. The order to load up on trucks came less than an hour after the last shot was fired. Regular Army troops and Marines had taken over the entire operation. Small convoys carrying platoons of infantry and scouts headed out from downtown every twenty minutes or so. Rumor had it that Guard soldiers were already being flown back to their armories from Edinburgh, but Nunez wasn't buying that one.

"I'm not telling you guys to give up," Nunez said to the truckload of anxious men. "But I'm telling you it's bad. The video makes it look like we murdered that guy after everything had calmed down. And it makes him out to be a regular working guy with a family, not a cartel fighter."

Someone muttered, "Shit." Nunez took a few moments to look each soldier in the eye before he went on.

"Guys, most of us are going to get arrested. Some of us are going to be charged with murder. When Lieutenant Quincy and I found out about the video, we decided that me, him and D'Angelo would take the hit for it. Now that D'Angelo's dead, and Lieutenant Quincy… "

Nunez swallowed. He didn't know what to say about Quincy. Quincy had been hurt worse than they first thought. His heart stopped as he was being loaded into a medic Humvee downtown. The medics brought him back, but Nunez didn't know if he survived the trip to Edinburgh. Quincy was so damn strong, though. If anyone could survive this wound, it was Quincy.

"We'll have to wait and see what the lieutenant says," Nunez said. "But I promise you, I'm going to tell the investigators that I ordered the platoon to burn the prisoner's body. D'Angelo was out of his mind when he killed the guy, and the cover up was my fault. Allenby, Eckert and Mireles burned the prisoner, and two of them are dead. I'm going to say I ordered Eckert to burn the prisoner, so he won't go down for it. The worst thing any of you did was kick the guy's ass. They'll say you should have reported it, but you can say I ordered you not to. The only people who should have to worry about going to prison for this are me and maybe Lieutenant Quincy. If he lives."

After Nunez finished speaking, the other soldiers sat on the benches in silence. A few smoked cigarettes, Gordon held a cracker in his hand but didn't eat it. Nobody looked at Nunez. His men focused on the floor.

"Don't get me wrong, guys," Nunez said. "We'll all probably get arrested. No matter what, every one of you is gonna get dragged into the investigation. You might get threatened with prison for withholding information, you're going to go through hell even if you never spend a day in jail. But you'll be okay in the end, I think. Just stick to the story. I ordered you guys to stay quiet about the murder. You didn't murder the prisoner and you couldn't report it. It wasn't your fault."

Gordon said, "It wasn't your fault either, Sarge. You shouldn't go down for it. Not by yourself, anyway."

"It was my fault, Gordo. I'm one of the guys in charge. I'm supposed to stop shit like that from happening. And it's alright if I get locked up. It is. Going to prison might be my best option anyway. There's no way I'll keep my job as a cop if I've been charged with covering up a murder. And I'm sure my wife left me when I took off for the armory in Round Rock. I got nothing to go home to. No wife, no family, no job. In prison they'll probably put me in protective custody or something. It won't be so bad. Maybe I'll get a free education out of it. If I ever get out I can be a doctor or massage therapist or something."

Nobody laughed. Nunez shrugged and said, "Lighten up, guys. It'll be okay."

A few men turned away. Conway mumbled, "I didn't even fucking do anything. I was driving a Humvee when you guys killed the prisoner. I never even saw him. I shouldn't go to jail for shit. It's not fair."

Nunez turned away. Conway was right, it wasn't his fault and it wasn't fair that he should be facing jail time. But it was what it was. Nothing could change their situation now.

"When do you think they'll arrest us, Sarge?" Sergeant Cuevas asked. "Like in a week or something?"

Nunez looked down and shook his head slowly. "No. Like when we get to Edinburgh."

A minute of silence passed. Nunez kept his eyes down. He felt ashamed. His men were in danger of going to prison because of his failure to lead.

"Sarjant Nunez."

Nunez looked up. Berisha squinted at him through swollen eyes, head turned slightly so he could see past the bandage covering one side of his face.

"My father and his brothers fought the Serbians during our wars in Kosova and Macedonia. Terrible crimes were committed, by both sides. Such things happen in war, Sarjant. My people know this, the Serbians know this. Those who fought to free the Albanian people are not considered criminals by the Albanian people, nor are the Serb soldiers considered criminals by the Serbs."

Nunez looked around the truck at the other survivors. Most weren't looking at Berisha, the few who were seemed annoyed or puzzled.

Berisha went on, "Do you know of the Ottoman Empire's attack on Austria? The Turkish army almost reached Vienna before Christian armies turned them away. Many Turkish soldiers were tortured and killed by the victors. But today, do the Austrians remember those terrible acts committed by their defenders in 1683? No, Sarjant Nunez. They do not. They know only that their soldiers protected their homeland. And they are grateful."

Nunez squinted back, wondering *What the fuck does that have to do with anything?* He gave Berisha a deadpan look and asked, "Berisha... why are you telling me this?"

"Yeah, Berisha," Cuevas said. "You're a Muslim. You should be pissed at the Austrians for killing your people."

Berisha shook his head. "Those are not my people, Sarjant Cuevas." Gesturing at his comrades, he said, "You are my people. Texans are my people. Americans are my people. Arriago is our Vienna. And we repelled those who tried to conquer it. If I am to be imprisoned for defending my people, so be it. The accusation of 'war criminal' will last only my lifetime. But the title 'defender of my people' remains forever."

He looked straight at Nunez. "I am happy with this, Sarjant Nunez. I defended my people."

A few soldiers nodded understanding. Nunez gave Berisha a sad smile.

"You're damn right you did."

Voices yelled outside. A fresh-looking young soldier from another unit climbed onto the tailgate to announce, "We're set to go! You boys ready to head back to civilization?"

Nunez's men gave him blank stares in response. Nunez gave him a slow nod, no words. The soldier crinkled his eyebrows and muttered, "You guys don't seem too excited to be getting out of here," before he jumped down.

The truck's doors opened and two soldiers climbed into the cab. Engines rumbled to life. Orders buzzed over the truck's radio. Nunez and his men breathed in exhaust for a minute or two, then the truck lurched forward and knocked the soldiers into one another.

The small convoy moved north on Nogales. Nunez looked out the back of the truck, watched anxious soldiers and Marines mill around Humvees, trucks, M1A2 Abrams tanks and M2 Bradley fighting vehicles. The afternoon sun shone on three full battalions clearing every last structure in Arriago. The city limits sign slid by the side of the truck and faded out of view among the sea of trucks, tanks and armored personnel carriers. For almost a mile north of town, soldiers and their vehicles spread along both sides of the road. Nunez shook his head and asked himself a question.

Why couldn't we just wait one more day? Was it worth losing all those fucking guys, just so we could say we took the town back instead of the regular Army?

Soldiers rocked back and forth in tune with the truck's starts and stops as it wound through the checkpoint north of town. Police officers waved at the convoy as it passed. Nunez didn't wave back. No more brotherhood of law enforcement for him. He had given that up when he told Quincy to burn the prisoner's body.

Nunez leaned back against the seat and rested. He realized this truck ride might be the last he'd ever have as a free man. Next time, he'd probably be in cuffs and leg irons, sitting next to some convicted rapist in the back of a prison bus.

Whatever. Maybe Berisha was right. If he spent the rest of his life in prison, that was that. Someday he'd be remembered as a soldier who did what he had to for his country.

That thought helped him nod off for half the thirty minute trip back to Edinburgh.

****

"Hey Sergeant Nunez. We're here."

Nunez forced his eyes open. A gate and portable towers that hadn't been there when he last saw Edinburgh loomed ahead of the lead vehicle. Military police stood on both sides of the gate. Belts of concertina wire stretched from the gate. Inside the wire, hundreds of military vehicles and dozens of police cars filled the mall parking lot. The beating of rotors increased and ebbed as a huge Chinook helicopter took off from blank section of parking lot and flew into the distance. Nunez felt a little disgusted when he saw "Forward Operating Base Edinburgh" stenciled onto a huge wooden sign beside the gate, over the words, "THIS IS A SALUTE ZONE." Garrison had broken out, in the middle of a real war inside the United States.

Nunez sat back. He heard guards walk down the line from the gate, checking the ID cards of every soldier in each truck ahead. A few of his men dug out their IDs and got them ready. Nunez didn't bother.

An MP climbed onto the tailgate and yelled an order.

"Everyone get your I –!"

The MP's eyes rose above the tailgate and he cut himself off. Eleven filthy, angry, bloodstained soldiers with blackened, unshaven faces stared back at him. Nunez wondered if the MPs were about to order them out and arrest them all. Instead the young military police officer looked around at everyone, then climbed down without a word. A minute later the convoy rolled through the gate.

Their truck halted with a blast of air brakes outside the main doors. Nunez heard cheering. He reached over and unhooked the troop strap stretched above the tailgate, stood up and looked out from the back of the truck.

Combat soldiers from different units climbed down from the other trucks as support troops shouted and clapped. Civilians wearing USO T-shirts stood behind a desk, handed bottles of Gatorade and bags of cookies to their returning heroes. Majors and colonels shook hands with several of the men.

The truck driver and his assistant dropped the tailgate, then stood back and waited for Nunez's men to dismount. Soldiers behind Nunez rose and grabbed their gear. Nunez told them, "Hold on. Wait for the dog and pony show to finish."

Shouted congratulations rang out down the line of trucks as men filed into the mall. Nunez sat back and waited for the commotion to quiet down. He didn't know where he was supposed to go anyway, and didn't want to climb down in the middle of that crowd and wander around like a lost puppy. And the last thing he wanted was for anyone to pat him on the back and tell him what a good job he had done.

"First platoon, Alpha Fourth of the One-Twelfth! Where are you?"

Nunez gave a resigned sigh and closed his eyes. He forced himself to his feet and leaned out of the truck. A short, fat captain stood outside the mall's doors, searching the crowd. Nunez mumbled "Fuck" and managed a dejected wave.

"Here, sir. We're right here."

The captain puffed up and put his hands on his hips. "You men come with me."

Nunez looked back at his men. "Here we go, guys. Hang in there."

He climbed down the tailgate, then took weapons and packs handed down by his soldiers. The men climbed down two at a time. Berisha and Cowan had minor leg wounds, not enough to keep them off their feet but enough to make them struggle to get down from the truck and limp away. Support troops and civilians cheered, but Nunez heard a few *Goddams* and *Man, those guys look fucked up* from the crowd.

After the men climbed down and Nunez helped them lift their packs, he noticed one soldier in the crowd of fans whisper to another. The second one whispered back with a questioning look on his face. The first man nodded. The second soldier stopped clapping, looked at Nunez and turned to another beside him. The whisper was passed, the cheering tapered off. By the time the last men climbed down the cheers and claps had stopped. Nunez's men found themselves surrounded by a throng of silent men, staring at them like they were exotic animals in a zoo.

Nunez looked over his men. Filthy faces and hands, uniforms torn and stained black, bandages on arms, legs and heads. Dirt-crusted, battered weapons hung from slings on their chests, equally dirty packs were slung over shoulders. They had taken their helmets off, exposing overgrown, matted hair. All looked on the verge of collapse from exhaustion. Reddened eyes were barely open and heads sagged. They almost looked beaten.

Nunez leaned in close to them. "Pick your heads up. We won that fight. Look proud of yourselves."

Heads and eyes rose. Nunez nodded, turned around and walked to the waiting captain. The captain squinted and pointed to each of Nunez's soldiers, making a count.

"Is this all of you?"

Nunez looked back. "Yes sir. We're all here."

The captain's eyes widened. "Eleven men? Where's the rest?"

Nunez gave him a tired, exasperated look. "They're casualties, sir."

"All of them? No more are coming?"

Nunez said, "All of them, sir. No more are coming."

"Jesus Christ. Alright, let's go."

The captain opened a door to the mall and walked in. Nunez grabbed the door to hold it open and a hand jerked it out of his grasp. He turned to see one of the support soldiers staring at him.

"I got it, Sergeant. Good luck to you guys. We're pulling for you."

Nunez gave a slight nod, waited for his men to walk in and followed them. The door led into the main area of the mall, a short distance from the 56th Brigade Combat Team headquarters at Sears. Soldiers and Marines were everywhere, running messages back and forth, eating or sleeping on tables and benches in the common area of the mall.

All the chatter and hustle of activity stopped as Nunez led his men toward Sears. People stopped what they were doing and watched the small group of survivors marching, not in step because a couple limped instead of marched. Nunez tried to ignore the eyes on them but still felt the sensation of being an oddity on display.

They walked through the wide doors into Sears. Now most of the men running around were officers instead of enlisted. They stopped and stared as well. Nunez ignored them and focused on the fat captain in front. He led them through the main showroom, past customer service to an office with "Security" on the door.

The captain held the office door open but didn't go inside. Nunez and his men walked into the small room. Inside were a table, a bench and a single chair. As the men dropped their packs the captain said, "Wait here, someone will be here to talk to you guys soon."

The captain closed the door. Nunez's men sat on whatever was closest. A few spoke quietly to their nearest comrades, nobody got comfortable. Nunez stayed on his feet by the door. Minutes passed, nothing happened.

"Sergeant Nunez."

Nunez turned to see Corley looking up at him. "They didn't take our weapons or ammo. Think that means anything?"

Nunez thought it over and decided not to be hopeful. "No, Doc. I don't think it means anything."

Harsh footsteps approached. The doorknob turned and door cracked a bit. Nunez heard a booming voice say, "No Captain, there's no need. You can take them yourself." Nunez didn't recognize the voice, but it carried the weight and authority of a senior officer. He guessed it was some anonymous colonel from division staff.

The door opened and a tall, white-haired man with a Beretta pistol in a thigh holster walked in. The man had an air of dignity about him, like he didn't have to yell and scream to get things done. A single black star adorned his rank insignia patch. The man's nose crinkled for an instant and Nunez saw him recoil slightly, but to his credit the man brought himself back under control and ignored the soldiers' stench. Nunez had never seen the man before, but he recognized the name on the man's uniform. Brigadier General Koba, commander of the Texas Army National Guard.

Nunez brought himself to attention and said, "Platoon, atten-hut."

The men rose and shuffled into the position of attention. General Koba waited for them to finish, then said quietly, "Stand at ease, men."

Everyone moved to parade rest, feet spread and hands at the small of their back. Nunez went through the motions, showing respect because military protocol demanded it. He didn't think much of General Koba. As far as he knew, Koba hadn't been anywhere near the fighting, but he was about to tell Nunez what he and his men should have done in combat. Nunez felt the resentment build as he waited for the inevitable.

Koba spoke in a soft voice, "First, I want you to know your casualties are being taken care of. Everything that can possibly be done for your wounded is being done. Our first concern is for the lives of your men. Understood?"

Men nodded and mumbled, "Yes sir." Nunez asked, "Sir, do you know anything about Lieutenant Quincy's condition?"

"I know that he left here alive on a medevac chopper and should have landed at Fort Sam Houston by now. Unfortunately, I don't have any updates. Specialist Eckert died here. I don't know the status on the others, but some of them are in bad shape. I'm praying for them."

Nunez had an acid thought. *Well, isn't that fucking special. You're praying our wounded will survive so you can put them in prison. Fuck you, General Koba.*

Nunez fought to hide his reaction to the General's words. Koba looked down for a moment and pursed his lips, like he was searching for the right thing to say. Nunez wished he would just come right out and tell them what everyone knew he was going to tell them.

"Men, there are some things you should know," Koba said. "I'm sure by now you've heard about the video. Maybe some of you have even seen it. You know the body of the prisoner was brought back here, but you might not know the FBI has it now. And you might not know this has become a high-level investigation that has the President's attention. Or the President and Joint Chiefs of Staff have demanded that those responsible be immediately arrested."

Nunez sighed and looked to the side. Nobody spoke. Nunez finally said, "We knew there was a video and that a body came back here, sir. That's all."

"Uh huh. Well, I don't see how this news could surprise you. We've all been trained on the Law of Land Warfare and Geneva Convention. We know the standards of conduct we're sworn to uphold. When we fail to live up to those standards, we expect to suffer just punishment. Whatever happens to you from this point forward, I expect you to own up to it. Either to the killing, or the intentional effort to hide it."

Conway sobbed out loud. Nunez looked at him and saw his eyes water. Twenty years old, and Conway was facing prison for a murder he didn't commit and a cover up he didn't order.

Nunez bit his lip. "Sir, nobody needs to pay for anything except –"

"Stop!" Koba ordered. "Don't say anything else about it. When I testify, I'm going to tell the truth. And I don't want to raise my hand and say you incriminated yourself. So don't say anything about what allegedly happened. Just listen."

Nunez blinked in surprise. Koba said, "When this video surfaced, I was ordered by the Pentagon to identify those responsible and have them detained as soon as possible. I'm complying with that order. As soon as the soldiers in the video have been positively identified, I will have them detained."

Nunez cocked an eyebrow. *What the hell did that mean?*

Koba continued, "Unfortunately for the Pentagon, we've been a little busy with this war and haven't had the opportunity to conduct a proper forensic analysis on the video. We have opinions about who's on that video, but nothing definite. There has even been speculation the soldier who committed the murder was later killed by friendly fire from an Apache. But we don't know for certain."

Nunez looked down and swallowed hard. He wasn't sure where General Koba was going with his speech and didn't want to misunderstand anything. But at the very least, it wasn't what Nunez expected to hear.

"I have responded to the Pentagon and told them my priority, by far, is the successful prosecution of this war and protection of American lives. Criminal investigations can wait. But don't get me wrong, men. I *will* comply fully with this order, and I *will* detain those determined to be responsible. But I'll do it when the real work of this war is done, and not a second before then. Understood?"

Nunez and his men mumbled "Yes sir" again. Koba nodded and said, "Good. One thing I didn't tell the Pentagon, because it's something they should know already, is that they're fucking crazy if they think I'm going to jump through my ass to arrest men who beat hostile fighters inside Texas. At least, they should know I'm not about to have anyone arrested before they get some well-deserved time with their families."

Nunez tilted his head. That statement was a shock.

Koba went on, saying, "You men fought the hardest fight, in the hardest hit town, against the toughest and most determined enemy force. You suffered the worst losses and experienced the worst horrors. You have earned the right to go home to your families as heroes. That might only last a day before someone knocks on your door and takes you away, but that one day will be one of the most precious you will ever have. I am not going to take that day away from you.

"So here are my orders. You will go to the landing zone and wait for a helicopter to take you back to your armory in Round Rock. When you get there, turn in your weapons and go home. Spend a day with your parents, wives and children. Make it a day to treasure forever. When that knock on the door comes, walk out of your house with pride and dignity. Cooperate with the investigation. Whether or not any crime was committed, you voluntarily fought a horrible, brutal war to defend our own land and people. Nobody can ever take that from you. And if you do find yourself behind bars somewhere, know that I, Governor Mathieu, every officer in your chain of command and the entire state of Texas will fight for your release. Hooah?"

Everyone gave an enthusiastic "Hooah!", even Nunez. He had a hard time believing it, but it sure as hell sounded like they were free men, for the time being anyway.

"Alright. My assistant Captain Petrovik will take you to the landing zone. If anyone without a badge tries to give you orders to do anything other than what I said, tell them General Koba said they can go fuck themselves. From this point on, you follow my orders and no one else's. Good luck to you. You've made me proud to be a Texas soldier."

Koba stepped forward and took Nunez's hand. Nunez returned the handshake with a weak, halfhearted squeeze. He still half expected the worst case, for MPs to rush into the room and start throwing cuffs on his people. Koba patted Nunez's shoulder, said "Take care of these men, Sergeant," and went around the room to every soldier. When the handshakes and wishes of good luck were finished, he walked out the door and yelled for Captain Petrovik.

Nunez gave his men a look of disbelief. A few smiled at him. Conway was in tears. They weren't out of the woods yet, but they had survived the war and this first hurdle. They were going home.

Petrovik stuck his head in the door. "Get ready to leave. I'll be right back."

Nunez fidgeted, wanting to get out of Edinburgh before someone changed their mind and decided to arrest him. The few minutes before Petrovik came back to the room felt like an hour.

The door creaked open. Petrovik said, "Come with me."

The soldiers filed out of the room, back through Sears and into the common area of the mall. This time several soldiers and Marines approached and shook hands with the men as they passed.

"Good luck to y'all. Stay safe."

"We're praying for you guys, don't give up."

Nunez nodded back to the well-wishers, a few of his soldiers gave quiet thanks. Captain Petrovik led them out the door toward the landing zone, a roped-off square in the parking lot. An olive drab Chinook helicopter sat on the LZ, its twin rotors beating the air into a racket that could be heard for miles. As the platoon passed scattered troops and clusters of vehicles, Nunez saw soldiers and police officers stop what they were doing and stare at him and his men. A few spectators climbed onto the hoods or roofs of Humvees to watch the platoon pass.

Nunez's breath quickened. *Is that our ride out of here?* But as they closed the distance he saw several platoons staged outside the white engineer tape that marked the borders of the LZ. The platoon at the head of the line was on its feet with weapons and packs slung, ready to go. Nunez deflated. Depending on what the delay was between flights, his platoon might be waiting for hours before their turn. A lot could happen during that time.

Captain Petrovik stopped the platoon fifty feet from the LZ, away from the waiting platoons. A staff sergeant stood at a gap in the engineer tape holding a clipboard. Nunez watched a helicopter crewman wearing aviation fatigues and a flight helmet jog from the back of the Chinook to the staff sergeant. The staff sergeant pointed at something on the clipboard, the crewman read it and gave a thumbs up. The staff sergeant and crewman both gestured to the waiting platoon. The crewman jogged to the rear of the Chinook, the platoon followed in two columns.

Soldiers in the platoon raised triumphant fists as they headed to the helicopter. Nunez saw some of them open their mouths and scream words that were lost in the crushing noise of the rotors. Men in the parking lot clapped and shouted unheard cheers of support.

The departing platoon loaded up. The rear ramp rose and a crew member sat behind his M240 machine gun. A minute later the Chinook's engines revved higher, blowing dust and sand in all directions. Nunez and his men lowered their heads and covered their faces with one hand as the Chinook lifted off and headed north.

By the time that helicopter disappeared from view another headed in. Petrovik conferred with the staff sergeant before it landed. The next platoon in line rose to their feet and prepared to mount up in the helicopter.

The Chinook floated to a landing and the rear gunner jogged to the staff sergeant. They conferred briefly and the staff sergeant waved a platoon forward. Nunez's platoon, not the platoon that was ready to go. It took a moment to sink in. Nunez and his men had been moved to the front of the line.

Nunez's men rose and jogged onto the LZ. The crewman led them to the ramp. Nunez stopped and turned around to count his men as they loaded up. What he saw made him freeze for a moment, dumbfounded.

Almost everyone in view was on their feet, clapping or pumping fists in the air. Many held weapons over their heads and bellowed words Nunez couldn't hear. He forgot to count the men as they rushed past him. General Koba stood at a distance, surrounded by his staff. He raised his hand and gave a plain, simple wave. Beside him Nunez saw another soldier, holding one arm over his head. It took Nunez a moment to recognize him.

Sergeant First Class Lacey. Nunez hesitated, then waved back before heading into the Chinook. His men stared through the opening at the back of the helicopter toward the sea of cheering soldiers. They looked as dumbfounded as Nunez felt.

Nunez counted his men and sat down. The ramp rose, the gunner sat behind his gun and Nunez felt the vibrations through his feet as the pilots powered up and lifted off. Nunez watched the cheering soldiers drop from view as the Chinook rose.

He looked around at his men. Their expressions ranged from stoic to hopeful, pained to relieved. Nunez wasn't going to allow himself to feel relieved or hopeful, and he sure as hell wasn't stoic about anything. He understood that what the platoon received was a reprieve, not a pardon. They were going to pay for the prisoner's murder sometime. Just not right this moment.

Edinburgh faded into the distance. After a few minutes, men nodded off. There wasn't much else to do in the back of a helicopter. Movies that showed soldiers having calm conversations in a flying chopper were pure fantasy. You couldn't hear yourself if you bellowed at the top of your lungs.

Nunez stayed awake for half an hour until the heat, noise and vibration lulled him to sleep. He woke to a slap on his arm. After straining to get his eyes open, he saw a crewman standing above him pointing to words scribbled on a dry erase board.

round rock 5 min

Nunez nodded and stuck a thumb up. The crewman went to a soldier on the other side of the helicopter. Nunez turned to Gordon in the seat beside him, slapped his thigh until he woke up, pointed at his watch and showed him five outstretched fingers. Gordon nodded and passed the word.

Through the back of the helicopter Nunez glimpsed the setting sun as the pilot brought the Chinook in a circle around the armory. Unlike some Guard armories that were dead center in the middle of their towns, Round Rock's armory was at the edge of open fields and woods just outside the city limits. The pilots had space behind the armory to touch down. The helicopter leveled off, hung motionless and began its descent.

Nunez looked out the window. No activity, nothing going on around the armory. He had worried that dozens of police cars would be there waiting to put them in jail. Instead, it seemed as if nobody knew or cared that they were coming.

The Chinook touched down with a slight sideways shudder. Nunez waited for the ramp to drop and rear gunner to motion them out. He stood to the side so he could count his men again, then walked off the ramp behind the last one. The gunner stopped him, shook his hand and mouthed with exaggerated words, *Good luck.*

Nunez mouthed *Thank you* back to him. He walked toward the armory behind his men, all the while being pelted by dirt and tiny pebbles being whipped around by the rotor blast. By the time they reached the door, the helicopter was taking off.

The loading bay door whirred open on its electric motor. Sergeant First Class Borden, their full-time soldier who ran the unit between drills, stood inside the armory shielding his eyes from flying dirt. Some full-timers were sharp, some were worthless losers soaking up a paycheck. Borden was the latter.

The eleven soldiers walked inside and Borden lowered the door. "Man, I'm glad to see you guys," he said to Nunez. "Shit's been going crazy around here since you left. Battalion's been calling every day wanting numbers and locations for all our people, and I haven't been able to tell them shit. You know nobody's sent me a personnel status since you guys left? I mean, not even one time. This morning Captain Harcrow called and said everyone would be coming back today or tomorrow. I told him that was great, 'cause I need you to get on some of these reports that need to be done."

Nunez gave him a blank stare and said nothing. Borden's gaze shifted from Nunez's face to his uniform, then he looked at everyone else and realized what condition they were in. Epiphany lit his face.

"Damn, you guys are dirty. They didn't have showers or nothing out there for you?"

Nunez looked at Corley. They exchanged unbelieving expressions, and Nunez walked past Borden toward the administrative office. The men followed. Borden tagged along beside Nunez, seeming oblivious to what had happened on the border for the last week.

"Nunez, you have all the numbers I need, right? We have some spreadsheets to work on. But I guess you'll want to shower and change before we get started. I mean, our office furniture is new. You know, we don't want to get dirt on it or anything."

Nunez walked into the office, popped the bipod on his carbine and set it on the floor. He ordered, "Everyone put your weapons in a row here with mine. Ammo can go in that corner."

His men set their weapons in a neat row. Borden watched them and said, "You know we can't store ammo here. I don't care what you do with it, but we can't keep it in the armory." He leaned down and picked up a carbine. "These things are filthy. You're cleaning them before I put them in the arms room."

Nunez dropped his magazines in the corner. His soldiers dumped their magazines in a messy pile on top of it. Borden put the carbine down and huffed, "I just fucking told you you can't leave ammo here. Get rid of it."

Nunez asked him, "Where'd you put our car keys?"

Borden blinked rapidly. "They're in my desk."

"Which drawer?"

"I put first platoon's in the middle right one. Why?"

Nunez walked past him to the desk, opened the drawer until it stopped and then yanked on it until it broke off its rails and came all the way out. He flipped the drawer and dumped the keys on the desk.

"Everyone grab your keys. Make it quick."

His men crowded in and dug through the keys. Nunez took his after they retrieved theirs. More than twenty sets of keys remained. More than twenty men, killed or badly wounded.

"Let's go."

Nunez walked out of the office. Behind him, Borden asked, "What the fuck are y'all doing? You can't just dump this shit here and take off."

Nunez thought, *General Koba says to go fuck yourself.* But he kept his mouth closed and walked to the parking lot. When they were all outside, he said, "Huddle up, guys."

The men closed in. Nunez put his arms around Gorham and Berisha, the two closest men. Other soldiers did the same, until they were in a tight circle. Nunez looked them all in the eyes and said, "Guys, go home. General Koba was right, we need to make this last day with our families count. When they come for you, if they come for you, don't fight or cry about it. Show dignity and pride. We defended America, guys. We defended Texas. Nobody meant for that shit with the prisoner to happen, and it doesn't take away what we did for each other and our people."

He squeezed Gorham and Berisha's shoulders. "We'll be together again soon. Til then, good luck and stay safe. I'll call you tomorrow to make sure you got home. Hooah?"

The men answered, "Hooah." Nunez stood up. Without warning, Berisha turned to him and gave him a hug. He returned it, and as soon as Berisha let go Gorham jumped in. Then Corley. Then Cowan.

Every survivor hugged Nunez. He saw that they were all hugging each other as well. They looked like a loving family leaving a once-a-year gathering.

Behind them, Borden yelled, "Hey! You guys can't leave until I get accountability and the captain says you can leave!"

Nunez turned and walked to Borden as the soldiers said their last goodbyes. He pulled out a notepad and asked Borden, "You want accountability? You want our numbers? Here they are."

He flipped to a folded-over page. "Just from my platoon, nineteen KIA. Seven wounded and evacuated. Some of those might die. Out of the eleven of us here, three are walking wounded. We had one attachment from a different unit who was killed by an air strike. The same air strike blew Lieutenant Quincy's arm off. All of us who lived will probably wind up in prison for murdering a prisoner. So how's that for numbers? Good enough?"

Borden gulped. "Holy shit. Your losses were that bad? Nobody told me anything. I didn't know."

Nunez tore open his body armor and shrugged it off his shoulders. "Second platoon lost ten killed, I think. Third platoon never fired a shot or lost anyone. You'll find out more later. Right now, we're going home. If you have any brains, you won't try to stop us."

Nunez turned and walked to his Jeep. Borden didn't say a word. Nunez unlocked the doors and threw his pack and body armor in the back, then climbed in the driver's seat. His men waved as they drove past him. Nunez pulled out of his spot, waited for cars to pass and drove out of the parking lot, heading to Houston. Three and a half hours to home.

The first half hour on the road, all he did was look at American and Texas flags dotting the highway, and think. No listening to music or news. Just dead time, the first quiet moments alone since arriving at the armory Saturday morning. It was Wednesday afternoon now. His entire universe had been transformed during the last four days.

He wondered if his wife would be home when he got there. He had no doubt she had followed through with her threat to move out if he reported for duty this time. She was sick of the military, sick of Nunez's trips to war. Sometimes their entire marriage seemed like a series of arguments about it. She insisted he put the Army before his family, he insisted his service was part of taking care of his family. They never reached a compromise.

She might have come back, though. She had to have seen the news about how bad the fighting was. She loved him. If she thought he was in danger, she'd be there for him. He had to fuel up on the way, and at the gas station he'd buy a charger for his phone and call her. She'd answer this time. He needed her to answer.

But what would she say when he told her about the prisoner? Would she think less of him for his snap decision to lie about it? Or would she tell him what she told him before Iraq and Afghanistan, *I don't care what you have to do to. Just stay alive.*

He rolled his shoulders and tried to relax. She was a smart woman. From listening to him she knew enough about war to understand that things happened sometimes. Things that should be expected when thousands of men are using thousands of weapons to kill one another in any way possible. She'd forgive him for his failures. Maybe.

Hey, maybe this whole thing will slide off. They might just decide to drop it.

Nunez let the thought settle, then got angry at himself for even considering it. There was no way in hell he wasn't going to prison. Maybe it wouldn't be for long, but he was going. And that meant dishonorable discharge, having his rank stripped, all of that. He'd be kicked out in disgrace.

Nunez's fingers tightened on the steering wheel. He told himself, *Stop think-*

ing about that. It's going to happen whether you dwell on it or not, just take it as it comes. No need to put yourself through it now. Someone else will put you through it later.

Nunez reached to the radio and pushed the knob. Music might get his mind off his situation. The radio was tuned to his favorite Austin station, one that always played good rock. But the station wasn't playing music. Instead, several DJs were having a discussion.

"–now is good. The President says major combat operations are over, the invaders have been killed or forced back into Mexico. I personally don't think it's over, but that's still good news, isn't it?"

"It is, Rick. We all know it's going to take a while to search through all these towns for any bad guys who might be hiding, and who knows how many dead civilians they'll find. There's still going to be bad news coming, but at least the worst part of the war is over."

"Yeah, true that. So what do you guys think will happen to those guys on that video? Think they'll get off? Or are they screwed like everyone says they are?"

Nunez's eyes jerked to the radio, as if he could see the DJs talking on it. A DJ said, "Oh, they're screwed all right. They deserve to be screwed. I mean, I know it was a bad war and all that, but damn. How do you justify doing that to someone? These guys are trained, they get paid to fight. They should have been able to handle that situation without going crazy and killing some innocent guy."

A third voice jumped in. "Whoa, dog, hold on! Where do you get that this guy was innocent? Did you hear what happened right before they captured him? That wasn't some innocent guy. Come on, man."

"Hey man, I watched that video just like you. That guy didn't even have a weapon. And those so-called 'soldiers' had plenty of time to calm down after they got attacked, or whatever it was that supposedly happened to them. I mean, we saw them attack that house. And by the way, what kind of a moron goes shooting into a house that civilians might be inside of? But they tear up this house, kill those hostages that are allegedly tied up, take all the bodies outside, capture this guy and then kill him? How long did it take to bring those people outside? Fifteen minutes or so? And after that, they're supposedly still so charged up they go crazy and kill the guy? I don't buy it. Don't get me wrong, I guess I'd get mad too if I screwed up and killed a bunch of innocent people. But I wouldn't go grab the nearest Mexican laborer and murder him to make myself feel better."

"Man, you're insane. You think it was that simple, or that the video shows exactly what happened? I guess you've never heard the term 'propaganda,' have you?"

"I'm hearing propaganda every day, man. Every time I hear the government tell that BS cover story, that these guys committed this murder 'in the heat of battle.' We saw the fight was over. They had time to calm down. If I had been there, I wouldn't have done anything like that. So I don't have any sympathy."

A horn blasted ahead. Nunez looked up from the radio and was shocked to see that he was halfway into an oncoming lane. He jerked the steering wheel right and a pickup missed him by a foot.

"Holy cow," a DJ said. "How the hell do you know what you would have done if you had been there? Listen, dude, I'll admit I'm a coward. The last thing I'll ever do is put on a uniform, pick up a gun and go fight in a war. But I'm up front about it, I ain't about to say 'In a war I'd do this' or 'I'd never do that.' That's nuts, man. You don't know what happened to those guys. And you don't know how it would affect you. You go ahead and volunteer to throw the switch on these guys, as far as I'm concerned they fought a hard fight for us. I'm on their side until I find out they murdered someone just for fun."

"See, that's why soldiers got away with all those crimes they committed in Iraq and Afghanistan," the first DJ said. "They were running around raping and murdering people, and guys like you give them a pass because 'they're protecting us.' What a load of crap. It was wrong for them to murder people over there, it's wrong for them to do it here. I'm not giving any of them a break. They murdered someone, screw them. They don't deserve to be called soldiers. They're more like gang members."

Nunez hit the search button so hard he almost broke it. *All the radio stations aren't like that,* he told himself. *Other stations are on our side.* The next station had music. Nunez felt relieved, until he realized the music was just a lead-in.

"Good evening, folks, glad you could join us tonight. I'm Bobby-O with the news, and we know what the news is, right? The war is over. Our guys won. First thing I want to say is, 'God bless our troops.' Thank you guys for what you did. We've heard that dozens of our soldiers were killed down there, along with hundreds of civilians and, like, a hundred and twenty cops and a bunch of firefighters. Our troops are awesome, they went down there right away and did what had to be done."

Nunez breathed in and out, trying to bring his heart rate down. The DJ went on, "Alright, let's take a few callers. I'd like to hear some opinions. First caller is, uh, Larry from Leander. Go ahead, Larry."

"Bobby, I want to give a shout out to my brother in the National Guard. Sergeant Edward Masten, from the 155th Artillery Battalion. He went down south on Monday and we haven't heard anything from him since. If you're listening Ed, we're all behind you and we know you're doing your best down there. Stay safe and come home."

"Thanks Larry, good luck to you and your brother. Next caller, Will from Bastrop. You're on, Will."

"Hey Bobby, I just want to say all this bull corn about those guys killing a prisoner is a joke. Who cares if some cartel guy was murdered? You ask me, we should kill all the prisoners, and then kill all them illegals trying to get across the border."

The DJ cut him off. "We're not going there. Our soldiers aren't going to murder illegals because they're better human beings than that. You're gone, Will. Next caller, Angela from Round Rock. Angela, what's on your mind?"

A sweet, elderly female voice came over the radio. "Hi, Bobby. What's on my mind is that horrible video they've been showing on the news. Do you think it's real? I heard the President said it's real and that he's going to put some of our soldiers in jail over it. Do you know if that's true?"

"Angela, I hate to say this, but the video is real. Some of our soldiers did kill a prisoner and burn the body to cover it up. I'm not going to pass judgment yet, because we don't know all the circumstances behind that prisoner's death, or how much the video was doctored. But it happened, and it has to be dealt with. If those soldiers murdered a prisoner, what else can we do but prosecute them?"

Nunez turned the radio off. *Son of a bitch,* he thought. *There doesn't seem to be much support for us out there.*

He made the turn onto highway 290 in Elgin. Everything there looked so normal. The sun set on a typical small Texas town, full of barbecue restaurants, cowboys in pickup trucks full of cattle feed, teenagers hanging out at Sonic. Nunez looked at his watch. Just a few hours ago he was hunched down below the edge of a berm, shooting into a mass of enemy fighters trying to overrun his platoon. Now he was driving in regular evening traffic in a town that didn't look like it was even aware of what had happened just a few hours away.

Nunez crested a hill. At a gas station on the right side of the road a Texas flag hung beside the front door, a banner strung from the awning. As he passed the gas station, he could read the words on the banner.

DEFEND THOSE WHO DEFENDED US

Nunez put his eyes back on the road. He wasn't about to let that banner get his hopes up. The decision whether to put him and his men away forever didn't rest with the owners of a gas station in Elgin, Texas.

Hours of silence passed. Nunez recounted details of the fight over and over, remembered the expression on the face of every man he lost. He wondered if the murder meant his soldiers who deserved medals for bravery would receive nothing. D'Angelo survived the massacre of his company and stayed in the kill zone to put information out, then fought for three days when he could have gone to the rear and safety at any time. His actions, more than any other soldier's, kept the platoon from being overrun. He died protecting Nunez's side of the perimeter, not protecting himself. Should his heroism be ignored because he lost control and killed someone who they all thought deserved it?

And what about Berisha? Twenty-two years old, an immigrant who struggled with English and was using the GI bill to get through college. He wanted to be a European history professor someday. Berisha had never deployed, the border war was his first. But he did far more than just his duty. He grabbed a grenade to throw it away from his friends and was almost killed when it exploded. When his position was overrun he held his ground and kept fighting. And he didn't kill the prisoner. Berisha deserved recognition, not prison.

Darkness fell. Nunez's thoughts carried him west on Highway 290, past Giddings and Brenham. By the time he reached Prairie View his tank was almost empty. He dreaded the thought of stopping at a gas station and being stared at by horrified civilians. Other soldiers had stared at him like he was an exotic animal, civilians would probably think he was an alien from another planet. And he knew he smelled like crap. But he had to stop. He had to go to the bathroom, too. That meant going inside. Either that, or find somewhere on the side of the road to do it. And Highway 290 was wide open, no place to hide.

Nunez exited the freeway in Prairie View and pulled into a gas station. The first thing he saw was another banner proclaiming, *Defend those who defended us.* The second thing he noticed was the station was so well-lit it was ridiculous. He stopped as close as possible to a pump, then sat in his Jeep for a minute and looked at everyone around. Customers were everywhere. Nunez opened the door, left it open and stayed behind it while he fueled up. A few customers looked his way, nobody paid much attention.

The pump stopped. Nunez put the nozzle back in its housing and pondered whether he had to go into the station. If there was a bottle or something in his Jeep, he could just piss into that. He didn't want to go inside.

Shit. I still have to buy a phone charger.

Nunez closed his door, took a breath and started toward the gas station. As soon as he was clear of the pumps he felt eyes on him. He tried to ignore them. Ahead, a young yuppie couple was about to walk in. The woman was talking on a cell phone. The man looked at Nunez and grabbed his woman's arm to hold her back from the door. When she saw Nunez she recoiled and said, "Oh my God."

Nunez walked past them and pulled the door open. Two middle-aged women behind the counter stared at him with a mixture of surprise, revulsion and fear. One of them reached under the counter. An old farmer in worn coveralls set a beer on the counter, tilted his head down and looked at Nunez over bifocals. His expression was blank. Nunez saw the bathroom sign and headed straight for it. He passed a woman who was bent down looking at magazines and hadn't seen him. Her head jerked and she exclaimed, "What's that God-awful smell?"

Nunez walked into the bathroom. A little boy stood at a urinal with his pants and underwear down around his thighs. The boy's father leaned against the wall behind him. Both of them stared at Nunez in shock. The little boy reached down and pulled up his pants before he finished peeing.

Nunez walked between the boy and his father to an available urinal. The father hustled his son out of the bathroom. Nunez fumbled to get his pants open so he could piss. Then he noticed that his right pant leg was split, from his crotch halfway to his knee. He had no idea how long it had been that way.

He pissed as fast as he could, hoping nobody would walk in. Nobody did. When he got to the sink and looked up into the mirror, he got his first good look at himself in two days.

Holy shit. No wonder they're so freaked out. I look terrible.

Nunez stared at the mirror for a moment, taking in the sight of someone who looked vaguely like him. His reflection had blood and dirt smeared on its face, a swollen upper right lip, five days beard growth, sunken eyes circled by deep bags, and hair matted with dirt, sweat and blood.

He turned on the faucet and scrubbed his hands so hard they felt like they would bleed. Then he put his face near the faucet and rubbed soap and water onto it. A dozen small cuts burned at the touch.

He stuck his head under the water. Red and black mud ran down the drain. He stood up and tore paper towels from the dispenser. Before he got them to his face he saw a teenage boy lean into the bathroom, trying to peak around the doorway. He and Nunez locked eyes. The boy scampered away.

Nunez looked in the mirror again. His face was half clean, half streaked with red and brown suds. He wiped them off and walked out.

Fifteen or so customers stood in the gas station in silence, watching him. Nunez stared back. He was hungry and thirsty, and needed a phone charger. He went in there to buy something. But fuck that. He wasn't going to walk around in the store and be a freak show for these people.

"You come up from the valley, son?"

Nunez looked at the farmer with bifocals, nodded and said, "Yeah, I did."

The man nodded back. "I heard it was bad down there. Glad you made it." Then he turned to one of the employees and said, "Gladys, I'm getting the man a beer. I'll pay you later."

Nunez had quit drinking and smoking years earlier, after he got married. He thought about refusing the offer, but a beer sounded damn good right then.

The farmer opened a cooler door. "Bud Light alright with you, son?"

"Yes sir. That's fine."

"You want anything else?"

Nunez leaned his head back and closed his eyes for a second. "A pack of Marlboro Lights would be great, sir."

"Gladys, fix him up."

The woman tossed him a pack of cigarettes and a lighter before the farmer handed him the beer. The farmer shook his hand and said, "You boys did good down there. No matter what you see on TV, we appreciate it. And if you know any of them boys that killed that guy they caught, you tell them we're on their side. That wasn't their fault. Stuff like that happens in war. Don't make it right, but that's just how it is. Trust me, I know."

Nunez nodded and swallowed. His eyes burned. He said, "Yes sir, I'll tell them. Thanks."

The farmer patted Nunez on the shoulder. Nunez walked past the other people who were still doing nothing but staring at him. Outside, a gray haired man standing outside an old blue pickup waved to him.

"I think you might need something stronger than a beer. This'll take the edge off a little."

He held out a bottle of Jack Daniels whiskey, about three quarters full. Nunez wasn't sure what to do. He took the bottle and stood in front of the man in awkward silence, whiskey in one hand and beer in the other. He couldn't even shake the man's hand.

"Take care, young man. Go home and spend some time with a woman. That's what makes us human again."

Nunez nodded and mumbled "Thanks" as he backed toward his Jeep. The gray haired man got into his truck. Nunez saw a Vietnam Veteran sticker in the back window.

He got back on the highway and thought, *I didn't get a stupid phone charger.* The beer sweated in a cup holder, Jack Daniels waited on the passenger seat. Nunez bypassed them both and tore open the pack of cigarettes. He was out of practice and fumbled with the lighter, but eventually the cigarette was lit. He inhaled and felt the pleasure of satiated addiction rush through his body, stress and anger take a step out.

Ten miles down the road the first cigarette was KIA. He lit another, then stared at the beer. It looked back at him with love in its eyes.

He popped the tab on the beer and took a long pull. The liquid was freezing, but it made him feel warm. Damn, it was good. It had been, what, almost ten years since he quit drinking? What the hell had he been doing for pleasure all those years? Other than going to war and fighting with his wife, he couldn't think of anything.

Ten more miles down. The beer can flew into the backseat, empty and crushed. Home wasn't far now. If Laura was there, she'd be pissed when she smelled smoke and alcohol on him. He better quit now if he didn't want another fight on his hands.

But he'd have one more cigarette. He lit it up and wished for one more beer. The farmer even asked him if he wanted anything else, he should have asked for two beers. Or a six-pack.

Jack Daniels shouted from the passenger seat, *Hey buddy, don't forget me. I'm here for you.* Nunez reached over and grabbed the bottle, steered with a knee and unscrewed the cap. *One swallow should be enough,* he thought. *If Laura's home, I'll leave it in the Jeep. If she's not, I'll finish it at the house.*

He took his one swallow. It burned hotter than he remembered. He grimaced and tensed up, then the burn softened. It felt fucking great. He hadn't been much of a whiskey drinker back in his single days, but now he realized he should have been. There was nothing like good whiskey.

He took a few more puffs and basked in the glow of the one swallow he had allowed himself. One beer and one shot of whiskey, and that was it. That showed a lot of willpower, especially for a guy who had flirted with alcoholism in his youth. He had complete control of himself. And that triumph of self-control was worth celebrating with a second shot. And maybe one after that.

By the time he turned onto his street he was plain fucked up. The Jeep weaved a bit as Nunez crept down the street at ten miles an hour, mumbling, "Be there, Laura. Please be home." His foot bounced compulsively on the floorboard, but the rest of him was so worn out from alcohol and lack of sleep he thought he might pass out. If Laura was home, he'd collapse into her arms, beg forgiveness for his relapse, take a shower and fall asleep with her and the kids. That was all he wanted. It wasn't asking all that damn much.

His tire bounced over the curb as he made the turn into his driveway. No lights were on in the house. But it was late, wasn't it? They had to be asleep. Laura always parked way at the back of the house, beside their neighbor's privacy fence. He craned his neck to see around the corner as he turned. The headlights lit up the length of the driveway. Laura's car wasn't there.

Nunez jerked his hands from the steering wheel and clenched them in fists behind his head.

Motherfucker. Now what do I do?

He stopped the Jeep and sat there for a few seconds. Maybe her car was in the garage. *Bullshit,* he thought. *She never parks it there. You're fucked and she's not here for you.*

He kicked the door open, got out cursing and realized he was about to piss his pants. He peed right there in the driveway, buttoned his pants and grabbed his pack from the back of the Jeep. When he slung it onto his back the weight threw him off balance and he fell on his ass. The impact made him angrier.

He mumbled insults at nothing and stumbled to his feet, then to the door. It took forever to find the right key and get it into the lock. As he turned it he made one last silent plea. *Be inside, Laura. I need you.*

He opened the door to a silent house. His pack fell to the floor with a thud and he kicked the door closed behind him. When he switched the light on he saw furniture and a TV in the front room. But the kids' clothes and toys that made their house a home were all gone.

"Son of a bitch. Come on, Laura. Don't do this to me."

He walked on shaky legs to the master bedroom. It was clean. Laura's clothes were usually all over the place. He went to the kids' rooms. Old clothes that he knew didn't fit them anymore hung in their closets. Everything else was gone.

He went back to the living room and sat on a sofa. Laura would be pissed if she knew he was ruining their sofa with his dirty pants. He wished she was there to yell at him about it.

He put his palms flat against each other in front of his face, then held them against his lips. He stared past fingertips at nothing. He didn't know what to do. Maybe he hadn't believed Laura would take the kids and go. Now that he knew she left, he was almost in shock. He would rather have been back in the fight in Arriago than sitting alone on his sofa, accepting that his family had dissolved.

My phone.

Nunez stood up and scrambled for his patrol pack. His cell phone had been inside, wrapped in a T-shirt and stuffed in a pouch for the entire fight. He dug through the pack like a dog digging up a bone, pulled the phone out and whipped the T-shirt away. With the phone gripped tight in his palm, he rushed to his bedroom. He leaned off balance as he went through the doorway and knocked the heck out of his shoulder.

His charger was plugged in next to his side of the bed. He found the middle of the cord, followed it the wrong way to the wall and then back the other way to the end. He jabbed the plug into the jack and pushed the power button. The screen lit up.

Nunez mumbled "Hurry the fuck up" as the phone booted up. When the display stabilized Nunez saw notification messages at the bottom of the screen.

Seventeen waiting text messages

Twenty-four missed calls

Seven new voicemails

Nunez beat on the arrow buttons to highlight the texts and managed to knock the phone out of his own hand. He dropped to the floor to pick it up and pounded the down arrow again. The first text popped up.

Jerry, we heard about you getting called up. I need to know you're alright. We're worried about you. Love, mom.

Not now, mom. He arrowed down to the next text.

Sergeant Borden, from Saturday. *Nunez, I need the fuel status for your vehicles. Call me ASAP!*

Nunez hissed, "Fuck you, Borden," and went to the next text.

Jerry, we need to talk. Call me when you can. From Laura. This morning. He rushed to the next one.

I saw the video and recognized you. Please, Jerry, call me.

Next.

Jen and I are watching the news about the fighting in Arriago. I just know you're there. Call me.

Next.

OMG Jerry, they just said more than 90 soldiers were killed in Arriago. CALL ME RIGHT NOW. Me and the kids are going crazy. Love you.

Nunez scrolled through the rest of the messages. All were from Laura. She was worried to death about him. She loved him. After reading the last message, he pulled up her number to call.

The phone vibrated and rang, startling him. Another number popped up on the screen. The alcohol dulled his comprehension. After a few rings he realized someone was calling him. The name on the screen said *Vic Corley.*

Nunez answered with an abrupt, "What?"

"Sergeant Nunez? Is that you?"

"Yeah. What do you want, Doc?"

"Are you home?"

"Yeah, why?"

"Are you watching TV?"

"No. I'm busy."

"Turn on your TV, Sarge. Any of the major networks, they're all showing it. The President's about to give a speech about the war. You need to watch it."

"What the fuck do I need to watch that shit for?" Nunez demanded. "We lived it. I don't need anyone to tell me about it."

"Sarge, sober up."

Nunez held the phone away from his ear for a second and looked at it in confusion. How the hell did Doc know he was drunk? Did he sound that bad?

Corley went on, "This is important. Trust me. The President's going to talk about us."

Nunez didn't speak. After several long seconds Corley asked, "Sarge, you there?"

"Yeah. I'm here. I'll watch the speech."

"Alright. Call me later. Out."

Corley hung up. Nunez left the phone charging on his bed, took three steps toward the living room and banged his head on the edge of the doorway. He grumbled, grabbed his head and wandered around looking for the remote. When he turned the TV on it was already on CNN.

The screen showed an empty podium embossed with the presidential seal. The chatter of waiting reporters buzzed from the TV's speakers. At the bottom of the screen, the newsfeed proclaimed, *President Lemoine to speak about alleged war crimes committed by American soldiers.*

Son of a bitch, Nunez thought. He sighed and dropped onto the sofa. For two minutes he worked at convincing himself that he was wrong, it wasn't bad news. Maybe the President would announce that no crime had occurred. Or not enough evidence existed to prosecute. Or the son of a bitch they killed flat out deserved it, and fuck anyone who said otherwise.

The President walked solemnly to the podium and faced the camera. The reporters' chatter ceased. The President looked tired, maybe a little frustrated. Nunez struggled to force the alcohol's effects from his brain so he could better read the man's face.

"Citizens of the United States, good evening," the President said. "Tonight I have two important matters to discuss. Unfortunately I don't have much time to do so, because of the continuing operations our military is conducting and the need for me as the commander in chief to monitor them. So this will be brief.

"I am pleased to announce that as of this afternoon, major combat operations on our border have come to a successful conclusion. This conclusion was not an easy one, however. It comes at a high price in lives of our soldiers, first responders and innocent residents of the affected cities. Due to the constant flow of new and changing information, I am presently unable to give definite numbers of lives lost. But I can say we have lost hundreds of private citizens, over a hundred first responders, and at least scores of soldiers. It will be several weeks before we know our precise losses.

"But, major combat has ended. Each of the eight affected towns has been occupied by thousands of our soldiers and Marines, and is being cleared house by house as we speak. Since the last large enemy forces withdrew or were destroyed today, there have been no further engagements. Our troops are encountering only the occasional straggler, and thus far all of those have surrendered without resistance. We can only hope all the towns will be fully cleared without further loss of life.

"The success of our operation on the border can be attributed to one thing, and one thing only: the bravery of our men and women in uniform. Early reports show that our troops engaged in battles whose ferocity was equaled only by those fought in the Second World War. One Texas National Guard platoon lost more than half its men killed, and many more wounded."

Nunez's eyebrows rose. The only platoon he knew of that lost more than half its men killed was his own.

"And the maintenance company that was ambushed Sunday in Arriago lost every man, save one. One single survivor, out of an entire company. I trust that the American people appreciate the horrors experienced by those brave young men. From the office of the President down to the local government level, there is not a soul who doesn't hold in the highest regard the sacrifices and accomplishments of our troops."

Nunez dropped his face into his palm, knowing what the next sentence would start with. *The troops are great, amazing, wonderful, we so cherish them... BUT...*

"But, there is a serious matter I must address," the President said. "Early Tuesday morning I was shown a video of an alleged incident that occurred in Arriago on Monday morning. Initially, I and many others thought this video was a fake, that it was nothing more than enemy propaganda.

"Unfortunately, careful analysis of the video and significant physical evidence proves the video shows a real incident. We have established, beyond a shadow of a doubt, that American troops captured and murdered an enemy prisoner, and made a deliberate effort to conceal the murder afterward. The video likely does not portray all the circumstances surrounding the incident, and we are sure the sequence of events has been altered. But the main focus of the video, the murder of a prisoner, did in fact occur.

"Ladies and gentlemen, we know and understand the stresses on the soldiers involved. They had just suffered a horrific ambush that killed or badly wounded seven of their comrades. We know they returned fire into a house they took fire from, and in the process unintentionally killed three civilians and a captured soldier who were placed in the house as human shields. The hostages may have been placed there specifically so our troops would kill them when they returned fire. We believe the entire event was engineered by the enemy to create an incident that could be used to cast our troops in a bad light. We understand the soldiers didn't enter Arriago with the intent to commit murder. The killing was an unplanned incident that occurred in the heat of combat. These factors have been considered. But they are not an excuse.

"The stress of combat, the anger brought on by the loss of friends, and the guilt they must have incurred from the deaths of innocent hostages, however traumatic they may be, do not justify murder. We must, under all circumstances, hold our fighting men and women to the highest standards of ethical and legal conduct. This line cannot be crossed if we wish to preserve our standing as the example of moral behavior to the rest of the world.

"Therefore, I have ordered Secretary of Defense Morrison to carry out a full and unbiased investigation. The result of this investigation will not come for some time. But the investigation has progressed far enough that we have identified, by name, rank and unit, each soldier shown on the video. Earlier this afternoon Governor Mathieu and the Texas Army National Guard were ordered to detain those soldiers. I have been told the soldiers in question were not detained. Because of this failure to comply with my direct orders, as of one hour ago the commander of the Texas Army National Guard has been relieved. The investigation is now in the hands of the FBI and the Army's Criminal Investigation Division. Arrest warrants for the named soldiers have been issued, and the arrests are being carried out as we speak."

Nunez leaned forward, put his elbows on his knees and his head in his hands. Arrests were being carried out. General Koba was wrong about them having a day of freedom. His wounded soldiers who were still on their feet, like Drake, were probably already in jail. Nunez imagined there were military police outside Quincy's hospital room, standing guard until he was well enough to be arrested. All his men who had been wounded and evacuated were probably in some type of custody already.

Looking somber, the President said, "This is not something I take lightly. I feel no pleasure giving these orders. I wish nothing but the best for the men and women who sacrificed so much for our safety and freedom. But I have no choice, legally or morally. And even if there was an alternative, I would still choose the route we are taking. Because it is the right thing to do.

"For the moment, I have no further information. I or my press secretary will keep you informed of future developments. I wish good luck and a safe homecoming to the troops who rose to the task and defended American soil from hostile invaders. Thank you, good night, and God bless America."

The President stepped back from the podium, turned and walked off the stage. Reporters shouted questions that went unanswered. The newsfeed at the bottom of the screen changed to *President Lemoine announces arrests of US troops charged in murder of Mexican immigrant.*

The screen shifted to a shot of Governor of Texas Lawrence Mathieu, seated at a desk in a large room, staring off to the side. The words *Texas Governor Lawrence Mathieu, Emergency Command Post, Edinburgh, Texas* displayed briefly at the bottom of the screen. Mathieu was unshaven, tired-looking and pissed off. There was no polish to his appearance. He wore a wrinkled polo-style shirt and looked nothing like the President in his tailored suit. Behind him soldiers and police officers rushed about like ants in a kicked-over anthill. The Governor shook his head in obvious frustration and turned to the camera. Nunez realized he had been watching the President's address as well.

An unseen reporter's voice asked, "Governor, now that you've heard the President's comments about this allegation, what is your response?"

Mathieu bit his lip. Anger was obvious on his face. He spoke in a tense voice, like he was on the verge of venting a boiling fury.

"First, the President is misinformed. Our troops are still in contact. We lost two more this afternoon in Verdele. These losses were reported up the chain hours ago. The President's responsibility, as the supposed 'commander in chief,' is to know what his troops are facing. Second, I have no idea, none at all, how the President can possibly fathom ordering the arrests of American soldiers while our troops are still conducting combat operations on Texas soil. The President needs to check his priorities.

"Third, is the President going to acknowledge that the enemy forces who attacked us were composed of cartel fighters and Muslim extremists? Some of the groups withdrew intact into Mexico and are still a threat to our citizens. It defies belief that at this time, when our country has been attacked and the enemy is just across the Mexican border, our President is focused on prosecuting our own soldiers.

"I want to go on the record with the following statement. Our President is taking action against American troops while those troops are fighting and dying to defend this state and this country. This is, I think, an act just short of treason.

"The President's view of the war from his exalted throne in Washington may be rosy and free of moral gray areas. My view from Edinburgh, and from the affected towns I've been to, is not. I have seen firsthand the devastation wrought by the invaders. I've seen the murdered men, women and children. I've seen what was left of the captured soldier who was beaten, made to wear a bomb vest and blown apart when he refused to approach our troops. I've stood outside the field hospital as wounded Texas Guardsmen were carried screaming in agony from the backs of shot-up Humvees. And I've watched our dead soldiers being carried with great reverence from those same Humvees to the makeshift morgue, and laid alongside dozens of their fallen brothers and sisters. I know what this war is. The President does not.

"The President himself admitted this videotaped event was engineered by the enemy. The platoon that was involved in this event is the same platoon that lost more than half its soldiers killed in three days of terrible fighting. One of the men on that video was one of the only survivors of the maintenance company ambush, and he chose to stay in the fight rather than be evacuated to a safe place. This brave young man was killed during the final battle in Arriago when his adopted platoon was overrun. And the platoon sergeant is the hero who singlehandedly killed the terrorists who committed the freeway massacre in Houston. These are the kind of men the President wants to put in prison."

Nunez's ears perked like a dog's. To anyone who knew anything about the Houston terrorist attack, he had just been identified.

"The President relieved General Koba for not immediately arresting the soldiers involved. Well, the President can't relieve me. My loyalty is to the citizens of this state and the fighting men and women who are dying to defend them. Criminal prosecution for any alleged, engineered 'war crime' is far down the list of my priorities, as it should be on his."

The reporter jumped in. "But Governor, don't you think the President has a point when he says –"

Nunez turned the TV off. Evil, bitter thoughts rolled through his mind. Alcohol produced mercurial changes in his mood. He knew the alcohol caused it, but his moods changed anyway. He sat in silence for a while and tried to fight off an idea that nobody would understand, nobody would forgive him for.

He dropped the remote onto the floor and walked through his bedroom to the walk-in closet. He shoved clothes aside, spun a dial on a heavy steel box, turned a knob and opened the fireproof door. He searched about in the dark recesses at the top of the safe until he found it. He walked back to the living room and sat down. After a few seconds he found the will to grab the slide and load a round into the chamber.

Images from suicides calls he had responded to floated across his mind. Bodies laid back against headboards, pistols held tight by rigor. Hysterical family members shrieking, *How could he have done this to us?* A mother dead in the back of an ambulance, suffering a heart attack after finding her son hanging in his room.

Nunez asked himself, *Are you going to do this? Here in the front room? What if Laura and kids come home and find you? At least have the decency to do it in a bathroom. You can put a sign on the door warning them not to come inside or something.*

Nunez stood and mumbled, "I need a pen and paper." He stuck the pistol into his waistband at the small of his back and went to the kitchen. There had to be a pen and something to write on in a junk drawer. He turned on the light and pulled open a cabinet drawer.

Someone knocked on the front door. Loud. Three times.

Nunez froze. His heart pounded. He stayed still, breathed in ragged gasps. When he finally did move, it was just to turn his head to the kitchen window. The night was solid black, he couldn't see anything outside.

He exploded toward the light switch and beat it until he got the light turned off. Another two loud knocks rang out from the front door. Nunez knelt in the shadows and wondered what he should do.

Turn the lights off. They know you're here already, turn all the lights off so they can't see you.

Nunez crawled on hands and knees into the living room. When he reached the right spot he jumped up and slapped the light switch. The house went dark. He squatted down again and looked out the nearest windows. Still too dark to see outside. But he had served enough warrants, he knew at least one officer would be in the back covering any escape route.

He could still risk it. He could sneak to the back door, fling it open and haul ass toward the back fence. The officer would have trouble climbing over it if he had all his gear on. And Nunez knew the neighborhood, knew where to go. A bayou was two blocks away, if he got into that it would lead him to a shopping center. He could hide out behind the shopping center until the stores closed, then break into one and steal whatever clothes he needed. Or he could just call a friend to pick him up. He could escape.

Hey, you fucking idiot. You're operating on like ten hours of sleep in five days. You're wearing heavy boots. And you're fucking drunk. The fattest, slow-est cop you've ever known could catch you. And what if they have a K9? Then not only do you go to jail, you go to jail bitten and bloody. And everyone will talk about the stupid, drunk-ass cop who tried to run from a K9. And even if you get away, where are you going to go? Fleeing to Mexico just might be out of the question. Make a plan B, dipshit. This one ain't gonna work.

Nunez lowered his head and clenched his jaw in frustration. Okay, running was out. He looked up to the ceiling and pictured his attic. There was enough crap up there to hide behind. He could even do what he saw a suspect do once, burrow under insulation. Maybe they wouldn't find him.

Sure they won't find you. This is just some minor little warrant, it's not like the President signed it. They couldn't possibly think to look in the attic. They'll just look around for a minute, give up and leave. Yeah. That's what'll happen. Moron.

"Fuck me," Nunez whispered. What was there to do now? Running or hiding wouldn't work. So his options were down to three. Give up peacefully, fight, or do what he had planned to do, less than two minutes earlier.

He reached and felt the pistol in his waistband. The impulse to shoot himself vanished. He couldn't even imagine doing it now. The thought was ridiculous. The alcohol must have put that idea in his head. For a moment, he felt just as stupid as every drunk he had ever dealt with as a cop.

The doorbell rang. Nunez swallowed hard. His ears burned. One option had been eliminated, two remained. Fight or surrender? Did he have it in him to fight some federal agent? Maybe it was better to just give up anyway. Show some dignity, walk into jail with pride, like he had told his men to do. If he ran or fought, he would look guilty to the entire world.

The doorbell rang again, twice. Nunez sat back against the wall. He figured they'd kick in the door within a few minutes. They might have even brought a full SWAT team with them. After all, they were going after a street cop and hardened combat veteran, known to be armed, who had committed a murder and probably had mental problems. You know, like all veterans of Iraq and Afghanistan supposedly did.

Giving up only made sense. Making himself look guilty by trying to get away wouldn't help him or his soldiers. He could fight this case from jail. Governor Mathieu might even step in on their behalf.

But if he went to jail, scumbags just like most of the people he had arrested would be waiting for him. They'd know he had been a cop. He'd probably get raped the first night there.

Fuck that.

He stood up and pulled the Glock from his waistband. Another option pushed its way forward. There was always suicide by cop. If he aimed carefully, he could make sure he only hit the officers in their vests. They'd blow him away, and none of them would be hurt.

His phone rang in the bedroom. Nunez jumped in surprise. He rushed to his bedroom, grabbed the phone and ducked down, worried the officers outside would see the flashing lights. The screen showed a name.

Laura

He hit answer and slapped the phone to his ear. "Laura? Are you there?"

"Jerry! I've been worried sick! How are you, are you in Edinburgh?"

"No, baby. I'm at home. I got here a little while ago. God, I was hoping you'd be here. I need you."

"I need you too, baby," she said, her voice soothing. "I'm sorry I got mad and left. I'm coming home soon. I just thought we'd stay here at my parents' while you were in the valley. The kids worry less when they're here."

Nunez nodded and closed his eyes. The doorbell rang again. Then three loud bangs sounded. A stern, commanding voice said, "Sergeant Nunez, open the door. We know you're inside."

Laura asked, "What was that? I heard a noise."

Nunez groaned a little. "Laura, I'm in trouble. The police are outside. I'm… sitting in the dark in our bedroom. They keep knocking on the door. I haven't answered."

Laura sighed into the phone, "Oh my God Jerry, I was so scared this would happen. I saw you on that video. What are you going to do?"

"I don't know, Laura. I was thinking… maybe it would be better if I didn't go to jail."

Laura stayed quiet. Nunez swallowed and listened to his heart beating in his ears.

"Jerry, what do you mean? You have to go with the police. They'll take you to jail and we'll do whatever we have to to get you out."

"Laura," Nunez said. "Listen to me. I shouldn't go to jail. I didn't do anything wrong. I mean… I did, but I'm not a criminal. If I go to jail, real criminals in there will tear me up. So I'm not going."

"Jerry, if you don't go with the police, what are you going to do?"

Nunez didn't answer. As he listened to Laura breathing over the phone, a flashlight beam shone in through a window, then turned off.

"Laura, I'm not going to jail. I'm sorry, baby."

"Jerry, are you drunk?"

Nunez threw his head back into the wall. "Goddamn it, what fucking difference does it make if I'm drunk? I'm not going to jail. That's it. I love you, Laura. You and the kids deserved better than this. Kiss them for me, tell them I love them and that I didn't want them to have to tell their friends their daddy is in prison."

Laura started to protest and he cut her off. "I have to go. They'll come in soon. Don't come home until they clear the crime scene, I don't want you to see me. I love you. Bye, baby."

"Jerry, don't –"

Nunez hung up, held the phone against his forehead and closed his eyes tight. He remembered his wedding day, remembered watching in amazement as Laura gave birth to his son and daughter. He started to cry. The tears just made him madder at himself.

The front door handle squeaked as someone tried to open it. Nunez put the phone on the floor and stood up. Someone pounded on the door again, then hit the doorbell about ten times. Nunez wiped his eyes and walked to the front door. He reached for the deadbolt, changed his mind, went to the light switch and turned the entry light on. If he wanted the cops to shoot him, they had to be able to see him. Now all he had to do was open the door, point his pistol at one of them and wait for the end. If they didn't shoot, he would. That would do it.

Nunez grabbed the deadbolt knob with his left hand, held the Glock by his side with his right. This was it. After everything he had done, it had come to this moment. Nineteen years of being a soldier, fifteen years as a cop. A year of running dusty, bomb-strewn highways in Iraq, nine months of firefights and frustrations in Afghanistan. Five horrifying minutes running around a jammed highway in Houston, trading shots with two terrorists mowing people down. Three days of brutal combat in Arriago, Texas. A marriage, two children, life in a quiet neighborhood. All the details of a life about to end.

No regrets. It's been a good ride.

Nunez took a deep breath. These were the final seconds of his life. He looked around his home for the last time.

Two things jumped at him. A family picture, taken the previous Christmas. And a mirror on the wall to the side of the door.

Nunez looked at his family, and at himself. Back and forth, picture to mirror and back. Outside, a voice commanded, "Sergeant Nunez, open the door."

Nunez recognized his own voice coming from the man outside. Nunez had served a million warrants, including some on people he didn't think needed to go to jail. He had just done his job. Just like the guys outside.

You aren't going to shoot a cop. You're not even going to point a weapon at one. You know it and they know it.

Just a few hours ago he had told his men to show some dignity if they were arrested. He had promised them he would take the heat for them. If he forced the police to shoot him, they'd have to deal with the investigation on their own.

The man who promised to stand up for them would have gone out like a coward.

Just give up. Go to jail. Be a man about it.

Nunez stepped back from the door. The flashlight shone through a small, narrow stained glass window into his face.

Fuck this shit. At the least, these guys are getting a good fight out of me.

Nunez raised the pistol, cocked his arm and flung it into the mirror. The glass shattered with loud crash. The flashlight turned off and a voice asked, "What the hell is he doing in there?"

Nunez grabbed the deadbolt, turned it and yanked the door open so hard it slipped from his grasp and hit the wall. Two middle-aged men in suits jerked back from the door in surprise. They had to be federal agents, the idiots were standing right in front of the doorway instead of off to the side. Their weapons weren't even in their hands. Nunez locked eyes with one of them and yelled, "What?"

The man on the right asked, "Sergeant Jerry Nunez?"

"Yeah, what the fuck's it to you?"

The man looked surprised at Nunez's tone. "Sergeant Nunez, you need to come with us. Grab whatever you need so we can go."

Nunez squinted at the man. "Grab whatever I need? What the hell would I need to bring with me?"

The men looked at him in amazement. Nunez wondered, *What kind of bozos did they send to get me?* He demanded, "Who the fuck are you guys anyway?"

"I'm Sergeant Webb and that's Officer Burton. Sergeant Nunez, we're pressed for time. We need to leave as soon as possible. Please, get your things."

"Oh? You're pressed for time? How fucking tragic. God forbid I jack with your tight schedule. What agency are you with anyway? I don't see a fucking badge."

Webb pulled a leather wallet from his pocket, opened it and held it toward Nunez. Nunez leaned in and read *Texas Department of Public Safety-Capitol Police.*

"Holy shit. They sent two capitol police to take me? They couldn't send real cops?"

Webb looked puzzled. He asked, "Sergeant Nunez, did anyone call to tell you we were coming?"

"Nobody told me shit!" Nunez yelled. "The fucking President told the whole world I was going to jail, but nobody told me a Goddamn thing! So you dickheads want to take me?" Nunez stepped back from the door. "Come on in and take me, motherfuckers! But I'm not going without a fight, and I'm not going to hurry so you can get off shift on time. You want me, you have to earn it. So come on. I'm ready."

Webb held out a palm. "Whoa, hold on, Sergeant Nunez. You're a little unclear on the situation. The Governor has told us to do something we're not sure we want to do, and we're just following orders."

Nunez raised his hands into fists. "Fuck you and your orders. You want to take me to jail, come on in and take me. We'll all go to the hospital first though."

The other man's face tensed in anger and exasperation. He took a step in the door and yelled, "Hey, asshole! We're not here to arrest you! We have orders from the governor to protect you from any federal agency that tries to take you into custody. That means we have to get your stupid ass out of here before the Feds show up. So get your shit and get in our fucking car. Now."

Nunez's hands and jaw dropped. He stared back at the man with an expression even he knew looked stupid. Suddenly he felt light-headed.

Are they serious? Is this a trick?

Nunez slurred, "Dude, don't fuck with me. Don't trick me into cuffs."

Webb stepped in and said, "Sergeant Nunez, if federal agents do come I don't know that we can stop them from taking you. Governor Mathieu's orders are easier said than done. So please, grab whatever you need. We have to go."

Nunez's breath quickened. The image of the two men before him blurred. They were serious. He was being rescued.

"And... and my men? What's happening to them?"

"They're being picked up too. The ones we can get to before the Feds, anyway."

Nunez's mind reeled. He reached out and tried to take a step forward. He went sideways instead. He felt his head fall forward a bit, as if he was sitting at a high school desk fighting sleep. His eyes narrowed of their own will. One of the men blurted, "Grab him!"

Nunez's knees buckled. His vision went black. He was out before his head hit the floor.

The next few minutes, until he woke up sprawled across the back seat of Webb's car, were the most peaceful of his life.

CREDITS AND CONTRIBUTORS

Publishing: Tactical 16, LLC
CEO, Tactical 16: Erik Shaw
President, Tactical 16: Jeremy Farnes
Cover Design: Javier Muñoz
Cover Photo: Tara Plybon

ABOUT THE AUTHOR
Chris Hernandez

Chris Hernandez is a former Marine and veteran Police Officer, currently serving in the Texas Army National Guard. He is a combat veteran of Iraq and Afghanistan, and served 18 months as a UN police officer in Kosovo. Chris lives with his wife and children in southeast Texas. Line in the Valley is his second novel and is the follow up to Proof of Our Resolve, the first in a series of several books.

ABOUT THE PUBLISHER
Tactical 16, LLC

Tactical 16 is a Veteran owned and operated publishing company based in the beautiful mountain city of Colorado Springs, Colorado. What started as an idea among like-minded people has grown into reality.

Tactical 16 believes strongly in the healing power of writing, and provides opportunities for Veterans, Police, Firefighters, and EMTs to share their stories; striving to provide accessible and affordable publishing solutions that get the works of true American Heroes out to the world. We strive to make the writing and publication process as enjoyable and stress-free as possible.

As part of the process of healing and helping true American Heroes, we are honored to hear stories from all Veterans, Police Officers, Firefighters, EMTs and their spouses. Regardless of whether it's carrying a badge, fighting in a war zone or family at home keeping everything going, we know many have a story to tell.

At Tactical 16, we truly stand behind our mission to be "The Premier Publishing Resource for Guardians of Freedom."

We are a proud supporter of Our Country and its People, without which we would not be able to make Tactical 16 a reality.

How did Tactical 16 get its name? There are two parts to the name, "Tactical" and "16". Each has a different meaning. Tactical refers to the Armed Forces, Police, Fire, and Rescue communities or any group who loves, believes in, and supports Our Country. The "16" is the number of acres of the World Trade Center complex that was destroyed on that harrowing day of September 11, 2001. That day will be forever ingrained in the memories of many generations of Americans. But that day is also a reminder of the resolve of this Country's People and the courage, dedication, honor, and integrity of our Armed Forces, Police, Fire, and Rescue communities. Without Americans willing to risk their lives to defend and protect Our Country, we would not have the opportunities we have before us today.

Proof of Our Resolve

By: Chris Hernandez

Love Me When I'm Gone

The True Story of Life, Love, and Loss for a Green Beret in Post-9/11 War

By: Robert Patrick Lewis

And Then I Cried:

Stories of a Mortuary NCO

By: Justin Jordan

SHADOW WORKS

"LIVE OUTSIDE YOUR COMFORT ZONE!"

Living the action sports lifestyle, Shadow Works in an action sports brand for men, women, and children who believe in working hard and playing harder! Started by former Navy Seal, Geoff Reeves, Shadow Works challenges others to "LIVE OUTSIDE YOUR COMFORT ZONE!" Shadow Works is a patriotic infused brand that encourages smartly pushing limits and challenging the human spirit.

www.shadowworksgroup.com

"The Bullhorn for R Brave"

American Soldier Network is a 501(c)(3) non-profit organization with the goal to raise national awareness and support for US troops. ASN embraces all who are truly impacting US veterans and currently serving the military and their families. ASN's utilizes television as the platform to accomplish this goal by capturing real stories and giving troops a true voice in broadcast media. ASN urges all Americans to help support the troops.

www.americansoldiernetwork.org

CPSIA information can be obtained at www.ICGtesting.com
Printed in the USA
BVOW05s0041271115

428177BV00007B/66/P